THE RITUAL

Books by Stefán Máni

<u>Iceland:</u>
Skipid
Odadahraun
Nautid
Svartigaldur
 (Grímsson Series)
Krysuvik (Grímsson Series)
Adventa (Grímsson Series)
Horfnar (Grímsson Series)
Daudabokin
 (Grímsson Series)
Hyldypi (Grímsson Series)
Husid (Grímsson Series)
Feigd (Grímsson Series)
Grimmd (Grímsson Series)

<u>USA:</u>
The Ritual (Grímsson Series)
Deathbook (Grímsson Series)
Dust in the Wind
 (Grímsson Series)

<u>Australia:</u>
The Ship

<u>France:</u>
Noir Océan
Noir Karma
Présages (Grímsson Series)

<u>Germany:</u>
Das Schiff
Der Stier und das Madchen
In Schwarzen Spiegeln
 (Grímsson Series)

<u>Denmark:</u>
Skibet
Ödeland

<u>Sweden:</u>
Skeppet

<u>Poland:</u>
Statek

<u>Italy:</u>
Nero Oceano

THE RITUAL

By Stefán Máni

Grimmson Series
Translated by Philip Roughton

The Ritual

You can reach the author at:
Website: stefanmani.is

Dedication

This book is dedicated to The Shadow

Special thanks to:
Stefán Eiríksson, former police chief
Jóhann Páll, duty officer at Litla-Hraun Prison
Haukur Ingvarsson, literary scholar
Matthías Viðar Sæmundsson, RIP

"In the opinion of the authorities, such a book led to fire and damnation; such lore was dangerous and cursed. Any person who had such a book in his possession was the scum of humanity, worthy only of hellfire, and in fact, a brutish devil in human form, sent by Satan from the depths of Hell; and he incited the wrath of God, who could sink the land like a lead ball into the bottomless abyss if nothing was done."

—from the preface to the book Sorcery in Iceland, *by Matthías Viðar Sæmundsson*

A Dark Reflection

In a gloomy room, flames burn on two black candles standing half a meter apart on top of an old dresser. Between the candles is an old human skull, brownish-colored and missing both its lower jaw and a few upper teeth. Behind the candles and the skull is a black mirror.

The skull is facing a young man sitting straight-backed in a chair in front of the dresser. Blackness fills the skull's eye sockets. The young man is blond and blue-eyed, and is wearing a black jacket, red t-shirt, stone-washed jeans and white sneakers. On his forehead is an old scar resembling the Nike Swoosh. His palms rest on his thighs and he has small earphones in his ears. He stares into his own eyes in the black mirror. His pupils are dilated. In his ears a voice sounds, deep and monotone.

"You see three things," says the voice, deep enough to tickle his ears. *"Two candles and a skull. The skull is a gate; soon we will embark on a journey through it. You see two things. The candles have merged into one. Inside of you, the gate opens; now it would be good to relax and sink deeper. You see one thing. It's the flame, flickering before you. The skull is gone. You are the skull—it is empty because your consciousness has sunk. You relax and allow your consciousness to sleep. You are empty, you feel good. Enter Eckankar!"*

He's empty, he's falling. Inside the skull is an entire universe of nothingness. A dark universe, cold and empty, like himself. Images rush through this universe, through the skull, through his mind. The images are old memories, refractions of his life. He's no longer a person with consciousness and feeling, he's a glass half-sphere, full of water and white particles for snow that swirls in circles as it settles. Each snowflake is a memory, a refraction, an old moment that he experiences again and again. These aren't memories; he realizes that now. They're real moments, instances, incidents from the past that come to life in him, or he in them. Time is a broken image, it scatters everywhere, a million glass fragments that shoot through the void, flashing like flares, lightning, a nuclear explosion in his soul. Unless it's his soul that is broken, that is strewn like a rain of shards through the universe inside his skull.

He's holding a knife. He looks, he breathes. He's going to kill someone; he just doesn't know whom. But *he* knows it. The other he. The one that whispers like a blazing conflagration behind the walls of a nightmare …

Standing in the lumpy lava fields south of Hafnarfjörður are old fish-drying racks, dilapidated for the most part, having not been looked after for a number of years. The racks form long, wide corridors. The weathered posts support eight-meter long poles that have turned white with age, but which, over the years, held many tons of strung cod. Poles lie here and there on the ground, sodden and decaying. The fishless racks have a ghostly air.

It's night. Clouds drift over the moon; the air is cold and a delicate drizzle falls over lava and moss.

Beneath the racks, seven young men stand staring at an eighth, who has a noose around his neck and is perched atop a pallet standing upright on one edge. The youth is blond and blue-eyed, bare-chested, with duct tape over his mouth and his hands tied behind his back. His chest and back are riddled with burns and open sores, and terror fills his gaping eyes. The noose is tied to one of the poles. The drizzle accumulates into drops that run down the rope, over the young man's pale face and bruised and bloody chest. His legs tremble and twitch, the pallet wobbles to and fro, ever on the verge of toppling.

If the pallet topples, he'll fall straight down—and the noose will tighten around his neck and stop him with a jerk halfway.

The seven men watching this are clad in black from head to toe, from their tightly laced combat boots to the cloths covering their noses and mouths. They all stare at their peer as he fights for his life. In most of their eyes, however, there's neither hatred nor malice. They're empty, slightly bored—even doubtful. What's happening isn't what they want, but they know that it can't be avoided. Not as things stand. It's out of their hands—like so much else in their lives. They would stop if they could—but they can't.

In any case, they *do* nothing. They seem paralyzed.

"I know what you're thinking," says one of them, sheathing the tapered, blue-handled knife that he's holding. "And those thoughts are weeds that need to be torn up and tossed into the fire. Weeds, like the one standing here incarnate on the gallows."

He pulls the cloth from his face, turns to his companions and regards them one by one. They blink, but don't dare look away from the eyes staring at them—*into* them, dark, cold, and focused.

"When one wolf starts limping, the others attack and kill it. A lame wolf is a liability. It doesn't help the pack; it slows it down and *weakens* it. Weakness is contagious. Removing a weak link from a chain isn't evil, it's rational."

"Aron …" says one of the masked youths. The smallest in the group.

"Yes?" asks Aron coldly.

"Wasn't it enough to …" says the small one. "Do we really need to …"

"Are you questioning this?" snaps Aron. "Having second thoughts? Maybe you want to quit, too? Does Little Mummi want to be next in the noose?"

"No, but …"

"If not, then the honor is yours." Aron steps aside with dramatic flair and gestures to Mummi to step forward.

"What?" asks Mummi, nearly tongue-tied from stress.

"Kick the pallet out from under him," orders Aron.

Mummi shakes his head. "No, not me!"

Aron pulls the knife back out of its sheath. "Do it, or I'll cut your throat. I swear to you I will."

"But …" Mummi steps forward hesitantly. He looks up. The drizzle falls in thin veils. The pallet creaks as it wobbles back and forth beneath the condemned person trying desperately to keep his balance. The veins on his arms and neck bulge, his face is blood red and his eyes are filled with terror and desperation.

"Now!" barks Aron.

Little Mummi hesitates, and then kicks at the pallet, knocking it over; the man falls and the pole creaks as the noose tightens around muscles and tendons and the weight of the man's body severs his spine.

Mummi runs off, throws himself on his knees, screams in horror and pukes into the cloth over his mouth. The others turn their backs on the horrific scene and gather closer in silent denial. All but Aron, who stares as if captivated as life ebbs out of the body of the hanged man. He stares with a composed, bovine expression at the swollen face, at the skin as it turns blue and black, and at the legs that twitch as they hang there in the air.

TUESDAY

Hörður Grímsson is sitting in an old swivel chair at the Barber Shop on Klapparstígur Street, looking at himself in the mirror. Or rather, he's trying *not* to look at himself in the huge, well-polished mirror. He isn't much for self-admiration; in fact, he feels as if there's nothing to admire. First of all, he's over two meters tall, which makes him conspicuous. He really dislikes attention. Secondly, he's too thin. At least he *seems* thin, because of his height. He actually weighs well over a hundred kilograms, but that weight disappears when divided into all those centimeters. His skin is colorless, as if he were chronically ill, if not simply dead. His face is rough-hewn and dramatic, even harsh-looking. He has a constant five o'clock shadow, despite shaving every morning. And then there's his hair: dusky red and coarse, like a horse's.

It's been only three or four weeks since his last haircut, and his relatively short hair sticks straight up all over his head. The back of his neck is covered in a shaggy growth mainly resembling wool.

No, it would be wrong to say that Hörður is his greatest fan. There's very little in that blessed reflection of his to please the eye, in his opinion. Except his eyes, perhaps. They're emerald green, deep, with a dark undertone. He likes their green color because it reminds him of his dearly departed mother and sister, both of whom also had green eyes. But he doesn't like the dark undertone as much. It holds both difficult memories and all sorts of *phenomena* that he doesn't want to have to think about.

"Well, what can I do for you?" asks the barber cheerfully. It isn't a man, but a woman. *A young* woman, even. Short, dark-haired, and slightly chubby. Her hair is cut short, her voice is warm and her smile beautiful. She's just over twenty, Hörður guesses. He himself is still under thirty, but looks ten years older.

He clears his throat. "Just a little trim. Short on top. Cropped at the neck. The usual."

"So you're a regular?" asks the girl. She sprays his hair with water and runs her slender fingers through it. Her touch is pleasant; a cozy feeling spreads through him. He could imagine sitting there forever.

"Yes," says Hörður, before letting silence settle over his tongue. Should he say something else? Sure, but what? Feeling awkward, his pale neck flushes red.

The chair is in its lowest position, yet the girl still needs to lift her hands to cut the hair on his crown. The scissors click in a speedy rhythm, *clip clip clip*, as the girl's fingers dash through the man's damp hair. Moist locks fall onto the nylon smock covering him. He lets his eyelids droop and tries to relax, but is unable to do so. His heart is pounding and he's all agitated inside, restless and dry-mouthed.

She's so close to him that he can feel her warmth. She has a pleasant presence, and smells so good.

"Have you been a cop for a long time?" the girl asks. Hörður sits up, and they look at each other in the mirror. Her eyes are big and brown, warm, like a late evening in Spain. He looks away, blinking.

"Yeah, kind of," says Hörður. Beneath the nylon smock, he's in his uniform, a light-blue short-sleeved shirt and dark-blue trousers. His duty belt is pinching his lower back, and in his right ear is a headphone attached by a cord to his radio. His jacket and cap are hanging on a rack near the door. They're on the day shift, he and his partner Vigfús, who is sitting in the same type of chair on the other side of the room and conversing energetically with his male barber. Vigfús is in his forties, broad-faced and blond, with a well-groomed beard and a potbelly.

"What made you want to become a police officer?" asks the girl.

Hörður swallows and his entire body stiffens. In his head, words and sentences swirl in circles, like shriveled leaves in an alley. But the words won't line themselves up properly, let alone find their way out of the man's head, down into his mouth and then out of it. Instead of answering, he reddens and feels even more awkward. The words seem to buzz loudly in his head, before going up in smoke, turning into nothing.

"I'm sorry, I didn't mean to pry," the girl says hurriedly. She continues to cut Hörður's damp hair, her scissors clicking even faster.

"No problem," mutters Hörður, his voice gravelly from stress. He shuts his eyes and pretends to relax, but wishes he could leap to his feet, run out of there and never come back. Damn, what a gigantic loser he can be!

October in Reykjavik, a light northerly wind and cold. The trees are leafless and the streets dusty, the sun comes up late, apricot-yellow, and sets soon after, a deep blood-orange color. Night descends early, slowly and calmly, like the night of all nights. In two months, the darkness will be nearly unbearable, despite all the Christmas lights, or perhaps precisely because of them. It's the light that creates shadows.

Autumn is a slow death; it is nature depressed.

"Do you think it's fish today?" asks Vigfús as he parks their squad car in front of the Múlakaffi café on Hallarmúli Street. There are four other police cars in the parking lot. At dinnertime, there are even more, when the spacious place is packed with the guardians of the law.

"Could be," says Hörður dryly. He's still thinking about the girl at the barber shop, the one with the beautiful smile, brown eyes and magic fingers. Does he have a crush on her? Maybe. But it doesn't matter. He blew it. He was so gruff—giant oaf that he is. There's no way she'd be interested in him, not after that introduction—that's for sure. And she probably has a boyfriend, anyway.

Vigfús shuts off the car, they step out and put on their caps.

Inside Múlakaffi, it's loud, warm, and rather smoky, from the frying of the breaded fish for the Tuesday special.

"As I was saying!" declares Vigfús, gloatingly.

Hörður forces a smile. They join the line, grab trays and go through their daily routine. Vigfús banters with the girls behind the counter, as Hörður, saying nothing, moves along.

They take seats at a long table where five of their colleagues are already sitting. The men nod and say hello and the like.

"Wow, new haircut!

"Look at you!"

"Flashy, aren't we?"

Vigfús is in his element here. He immediately starts chatting with his colleagues about this, that and the other, the weather and work, in between shoveling bites of fish into his mouth, which he washes down with cold milk. Hörður doesn't understand how people can talk endlessly about everything and nothing. He would prefer to sit somewhere by himself and eat in silence. But if he did so, he would be accused of being unsociable, or even worse, of thinking that he was better than everyone else. He knows this because he has repeatedly experienced such a reaction, both at work and in school.

Hörður can't stand how Vigfús eats, greedily and smacking his lips loudly, besides talking with his mouth full. He often loses his appetite just by sitting next to him. Hörður reaches for a folded copy of the *Morgunblaðið* daily, opens it and pretends to read as he forces himself to eat. Vigfús is saying something about their elective shift system, with which he seems to be obsessed, while Hörður tries to let the man's monologue go in one ear and out the other. He's heard this all before.

"Is there anything in the paper?" asks the officer sitting opposite Hörður. He's a man of Hörður's age, a former team-handball player whose name he doesn't remember.

Björn? Bjarni?

Hörður, who's been pretending to be immersed in his reading, looks up slowly. "Huh?"

His colleague grins. "You sure are focused today."

Hörður forces a smile and taps his finger on the paper. "Yeah, it's the chess puzzle. I like trying to solve it."

"Okay," says his colleague indifferently. "But talking about sports—though chess can't really be called that—we're planning on meeting at Ölver tonight to watch the match. Do you want to come?"

"The match?" asks Hörður, before glancing over at the nearest table, which is occupied by two plainclothes members of the criminal investigation department, Jafet Sigurðsson and Engilbert Gústafsson, called Betti. He knows their names because he's well acquainted with their department, its methods and work. His greatest dream is to become a detective—but this dream, which is around ten years old, he has never told to anyone else.

Jafet and Betti sit silently at their table. Jafet is reading a book, whose author appears to Hörður to be lyrical master Gyrðir Elíasson, while Betti is fiddling with his cell phone, probably sending a text message. They're serious and respectable-looking, unlike the clowns with whom he's sharing a table. Was this Bjarni saying something?

Hörður starts from his own thoughts. "What's that?"

"Ajax versus Arsenal," says Bjarni, or Björn, irritatedly. "The Champions League, man! Weren't you listening?"

Handball? Football? He has no idea.

"Yes, I just ..." Hörður stops and glances down at his plate, where his fish is cooling and its grease solidifying.

Social interaction is difficult for him. He *knows* this well, but has to *do* something about it. Otherwise, he'll never get ahead. It's all about relationships: being respected, and preferably popular. Diligence and vigilance aren't everything. Unless he wants to be a street cop all his life, he's got to make improvements in this area. He has aspirations, damn it!

Hörður clears his throat, looks up and smiles widely. "Yeah, it sounds exciting. Of course I'll come."

"Great," says Bjarni or Björn. "We have a betting pool—a thousand krónur per person. We write down what we think the score will be, and whoever guesses right wins the pot."

"Okay." Hörður nods. Of course! That's why they want him to go, to put more money in their betting pool. "No problem. Arsenal will win."

"Arsenal, he says," mutters Bjarni or Bjorn, pulling out a folded sheet of paper and a pen. "The score?"

"The score, yes," says Hörður, thinking about it. Arsenal is a football team; he's pretty sure of that. "Let's just say 3-1."

Hörður and his partner have barely sat back down in their car when the radio crackles. "*Dispatch calling unit 213, come in?*"

Vigfús answers. "Unit 213 here, over."

Hörður shakes a cigarette from a pack of them and lights it, before lowering his window halfway.

"*A skull has been found at a self-storage facility out on Grandi. Can you go check it out, over?*"

Hörður's eyes widen, and he blows smoke out his nostrils. Before answering, Vigfús gives Hörður an inquisitive look and shrugs his shoulders. "On our way, over and out."

"A skull?" asks Hörður.

"No two days the same," says Vigfús philosophically as he drives off. "I've said it often before, and will say it often again. No two days the same."

Hörður rolls his eyes.

The self-storage facility Geymslur is housed in a newish, square-shaped building on landfill at Grandagarður, close to the Króna supermarket and Byko hardware store, on the other side of the street from the fish-liver oil production facilities of Lýsi Ltd. A rock wall protects the area from the choppy waves of the Atlantic, from which come a salty wind and seagulls that glide through the grayish sky, which smells of marine and fish oil.

They walk through a gate in the chain-link fence and along a flagstone-paved path. The man who meets them is named Guðjón, the same who called about the skull. He's around sixty, short and bald, wearing a nylon jacket, baggy jeans and wooden clogs. A typical custodian.

Guðjón leads them down a cold-looking corridor, his clogs clicking on the concrete floor and keys jangling on his big key ring. "I thought I should let you know about it. It may be nothing, but I was alarmed. What's someone doing with such a thing? I've got to empty out the unit; the tenant's in default. People can't be storing all sorts of goddamn crap here without paying!"

On both sides of the corridor are closed storage units, all with yellow sliding doors and padlocks. The custodian's footsteps echo through the building. Hörður and Vigfús are wearing rubber-soled Ecco shoes.

"It's here." Guðjón unlocks one of the sliding doors and pushes it up, then switches on the storage unit's light. "This is one of our locks. I cut open the other lock, the one that the tenant was using. The account is delinquent, which is why I cut the lock. I had every right to do so. Tenants have to pay!"

"Thanks, wait out here while we take a look," says Vigfús. He goes into the unit, which is like a half-size garage. Hörður follows right behind him.

The unit is mainly empty; the little that's being stored in it could easily fit in the back of a station wagon. Against the far wall is a single piece of furniture: an old dresser with narrow legs and two drawers. On top of it is a human skull, and lying next to the skull is a black cloth. On either side of the dresser are garbage bags stuffed full, three in all, and four full cardboard boxes. Leaning against one of the side walls is a large mirror in an ornate frame.

"I didn't touch it," says the custodian. "I only pulled the cloth off it, and got quite a fright. Then I called you right away."

"That was exactly the right response," says Vigfús. He takes a look at the skull, as does Hörður. It's brownish, rather dark, has cracks and holes and is missing quite a few teeth. There are cut- and burn marks on top the dresser, and a large part of it is covered in black wax. There are solidified pools of wax on either side of the skull, with short, slender iron pins stuck in them—headless nails, guesses Hörður.

"It's old, this skull." Hörður takes a pair of disposable gloves from a compartment on his duty belt and pulls them on. "Decades old, I would say. And foreign, most likely from an old tomb. It doesn't appear to have ever been in the ground."

Vigfús nods. After putting on latex gloves as well, he lifts the black cloth, which turns out to be the size of a large handkerchief, and shakes it before setting it aside. Then he pulls out the dresser's top drawer. In it are black candles, a few knives of various makes, a packet of incense and some small bottles of essential oils. Further back in the drawer are three black rag dolls with pins stuck in them—voodoo dolls.

"What the hell is this?" mutters Vigfús.

"Mumbo jumbo," says Hörður.

"What do you mean?" exclaims Vigfús.

"Black magic," says Hörður.

"Black, white," says Vigfús disdainfully. "All magic is the same. Just the same old superstition and stupidity!"

"Yes and no," says Hörður. "White magic usually has to do with herbal medicine, love potions and the like—to heal and help. Black magic is connected with the powers of Hell. It's selfish by nature and is all about personal gain, usually at the expense of others. It's used to damage, destroy and kill."

"How do you know this?" asked Vigfús in surprise.

"Know thy enemy?" says Hörður, with a shrug. He grabs two black candles and sticks them onto the nails on the dresser, then takes the mirror and puts it on top the dresser, behind the skull and candles, leaning it against the wall. "Now it looks like an altar, doesn't it?"

"What gave you this idea?" asks Vigfús, bewildered. "And *what's* it supposed to mean?"

"I just found it kind of obvious," replies Hörður. "But maybe I'm barking up the wrong tree. There's always a certain group of people who practice all sorts of mumbo jumbo and black magic. It's in mode, apparently."

"In mode? Are you Danish, or what …? Do you mean it's in fashion? It's only old women who sprinkle their language with Danishisms."

"Whatever," says Hörður. His mother used a lot of Danishisms, like her mother before her.

"And these days it's all English words," says Vigfús, scandalized, before turning around. "Who's renting this unit?"

"Guðmundur Vífill Marínósson," says Guðjón testily. "But he didn't give us his correct address, and his phone is never turned on—if in fact he gave us his real phone number, the bastard. He paid in advance for six months, but now owes for two, soon three."

"Little Mummi," mutters Vigfús.

"He's dead, isn't he?" says Hörður.

Vigfús nods.

"He's what?" asks Guðjón.

"Guðmundur is dead," says Vigfús. "He took his own life earlier this year. In January, as I recall. Probably about the same time as he rented this storage unit."

"Damn!" says Guðjón. "Why do people do that? Make commitments knowing that they won't stick to them. Why should I have to pay the price for it?"

"Listen," says Vigfús dryly. "Do you have a plastic bag we can use? We'll take the skull with us."

"Yes, I suppose so," mutters Guðjón irritatedly, before sauntering off in his clogs, his footsteps echoing like slow, metallic drumbeats.

Hörður looks into one of the trash bags, which is full of t-shirts, underwear and socks. "Didn't Mummi have some psychological issues?"

"Yes, he was touchy, the poor fellow," says Vigfús, re-covering the skull with the cloth. "One of those who never had a chance. Up to his ears in drugs and crime since he was a teenager."

"And the occult, apparently," adds Hörður. He looks in the cardboard boxes but sees nothing of note, just CDs and books, mainly heavy metal and fantasy. One box also contains two framed photos, upside down. He turns them over. One of the photos is black, as if the back of the glass covering it has been painted black.

"Framed darkness," mutters Hörður.

"What's that?" asks Vigfús, as he pulls out the dresser's lower drawer.

"Nothing." Hörður scrutinizes the other photo. It's of a short young man standing next to a huge side of beef hanging on a meat hook in a large cold-storage unit. The young man, who looks to be about sixteen or seventeen years old, is wearing a blue smock and white boots, with a hairnet on his head. He's smiling at the camera and seems to be extremely proud of something. Behind him, knives hang in wall-mounted sheaths.

Hörður holds out the photo. "Isn't this Little Mummi?"

Vigfús looks up from the drawer. "Yeah, that's him."

Hörður puts the photo back in the box. "Anything else in the dresser?"

Vigfús snorts. "No, just some books. Some sort of occult bullshit, it seems to me."

"Can I see?" Hörður pulls the drawer out farther and examines its contents: basically a small library, including a few typical textbooks and handbooks for fringe dwellers and occultists. *The Satanic Bible*, *Necronomicon*, and so on. Mostly paperbacks, but one or two hardbound books.

"What a bunch of crap," mutters Vigfús.

"You can say that again," says Hörður with a grin, as he hands his partner an old Bible.

"Watch what you say, boy," says Vigfús gloomily as he takes the sacred book. He's a member of the Pentecostal church, but it has to be handed to him that he says next to nothing about that side of his personality while on duty.

Hörður keeps rummaging through the books. Among other things, he finds the dictionary *The Place of Words*, by Jón Hilmar Jónsson. "Isn't this up your alley?"

"What's that?" Vigfús looks up from the Bible.

Hörður hands him the book, which is both big and heavy. "Some dictionary. Aren't you an Icelandic-language fetishist?"

"Fetishist?" exclaims Vigfús, looking incredulous as he takes the book.

"You know, a language purist or whatever it's called," mutters Hörður, as he continues to rummage through the drawer. At the bottom of the stash of books he finds a few interesting titles, such as *How I Learned Soul Travel: The True Experiences of a Student in Eckankar*, *The Ancient Science of Soul Travel* by Terill Wilson, *Become Superhuman—Master of Hypnosis* by Doctor Hypno and the professor and *How to Hypnotize Anyone—Confessions of a Rogue Hypnotist*, by someone who calls himself The Rogue Hypnotist.

"Soul travel and hypnosis," mutters Hörður. He straightens up again, holding the latter book. *How to Hypnotize Anyone*. Indeed. Written under a pseudonym. The Rogue Hypnotist. Doesn't rogue mean con artist in this instance?

He leafs quickly through the book, which is a tattered paperback, before examining the front flyleaf. The book is marked as belonging to someone named Aron. Just Aron, no patronymic. And around the "A" is a circle, making it resemble the anarchist symbol.

Heavy footsteps sound in the corridor, drawing nearer.

"Did Mummi have a friend named Aron?" asks Hörður, looking at Vigfús, whose cheeks are flushed. Vigfús snaps the dictionary shut.

"Everything all right?" asks Hörður in surprise. "You look like you've looked up the word *homosexuality* or something similarly unchristian."

At the same moment, Guðjón reappears, holding a gray plastic bag. "Well, here's your bag."

Vigfús sticks the dictionary under his arm and takes the plastic bag from the custodian. "Thanks."

"So what do I do with this crap?" asks Guðjón.

"You can try contacting Guðmundur Vífill's parents. But if no one wants to claim this stuff, you should just take it to the recycling center." Vigfús holds the plastic bag open and nods toward the dresser. Hörður, understanding the gesture, picks up the skull in its cloth and puts it in the bag.

Hörður takes The Rogue Hypnotist's book. "I'm going to keep this, if it's all the same to you? It doesn't belong to the late Mummi, anyway."

"I couldn't care less," says Vigfús, gruffly. "I'm taking the dictionary."

"Oh?" says Hörður.

Vigfús's face reddens again. "I'm a language purist, as you pointed out."

Hörður bursts out laughing. "I'm starting to think it's some sort of dirty book. Can I see it?"

"Stop being an idiot," says Vigfús, as he storms down the corridor with the book under his arm.

It's two o'clock in the afternoon. Only an hour left on their shift. Their squad car is parked halfway up on the sidewalk at the intersection of Bjarkargata Street and Hringbraut Road, at the southwest corner of Hljómskálagarður Park in central Reykjavík. Vigfús raises his radar speed gun and aims it at the cars driving west, from the big intersection at the edge of the Vatnsmýri area to the roundabout on Suðurgata Street, where the National Museum stands on the outskirts of the University of Iceland campus.

Hörður is leaning against the squad car and thumbing through the hypnosis handbook, which he abruptly tosses through the open window into the passenger-side front seat. For some reason, Vigfús put the dictionary in the car's trunk, along with the skull. They delivered the skull to the medical laboratory of the National and University Hospital.

Hörður saunters over to him. "It's a pretty interesting book—at first glance, anyway."

"Is it?" says Vigfús, indifferently.

"Yeah, kind of." Hörður goes and stands next to him. "More sort of out there, unconventional, than scholarly, you know, but that's exactly what makes it interesting. It has a kind of wild tone; it's powerful, like rock n' roll."

"Yeah, okay," says Vigfús, who has extremely limited interest in things that are out there, rock music and actually anything else that people have come up since the end of the Second World War.

"No bites?" says Hörður. He shields his eyes and looks toward the intersection of Hringbraut and Njarðargata Street, which is two to three hundred meters away. Beyond it is the airport in Vatnsmýri. The autumn sun reveals exhaust fumes and airborne particulates.

"We're not fishing," says Vigfús.

"I guess not." Hörður watches a white sports car approach at a speed that is probably well above the limit. "What about him?"

"Seventy," mutters Vigfús.

"Shouldn't we stop him?" Hörður throws up his hands. If there's one thing he can't tolerate, it's rich show-offs who think they own the world.

"Oh, it isn't worth it," says Vigfús. He lets the radar speed gun sink and looks at his watch. "Let's wrap this up. We still have to return the car, write up a short report about our visit to the storage facility and clock out."

"Right, but ..." Hörður stops in mid-sentence, takes two steps forward and shields his eyes. He stares at the intersection his senses open wide, and it's as if his eyes change into zoom lenses. The lights are green and cars drive east and west, but it is neither the lights nor the cars that capture his attention—instead, it's the lonely shadow standing in the middle of the intersection. It's the silhouette of a man, a black ghost that then flickers, fades, and turns to nothing.

"What?" asks Vigfús.

A chill runs up Hörður's spinal cord. "Call an ambulance."

"An ambulance?" exclaims Vigfús. "Why?"

"Just do it," says Hörður, before running off toward the intersection. The lights are red. Cars drive south and north. Many turn onto Hringbraut, either east or west, while others continue to Vatnsmýri or toward the city center.

Hörður runs as fast as he can. The lights turn yellow and then back to green. A black SUV comes tearing in from the east, clearly on its way to shooting through the intersection without slowing down. At the same moment, another car runs the red light. It's a Japanese compact car, heading south down Njarðargata.

But the compact car has barely entered the intersection when the black SUV smashes into it. The crash sounds like a cannon blast; tires screech, glass shatters in all directions and a huge cloud of smoke erupts. The cars spin, slide forward and end up standing side by side in the middle of Hringbraut. Other cars slam on their brakes, steer clear, and stop here and there. It's a chaotic situation, and then all traffic stops and smokes covers the scene.

Hörður runs straight to the compact car, which is so utterly wrecked that it's nearly unrecognizable. Inside it is only one person: the young man who was behind the wheel.

Now, he's no longer sitting, but lies doubled up along the front seats, with the wheel no longer in its place.

Hörður manages to pull open the passenger-side door. He catches his breath and looks sadly into the car, whose interior is covered with shattered glass, blood, and bits of brain. The young man is dead, as Hörður knew beforehand that he would be.

The sports bar Ölver is packed with people, as always whenever there's a Champions League match on; almost all of them men, and at least every other one wearing an Arsenal jersey. Fewer of them support Ajax. The room has ten four-person tables, with every seat taken, and a group of people is sitting and standing at the bar. The match is being shown on a big screen on the end wall, the sound pouring over the crowd from large speakers.

Hörður and three of his colleagues are sitting at one of the tables on the right side of the room. Their group includes the officer named Bjarni or Björn. Hörður is wearing a green army jacket, a turtleneck sweater, dark-blue army pants and motorcycle boots. Wrapped around his neck is a keffiyeh. His helmet is under his chair, with his gloves lying on it. Hörður takes a sip of his warm coffee, then gloomily leans forward on his elbows. He doesn't feel well. What a day.

His self-esteem is in pieces.

On the one hand, he feels like a complete loser because of the way he acted at the barber shop. His hair was being cut by a cute girl who was open and fun, but he could hardly say a word because he panicked, as he always does whenever he feels attracted to someone. Why didn't he say anything?

Loser, that's what he is!

On the other hand, he feels like a fucking *freak* because of the shadow that he saw at the intersection. Because of his *premonition* of the fatal accident. He thought he'd outgrown that. Seeing something for the first time on the deck of a boat when he was seventeen, shortly before the boat sank, along with its skipper. Two years later, having a premonition of the avalanche that fell on the village of Súðavík. Back then, he saw numerous shadows, as a lot of people died that time—among them his parents and siblings.

Hörður downs the rest of his coffee in one gulp. It's been standing too long and tastes acrid. He's dying for a beer, or a whiskey—a beer *and* a whiskey. Something to deaden his pain.

Loser, freak.

Freak, loser.

Why can't he be like other people? Why can't he talk to girls and do his job without experiencing shadowy premonitions? Why can't he be cheerful and upbeat and be interested in ordinary things like football?

All of a sudden, the Ölver patrons shout in delight, leap to their feet and throw up their hands.

Hörður starts in alarm. What's all this about? He looks up at the screen, which shows players celebrating. Red-clad football players run around, one takes a running slide across the grass on his stomach, and the others throw themselves on top of him.

Ajax versus Arsenal. Hörður starts thinking about the soap Ajax, the cleanser that's mixed with water and used for scrubbing floors and the like. His late mother always used Ajax. Ajax comes in white containers labeled with an illustration of a dirty floor, with a clean, gleaming swatch where the floor has been wiped with a sponge, presumably soaked in Ajax. Also on the container is a picture of a spirit smiling self-confidently; in television ads for the product, he spins in a circle like a whirlwind, magically making everything sparklingly clean. Hörður remembers the smell; he can feel it in his nose, as if someone were scrubbing the floor of Ölver with Ajax just then. An arsenal is a place where weapons are stored. The team's logo is a cannon. Arsenal's players are soldiers waging war on a green battlefield, armed with cannons. They shoot, they blow things up, they change the beautiful field into a dirty, bloody mire. Corpses everywhere, smoke, earth, and death. Then comes Ajax, a whole troop of energetic, cleansing spirits who whirl around and clean up after the battle. The field becomes like new; it is fragrant with cleanliness.

When the celebration dies down, Hörður gets up, taking his coffee cup with him. He walks toward the bar, which is at the back of the room. Standing there among the others are two young men wearing dark hoodies, looking more like small-time crooks than football enthusiasts. One of them has his hood pulled over his head, and the other has a spider-web tattoo on his neck. These two fellows appear to have little or no interest in the match—no more than Hörður himself. He saunters past them, puts his cup down on the bar and goes to the bathroom.

There's a line to use the urinals. Hörður waits patiently. He's in no hurry. It's less noisy in the bathroom. His turn, however, soon comes. A young man flushes a urinal, zips up his pants and turns around slowly. He's of medium height, blond and blue-eyed, wearing an Arsenal jersey beneath a black blazer, stone-washed jeans and white sneakers. On his head is an old, prominent scar resembling the Nike Swoosh.

But instead of stepping aside to let Hörður use the urinal, the young man stares at him vacantly.

"Would you mind?" Hörður asks politely, gesturing to the young man to step out of the way.

But the young man stands there as if paralyzed.

"Hello?" says Hörður, waving one hand in front of the young man's face. Only then does the fellow blink, before stepping clumsily aside and walking stiffly out of the bathroom, without stopping to wash his hands.

Hörður shakes his head and sighs. Nothing but idiots and zombies here, he thinks, taking his place at the urinal.

The sounds of loud cheering come from the main room, and the floor trembles as the crowd jumps around in celebration.

It's all the same to Hörður. Leaving the bathroom, he heads straight to the bar. The dark-clad men are gone. Hörður is about to order another cup of coffee, but stops. Shouldn't he just go home?

He goes and gets his helmet and excuses himself from his colleagues, who are too preoccupied with the match to pay him any attention.

Hörður leaves the bar and walks into the parking garage next to it, where his motorcycle is parked along a gray concrete wall. The bike is a 400-cubic-liter Suzuki Enduro, yellow, with scratches, dents, and a broken clutch lever. He wraps his keffiyeh around his neck, puts on his helmet and gloves, mounts the motorcycle and starts it.

The night is freezing cold and pitch-black.

Murder

The clock on the Cathedral tower reads twenty minutes past ten. Austurvöllur Square is empty, though now and then someone walks past the statue of independence hero Jón Sigurðsson, proudly keeping watch on the Parliament House. Those out and about, people on their way either to the city center or home from there, are dressed warmly and walk quickly, it being chilly outside. The Parliament House is lit by floodlights, especially the new annex, which has both more and larger windows than the old stone-walled building. Meetings are finishing, and an MP or two leaves that historical workplace. Most go straight down to the underground parking garage and drive off without stepping a foot outside, while one or two walk out into the darkness of the night and head toward the city center, perhaps on their way to their party office or to meet with friends or colleagues at a café or bar.

Loitering in the darkness to the east of the Parliament House is a young man. He's surprisingly lightly dressed for the weather, bare-headed and wearing an unbuttoned jacket and thin red shirt of synthetic fabric. He sticks to the shadows behind one corner of the building, shifts his weight from one foot to the other and keeps close watch on people's movements at the annex. His right arm hand at his side, while his left is hidden beneath his jacket's right lapel.

The door of the annex opens and a woman in her thirties walks out onto the flagstone-paved sidewalk. It's Ingigerður Ásmundsdóttir, of the Social Democratic Alliance, an MP for the Northwest Constituency. She's wearing a Burberry coat and carrying a purse over her shoulder. The young man steps out of the shadows, while avoiding the light of the floodlights illuminating the building. He hesitates and stares at the MP, before stepping back into the shadows.

At ten thirty, the door opens again and out walks an MP for the Reykjavík Constituency, Þórólfur Hannesson of the Independent Party. He's dressed in jeans and black leather shoes, a black shirt and gray jacket, but no tie. Þórólfur has a full, groomed beard and wears glasses, and is carrying a laptop backpack over his right shoulder. Walking briskly, he heads toward the city center.

Without hesitation, the young man emerges from his hiding place. He steps across the sidewalk in his white sneakers and approaches the MP from behind. His gait is jerky and somewhat unusual. He lifts his feet slightly too high, as if his shoes are far too big or he's walking on a soft surface. His left hand appears from beneath his jacket lapel; a knife blade gleams in the glow of the floodlights.

"Excuse me!" says the young man. His voice is piercing and authoritarian, but also somewhat slurred, as if he doesn't have full control of his tongue or vocal cords.

"Yes?" The MP stops and turns halfway around. Then the young man seizes his opportunity; he lunges forward, bends his back and drives the sharp knife hard into the MP's belly, not just once, but twice, and finally a third time, before stepping back and straightening up.

The MP collapses, groans loudly and grabs his abdomen with both hands. Blood pours out, drenching his shirt, and the dark, vital liquid forms a puddle on the flagstones. His face is deathly pale, his mouth gapes, and his glasses are perched crookedly on his nose.

On Austurvöllur Square, a woman screams.

The young man lets go of the knife, which bounces twice on the sidewalk at his feet, and then he walks off, stiffly and awkwardly, and hurries away. Above him, the moon appears and disappears behind clouds.

The moon that is over three quarters full.

WEDNESDAY

It's eight in the morning. The sun hasn't risen yet, but the scene of the murder at the Parliament House is lit up from all sides. Besides the floodlights already there, the criminal investigation department has added four powerful, freestanding spotlights. Yellow police tape cordons off the scene, and police cars, lights flashing, are parked at all the intersections, as over a dozen uniformed police officers stand guard over the area—and a good thing they're doing so, too. The first few hours, there was hardly any peace to work what with all the reporters and photographers, to which was then added curious members of the public. Behind the yellow tape, members of the CID are still working, besides a photographer and two members of the Forensics Unit. At the center of the area is a large patch of blood that has turned black, surrounded by smaller patches and sometimes just drops, each and every one marked with a little yellow tag with a number on it. The photographer clicks away from all possible angles, the forensics team measures distances and fine-tooth combs the entire area, while the detectives from the CID crouch on the ground, thinking things over.

The victim is awaiting autopsy; the killer is still on the loose. Hörður and Vigfús stand guard by the yellow tape where it divides the area between the Parliament House annex and the grounds of the Oddfellow House on

Vonarstræti Street. The two men are wearing neon-green vests over their jackets. Now and then, curious wayfarers stop at the scene, and are asked politely to keep their distance. A few members of the media are still around, but their numbers are dwindling.

"Is anything known about the murderer?" asks Hörður. Without making a show of it, he slaps his arms against himself to warm up. It's chilly, and he slept rather badly.

"There's just the description that was distributed this morning," says Vigfús. "But from what I understand, the coroner thinks the attacker is left-handed. That seems to fit with the statements made by witnesses."

"What the hell are we doing *here*?" asks Hörður, disappointed and irritated. "Shouldn't we be out searching for the murderer, instead?"

"Others are doing that," says Vigfús. "The most comprehensive search was conducted during the night, from eleven o'clock until early this morning. But they've got few leads."

"Who were the witnesses?" asks Hörður.

"Two women on their way home from the city center," replies Vigfús. "They were able to provide a decent description of the perpetrator, but were apparently in complete shock."

"I see," says Hörður. "Do you have the description?"

Vigfús sticks his glove-clad hand into his pocket and hands his partner a folded sheet of paper.

"Thanks." Hörður unfolds the sheet and reads the witnesses' description of the murderer. *Guessing twenty to twenty-five years old. Average height. Blond, possibly with a scar on his forehead. Wearing light-colored jeans, white shoes and a black jacket. In a red shirt.*

Hörður reads the text twice, and thinks things over. "Fuck!"

"What?" asks Vigfús.

"He was at Ölver yesterday," says Hörður. "I could swear it."

"Are you sure?" asks Vigfús, skeptically.

"Pretty sure," says Hörður. "Who's leading the investigation on this case?"

"I think it's Engilbert," says Vigfús.

Hörður looks over the scene and soon sets eyes on Engilbert. He's standing next to one of the spotlights, wearing a trench coat, with disposable latex gloves on his hands and blue plastic covers over his shoes. "Hello! Engilbert! Betti!"

The detective looks up slowly, before going over to the police officer. Judging from his expression, he doesn't really appreciate the disturbance. "Yes?"

"I saw him, the murderer," says Hörður. He's worked up, but tries to stay calm. "He was at Ölver yesterday. There was a Champions League match on, Ajax versus Arsenal. He was there, this kid. The description fits perfectly. The red shirt is an Arsenal jersey. And he *does* have a scar on his forehead. It's shaped like the Nike Swoosh."

"Are you sure?" asks Engilbert.

Hörður shrugs. "The description fits."

Engilbert stares hard into the officer's eyes, before nodding abruptly. "I'll look into this. Thanks ..."

"Hörður," says the red-haired giant. "Hörður Grímsson."

Engilbert nods again and walks back onto the floodlit scene. He takes out his cell phone, selects a number and holds the phone up to his ear.

"He seems to have taken you seriously," says Vigfús.

Hörður has second thoughts. "I just hope I'm not mistaken."

"I guess we'll find out, won't we?" says Vigfús. "It would be worse to keep quiet about some far-fetched idea that turned out to be a lead."

"True." Hörður stamps his feet to get his blood moving, and looks at his watch. "When are our replacements showing up?"

"Any time now," says Vigfús.

"I could use some hot coffee," says Hörður.

"Same here," says Vigfús, before pointing at two police officers approaching them from Vonarstræti Street. One of them is the officer named Bjarni or Björn.

"Hi, fellows," says Vigfús.

"Anything going on?" asks one of the officers.

"No, nothing," says Vigfús. "But it would be good if something did. This is one of the most cold-blooded murders anyone's committed here in a long, long time. The CID is under enormous pressure. They'll have a hard time getting their work done, what with all the media attention."

"You just disappeared yesterday," says Bjarni or Björn.

"Yeah, I was a bit under the weather," says Hörður. "Thought maybe I was getting sick. Which didn't turn out to be the case."

Bjarni or Björn hands him an envelope containing a wad of bills, fifteen thousand krónur in total. "Here's the pot. You guessed correctly. Congratulations."

"Huh, I did?" Hörður takes the envelope hesitantly. He's never won anything before.

"You take over at ten o'clock, don't forget," says Bjarni or Björn.

Hörður and Vigfús head over to their squad car.

"What's his name again, the one who gave me the envelope?" asks Hörður. "Bjarni? Or is it Björn?"

Vigfús gives him a puzzled look. "Are you kidding, or …? His name is Fritz!"

They go to Björn's Bakery on Hringbraut Road and buy coffee in paper cups and donuts, take seats on barstools at a tall window table and watch the morning traffic as they warm up and enjoy their refreshments.

"Think about it," says Vigfús. "Not a single killing for ten months, almost a year, and then a member of parliament is murdered out on the street. In front of the Parliament House."

Hörður nods. "Outrageous."

"Let's hope he's found," says Vigfús, taking a sip of his coffee. "The public won't be too pleased having such a murderer running loose."

"There's something odd about this." Hörður takes a bite of his donut.

"What makes you say that?" asks Vigfús.

"If it was the kid that I saw, the one in the Arsenal jersey," says Hörður, "then I can't for the life of me imagine why he did it. I mean, he's just an ordinary kid, young, well-groomed, decently dressed. He's watching a football match with his favorite team, and then goes to the city center and stabs someone!"

"He must have psychological problems," says Vigfús. "They aren't really apparent from the outside."

"Yeah, maybe," says Hörður. "He actually did look a little peculiar. As if he were on drugs. Stoned or medicated."

"There you go," says Vigfús.

"Still." Hörður sips his coffee. "There's *something* peculiar about this."

Vigfús clears his throat. "Talking about peculiar things. We still haven't discussed the incident at the intersection yesterday. The fatal collision."

"Is there anything to discuss?" asks Hörður dryly.

"You ran off before the cars hit each other," says Vigfús. "You even asked me to call for an ambulance. How could you know there'd be an accident?"

Hörður's mood darkens. "I didn't know. I just guessed. Sometimes I just get a feeling about certain things happening."

"You guessed?" says Vigfús, incredulously.

"I don't want to talk about it," says Hörður. "There was an accident. A young man died. And whether I sensed it beforehand or not, there was no way that I could prevent it from happening. Unfortunately."

"No problem." Vigfús finishes his coffee. "Should we go do our rounds?"

"Yeah, let's do that." Hörður steps down from his stool.

"Thanks for the coffee and donut," says Vigfús, patting his partner on the back.

"You're welcome." Hörður smiles faintly. "The rare times that I win, I feel it's only natural to share my winnings."

They drive up Njarðargata Street, over Skólavörðuholt Hill and then down Laugavegur Avenue. The city center is quiet, with relatively few people out and about.

"Shouldn't we head back to the station?" asks Vigfús. "We still have to turn in a report on the discovery of the skull and a complete workup on the accident. I just wrote a short summary yesterday before we went off duty, for the insurance company."

"Yeah, let's do that," says Hörður. As they drive past the intersection at Klapparstígur, he looks out his window at the sign in front of the barber shop. Might she be working, that cute gal who cut his hair?

He feels strangely nervous and dry-mouthed.

"Would you mind writing the report on the skull discovery, if I take care of the accident?" asks Vigfús.

"No problem," says Hörður.

Vigfús turns right at the bottom of Bankastræti Street, and then drives up Hverfisgata Street toward the police station. He stops on red at the intersection with Klapparstígur. Hörður's heart starts beating faster.

When the light turns yellow, he gives Vigfús a poke, sort of off-hand. "Hey, would you mind turning up here?"

"Huh?" Vigfús hesitates, but then signals to turn right and heads up Klapparstígur. "Why? Weren't we going back to the station?"

He drives slowly up the narrow street.

"Just … no reason." Hörður leans forward and looks out the driver's side window, at the brightly lit windows of the barber shop.

"Do you need another haircut?" asks Vigfús, grinning.

"No, no, nothing like that," mutters Hörður.

Vigfús sees an empty parking space to the right and parks the car there.

Then he gives his partner a smile.

"What?" asks Hörður.

"Go in and talk to the girl," says Vigfús. "Get her phone number. Ask her out on a date. Put what you're thinking into action."

"Yeah, but …" Hörður's face turns bright red. "How did you know what I was thinking?"

Vigfús shrugs. "I didn't know. I just guessed. Sometimes I just get a feeling about things."

"But …"

"Stop thinking," says Vigfús. "You think too much, and you know it. Go and *do* something for a change. Now, do as I say!"

"You're unbearable." Hörður sighs, opens the car door and steps out. He puts on his cap, crosses the street and enters the barber shop.

Standing behind the reception desk is a young girl, but not the same one that cut Hörður's hair the day before. The air inside smells strongly of hairspray and cologne. Hörður's heart is pounding; he sees spots and has a buzzing in his ears.

"Hi! Can I help you?" asks the girl cheerfully.

"Yes," sighs Hörður. "She, um, cut my hair yesterday."

"Who cut your hair yesterday?" asks the girl.

"A woman," says Hörður. He looks around the room but doesn't see her just then. "Kind of small. Dark-haired."

"I think you mean Bíbí," says the girl, before standing on her toes and calling loudly: "Bíbí! There's someone here to see you!"

Hörður's face pales. "Yeah, no, it's all right. I'll just come later. It's not important."

He reaches for the door handle and is about to open the door and step out into freedom when a silky-soft voice addresses him.

"Yes?"

It's her. He recognizes her voice. And that voice now has a name. It's Bíbí. He turns around, takes off his cap and blushes brightly.

"It's you. Hello again," says Bíbí, smiling so beautifully that Hörður's knees grow weak and he nearly loses his balance. "You're not satisfied with your haircut? Would you like me to fix something?"

"Yes, no, not at all," he says hoarsely. "I was just wondering, see. Um, I'd like to apologize."

"Apologize?" says Bíbí, in surprise. The girl at the reception desk is all ears. "For what?"

"I, um." He clears his throat again. "I was a little gruff. I didn't mean to be."

"Oh, dear—don't worry about it," says Bíbí, laughing. "It's just natural to want to relax in the chair. Not everyone wants to chat. I'm the one who should watch myself, just blabbing away all the time!"

"No, not at all," says Hörður. "There's nothing wrong with you. Absolutely nothing."

"Oh, well." Bíbí smiles warmly and her brown eyes grow twice as wide. "What a lovely thing to say."

"Yeah, sure." Hörður looks away, turning his cap around in his giant hands. "But, um, yeah. Exactly."

Bíbí takes a business card from a rack on the reception desk and hands it to him. "You can make an appointment if it suits you better. I can cut your hair again, if you want."

He takes the card and looks at it. *Ester Guðmundsdóttir, hairdresser.* Below the name is the barber shop's phone number. "Yeah, I'll do that. Thanks, Ester."

"Bíbí," she says, smiling. "Call me Bíbí."

"Bíbí," repeats Hörður. Her name is light and short; it flits around and flies off into the blue like a little bird. Unlike his name, which is like a massive rock.

"Well, then, I'll see you later …" says Bíbí, opening her brown eyes wide, inquisitively.

"Hörður," says the massive rock, and then, it's as if his courage is all used up. He lifts his cap in farewell and turns around halfway, but then hesitates for a second before going for it.

"Hey, Bíbí?"

Hörður plunks himself into the squad car and exhales like a whale. His legs tremble, his hands shake, and his back is drenched with sweat.

"Well, and …?" Vigfús asks, grinning.

"Drive," says Hörður, hoarsely.

"Easy," says Vigfús, as he pulls out of their parking spot. "You didn't rob the joint, did you?"

Hörður looks at the business card, before sticking it in the breast pocket of his jacket. "Bíbí. Her name is Bíbí."

"Yeah, so what?" asks Vigfús. He turns right and they drive down Laugavegur for the second time in less than five minutes.

"I asked her out," says Hörður, in a surprised tone, as if realizing it just now.

"Good job!" says Vigfús. "When's your date?"

"Tonight." Hörður suddenly feels mildly dizzy. Tonight! Is he crazy? His anxiety is almost unbearable.

"You don't mess around. I'm proud of you!" says Vigfús. "And where will you go? To the theater? Out to eat?"

"The Vitabar pub, at eight," says Hörður. "I'll probably eat first. If I have any appetite."

"Vitabar?" exclaims Vigfús, frowning. "Why Vitabar?"

Hörður shrugs. "Just, I couldn't think of anything else. I'm always there, anyway. What's wrong with Vitabar?"

Vigfús sighs. "It's a damn dive, Hörður. Nothing but drunks, crooks, and cops. The only women who go to Vitabar are toothless and have hepatitis."

"I don't know about that," says Hörður annoyedly. "Maybe she won't come, anyway."

"Can the negativity," says Vigfús, in a paternal tone. "I'm sure she'll come. And when she shows up, you should suggest going somewhere else. Let her decide where you go."

Hörður nods. "That sounds good. I'll do that."

Around ten to twenty percent of the working hours of regular police officers goes into writing reports and doing other "housekeeping" work. It's the part of the job that Hörður hates most. He's been sitting at one of the computers in the communal work area for nearly twenty minutes and is practically dying of boredom. He's about halfway through his report on the discovery of the skull at the self-storage facility, but has long since lost interest in the topic, and along with it, his concentration.

Chewing on a match and longing to take a smoke break, he fidgets moodily in his chair. He takes a sip of lukewarm coffee and scowls. The work area is windowless, the air is dry and smells of stale sweat.

"Should I mention the books that we took?" he calls out.

"What?" says Vigfús, who is on the other side of the room, writing up his report on the fatal collision. He sits bent over his desk, his glasses on his nose, tapping at his keyboard with his two index fingers.

"The dictionary and the hypnosis book," calls out Hörður.

"Are you nuts?" calls Vigfús back. "Stick to what's important and forget about the rest."

"Yep." Hörður types something into the computer, and then his mind wanders. He grabs the paper that the custodian of the self-storage facility gave them. It's a copy of the rental agreement. The signature is shaky, yet still quite legible.

Guðmundur Vífill Marínósson

Better known as Little Mummi, a drug dealer and petty criminal. He gives his address as Baldursgata Street. It was there that he was found, in a vacant attic apartment. Hanging at the end of a rope tossed over one rafter. On the kitchen counter was his passport and a plane ticket to London. A very peculiar set of circumstances.

Hörður writes the name "Mummi" on a blank sheet of paper, and then closes his report file and opens Löke, the police database. He enters his ID number and password, then types Little Mummi's ID number in the empty window that appears.

The deceased Mummi had several complaints on record, most rather insignificant, all the way down to traffic violations. The most recent complaint had to do with a case of squatting on Vatnsstígur Street a year and a half ago. Two weeks before he hung himself, he was ordered to pay fines and damages. Mummi had been convicted three times, including two prison sentences, but he'd gone to prison only once, for the possession and sale of drugs. The previous sentence was suspended.

Hörður jots down several details before scrolling down. Mummi had filed a complaint once as well, thirteen months ago. It was against Ingimar Jósefsson, a retired pastor, for repeated sexual offenses. The offenses were allegedly committed in the YMCA summer camp at Vatnaskógur, when Mummi was eleven and twelve years old. This Ingimar turned seventy-five years old a month ago. He was questioned, but then the case was dropped.

"The poor kid," mutters Hörður, as he writes down the pastor's name on the sheet of paper.

He enters Ingimar's ID number into Löke, and finds that the old pastor has three complaints on record and one conviction. Four years earlier, a young man pressed charges against him for sexual assault. The offense was committed at Ingimar's home in the Laugarnes neighborhood. At the time, Ingimar was employed as an assistant pastor at Langholt Church. He pleaded guilty and was given a suspended sentence of three months. The other two complaints were thirteen months old, like the deceased Mummi's complaint, and for the same offenses: sexual abuse of juvenile boys at the YMCA camp at Vatnaskógur, where Ingimar was employed by the YMCA as a counselor. The charges were both deemed ungrounded and invalid.

"Fucking disgusting." Hörður closes Löke and opens the web browser. He tries Googling the pastor, but hardly anything comes up. Next he tries the Icelandic newspaper and magazine archive, *timarit.is.* A few results are returned, mainly links to articles in the *Church Journal.* Yet he does find one link related to the pastor's 70th birthday, which he celebrated in Florida with family members and friends, according to the article published in the daily *Morgunblaðið* in the birthday announcements section. The headline reads: "Hole in one, God willing." The article reports that the pastor is going to play golf on his birthday, along with his nephew, whom he says is incredibly skilled at the sport. The photograph accompanying the article is of the two of them, Reverend Ingimar and his nephew Gísli, who is around twenty.

"Great," mutters Hörður. He closes the article about the golf-crazed pastor and types the name Little Mummi into Google. His inquiry yields only one photograph: a passport photo of Mummi when he was a little over fifteen years old. A search was conducted for him after he and another boy ran away from his juvenile detention center. The photo is of a young boy who is not at all unhandsome, but with such a bewildered look in his eyes and depressed expression that Hörður cannot help but feel sorry for him.

The boy who ran away with him is also named. A good-looking boy with blond hair.

"Áskell Tyrfingsson," calls out Hörður. "Isn't that Sæli, the drug dealer who lived on Stórholt?"

"That's right," says Vigfús.

"They ran away together once from juvie, he and Little Mummi," says Hörður.

"Right."

"Didn't Sæli disappear?" asks Hörður. "Wasn't an alert put out for him? He was never found, was he?"

"No."

"Wasn't he supposed to have been killed?" calls out Hörður. "For drug debts? Didn't he owe the SS-brothers money? That's what I heard."

"That was just some bullshit story," Vigfús calls back. "Sæli's in South America. In Peru or Colombia. He's a kingpin there. A powerful cocaine dealer. Lays low. Has changed his name and everything."

"Is that right?" asks Hörður.

"Yep," says Vigfús.

"One's always learning something new," says Hörður. Well. Shouldn't he finish his goddamn report? He doesn't feel like it just now. He folds the paper holding his notes and sticks it in the breast pocket of his shirt.

Hörður looks at his watch. It's not like he's under any time constraints. He reads the news on *visir.is* and *mbl.is.* The murder is front-page news everywhere, but the deceased hasn't yet been named. After reading the news, he checks his e-mail inbox, where he finds a message from the medical laboratory of the National and University Hospital. The message is actually addressed to Vigfús, with Hörður cc'd. Preliminary results of the analysis of the skull, which are simple and clear: it is estimated to be one hundred to two hundred years old. Possibly Icelandic, but much more likely from a foreign tomb.

"It's foreign, the skull," calls out Hörður.

"That's good," answers Vigfús. "Then we don't have to give it any more thought."

"Where do people get skulls?" asks Hörður.

"It was smuggled in, I suppose," says Vigfús. "Or just ordered off the Internet, for all I know. People keep snakes and spiders as pets. The world is full of whack jobs."

"Yep," says Hörður. "In any case, I can complete my report now."

"Good," says Vigfús, before continuing to tap at his keyboard.

Hörður clears his throat. His report. Yeah, right. He'll finish it, soon enough. But first, he's going to browse a bit longer. He wonders if there are any photos of that squatting incident, which ended with arrests and charges. A group of young anarchists had taken over an abandoned house on Vatnsstígur Street. The house owners complained and the police were sent to clear the place out, which ended in a clash between the squatters and the police. Hörður remembers the incident quite well, but wasn't on duty when it boiled over.

He enters "squatting on Vatnsstígur" into Google. Quite a few photographs come up, as a large number of photographers had been on the scene. The squatters are dressed in black, most with a black cloth covering their noses and mouths. They wave black flags, shake their fists through the broken windows on the upper floor of the house, and throw various things at the police officers breaking down the door on the lower floor. Most of the conflict took place inside the house, and was, therefore, not photographed. But in three of the photos, several of the anarchists are being led in handcuffs out the door. Among them is the group's leader, whose name Hörður can't remember just now. Four police officers hold him tightly as they lead him away, screaming and shouting. He's in a terrible rage and his eyes blaze with fury.

Atli? Andri? No, the name escapes Hörður. He remembers only that this fanatic was given a three-year jail sentence for squatting, resisting arrest, and assaulting the police officers, or, offenses against the government authorities, as violence against officers of the law is called in the system.

The squatters had painted a huge sorcerer's stave on the front of the house with black paint. The stave was basically a cross inside a circle, with bent arms extending from the circle, each arm having numerous small lines on it, making them resemble flags or the old windspeed symbols on the television weather forecasts.

Is there no photo of Little Mummi? Hörður scrolls through the images, stopping finally at a group photo published in the daily *DV* two days before the incident. The photo accompanies an interview that a reporter for *DV* conducted with Aron Beck, the leader of the anarchists, after the owner of the house complained to the police.

Aron! As soon as he sees it, Hörður remembers the name. It rings a few bells in his memory. Didn't he see that name somewhere? Yes, of course! It was in the hypnosis book, which was marked with the name Aron, with a circle around the "A"—the same as the symbol for the anarchist movement, of which Aron is the head in Iceland—he should have realized this right away!

The photo shows seven young men: Aron, Mummi, and five others, all dressed in black fatigues, and most of them looking like crooks—with fierce looks in their eyes and tattoos on their hands or necks. No blurbs accompany the photo or the interview, other than the heading: *Aron Beck: "Anarchism is neither a political party nor a religion, but a revolution."* Mummi is noticeably the smallest of the six; he's standing to the right of Aron, looking furtively at the photographer out of the corner of his eye. Aron is standing spread-legged in the center of the group, holding a long pole with black flag on the end in one hand, and the other, clenched in a fist, over his chest. His head is shaved bald, his mouth is turned down in an arrogant scowl and his eyes, black and piercing, are fixed on the camera.

He could be a rock star, and this photo a portrait of his band. Their poses are typical of a little-known rock group that's determined to draw attention to itself in any way possible. They're at once nonchalant and provocative, indifferent and focused. Their leader looks like a combination of Charles Manson and Henry Rollins.

"The book that I took," says Hörður. "I know whose it is."

"Oh?" says Vigfús.

"It belongs to Aron Beck," says Hörður. "The anarchist who took over the house on Vatnsstígur. The one who's locked up in Litla-Hraun Prison."

Vigfús snorts. "Fucking dirtbag. He should never be let out again. Raving lunatic."

"Yep," says Hörður, just to say something. Vigfús has strong opinions, and isn't much for reasoned discussion or listening to others' opinions. But this is undoubtedly the right call on his part. This Aron looks to be both intelligent and half-crazy. A combination that can be extremely dangerous.

And exciting.

Hörður's curiosity has been aroused. He has a burning interest in both rock stars and criminals, and has read a lot of books about both. Ozzy Osbourne, Adolf Hitler, Keith Richards, and Ted Bundy, all of these people were born with some sort of undefined X-factor that distinguishes them from the average person and is the reason that they either became fame-obsessed rock stars or notorious dictators and mass murderers. Some of them were born with musical talent and the will to go far, but maybe the others just felt a longing for something, something missing—maybe they had a kind of inner emptiness or hunger, a brutish black hole that demanded endless human sacrifices, a need that could never be satisfied.

Hörður goes back to *timarit.is* and looks up the interview with Aron Beck by typing his name into the search field.

The group photo reappears, the same that showed up on his image search on Google. But this time, the photo is captioned:

Anarchists on the warpath. The photo shows, from left to right: Orri, Hákon, Guðmundur Vífill, Aron Beck, Tryggvi Leó, Þorsteinn, and Egill Þór.

The interview itself is neither long nor remarkable, just a typical *DV* shock piece, written and published to scandalize, amuse, and frighten—little or no risk of it being nominated for a Pulitzer Prize. No Truman Capote at work here. Yet despite the interview being no masterpiece in journalism, the interviewee's statements are well worth reading. He seems to have shown up much better prepared than the reporter. Which says everything about the working methods of both.

At the start of the interview, the reporter makes an attempt to inform the readers of the interviewee's past—his family history, education, work experience—but Aron slips from his grasp like a frantic snake. He claims to be self-made: *I created myself out of nothing, I am nothing and all will fear me. One day I will return to nothing.*

Hörður smiles faintly. This answer is pre-formulated and practiced, damn it. Nor is Aron any more tongue-tied when asked about anarchy: *Anarchy is truth and life; all else is either denial or sheer delusion. At its heart, life is savagery and chaos; that is plain to see. Outer space appears silent and still in photographs, and according to the standardized tastes of the civilized person, it's considered beautiful—but what is the universe other than immense cold and darkness scattered with galaxies, like scraps of garbage blown about in cold north winds! Collisions, nuclear explosions, black holes and screaming fires! We would not be as captivated if these actual horrors of existence were a little closer to us, as blessed creation would have wiped us out long ago—and indeed should have. And on our Earth, our blue Mother, chaos and the law of the jungle prevail, everywhere except in our so-called human culture—but what are humans but self-centered cockroaches in suits; hairless monkeys with delusions of grandeur? No, anarchy is the one true con-dition, and we are its heralds and servants. Education is a delusion, the work week is a lie, democracy is a tool used to control the people, and the people live under the illusion that they are free—whereas the truth is otherwise. You're the slaves of habit, the slaves of work, the slaves of religion and ideas, the slaves of luxury and lack, riches and poverty, the slaves of deception and lies.*

What a speech! Hörður has of course heard and read things far more ridiculous. Some of this was simplification and some of it dubious assertions, but basically, the doomsday rant made some sense, and it would be wrong to say that this Aron was stupid. Nuts, yes, but not stupid.

At this point in the interview, the conversation turned to the squatting incident on Vatnsstígur, to the ideas of ownership, capitalism, and the system, that great enemy of the anarchists. Aron blathered a bit about ownership being a crime, seeming to change for a moment into a bitter communist before taking aim at the system, *that three-headed giant representing oppression, injustice and violence,* according to the anarchist.

Are you talking about the separation of powers? asks the reporter.

I'm talking about the Enemy, with a capital "E," says Aron. *It's disgusting to see how the public in this country both feeds this giant and pretends not to see it. It's democracy in the form of a monster. Parliament ensures the continued existence of oppression and inequality in society, the courts dole out injustice like some hellish gospel, and the cops silence and beat anyone who dares to object to this abomination.*

Isn't this talk of some undefined giant the same as what's called standing up a straw man? asks the reporter.

Straw man? asks the anarchist.

A straw man is a term for a rhetorical fallacy, says the journalist. *When one person or group attempts to refute another's contrary opinions, sometimes a view not actually held by the refuter's opponent is presented and attacked instead—this is called standing up and knocking down a straw man. Usually, resorting to this fallacy is indication that the party doing so actually holds an untenable position.*

"Aha," mutters Hörður. The reporter is apparently not as dense as he thought. Hörður scribbles down his remarks on the straw man, before continuing his reading.

Aron seems not to understand this about a rhetorical opponent and untenable position. In any case, he says nothing about these, but seems to like the term straw man, which he feels suitable for describing those slaves to the system who control everything—*scarecrows in suits,* he says, laughing. Then he cuts loose:

The rich are made richer, ownership is nothing but violence in the form of laws, public assets are raffled off to the chosen few, and criminal complaints filed in response to the rape of children and teenagers are dismissed because the offenses have passed the statute of limitations! In return, I ask: When does the shame pass the statute of limitations, when do the damage and the pain become null and void?

Are you referring to a particular matter? asks the reporter.

Yes and no; this happens on a daily basis, says Aron. *And it doesn't matter whether it's women or men who file complaints. Children don't file complaints; they're scared, and feel threatened and intimidated by their abusers. But when they come of age, have matured and gained courage, then, perhaps, they may step forth, but only to be humiliated again. Whereas the abusers go free and continue to work, teach, and proclaim the word of God. May they all burn in Hell, if Hell in fact exists.*

He's talking about that pastor, that Ingimar who abused Little Mummi, thinks Hörður. He's as angry as he is because his friend was abused. And who's to blame him?

The system is like a mean-spirited child who pulls the wings off of flies just to see them suffer, adds the anarchist. *Things are boxed but not forgotten. When the Revolution takes place and the oppressed come to power, the oppressors will not be squashed like bugs, but instead, they'll be given a taste of their own medicine.*

Aron is asked to say more about the proclaimed revolution and the system to be overturned.

Children and animals are innocent and don't know any better, he says. *But every single person over the age of eighteen who doesn't fight against the system, the three-headed giant, is a part of the system and thereby our enemy, an enemy of life.*

When the reporter asks Aron if he's worried about clashing with the police and perhaps ending up in prison, he replies:

They can beat us, they can oppress us, bend us and break us. They can lock us up in their institutions, but they can never defeat us! We aren't men, but evil spirits; no walls can hold us, we slip out everywhere. We are not of this world; we're the sons of darkness!

And at those words, the interview concludes.

Hörður laughs out loud. In fact, he'd hit the nail on the head when he compared the squatters to a rock band.

Those final statements could have been verbatim quotes from Glen Benton, the leader of the notorious death-rock band Deicide. This Benton sometimes slathered his own face with pig's blood for photo shoots and had an upside-down cross branded on his forehead. He talked a great deal about Satan and himself as his servant, and said that he was going to commit suicide after living one year longer than Jesus had done.

Naturally, though, he didn't follow through on that, and before he knew it, he was a fat, middle-aged man, a father who had to attend PTA meetings with an upside-down cross on his forehead.

"What's so funny?" calls Vigfús from across the room.

"Nothing, I was just reading an interview," answers Hörður.

"How's it going with your report?" asks Vigfús.

"It's getting there." Hörður closes the browser and re-opens the document he was working on. He picks up where he left off. A description of the storage unit, what they found, how they removed it and where they took it. What a boring job! He taps at the keyboard, but his concentration wavers and his mind immediately roams elsewhere.

Date tonight. The thought of it gives him butterflies. Is he in love? Or is it just anxiety? Ugh. What should he wear? Did he forget to buy razor blades? Does he have any aftershave left?

The crowd at Múlakaffi listens silently to the twelve o'clock news being read on the radio. The police in Reykjavík have custody of a young man suspected of killing another man outside the Parliament House the previous evening. According to the news bureau's sources, the suspect turned himself into the police after an alert for him was announced over the radio. He was to be questioned today. The police declined to comment on the case, other than the head of the CID, Axel M. Axelsson, who stated that it was at a sensitive stage, but was going well. The deceased's name was Þórólfur Hannesson, who was an MP for the Independent Party. He left behind his fiancé and daughter from a previous relationship.

"They caught him after the tip from Hörður," says Vigfús proudly. The silence gives way to the babble of voices and clinking of cutlery.

All eyes are directed at the red-haired giant from Súðavík.

"No, hardly," Hörður mumbles. He cuts a meatball lying in brown gravy, but has lost his appetite. "An alert was put out for him first thing the next morning, based on the witnesses' descriptions."

"The alert was changed after you spoke to Betti," says Vigfús. "They added the Arsenal jersey, and that the suspect had been seen at Ölver earlier that evening."

"Was he really there?" asks Fritz, whose name Hörður had thought was Bjarni or Björn.

Hörður nods as mushes his potatoes into the gravy. "I saw him in the bathroom. He was ahead of me in line. Just an ordinary guy. But he was on something. His eyes were like … they were just completely empty."

Fritz leans forward and lowers his voice. "Don't let it get out, but I heard that the murderer had ecstasy on him."

"Oh?" asks Vigfús hesitantly.

"Did he bring ecstasy tablets to the police station?" asks one of their colleagues.

"That's what I heard," says Fritz.

"He's crazy," says someone at the table.

"They're saying that it's political," says Vigfús, shoveling food into his mouth. "Because of that bill that he was going to submit, that Þórólfur."

"The alcohol bill?" asks Fritz.

"Yes," says Vigfús, through a mouthful of food. "He wanted to do away with the government monopoly on alcohol. It was, and is, highly controversial. Not everyone wants alcoholic drinks to be sold in the grocery stores."

"But that's no damn reason for murder, is it?" exclaims Fritz.

Vigfús shrugs. "That's what they said on Radio Saga."

His colleagues laugh, but Hörður just pushes at his red cabbage and peas with his fork. The name of the head of the CID echoes in his mind. Axel M. Axelsson. They met when Hörður was seventeen, he and Axel, but the mythical Steppenwolf, as Axel is called by Hörður's colleagues, probably wouldn't remember it. It was at a maritime inquiry in Ísafjörður, after the fishing boat María sank near the Djúpálinn trench. There were three on board: Hörður, his deceased father, Grímur, and the skipper, Pétur. Things had gone terribly badly for them that day; once they were aboard the lifeboat, Hörður suffered an intense asthma attack. He'd left his inhaler on the María, which was on the verge of going down. Pétur went to retrieve the inhaler, the María capsized and the old oak boat disappeared into the deep with the skipper aboard.

The inquiry was a huge ordeal. The representative of the insurance company was both mistrustful and dour. Adding to the pressure, he was accompanied by a representative from the criminal investigation department of the police force in Reykjavik. It was Axel M. Axelsson, who, at the time, looked like Clint Eastwood in the *Dirty Harry* movies. But instead of badgering the nervous, unhardened Hörður Grímsson, Axel came to his rescue at that moment of truth. Why, Hörður doesn't know, but he always feels as if he owes a debt of gratitude to that notorious hardhead.

Axel M. Axelsson was the reason why Hörður entered the police academy. When Hörður saw Axel at the top of his super-cool match, he knew for the first time what he wanted to be. He was going to be cop. Not a street cop, but a criminal investigator, a *detective,* as they called themselves. Members of the CID don't wear uniforms. Each has his own style. Some wear suits, some are sporty, and others wear leather jackets. They don't hang around in bakeries and at gas stations. They don't write speeding tickets and don't have to deal with cases of domestic violence or arrest teenagers for drunkenness and disorderly conduct. They used to do so at one time, but not any longer.

The detectives are beyond such work; they're past that—they're the elite.

Unit 07-213 has been assigned to traffic control on Sæbraut Road. Vigfús is behind the wheel, driving westward in the right lane when his cell phone rings. Hörður is in the passenger seat, gazing distractedly out his window toward Faxaflói Bay, Esja, Skarðsheiði Heath, and Akrafjall Mountain. The sun has already begun to descend; its orange rays are mirrored on the surface of the ocean. The sky is a deep, dark blue, with black clouds in the distance. The lights of the town of Akranes twinkle like the stars in the Milky Way on the opposite side of the tranquil bay.

Vigfús's cell phone rings over and over.

"What fucking commotion is this?!" Vigfús tenses. He signals a right turn and parks the car next to the sewer pumping station a short distance from Laugarnes, before fishing the ringing cell phone out of the breast pocket of his jacket. But he doesn't answer straightaway; he's too suspicious for that. He pulls his reading glasses from another pocket, unfolds the temples and puts them on. He stares at the phone's display, mutters something and then presses the green button with a trembling finger.

"Yes, hello?"

Hörður rolls down his window and lights a cigarette. He inhales the smoke deeply, and holds it in for a moment or two before blowing it out his nostrils.

"Speaking," says Vigfús to the caller. He speaks softly and quickly, as if he's worried that his partner is listening in.

But Hörður is distracted. He's standing on the pier in the remote fishing village Súðavík, looking out at Álftafjörður. Behind him looms the mountain Kofri, like a Nordic pyramid, and on the opposite side of the deep fjord is the steep Sjötúnahlíð mountainside. He thinks about the boat that sank, about the skipper who perished and his daughter María. He thinks about the avalanche that wiped out both buildings and entire families. He thinks about his mom and dad, about his sister and brother, about the cold, black tombstone upon which their names are engraved.

And he thinks about himself, the depressed giant who survives it all. About the sad soul that continues to live, despite occasionally lacking the desire to do so. In his opinion, he's simply "undead"—like a specter or zombie.

"Around five hundred, I guess," says Vigfús into his phone. "Blue, yes."

Hörður taps the ash from his cigarette out the window. He's back in Reykjavík. His mind turns to the murder case. The investigation must be drawing to a close. Having arrested the suspect, and all. Maybe he's being questioned now? Or will they let him stew in his cell overnight first? They've undoubtedly requested an extension of custody. It should be an open-and-shut case.

"Yeah, that sounds fine," says Vigfús. "When do you think that … the day after …? Not today …? What about tomorrow? Okay then, that should work. I'll call you. Yeah, okay."

Vigfús hangs up and sticks his phone back in his pocket.

"Lots going on?" asks Hörður, just to say something.

"Not really, no." Vigfús clears his throat and drives off, out of the parking lot and back onto Sæbraut. "That was my nephew. He's going to buy some of my old stuff. Old stamps. He collects them."

"I see." Hörður tosses the half-smoked cigarette out his window and shuts it. "Isn't it better to hold onto stamps? Aren't they always increasing in value?"

"Yeah, I'm sure they are," says Vigfús. "But the money will come in handy. He'll pay me a decent sum for my collection. They're going to be doing some renovations on my apartment building, which means increased expenditures, of a hundred thousand or more. It's not like I make a government minister's wages, do I?"

"No, no," says Hörður. "Certainly not."

"Why I'm in this line of work, I'll never know," says Vigfús angrily. "You put your life in danger every week and get nothing for it but ingratitude! I'll never understand why anyone would become a cop."

"Yeah, yeah." Hörður is in complete agreement with his partner, but the man's constant complaining is more tiring than the job he complains about. And if it's not his job that he's complaining about, it's just something else—the European Union, artists, bicyclists, the band Sigur Rós, vegetarians or Communists.

The changing room at police headquarters on Hverfisgata Street is like a cliché from an American movie. White walls, rows of metal lockers, and hard wooden benches. Hörður removes and puts away his duty belt, hangs his uniform on hooks in his locker and puts on his everyday clothes: army pants, a turtleneck sweater, and motorcycle boots. His helmet is on top of his locker, and in it are leather gloves. Hörður puts on his green army jacket over his sweater, wraps his keffiyeh around his neck, and shuts and locks his locker.

Out in the corridor, he runs into Þórhildur Sverrisdóttir, a friend of his and classmate from the Police Academy. Þóra Sverris, as she's always called, is as unlike Hörður as imaginable. She's short and thin, with dirty-blonde, shoulder-length hair and a face that's so plain it's almost indescribable. She's comely, without being downright attractive. But within her small, unpresuming body, there's more strength and intelligence than in an entire battalion of athletes and beauty queens.

"Hi, how are you?" says Þóra, giving Hörður a punch on the shoulder. He's not about to greet her in the same way. She'd undoubtedly be slammed into the opposite wall and fall in pieces to the floor.

"Just fine, and you?"

"Fine, thanks." They both head toward the staff exit, which is behind the building. "How do you like partnering with Vigfús?"

"Just fine," says Hörður. "He's old and tired, but overall, a decent guy. But, um … who's your partner, again?"

"Karl," replies Þóra. "He's fine, but I think he finds it pretty dull hanging around with a woman all day. He's more used to sharing dirty jokes and stories with other guys."

"Can't he tell you his dirty stories?" asks Hörður.

Þóra shrugs. "Yeah, yeah. But he won't. I don't think he dares. Maybe afraid that I'd file a complaint against him for sexual harassment."

"It's a hard world we live in," says Hörður. They've reached the exit, but instead of opening the door, Þóra stops and grabs Hörður's jacket sleeve.

"Listen," she says. "What shifts are you working this weekend?"

"I'm off this weekend," he says. "I start evening shifts on Monday."

"Okay, great," says Þóra. "I need to ask you a favor. Nothing bad, mind you. Actually, it should be really fun."

Hörður sighs. This doesn't sound good. But he knows that he'll have a hard time saying no, no matter what the favor involves. He owes Þóra one. No, not one—more like a hundred. He would never have made it through Police Academy without her help. She pushed him through the practical courses, and they studied together for the written exams. She literally got him back on his feet when he was hungover, and numerous times prevented him from going on benders.

In return, he was always there for her during their Academy years. She wasn't only the smallest person in their class, but also the least popular. As a former member of the national women's football team, she was judged to be a privileged bitch and a snob, neither of which was justifiable. And on top of it all, the fact that she was openly gay complicated things even further, because other female students were uncomfortable being around her in the changing room, and the guys acted as if she were invisible.

Hörður was unsociable and had few friends, but because of his size and temperament, he was mainly left alone. He felt sorry for Þóra, who put more pressure on herself than most others without reaping any respect or praise for it, and took her under his wing. She repaid his kindness with unconditional friendship. They were and still are considered an extremely unusual pair, but they themselves couldn't care less.

"Are you doing anything on Saturday evening?" asks Þóra.

"Nothing planned, no," Hörður answers conscientiously. If his date with Bíbí goes well, however, maybe they'll end up doing something together on the weekend, go to the movies or out to eat—but he's worried about jinxing that extremely exciting possibility if he starts hoping for it now.

"Then come with me to the wedding," says Þóra, smiling widely.

Hörður is dumbstruck. "Wedding? Are you out of your mind? Not a chance! Weddings are unbearable. And besides, I don't have the clothes for one. You can forget it, unfortunately."

"Listen to me," says Þóra. "It's not as you think. In the first place, the ceremony isn't in a church, but outdoors, in a clearing by Elliðavatn Lake. The reception is being held in a party tent up there. And it will all be extremely relaxed, no fancy dresses or anything like that. It's a country wedding! At most, you'd only need to buy yourself a leather jacket or wool overcoat."

Hörður sighs. Damn, these women can be a pain! Maybe he should skip his date. What if he and Bíbí became a couple? Before he knew it, he'd have to start going clothes shopping at the Kringlan Shopping Mall, attend family events and weddings, go to the theater and out to eat at restaurants that serve fancy tidbits in place of proper food.

Isn't it better just being single?

"What do you say, you old oaf?" says Þóra, energetically. "Do you have something better to do than go with your best friend to a rural feast where the tables bend under the weight of game meats and alcohol?"

Hörður's eyes widen. "Game meats?"

Þóra nods. "It's going to be great. And you *have* to come with me! I don't have anyone else to go with, and there'll be people there that I really don't want to have to talk to if I go alone."

"What people?" he asks.

"My ex," mutters Þóra.

"Which one?" he asks.

"Idiot!" says Þóra with a laugh, punching him in the arm at the same time, so hard that he nearly cries out.

"Easy," mutters Hörður, rubbing his arm. There's no way he's up for this. No way in hell.

"Do it for me, okay?" says Þóra, making puppy eyes at him. "For your dearest bestest friend."

Hörður growls annoyedly. "Fine, then. But I'm not going to go and buy a new jacket for it—out of the question. I have a black jacket that'll do just fine. But if it turns out to be as boring as I think it will, I'm going to be pissed."

"You're the best." Þóra jumps at him and tries to hug him, but her arms barely reach halfway around the big man.

Hörður lives in a small, rented basement apartment on Bergþórugata Street, in a long apartment building that starts at the intersection with Vitastígur Street and ends down at Barónsstígur Street. He drives his motorcycle in through a narrow gate and parks it on a little sidewalk in a shabby-looking back garden, next to four trash cans. He takes off his helmet and gloves and walks around to the front of the house. Across the street is the Vitabar Pub, at the opposite corner of the intersection. Painted on the wall above him is the year his apartment building was built: 1927.

The door is painted black, and is set with a vertical window. Next to it is an intercom with four labeled buttons. Scribbled on the lowest, in ballpoint pen on the little slip of paper behind the smudged plastic cover, are the initials HG.

Hörður stops on the sidewalk in front of the door, finds the right key among those on his keychain and opens the door. He steps into the entryway, kicks away a pile of newspapers and junk mail, shuts the door behind him and switches on the light. He's halfway down the stairs leading to the basement when the door opens on the ground-floor landing and someone calls to him.

"Hörður Grímsson, is that you?"

Can he never be left in peace? Hörður sighs, turns around and forces a polite smile. The person who appears in the entryway is precisely the one whom he cares least to meet—the nervous dwarf who lives on the ground floor, right side. He isn't really a dwarf—but is just so damn small and skinny. Maybe more elf than dwarf. Nothing but skin and bones, always dressed in pressed trousers and an ironed shirt. Pale as milk, just as bloodless as the vegetables he lives on. Vigfús should meet him. He undoubtedly supports Iceland's admission to the EU, and for all Hörður knows, he may have been in that dreamy band, Sigur Rós.

But what's his name, again? Hörður can't remember—of course; he's terrible with names, absolutely terrible. But he has a system for remembering the names that he needs to, and this dwarf-neighbor of his is in fact in the system. In his system, Hörður focuses on some feature in the demeanor, appearance, or physical features of a particular person, something characteristic of that person and rhymes with his or her name or forms a kind of bridge over to it, logically, phonologically, or literally. The system is both far-fetched and complicated, and no one understands it but Hörður—and sometimes even he can't quite figure it all out.

"Hello!" says the dwarf.

Hörður doesn't answer, but just stares intently at his neighbor and tries to recall what his keyword is in his good old system. He's a dwarf, he's small, he's almost nothing. Just half a man, sorry-looking, miserable—what was it again?

Looking as proud as if he'd just won the Nobel Prize, the dwarf holds up two window envelopes. "I've got your mail here, neighbor. It'd been lying here neglected for two days, and I was worried that someone would throw it into the blue bin along with the junk mail. So I rescued it."

He hands the envelopes to Hörður, who is still lost in thought. Did it have to do with food? He's not a whole meal, just a half? No, that wasn't it. Yes—he remembers! Leftovers, little bits left on the plate … which could actually just be called … leavings! Exactly, he's just leavings, because his name is …

"Leifur!" says Hörður triumphantly.

"Yes," says Leifur hesitantly. "That's right. But, um, do you want your mail?"

"Oh yeah, sure," says Hörður, taking the envelopes. "Thank you, Leifur."

"Don't mention it," says Leifur cheerfully. "That's what neighbors are for, isn't it? We help each other out."

"That's right." Hörður ambles down the stairs. The basement ceiling is low enough for him to have to bend his head, and the place is half dark and smells of sewage and laundry detergent. To one side are several locked storage rooms, and to the other is the residents' laundry room. Straight ahead is a blue door with a night latch, behind which is a small apartment once used as a storage room for garden tools, bicycles and the like.

"It's good to know you're here in this building, Hörður," calls Leifur after him. "Not everybody lives so well, having a police officer at the bottom of their stairwell."

Hörður can't be bothered to answer this. He uses a small key to open the door to his apartment, and switches on a naked lightbulb hanging from the ceiling. His apartment is at the very margin of what is considered habitable accommodation, it being unapproved and the rent accordingly low; the landlord doesn't report his rental income on his taxes. Hörður takes off his helmet and places it on a low bookcase, then shuts the door and hangs his jacket on a nail in the back of the door. Next, he sits down on his cot and pulls off his motorcycle boots. Above the cot is a horizontal window looking out on the garden, through which, however, nothing can be seen but grass in the summer and snow in the winter. Covering the window is a green curtain that Hörður never pulls open. Next to the bed is a small dresser, on top of which are stacks of CDs and books, as well as an overflowing ashtray. On the floor in front of the dresser are a travel CD player and headphones. Across the room, a meter-and-a-half away from the cot, is a small refrigerator. On top of the refrigerator is an electric burner, covered with coffee stains, and a battered moka pot sitting on the burner. Hörður's cup is hanging on a nail in the wall above the burner and the fridge. The floor is littered with dirty clothes and plastic bags full of trash and beer cans. Next to the fridge is the door to the bathroom, hung with a light-blue sheet. The bathroom is tiny; just barely fitting a toilet, wash basin, and showerhead. On the far wall is the intake for cold and hot water for the entire building—the pipes buzz loudly, and the meters labeled Reykjavik Energy tick constantly, day and night. The drain is in the middle of the floor and Hörður can't take a shower without flooding the place, which is why he doesn't shower at home. Sometimes he takes a shower at the police station on Hverfisgata Street or goes over to the Sundhöllin swimming pool, which is a two-minute walk away.

Hörður screws apart the moka pot, dumps the coffee grounds into an open trash bag, rinses out the top part in the bathroom sink and fills the lower part with water. Then he puts Italian coffee in the filter basket, screws the contraption together, places it on the electric burner and sets the burner at the next-highest temperature. Stooping, he paces his abode, taking care not to run into the lightbulb—instead circling it like a demon orbiting the sun.

He sits down on the cot, opens the CD player and puts *Closing Time* by Tom Waits back in its sleeve—he's listened to this old masterpiece for several days in a row now. Then he runs his eyes over his CD collection in search of some other ear candy. His attention quickly turns to his CDs of Type O Negative, as so often before. They draw him in, those green CDs—a particular shade of dark green is one of the trademarks of this favorite band of Hörður's. The band is from Brooklyn, the capital of cynicism, and plays so-called Goth rock—the band's musical world is dark and gloomy, dramatic and elegant at once, like a leather-clad Gothic cathedral constructed of guitar and organ chords. The lyrics are genius and written with the heart's blood, as well as other bodily fluids—melancholy, bitter, lovesick, ironic, self-critical, and sometimes extremely amusing, even funny. The band consists of four impulsive types—The Drab Four as they sometimes call themselves, which is their version of The Beatles' nickname, The Fab Four. First among these equals is the depressed sex symbol, Peter Steele. He's a hulking giant of a man, with long black hair, thick lips, deep, dark eyes and facial features reminiscent of Frankenstein's monster. He writes both the music and the lyrics, plays bass and sings in a deep, plaintive voice that swings from a dark mumble to a desperate falsetto. Peter is as imperfect as he is big; his self-confidence is built on sand, doubt about his own talent and excellence runs deep within him, he drinks and is addicted to cocaine, and is so depressed that death is his best friend and main subject.

Hörður has long looked up to the giant from Brooklyn; he's his role model and idol number one—he connects with him in spirit as well as flesh—each lyric is as if pulled from the head of the red-haired giant from Súðavík, and the music harmonizes with his inner essence, what some people call the soul.

He chooses the CD with the name appropriate to four certain weeks per year, the great magnum opus *October*

Rust—the month of decline, broken hearts, and turning leaves, whose color can in fact resemble rusty iron. He presses play, puts on headphones, cranks the volume all the way up and stretches out on the cot, with his head against the wall and his feet dangling off the other end. The disk starts with a little antic piece in the spirit of The Drab Four, but then the poetic and powerful drama begins, in all its divine power. The first actual song on the CD is the classic "Love You to Death," which begins with a fragile piano melody in a minor key, but then takes flight with a pounding bass, guitar, organ, and drums. *"In her place, one hundred candles burning, as salty sweat drips from her breast. Her hips move and I can feel what they're saying, swaying. They say the beast inside of me's gonna get ya, get ya, get …"*

Feeling somewhat ashamed of himself, Hörður rinses the moka pot in the bathroom sink. Of course—he'd spaced out and then fallen asleep with the music in his ears, and the coffee boiled over, spilled out onto the burner, splattered onto the wall and the floor, boiled away and finally burned. The maker had nearly melted from the heat, the rubber ring inside it was ruined and now the little apartment smells of hot metal and burnt coffee. He has an extra ring for the maker—it's not as if this hasn't happened before—he puts it in, but decides not to make a new batch. Instead, he opens the fridge and takes out one of the three cans of Egill's Gull beer in it. Actually, the fridge has nothing else in it.

He opens the can, takes a big drink of the cold beer and breathes a sigh of relief. Nothing calms the nerves as quickly as an ice-cold, sparkling beer. He sits down on the cot, puts down the beer can, pushes the travel CD player aside and opens the dresser's lower drawer. What clean clothes does he have? Hidden in the drawer are a few t-shirts, all prin-ted with the logos of rock bands except for one that's plain white, two crumpled shirts and one pair of jeans that look fine but are just slightly too tight at the waist—he hasn't been able to button them since last spring. At the bottom of the drawer is a single black jacket that he actually never wears, except for funerals—he guesses he'll just have to wear it for this goddamn wedding. The jacket is decent-looking, but is actually one to two sizes too small. The garment fits him only as long as he doesn't move too much while in it.

He actually has no other shoes besides his motorcycle boots, apart from his tennis shoes, which are so worn and dirty that it isn't even funny. The boots are newish, at least, that is, compared to everything else he owns, apart from the fact that they're terribly cool, in the opinion of their owner.

The upper drawer holds his underwear and socks, all faded and worn after a million washes and more or less full of holes, half a carton of Camel filters, a nearly empty glass of Jovan musk cologne, and a squashed tube of stiff hair gel.

Could be worse, he thinks to himself. It's nearly three-thirty. Three and a half hours until his date. All he has to do to get ready is shave and change clothes, which will only take fifteen, maybe twenty minutes. What should he do for three hours? A sudden feeling of emptiness and anxiety overwhelms him. He chugs his beer, lights a cigarette. Just relax; he needs to relax.

The Vitabar Pub is on the first floor of an old residen-tial building at the intersection of Vitastígur Street and Bergþórugata Street, and is partially underground. The entrance is at the corner of the intersection, and the place itself is L-shaped. The longer part of the L lies alongside

Vitastígur; this part has four tables on the window side, with the bar across from them. In the inner corner is a television set, where live broadcasts of sporting events are shown. The shorter part of the L lies along Bergþórugata and is below ground. It has fewer tables, but also the bathrooms, which are shabby and smell of urine and strong perfumes that seem to do little other than highlight the urine stench. The place is painted dark green on the inside; on the walls are copper lamps with yellow shades and the old wooden floor undulates slightly here and there.

Vitabar is famous for two things: its bleu-cheese burger, which is called the Forget-Me-Not, and its Premium Beck's on tap. It's also notorious for two things: the suffocating cloud of smoke that always fills it, and its rather shifty crew of regulars, who are in fact the reason for the heavy air, which is approximately two-thirds tobacco smoke and one third smoke from the grill. The regulars are unemployed alcoholics who occupy the same tables from the time the place opens around noon, sipping whiskey and beer and chain-smoking cheap cigarettes, until it closes around midnight. Mingled with the boozers are young people from the Technical College, crooks, and cops, along with family types from the neighborhood who occasionally come in for a beer or bite to eat in the afternoon or stop to pick up their to-go orders.

Hörður sits at his favorite table, which is in the shorter wing of the place, and nearest the entrance. He takes one last drag on his cigarette before stubbing it out in an over-flowing ashtray. Overhead, a fan diligently stirs the place's foul air. Hörður usually turns his back to the entrance, but now he's sitting on the opposite side of the table, waiting nervously and excitedly for Bíbí to appear in the doorway.

Above the door is a little copper bell that rings every time someone comes in or goes out—the door hits the bell and causes it to jingle brightly. It's now ten past eight, and he's been waiting there since seven fifteen. He's eaten a hamburger and fries and drunk two dark Beck's, and is now starting on his third. First, of course, he finished the three beers that he had in the fridge at home, having had nothing other to do than listen to music, chain-smoke cigarettes, and drink beer. He'd played The Kinks, the Rolling Stones, Led Zeppelin and Deep Purple.

Good old rock n' roll.

Vitabar is packed with patrons. Loud laughter, the clinking of glasses, and noisy chatter bounce off the walls; greasy smoke wafts from the kitchen and the cigarette smoke has turned into a thick, acrid fog that burns the eyes and throat. The heat is stifling.

Hörður is so stressed that he feels like he's losing it. He blows smoke from his nostrils and stubs out his fifth cigarette in around twenty minutes. He's wearing his black jacket over a stone-gray shirt, his face is pale and his forehead is beaded with sweat. He realizes why Vigfús found it a bad idea to invite a woman here on a first date. It's not exactly the coziest place in the city center. He's determined to take his partner's advice and suggest to his date that they go elsewhere.

That is, if she even shows up.

Hörður looks at his watch. A quarter past eight. No, he guesses she's not coming. Which may just be for the best. What have women brought men, other than pain and trouble throughout history? Or is that just a blues-song cliché? He takes a big swig of beer, gulping it just as the door opens; the bell rings and Bíbí appears in the doorway, wearing a white coat, white trousers and a pink kerchief around her neck, like an angel in the vestibule of hell.

The beer catches in Hörður's throat, causing him to cough and nearly spit it out over the table. His throat burns and his nose fills with foam.

"Hi!" says Bíbí, smiling at him. "Sorry I'm late. I was stuck on the phone, and then it took me forever to find a parking spot."

"Hi." Hörður manages to swallow the beer and maintain his composure. He gestures to her to take a seat, but realizes that it might be appropriate for him to stand up and greet her like a gentleman. He hesitates, then pushes his chair back and gets to his feet, in all his might.

"Oh!" Bíbí is startled; she didn't expect this. She's halfway out of her coat when he steps over to her, insecure and awkward. She gets tangled in her coat; it's as if she's wearing a straitjacket, but she tries to make good of the circumstances and manages to turn her head in the right direction just as Hörður gently touches her left shoulder and kisses her on the right cheek.

"Good to see you," he mutters, before plunking back down in his seat. His face reddens and his hands tremble. Was that the right thing to do? He has no idea. He wants more than anything just to pound his beer in one gulp and wash himself down a drain with it—spin down the drain of his own throat.

Bíbí hangs her coat on a hook on the wall by the door, then sits down opposite him at the table and looks quickly around the room, before giving Hörður a wide smile. "Do you come here often?"

"Ye-eah," he says. "I live just across the intersection. I always eat dinner here when I'm on day shift. I'm not big on cooking. And my colleagues come here sometimes. It's kind of our place."

"I see," says Bíbí. "Kind of a cop bar. Like in the movies."

"Yeah, maybe," says Hörður, without knowing precisely what movies she's talking about. He never goes to the movies nowadays. He finds it stupid to pay to sit with strangers in a big room and watch a movie that will show up on television anyway after two or three years. He can just as well wait.

There was actually a cop bar in the movie *The French Connection*, he recalls. It was the movie's opening setting.

"I wouldn't be surprised if Humphrey Bogart stepped out from this cloud of smoke," says Bíbí, lifting her plucked, black-penciled eyebrows in a comical way.

Hörður can't help but smile. Not because of her comment about Bogart, who is one of his favorite actors, but simply with joy at the fact that this cute hairdresser should suddenly be sitting there. She came! This beautiful woman came to meet him. They're on a date. He has no idea how often he's sat alone at this same table.

Very, very often.

But now everyone can see that he isn't a lonely giant, but rather, a presentable man whom women want to meet. Or maybe no one has noticed?

"Would you like anything? A beer or red wine?" he asks. "I think they have red wine, and white wine, too. They sell it in little bottles."

"No thanks. No alcohol for me," says Bíbí. "I'm driving, as I said. Otherwise I would have been even later."

"No problem," says Hörður. "There's also soda and coffee. Would you like a coffee? We can also go somewhere else. Would you like to go somewhere else? You choose. I'm just going to finish my beer, and then we can go."

Bíbí smiles slightly. "I'm up for a coffee. Then we can maybe go somewhere a little quieter. For example, to the Sufi Café in Mál og Menning Bookstore. It's really cozy there. I always enjoy going to bookstores."

"Yeah, that's a good idea," says Hörður. A bookstore! Why didn't he think of that? But naturally, he didn't know that she liked bookstores. It's a definite plus. He likes going to bookstores, too. They have a soothing effect. "I'll go get you a coffee. Then we can stroll over to the Sufi in a bit."

"Okay," says Bíbí. "Sugar and milk, please."

Hörður stands up and goes to the bar. He gets the attention of the girl behind the bar and asks for a coffee for his date. He looks over his shoulder and smiles at Bíbí, who smiles back.

This is going pretty well, thinks Hörður. He breathes lighter, and is much less stressed than before. He can feel the effects of all the beers, but is absolutely not drunk, just tipsy. As the girl prepares the coffee, he drums his fingers on the bar and runs his sea-green eyes over the room. The regulars are in their places, and students from the Technical College fill other tables. In the darkest corner sits a young, unknown writer, writing in a notebook. His name is Ófeigur, which makes Hörður think of the word "ófleygur"—flightless—which evokes an image of a bird, and he is in fact rather birdlike, this drunken writer—his arms are long, his back bent, and his nose like those of the Romans in an Asterix comic. He's surly and arrogant, but decent as they come; Hörður has sometimes shot the breeze with him. He's a bit of a squawker, like many artists, but is definitely not stupid; far from it.

A squawker, exactly. Hörður smiles at his own humor. If the writer Ófeigur were a bird, he would most likely be a squawking skua, though he would doubtless consider himself to be an eagle, or at least a falcon.

Hörður's eyes flutter from one corner of the room to another, and stop there on a man of around forty sitting alone at the innermost table in the longer part of the place, by a window facing Vitastígur. The man is none other than Detective Inspector Engilbert. He has pushed away a plate holding a few fries and remains of sauce, and is looking at something on his laptop screen, in between leafing through some papers. He´s unbuttoned the top two buttons of his shirt and taken off his tie. A cigar lies burning in an ashtray in front of him, and the detective sips distractedly at a shot of whiskey and water. His trench coat is draped over the back of the chair next to him.

He's still working, thinks Hörður. Which isn't so strange, perhaps. Those rare times that murder is committed in the capital, the detectives have to work day and night, hardly taking a break until the case is solved. Hörður wonders if he's making any progress. Has the suspect confessed? He's probably been questioned for a few hours. Unless they've decided to let him stew first in isolation overnight, to break his resolve.

Hörður sighs. He longs so much to take part, be involved—to do *real* police work instead of traffic control and responding to minor calls. To interrogate suspects, gather evidence, construct hypotheses and theories, and then sit there on overtime pay at Vitabar late in the evening, having slept little and feeling rather jaded, sipping twelve-year-old whiskey on ice.

"Here you go!"

He's startled from these thoughts of his when the girl from behind the bar plunks a coffee cup onto a saucer.

"Should I put this on your account?"

"Yes, thanks," says Hörður. He brings Bíbí the coffee and sits back down at the table with her. "I hope it's not undrinkable. When it's freshly brewed, the coffee here can be pretty good, but sometimes it sits for too long and tastes like rat poison."

Bíbí smiles. "I'm sure it's fine."

"Okay, good." Hörður smiles back. She smiles so beautifully—she's a gorgeous woman. He hopes that she likes him. In any case, he definitely likes her. But he doesn't dare to be too optimistic. He's a realistic man.

Expectations are a recipe for disappointment; that's his bitter experience.

"Have you been a policeman a long time?" Bíbí asks.

"Yeah, kind of." Hörður takes a sip of his beer. "For three years, all told. I started as a summer employee and then went to the Police Academy. We worked as trainees in the summers, and took classes the rest of the year. It hasn't been long since I started full-time. Not long at all, in fact."

"And do you like it?" Bíbí fiddles with her cup, which rattles on its saucer, but she still hasn't touched the black coffee.

Hörður nods, as if distracted. In fact, he's thinking about Engilbert and the murder investigation. He'd managed to forget about both of them, but then Bíbí started asking him about his job and his mind turned back to the detective sitting at the other end of the room.

He really wants to go say hello to him, to ask if his tip did any good, how the investigation is going, and so on. Show a little interest, make his presence known and such.

Build relationships; *networking,* as it's called.

"And, umm, and you?" sputters Hörður. "Have you been at your job a long time, cutting people's hair, there on Klapparstígur?"

"No, not really," says Bíbí. "I had an apprenticeship at another hair salon, but took a job there after I finished school. I couldn't find anything better, but I'm planning on being there until I find something more exciting."

Hörður nods, in between glancing in the direction of Engilbert, who is half-hidden in smoke, but seems to be immersed in his work.

"I don't get much out of doing men's haircuts all day long," says Bíbí, laughing apologetically. "Naturally, I want to find a place in a nice salon and get to do hair coloring and style women's hair according to the latest trends."

"Exactly." Hörður sips his beer and shakes a cigarette from his half-empty pack of Camels. "Would you like one?"

Bíbí smiles faintly. "No thanks. I quit."

He sticks the cigarette between his lips. "Do you mind if I smoke?"

"No, not at all."

Hörður lights the cigarette with his butane lighter, inhales the smoke greedily and holds it in. He blows a few smoke rings, places the cigarette in the ash tray and points at the cup of coffee that he brought Bíbí. "Is the coffee okay? You haven't touched it."

"Yes, or, um …" Bíbí looks embarrassed. "It's missing both milk and sugar."

"Oh, stupid me!" Hörður strikes his forehead with his open palm. "I'm sorry. I'll fix this."

"All right," says Bíbí.

Hörður rushes to the bar and asks for milk and sugar. He looks over at Engilbert, who is typing something into his computer. Shouldn't he go and say hello to the detective?

A little pitcher of milk and a sugar bowl appear on the bar. Hörður brings Bíbí both and apologizes to her again, but then stands there hesitantly by the table instead of sitting.

"It's not the end of the world," says Bíbí, giving Hörður a quick little smile. She puts a spot of milk and two sugar cubes in her coffee.

Hörður snaps his fingers and points behind him. "I'm going to go say hello to one of my colleagues. I'll be right back."

"Yes, of course." Bíbí stirs her coffee with a teaspoon. "No problem."

"Good, I'll be quick!" He works his way through the crowded room and stops next to Engilbert's table. The detective pays him no notice.

Hörður clears his throat.

Engilbert looks up with an expression of curiosity tinged with irritation.

"I'm a police officer," says Hörður. "We met this morning—I'm the one who saw the suspect at Ölver yesterday. If it was in fact him."

"Yes, that's right." Engilbert leans back in his chair. "I didn't recognize you without your uniform. Though you seemed slightly familiar. You're that kind of person."

Hörður smiles sheepishly.

"But you were right," says Engilbert, shutting his laptop. "He was at Ölver, this Gísli Már, along with a few of his friends in the Arsenal Fan Club."

"Gísli Már," repeats Hörður. The cold-blooded, nameless murderer suddenly has a name, and at the same time, has become a person of flesh and blood. He feels somewhat familiar with the name, as if he's heard it before, but in an entirely different context. But he could be mistaken; he has such trouble remembering names. "And what? Did he turn himself in, or …?"

Engilbert nods. "A friend and schoolmate of Gísli's who was with him at Ölver called him after reading the description of the alleged perpetrator online. Gísli didn't show up at school this morning; he's studying computer science at the University of Reykjavík. Following the phone call from his friend, he turned himself in at the Hverfisgata police station. Shortly beforehand, the taxi driver contacted us. He said that he'd driven this boy from Hljómskálagarður up to the Grafarvogur neighborhood around eleven o'clock. The address he provided is that of Gísli's parents' home. The boy lives in their basement."

"I see. The time frame is right." Hörður pulls out a chair and sits down opposite Engilbert at the table. "And what did he say, this Gísli, when he turned himself in?"

"He was, and is, extremely upset," says Engilbert. "I just took a preliminary statement from him and then submitted a request for an extension of custody, which was, of course, approved. He was driven to Litla-Hraun Prison around dinnertime, and the actual interrogation won't start until tomorrow. I'm preparing for it now."

"I see," says Hörður. "He was upset, you say? Does he remember what happened?"

"Why do you ask?" Engilbert asks cynically.

"I saw him at Ölver, as you know." Hörður rocks in his seat, blinks, and speaks quickly and excitedly. "He was taking a leak, and then he turned around and looked me in the eye. I was next in line, see. And his eyes were empty, you know—like a doll's. The lights were on, but there was no one home, get it?"

Engilbert nods thoughtfully. "You guessed correctly. He remembers sitting down and watching the match, but then everything went black, according to him. He doesn't remember

Arsenal scoring, or how the match went. Actually, no one who was with Gísli at Ölver remembers seeing him after he went to the bathroom, which was early in the first half."

"Really?" Hörður smacks his lips. "Which means that he left the bar right after I saw him. I didn't see him after that. I myself went home shortly afterward. But still. He left before me; that's pretty clear."

"According to him, he came to his senses a short distance from Hljómskálagarður. He found himself sitting there on a park bench, without knowing how he got there or what he was doing there," says Engilbert. "He flagged down the first taxi that he saw and asked the driver to drive him home, which he did."

"Had he drunk a lot?" asks Hörður.

"He drove to the bar," says Engilbert. "He says that he drank two glasses of Coke, which his friends confirmed. His car was still in the parking garage next to Ölver. He didn't leave in it."

"How did he get to the city center?"

"That's one of the things we don't know," says Engilbert. "One of the numerous details under investigation."

"Did you have a blood test done on him?"

"Of course," replies the detective. "No sign of alcohol, but there were trace elements in his blood."

"Ecstasy?" asks Hörður excitedly. "I heard that he'd found ecstasy in his belongings and handed it over when he turned himself in. Is that true?"

"It's true," says Engilbert sulkily. "Sometimes it's as if my colleagues can't keep quiet about anything."

"Had he taken any ecstasy that evening?" asks Hörður.

Engilbert shrugs. "I don't know, honestly. What was found in his blood *may* have been ecstasy. We're waiting for the results of the study of the ecstasy that he turned over to us. Still, what was found in his blood suggests more that he took GHB—liquid X."

"The anesthetic?" Hörður is all eyes and ears. "That could explain the blackout. The drug is abused by the same group of people who use ecstasy, and of course it's also used as a date-rape drug, like rohypnol. It turns their minds to mush, making them like zombies, and they don't remember anything the next day."

"That's right," says Engilbert. "But the test only turned up traces of something that *could* be GHB *or* something else entirely. There are all sorts of toxins in ecstasy, and it certainly hasn't been ruled out that the tablets he had on him contain GHB."

"Did he say he just found them in his pocket, or …?"

Engilbert nods. "He handed over a small plastic bag. In it were three blue ecstasy tablets imprinted with a pentagram. But he says that they weren't his, that he'd never taken, had in his possession, or even so much as seen ecstasy before."

"Is that credible?"

Engilbert sighs. "Yes, in fact it is, I must admit. The boy has a clean record; he's hardly ever even skipped a day of school. Comes from a good home, does well in school and has been recognized for academic achievement. Was in both football and team handball when he was younger, in addition to being on the national youth golf team. He's you're your ideal Boy Scout, but still …"

The detective pauses and looks away, as if he feels he's said too much.

"Was there anything else?" asks Hörður in a low voice.

Engilbert shrugs. "Gísli had a tiny puncture wound on his right forearm. As if from a needle. It's recent, with bruising around it."

"Drugs? Steroids?" asks Hörður.

"For example," says the detective. "Or B-vitamins. Insulin? I'll find out later, or tomorrow, whether Gísli has diabetes. I'm also having it checked whether he's had any vaccinations recently, had blood samples taken, or received injections of any kind. Maybe it's just something like that. Something that doesn't have anything to do with the case."

Hörður nods thoughtfully.

"Are you convinced he killed Þórólfur?" he then asks.

"There's no doubt about it; not even the smallest," says the detective. "There were witnesses to the murder, and the description of the alleged perpetrator matches perfectly. Fingerprints were found on the murder weapon, and they all turned out to be from Gísli. Tiny drops of blood were found on the left sleeve of his jacket—and they turned out to be from the deceased. Gísli also had a wound on his left hand, which he probably got when his hand slipped during his attack."

"I see," says Hörður, with a thoughtful expression. "What sort of knife was it, anyway?"

"It has a blue plastic hilt and a slender, tapered, stainless-steel blade," says the detective. "A kind of industrial knife, possibly used in fish processing or something like that. It's being studied, like everything else."

"But the motive?" asks Hörður.

Engilbert shrugs. "At this point, I'm inclined to think it was a kind of temporary insanity. Gísli ingests some sort of drug and carries out this murder when he's high. This isn't just speculation. The facts of the case suggest that this is what indeed happened. The only thing that's still a mystery is whether he took the drug or drugs deliberately, or by accident."

"By accident, you say," mutters Hörður, distractedly. What if someone slipped Gísli some drugs? Weren't there some shady characters there at Ölver, at the bar?

"It'll all come to light." Engilbert sips his whiskey, licks his lips and sighs contentedly.

The smell of Engilbert's shot carries to Hörður's nostrils; his mouth starts watering, but he has trouble swallowing. His throat is bone-dry. He suddenly wants a beer, ice-cold and refreshing. Didn't he already have one? Did he leave his glass behind?

Where, then?

Bíbí! Hörður stands up so swiftly that he nearly topples the table. "Thanks for the chat, Betti. But I've got to leave you now; I'm here with someone—on a date, actually."

Engilbert puts down his shot glass and re-opens his laptop. "No problem. I'm busy, anyway."

Hörður hurries over to the table by the entrance, nearly shoving aside the people standing at the bar and forcing his way through the crowd. Bíbí looks up as he approaches the table. She has finished her coffee and appears to be just slightly bored. Hörður was worried that she might have left, but even more worried about being fixed with an angry stare or on the receiving end of a loud chewing-out.

His beer has gone completely flat and his cigarette has burned out in the ash tray.

Looking sheepish, he throws up his hands, plunks down in his seat and catches his breath, as if having run over mountain and dale. "I'm sorry, I didn't mean to be so long!"

"No worries." Bíbí smiles, but is obviously either offended or irritated; he doesn't know her well enough to be able to tell which one it is. But his absence has definitely bothered her; that much is certain.

"I was talking to Engilbert, who's in the criminal investigation department," says Hörður, lighting himself a new cigarette. "I met him this morning by the Parliament House, at the scene of the crime. He's leading the investigation."

"Yes, the murder—of course." Bíbí is half-embarrassed. "I'd forgotten about it. How could I forget it? A terrible thing, absolutely terrible. But I just go and forget about it right away! I feel so self-centered."

Hörður swigs his beer, quenching his thirst. "Don't think like that. Terrible things happen every day. But life goes on, doesn't it?"

"Yes, I suppose it does," she says.

"But anyway, I was there this morning, at the scene." Hörður blows smoke out his nostrils. "We were on guard there, my partner Vigfús and I. They put out an alert for the alleged perpetrator, and I realized that I'd seen him the night before, at Ölver, where I was watching a football match with my friends."

"What are you saying?" Bíbí's brown eyes widen. "Was he there? The murderer?"

Hörður nods. "I told Engilbert, the noose tightened around the alleged perpetrator, and shortly afterward, he turned himself in."

"So it's you to thank that he was caught?"

"You might say that, yeah," says Hörður, with pretend modesty.

"Holy cow," she says. "I'm just cutting hair all day long, while you're investigating murder cases. My life is so predictable, compared to the life that you live."

"I'm not investigating the case, not directly, anyway. More like assisting Engilbert," says Hörður, before rubbing the back of his neck and smiling slightly. "And don't make little of your job. This haircut suits me really well, at least in my own opinion."

Bíbí blushes. "Thanks. Yes, doesn't it? I think you look good with it like that … really good."

Hörður is embarrassed. He looks away, fiddles with his beer glass and then finishes the beer in one gulp, just to do something.

"Are you from Reykjavík?" he asks.

"No, I'm from out of town," says Bíbí. "From Hólmavík. With sea-salt blood in my veins."

"You don't say." Hörður smiles widely. "I'm from Súðavík. Dad was a fisherman."

"Really?" Bíbí laughs. "My dad, too. He's been hunting sharks for the last decade or so. He cures it, too. In midwinter, cured Guðmundur-shark can be bought in all the better stores and shops."

"Awesome," says Hörður. He's happy that she's from out in the countryside. Her being from the Strandir region is even better. City girls don't get him, nor he them. There's always a lack of connection, a kind of *understanding* that's impossible to explain.

"I actually grew up on a farm," says Bíbí. "With my grandmother and grandfather. I was there every weekend and throughout the summers."

"Really?" says Hörður, smiling. "My grandfather on my mother's side was a farmer. I have an incredible amount of good memories from the countryside. Especially from haymaking in the summer. I started driving tractors before I was confirmed, and both mowed and raked when I was fifteen and sixteen. Afterward, I spent much more time at sea, with my dad and his fellow fishermen."

"Does your dad go to sea anymore?" she asks.

Hörður's mood darkens. "He's dead. They all died in the avalanche of '95."

Bíbí lays her hand over her heart. "I'm sorry. I didn't know. How sad. My sincere condolences."

He smiles faintly. "Thanks. No problem. How could you have known?"

"But you?" she asks cautiously. "You survived the avalanche? Or you weren't at home at the time?"

"I don't want to talk about it," says Hörður. "Not now, at least."

Bíbí starts. "No problem. I'm sorry. I shouldn't have asked. I can be so impulsive."

They both fall silent, and the silence soon becomes both oppressive and awkward.

"What's your greatest fear?" Bíbí asks suddenly.

Hörður is surprised by the question, but says the first thing that comes to his mind. "To be shut in a room with unfamiliar people. To be stuck in a crowd. Hell is other people, as the man said."

"I see," says Bíbí. "But where do you feel best?"

Hörður shrugs. "Just at home, I think. Alone at home reading or listening to music. When I was little, I wanted to be the only person in the whole wide world. The idea seemed brilliant to me. No people, and I could just do whatever I wanted."

"So, are you planning to be alone your whole life?" asks Bíbí hesitantly.

"Yeah, or …" He blushes. What is he saying? "Not necessarily. Not my whole life. Though I do feel fine on my own."

"I understand," she says, smiling softly.

"Weren't we going to go over to the Sufi?" he asks, to change topic. "Or would you like more coffee?"

"No, that's fine," she says. "Yes, let's go. The smoke here is suffocating me."

"Oh, yeah, sorry," he says, putting out his cigarette in the stuffed ashtray. "And then I sit here chain-smoking in front of you."

"I'm sure I'll survive," she says. "But I'll be glad when smoking is banned in restaurants."

Hörður laughs. "That'll never happen. At least not in this restaurant."

"Maybe not," she mutters.

"All right then." He stands up. "Let's get out of here. But I'm just going to dry out before we go."

"What's that?" she asks.

"Oh, just a bad joke." He points sheepishly toward the bathroom. "I just have to pee."

"Okay." Bíbí puts on her coat, while Hörður goes and grabs the doorknob of the men's bathroom. The door is locked.

"There's a line," says a young man of around twenty who is standing at the door.

"I see." Hörður steps backward and stands behind the young man. His mind turns reflexively to Ölver, where he stood in line in the men's bathroom and waited for the murderer-to-be to finish peeing.

Incredible! In his mind's eye he sees the kid, the one in the blazer and Arsenal jersey, the blond, blue-eyed Gísli Már, who, at this moment, is locked in a small cell in the isolation unit at Litla-Hraun Prison. Just twenty-four hours ago, he was standing at a urinal emptying his bladder, presumably clueless about the terrible act that he was about to commit. He gave his dick a shake, zipped up his pants, flushed the urinal and turned around—with an expression like that of a lifeless doll.

Imagine it. He kills a man in cold blood, but first flushes a urinal. Only slobs don't flush after peeing. But tidy people flush their pee, and commit murder shortly afterward.

Does that fit?

Hörður scratches his head, as he does sometimes when he's sunk in thought. The murderer was left-handed, Gísli Már had a wound on his left hand, but …

The hairs rise on the back of Hörður's neck. Holy shit! He leaves the two-man line and goes straight back to Bíbí, who´s waiting with a smile by the entrance, her coat buttoned up to her neck.

"Decided against it?" she asks mischievously.

"No, but I need to have a word with Engilbert first," says Hörður. "Concerning a little thing I remembered. It's related to the murder investigation. I'll just be a moment."

"Okay." Bíbí forces a smile. "But if it's all the same to you, I'll wait outside. My eyes are burning."

"No problem—see you in a minute." Hörður elbows his way through the crowd at the bar and stops at Engilbert's table. The detective's eyes are focused on his laptop screen.

"Hey, Betti," he says, plunking down in the chair opposite the detective. "I just remembered something."

Engilbert sighs. "What was that, Hörður?"

At the same moment, the bartender brings the detective a new shot glass—a single whiskey on the rocks. "Here you go."

"Thanks, friend," says Engilbert.

"Anything for you?" she asks Hörður.

"Eh, yeah … just the same," he says.

"Of course," says the girl, before disappearing back behind the bar.

"Be quick." Engilbert's tone is dry and formal. "I'm busy, as you can see."

"One minute, and then I'll be gone," says Hörður. "I'm busy myself; my date's waiting for me."

"Then get to the point."

"Well, I realized something," says Hörður. "Gísli is right-handed. I'm pretty certain of that. He was ahead of me in the line for the urinal and I watched him flush it with his right hand. But if he's right-handed, why would he stab a person with his left?"

"Right or left—it changes nothing, in itself," says Engilbert irritatedly. "As I told you before, there's no doubt as to who committed the deed. It *was* Gísli Már. We have witnesses, a murder weapon, and the guilty party in custody. Period. The only thing we don't know is why he committed the murder. But that's irrelevant, as well."

"Okay, I understand." Hörður scratches his head. He moves to stand up, just as the bartender returns with the drink that he ordered. She places the glass on a small cork mat; the ice cubes clack softly and the whiskey glows with the color of melted copper.

"Here you are," she says. "Should I put it on your account?"

"Yes, thanks." Hörður takes a sip, and groans with delight. "Ah, this is good! Refreshing, with a kick. Are you a shot-man, Betti?"

"Call me Engilbert," says the detective coldly.

Hörður nods distractedly. "There's also the motive—the reason for the murder. I've been giving it some thought. He'd clearly been planning to attack the MP—otherwise he wouldn't have ambushed the victim at precisely that spot. I suppose he'd been waiting there in the shadows?"

"That's what the witnesses' statements suggest," says Engilbert.

"What puzzles me is the choice of victim," says Hörður. "Was it a coincidence or not? Was he waiting for this particular MP, or just any old MP?"

"That's one of the things that we don't know," says the detective.

"Another MP walked out the same door and across the parking lot in the same place shortly beforehand, true?" asks Hörður. "That woman from the Social Democratic Party."

Engilbert looks at his laptop screen. "Ingigerður Ásmundsdóttir, yes, that's right."

"She's almost entirely unknown. I didn't remember her name, and neither did you," says Hörður. "But Þórólfur is well known. He's been in the news a lot recently, in connection with his alcohol bill."

"Yes, and?"

"Maybe the murder was politically motivated, but I find the idea unlikely," says Hörður. "This Gísli doesn't seem to be the type who would kill a person over his political opinions, although that can't be excluded entirely—but as he doesn't remember his actions, I find it unlikely. If he meant to kill an MP, just *any* MP, then his choice of Þórólfur makes sense because he's heard of him and *knows* that he's an MP, whereas Ingigerður could just as well have been someone working in a parliament office. Do you see what I mean?"

Engilbert nods. "In and of itself, your reasoning isn't off-track. But think about this: even if Gísli Már says that he doesn't remember anything, that doesn't necessarily mean he doesn't remember anything. He could be playing us. That's why I'm working overtime. I want to take into account all possibilities. If I'm open to only one possibility, the most obvious one, the chances of the investigation missing something increase, and our case will fail due to lack of substantial evidence.

"Yeah, of course." Hörður sips his drink. "Did you think about using dogs—you know search dogs?"

Engilbert smiles condescendingly. "In order to find someone, the dog needs to be able to sniff the shoes or clothing that that person was wearing. All that we had was the murder weapon, the knife, which definitely wasn't enough."

"I didn't mean that." Hörður smacks his lips contentedly, relishing the aftertaste of his drink. "I mean after Gísli turned himself in. Not to trace his movements from the scene of the murder, but *to* him."

Engilbert pales.

"Where did he come from?" asks Hörður. "He could hardly have walked all the way from Ölver; that would have taken him an hour and a half. He didn't drive his own car. What car did he drive? Did someone give him a ride? Who then? And where did that person drop Gísli off?"

Engilbert clears his throat. "As I said, we're looking into all these things. We just haven't made any headway—not yet. Your idea about the dog is fine, in and of itself, but there's probably been way too much pedestrian traffic in the city center for a dog to be able to track the trail of one person who was there twelve hours earlier, at the very least."

"Yeah, maybe." Hörður drains his glass in one gulp. "But it wouldn't have hurt to try, would it?"

Engilbert's face reddens with anger. "Did you come here to criticize my work and challenge my abilities and education? Or just to waste my precious time, and that of the CID?"

Hörður is taken aback. "No, not at all. I just wanted to let you know what was on my mind. I apologize—I was just trying to help."

"Goodbye," says Engilbert brusquely, before directing his attention back to his laptop screen. "I have better things to do than listen to dog-logic from some know-it-all street cop."

Know-it-all! Hörður's temper flares, but he manages to control himself before doing something that he knows he'd regret. He stands up, snorts furiously and walks off without another word.

Hörður opens the door, causing the bell to jingle as he steps out into the chill of the evening. There's no one waiting for him.

He peeks around the corner, looks in all directions, but Bíbí is nowhere to be seen. Has she gone ahead of him to the Sufi?

Hörður saunters down Vitastígur, and then starts running.

"Bíbí?" he shouts, just in case. The only answer he receives is the sound of his own footsteps echoing off the buildings.

Hörður runs faster, but knows very well that it's useless. Bíbí won't be at the Sufi; she obviously gave up waiting for him and has gone home. He runs down to the intersection with Laugavegur Avenue, where he turns left. His jacket is so tight that he can barely swing his arms forward and back; the seams split and start tearing. First, the right sleeve tears halfway down from his shoulder, followed immediately by the left, and finally, the back seam gives way and the jacket opens from the collar down to the vent.

His heart is pounding and his lungs burn from the exertion; he gradually starts feeling nauseous and his legs are on the verge of stiffening. He slows down, breathless and sweaty, before coming to a full stop.

Bíbí is gone. He's lost her. But he never had her, anyway, to begin with. She couldn't possibly have had any interest in a man like him. That's obvious. Otherwise, she wouldn't have disappeared.

And he actually thought he'd had a chance.

Hörður laughs coldly at his own stupidity. Damn, what an enormous loser he can be! He plunks down on his ass, leans back against a building, and looks up at the night sky. Overhead, clouds drift over the moon.

The moon that will be full in four days.

Thursday

It's seven in the morning. The locker room is its usual noisy self during shift changes at the station. Those who were on the night shift change back into their civilian clothes as they talk about the events of the night and share information with those coming on day shift. Voices and laughter echo off of the metal lockers and stone walls; locker doors are slammed shut and duty belts clatter as they're either tossed into lockers or fastened around waists. A few people take showers, and the smell of soap and steam blend with the aroma of coffee and the odor of bad breath.

Hörður sits on the wooden bench opposite his locker and ties the shoelaces of his work shoes. He's sleepy, grumpy, and groggy—his head aches, and his temples throb. He might not have gotten drunk at the bar last night, yet did in fact have one drink too many. It was the damn whiskey; he should have skipped having it. Damn, that stuff is bad for one's head.

"So how was it yesterday, Romeo?" Vigfús asks, grinning.

Hörður's temper flares. This damn idiot can be so un-funny. It's just incredible. Can he never behave like a man? But Hörður mustn't let himself be provoked; that only makes matters worse.

"Just fine," Hörður mutters. He stands up, adjusts his shirt collar and puts on his duty belt.

"And? asks Vigfús mischievously. "And now you're enga-ged, or ...?"

"No, I guess not." Hörður wants so much to punch him in the mouth—to shut this stupid windbag up once and for all.

"Oh? You don't like her?" asks Vigfús.

"Yes, yes, kind of," says Hörður. "But I'm just not what she's looking for."

"Well, my man," says Vigfús, laughing. "So it was she who broke your heart!"

"Do I seem brokenhearted to you?" asks Hörður coldly.

"No, no, not really," says Vigfús, with a grin. "Is this a sensitive subject, or ...?"

"Not at all." Hörður sighs—he's pretty tired of this. "But you know how these girls are. The ones in the world of hair-styling and fashion. They might be attracted to a cop at first sight, you know, the uniform and all. But as soon as we start talking about our jobs, they lose interest. They don't want to hear stories about domestic violence, biker gangs, drug nests and kids who sell themselves for their next fix. They only want to talk about things that are cute and cozy. Do you know what I mean?"

"Yeah, I get you." Vigfús nods and pats Hörður on the back in a fatherly fashion. "Sorry to hear it. But one day you'll meet the right one. Like me."

"Yep." Hörður puts on his jacket and cap. "What are we doing today, by the way?"

Don't say speed monitoring at Ártúnsbrekka Hill, he thinks, sighing to himself at the thought. He would prefer to do traffic control near one of the city's elementary schools.

"Speed monitoring at Ártúnsbrekka Hill," says Vigfús. "Let's get going, so we make the seven-thirty rush."

"Awesome, man." Hörður pats his jacket pockets, checking to see if he has cigarettes. "But we need to stop at a shop first. I want a Coke, and I think I left my cigarettes at home."

When he says *want*, he means *need*—his throat is so dry that he may as well have eaten sawdust for breakfast. When in fact he hadn't eaten anything.

"We don't have time for that," says Vigfús irritatedly.

"Relax, man," mutters Hörður. Something crumples when he sticks his hand in one pocket, and he pulls out a folded sheet of paper. He unfolds it. It's the sheet of paper that he wrote a few things down on when he was Googling yesterday. *Points,* as he calls such notes. At the top of the sheet is the name Little Mummi, followed by a few points about criminal complaints and sentences. Below these is the name of the pastor against whom Mummi filed a complaint for sexual abuse:

Ingimar Jósefsson

The one who went to Florida to celebrate his 70th birthday. He was going to play golf with his nephew on his birthday.

Hörður feels a tickling at the back of his neck. It's as if he should be remembering something, but can't.

What was the name of this pastor's nephew? And why does he feel it matters? Is it something connected to golf?

"Are you coming?" asks Vigfús.

Was it Engilbert?

Hörður blinks. "Yes, or ..."

"Or what?" Vigfús asks brusquely. "We've got to get going, man! Especially if you have to stop at a shop."

Hörður waves the sheet of paper. "I need to do a little something first. Be right back."

"Do what, damn it?" barks Vigfús. "Out of the question—no matter what it is. We're wasting too much time."

"Have some coffee—relax a little," says Hörður grumpily. "I'll be right back. It's not the end of the world."

Vigfús exhales like a whale. "I'll have half a cup of coffee, and then I'm leaving, with or without you. Do you hear me?"

"Fine." Hörður goes over to the communal work area, sits down at a free computer, and logs in. Then he navigates to *timarit.is* and again looks up the birthday story in *Morgunblaðið*. He quickly reads over the interview with the pastor, then looks at the picture of him and his nephew.

The hairs stand up on the back of Hörður's neck. The nephew's name is Gísli Már Brynjarsson. The same Gísli Már who was on the national youth golf team, and is now in custody at Litla-Hraun Prison, under suspicion of having killed a member of parliament with a knife. In the photo, Gísli is wearing a golf glove on his right hand. So he *is* right-handed. Is that right? Does a right-handed golfer wear his glove on his right hand?

Maybe it doesn't matter, this fuss about right or left. Still, Hörður is convinced that it does.

Or what?

But whether Gísli is right-handed or left-handed, he is clearly the nephew of Ingimar Jósefsson, the man who abused Little Mummi. What does this mean? Is it just coincidence?

Or is it significant, in some way?

And in what way?

Hörður bites his lower lip. Should he just forget about it? Or should he let someone know? He drums his fingers on the table. It wouldn't do any harm to pass this information on, would it?

The CID is located on the third floor of the police station, on the western side of the building. Hörður walks down a windowless corridor and stops in front of the door to the department. He grabs the handle, but the door is locked. Next to the lock is an access-card reader. Hörður pulls his card from his breast pocket and runs it through the reader.

A red light flashes. He doesn't have access to this department.

On the wall next to the door is a tablet with a vertical list of the names of all the members of the department. In front of each name are two boxes, out and in. There's a green magnet in the in-box next to Engilbert's name.

Hörður hesitates, and then knocks on the door. After a few moments, he hears the faint sound of footsteps behind it, and the lock clicks and the door opens. In the doorway stands Jafet Sigurðsson, Engilbert's partner in the CID. Behind him, Hörður catches a glimpse of a row of work stations in a long office space. There are fluorescent lights on the ceiling, and the curtains are drawn over the windows that look out on Faxaflói Bay.

"Yes?" asks Jafet, with professional nonchalance.

"Sorry to bother you," says Hörður. "Is Engilbert here?"

"He's busy," says Jafet. "What's up?"

"It has to do with the murder investigation," says Hörður. "I've just realized a certain connection that might shed some light on the case, and might not. I just thought it would be better to let someone know, instead of simply forgetting about it. One never knows what matters and what doesn't."

Jafet thinks things over. "I'll check if he has a moment to spare. Who should I say is asking for him?"

"My name is Hörður Grímsson. He knows who I am. We spoke to each other yesterday—twice, in fact. It was I who saw the suspect at Ölver shortly before the murder was committed."

Jafet looks at the police officer as if he were an alien.

"Wait here. I'll go get Engilbert."

"Yes, I …" Hörður stops when Jafet shuts the door, and then reddens with anger. Fucking arrogant prick! He takes a deep breath and tries to relax, before looking at his watch.

Vigfús is going to be pissed.

He's startled by the door suddenly opening.

"What do you want?" Engilbert asks brusquely. His face is ashen and his eyes are bloodshot. His whiskey drinking has clearly taken its toll. He looks at the red-haired giant with acrid contempt, and Hörður recalls how their conversation at Vitabar had ended rather abruptly, to put it mildly.

"Hello." Hörður feels slightly awkward, and immediately regrets having disturbed the detective. "Thanks for the chat yesterday. It was very interesting. I hope that I didn't insult you or anything like that."

"Did you come to apologize to me for wasting my time last evening?" snaps Engilbert. "Or do you simply want to keep wasting my time and this department's?"

The police officer takes two steps back. Not only is the detective ill-disposed, but his breath stinks, as well.

"I just realized a certain connection," says Hörður. "I thought it better to report it than to keep quiet about it. But I probably shouldn't have bothered you."

"What connection?"

"It's Gísli Már," says Hörður. "He's a nephew of Ingimar Jósefsson, a retired pastor. Ingimar is a convicted sex offender. One of those who filed a complaint against him for sexual misconduct is Guðmundur Vífill Marínósson, better known as Little Mummi. He and two of his peers accused him of offenses that he supposedly committed when they were kids at summer camp. The case was dismissed."

Engilbert stares at Hörður. "And?"

"We were called to a storage facility on Tuesday—my partner Vigfús and I. A skull had been found there, and it turned out to be extremely old and foreign, as well. The stuff in the storage unit belonged to the deceased Mummi. Who turns out to have filed a complaint against the uncle of Gísli Már, who murders someone the same evening. This is just too freaky; so unbelievable. Probably a coincidence. But what do I know?"

"Probably a coincidence?" exclaims Engilbert. "We live in Iceland, you clown! Everyone here is more or less related. This is the biggest bunch of bullshit I've ever heard. Who Gísli's uncle is doesn't matter one bit. And Mummi is dead, as you yourself pointed out. Are you trying to piss me off? Or are you just dense?"

"I just thought I should let you know," Hörður mutters.

"Thank you very much. But next time you put two and two together and get something other than four, keep it to yourself!," says Engilbert, shutting the door.

Hörður stands there as if paralyzed, staring at the door, then walks dejectedly back down the corridor toward the elevator. He doesn't feel well at all, but doesn't know whether he's angrier at Engilbert or himself. The detective's response was both hurtful and unfair, but what he said was true, in and of itself—that is, leaving off his sarcastic tone and the insults.

He should have seen this himself. Of course there was no connection.

He's got to learn to think things through before plunging headlong into them and …

And what?

Hörður sighs heavily.

And making himself look foolish.

He steps into the elevator and pushes a button. The elevator door shuts, and jerks once before descending.

The elevator descends slowly. Whereas Hörður is heading downhill fast.

Vigfús is neither in the changing room nor the communal work area. Nor has he left ahead of Hörður, because their squad car is in its place in the alley. Hörður walks quickly down the corridors, with a bewildered expression, like a young boy who has lost his daddy. His conversation with Engilbert is really sticking in his craw. He's extremely hard on himself, often running the gauntlet between self-criticism and humiliation, leaving his ego resembling a worn-down car tire. The day began well—or rather, the opposite. He finally finds Vigfús in the place where he naturally should have started his search—in the cafeteria on the third floor, where he's been leisurely sipping his coffee while his partner rode the elevator up and down and back up again.

"You're not an easy person to find," says Hörður, with self-pity dripping from every word.

"You said I should get some coffee and relax." Vigfús is as calm as can be. He stands up and rinses his cup, before putting it in the dishwasher.

"Where's your stress?" asks Hörður in surprise. "Aren't we running way behind?"

Vigfús looks at the wall clock. "No, not at all. We need to be back by ten, which it looks to me we'll make easily."

"Back from where?" asks Hörður.

"From Litla-Hraun," says Vigfús. "We've been assigned to go pick up Gísli Már. "They're going to be questioning him all day."

Hörður has difficulty concealing his pleasure. That's a hundred times better than standing out in the cold, writing speeding tickets. To be sent on a long mission is always a godsend. But to go pick up a suspected murderer from custody is in his mind like winning the lottery. "Awesome! But why us?"

Vigfús shrugs. "Everyone else left already."

"So I'm to thank for this," says Hörður, feeling cheerful again.

"Easy, boy," says Vigfús authoritatively. "If you don't behave, I'm not stopping off at the shop."

They drive Suðurlandsvegur Highway eastward, past Hólmsheiði and up to Hellisheiði Heath. On both sides, there is little more than sand and lava, but ahead of them, the Bláfjöll mountains stand out against a pink background. The sun is rising and the lowlands are still dark, but the sky is rosy and gradually turning redder. The pleasant sound of the road beneath their wheels fills the car, blended with the incoherent blather of the conspiracy infected and often racist voices of Radio Saga. It's listener phone-in time, and a nervous-sounding woman is on the line, a stay-at-home housewife who is very worried about the mosque that the Muslims want to build in one of the best locations in the city.

Hörður finishes the half-liter bottle of Coke that he bought at the shop at Norðlingaholt. His thirst is bottomless; he should have bought two more bottles. But he feels a little better—the Coke settles his stomach and his headache is dwindling. "Shouldn't we listen to Channel 2, instead?"

"Hm." Vigfús grips the wheel with both hands, his eyes focused on the road. "No, not now. I'm listening."

Hörður sighs. One day he'll be in the driver's seat, with some poor new recruit sitting to his right. Then, the radio will be set permanently to X generation's rock station The X, with the volume cranked. Feeling bored, he gazes out his window at the desolate landscape. He should probably have brought a book with him to work.

Wait a minute—doesn't he have a book?

Hörður opens the glove compartment, and there it is: the book that he took from the belongings of the deceased Mummi. *How to Hypnotize Anyone*, by The Rogue Hypnotist. He switches on the light above his seat, leans back and starts reading. The book's purpose is to demonstrate that not only can anyone learn hypnotism, but that it's also possible to hypnotize almost anyone, except perhaps terrified individuals, brain-damaged people and those who are simply feebleminded. This is a *How-To* book, says its author, who writes in an easy, accessible manner.

At the start of the book, the author writes that the hypnotic state is common, and that everyone has experienced it in one way or another, without perhaps realizing it. He strongly emphasizes the idea that although the techniques of hypnosis are easy to learn, hypnosis is and will always be a *mystery* that can never be fully understood.

It's all about understanding on the one hand and technique on the other, it seems to Hörður, at least at a glance.

Understanding how the human mind responds to words, gestures, and the voice—knowing and grasping these basic elements of hypnosis, its techniques, is the key to another person's mind.

"Interesting," mutters Hörður. He continues reading. In some places, words and sentences have been underlined in pencil.

The book teaches the techniques step by step. First, the attention of the person to be hypnotize needs to be captured. The hypnotist uses a pre-determined script that is thought out in every last detail. To begin with, the subject's attention is focused on particular things, and then these things are reduced in number—the hypnotist controls what the subject thinks, and little by little narrows the field until a specific focal point is reached. The subject's consciousness gives way and the hypnotist speaks directly to the subconscious. Every word he says exerts great influence on the subject because the subconscious takes everything literally. By speaking directly to the subconscious, the hypnotist avoids all the conscious security checks of the brain, such as reasoning and judgment. The hypnotist's script is a combination of indirect instructions and specific commands. He plays the subject's mind as he would any other instrument. He gets the subject to relax completely, and orders him or her to fall into a trance. Vocal technique is extremely important—the author emphasizes this particularly. The voice should be low, one or two eighths lower than the hypnotist's normal speaking voice. Pronunciation should be monotone and flat, the voice should flow like a river that is calm on the surface, but below is both deep and swift-currented. Pauses are important. At the end of each sentence, the voice should drop, not rise, especially in the case of a command. The subject's mind is directed inward, into the expanses of his or her own being. Hypnosis takes place in the realm of the spirit, despite the techniques being bound to the physical world. The hypnotist speaks, and what he says is general and unclear. He put the subject <u>to sleep</u>, gets that person to <u>trust</u> him.

Take note of four things that you see in the room … four things … you may perhaps notice how the light falls on them … now take note of three things … now two things … finally, just one thing … that's right … then just gently … close your eyes … listen for four sounds around you … maybe a plane flying over … a clock ticking … now listen for three sounds …

The car's engine … the sound of the road … the voices on Radio Saga …

Hörður starts when Vigfús shuts off the car. He blinks, lets the book sink and looks out the window, with a puzzled expression. The car is in a large paved parking lot bordered by a double security fence. The outer fence is a dense chain-link mesh, topped by barbed wire on sharp metal spikes leaning outward. The inner fence is like a mirror image of the outer one, except that it's electrified with high-voltage current. A space of three or four meters separates the two fences.

Inside the double fence is Litla-Hraun Prison.

"Are we here?"

"What do you think?" says Vigfús, opening his door. "Were you sleeping, or what?"

"No, I was just …" Hörður stops, steps out of the car and shuts the door. He was just what? Engrossed in his reading? Distracted?

Or something else entirely?

The sky is pale blue, and clear. Surrounding them are gravel flats and fields that are as yellow as in a painting by Van Gogh. The village of Eyrarbakki is on their right. The houses are lined up along the shore, and merge with the spartan landscape. In the distance, four horses stand motionless on the other side of a fence.

The clatter of a diesel engine and heavy, rhythmic strokes tear through the stillness and echo off the buildings. At one corner of the horse fence stands a large tractor, with a pneumatic drill in tow. The road lying parallel to the southern gate of the prison fence is barricaded at its southeastern corner. A district road crew has torn up the road, and are just then breaking apart a boulder with a hammer drill.

Vigfús looks over his shoulder. "Are you coming?"

Hörður hadn't realized that Vigfús was walking away. It's as if he isn't entirely in full control of his senses. He must have fallen asleep in the car.

They walk along the fence and up to the gate. On one side is a narrow, separately fenced pathway that ends at a metal turnstile, and on the other, a sturdy gate for delivery trucks. Next to the turnstile gate is an intercom.

Vigfús pushes the button and waits. Hörður stands behind him. This is his first official visit to Litla-Hraun after joining the police. But when he was at the Academy, his class made a field trip here, to the country's largest prison. Accompanied by prison officers, they were given a guided tour of the place.

The intercom crackles. *"Control room."*

"Reykjavík police," says Vigfús over the intercom. "We're here to pick up a detainee."

A few seconds pass, and then the turnstile gate unlocks with a loud click. Vigfús maneuvers his way through the gate first, followed by Hörður. The gate is heavy, and the space between the bars confined. Hörður pushes with both hands on the stout bars, realizing at the same time that he's holding the hypnosis book.

From the gate, they head straight to a door marked VISITORS. To their left is the gymnasium, which is separate from the main prison building. The prison itself consists of several adjacent buildings, old and new. Atop the newest building is a tall guard tower, blue with outward-slanting windows on all sides.

Hörður leafs through the book. Its final chapters provide instructions for voice and breathing control, along with suggestions for hypnosis scripts. He opens the book to the title page and regards the symbol drawn there.

Aron, with a circle around the A.

The owner of the book is somewhere inside the walls of this institute. The anarchist Aron Beck. The evil spirit that no walls can hold, according to him. He who slips out everywhere.

Before going inside, Hörður glances up at the building's walls, which are thick and set with narrow windows. The prison is like hopelessness and depression in the form of concrete and steel.

The duty officer welcomes them in the control room. Here, three large flat-panel monitors are mounted on the wall, with each monitor display divided into numerous smaller displays, each of them a view from one of the prison's surveillance cameras. The images are black and white, and show either empty corridors and cells or prisoners doing various jobs in work areas, or else relaxing in common rooms.

In front of the monitors, a young prison officer is sitting on a worn office chair, distractedly fingering a key ring while keeping an eye on the displays. Numerous short keys and two long ones hang from his key ring, and hanging from a hook on the wall above the officer are two different key rings, with another empty hook between them. The officer's job is as uninteresting as it is thankless.

"Sign in here," says the duty officer, a man of around fifty. He points to a line in a large daybook lying open on a desk. They do as he says, writing down the date, time, and purpose of their visit, and sign their names. Lying on the table alongside the daybook are copies of the day's newspapers, *Fréttablaðið* and *Morgunblaðið*. The headline story of both papers is the same, although the presentation is slightly different. MAN IN CUSTODY, reads the enormous headline of *Morgunblaðið*. "The murder investigation is going well," reads smaller letters over the headline, and beneath it is a photograph of the murder scene. Where Þórólfur lay in his own blood, people have laid numerous flower bouquets in memory of the deceased. The photo was taken from a low angle, with the flowers in the foreground, and over them towers the Parliament House, like an unscalable cliff. THE PERPETRATOR TURNED HIMSELF IN, declares *Fréttablaðið*. This paper's cover page also displays a photo of the murder scene, but the view is from above, most likely from the balcony of the Parliament House. The photo was taken at eight p.m. the previous evening, when over a hundred people gathered to commemorate the deceased. The photo shows a little girl adding a bouquet to the pile that has already formed.

"Such a tragedy," says the duty officer.

"You can say that again," mutters Vigfús.

"One would think that some sort of monster did it," says the duty officer, with a sad expression. "But then they show up here with this poor kid. Of course I sympathize with the family of the deceased, but I feel really sorry for this young fellow, too. It's no small thing having such a horrendous deed on your conscious."

"True, true," says Vigfús, reluctantly.

"But anyway. The detainee is taking a shower at the moment," says the duty officer. "Would you like a cup of coffee while you wait?"

They nod and say yes, thanks.

"I'll go and get two mugs." The duty officer goes to the break room. He speaks slowly, and moves slower. At the prison, time stands still—no one has anywhere to go; there's never any rush. Prison is a monastery with bars.

Vigfús grabs the copy of *Morgunblaðið*; he sits down and starts flipping through the paper, while Hörður stares interestedly at the monitors. One of them shows two prisoners playing ping pong in a small space. One of the prisoners turns halfway toward the camera, which is clearly hanging up in one corner, near the ceiling. The prisoner is thin, with a dark complexion and quick movements, and wearing black sweatpants and a black t-shirt. He holds the ping-pong paddle in his right hand, and his left arm is in a cast from the knuckles up to the elbow. He carries himself clumsily, has to work hard to return his opponent's fast shots, and finally misses a return. Then he throws a fit, smashing the paddle to the floor and kicking at the ping-pong table. As quickly as he gets worked up, however, he calms down, shrugging his shoulders moodily and glancing straight and menacingly at the camera, smirking slightly.

"Is that …" Hörður steps closer to the monitor. "Is that Aron Beck? The one in the cast?"

"Yes, that's right," says the young officer.

"Is his arm broken?"

"Yeah, it is," says the officer. "He was pouring concrete and had an accident. Broke his wrist. Apparently, he's going to sue the prison."

"Is that right?" asks Hörður.

"So he says," says the officer. "But maybe those are just big words on his part."

Hörður scratches his head, and then shows the officer the book that he's holding. "Strange coincidence—this is Aron's book. Vigfús and I found it along with other things in a storage unit that we were sent to investigate. Long story. But maybe I should return the book to him, now that I've got it here with me?"

The officer shrugs. "That's all right with me."

"What are you talking about, man?" asks Vigfús. "You're not going to return the book! We're here to pick up a detainee. Period!"

"It'll only take a moment—what is the problem?" says Hörður. "It's his book, after all. And he's an interesting guy. I read an interview with him yesterday. I'd really like to find out whether he's as messed up as he pretends to be."

The officer stands up. "He's completely nuts, I can absolutely guarantee you that. But he's no troublemaker. Not here, in any case. He's no model prisoner, but isn't the worst by a long shot."

"What block is he in?" asks Hörður.

"Three," says the officer, lifting his key ring. "I'll take you to the Blue Door and let you through."

"Out of the question!" Vigfús gets to his feet, as heavily as a dinosaur. "We're here on official business, and not to return books to nutcases. Do you understand?"

"Calm down, man," says Hörður irritatedly. "What does it matter?"

Vigfús throws up his hands. "It just does! I don't want you going and meeting that idiot."

"Sit back down and relax," says Hörður. "I may not get to decide what radio station we listen to, but surely I get to decide what I do while we're waiting around, doing nothing. It's only a quarter to nine. We're not in any rush."

"You and your goddamn attitude!" Vigfús plunks back down onto his chair, and Hörður and the prison officer head down a long corridor. On either side of them are rooms with steel doors. On the left is a room where urine samples are taken from prisoners, another with clothing donations from the Red Cross, and a medical-exam room. On the right are interview rooms for professional consultants, and another room where prisoners are searched upon their arrival at the prison.

They stop in front of a blue steel door that's shut and locked. On the door is a closed hatch, at eye level.

The prison officer unlocks the door with one of his long keys and opens it. "It's straight ahead and to the left. When you're done, ring the bell and I'll come open the door for you."

"No problem. Thanks." Hörður walks into Block 3, and gets goose bumps when the Blue Door is locked behind him. He glances over his shoulder. The door is marked with countless scratches and dents, and on it is a greyish window with bulletproof glass. The window is dark, as the hatch cover on the opposite side is pulled down.

Block 3 is painted yellow, and smells of cigarettes and sweat. To both sides are cells, both open and closed. The doors are wooden and heavy, and are locked with steel latches. In the evenings, the latches are secured with padlocks. From the end of the corridor comes a rapid clicking noise, and the squeaking of the soles of shoes.

The common room is neither large nor luxurious. In it are a TV, a three-seater sofa and a coffee table, besides the ping-pong table. On the coffee table are coffee mugs and two ashtrays. Two cigarettes are burning in one of the ash trays, and the air is saturated with smoke. Aron's opponent is short and fat, and he bites his tongue lightly as he hits the ball over the net.

Hörður stops.

Both of the prisoners stop playing and look at him. The ping-pong ball bounces onto the concrete floor and rolls under the sofa.

"Who the hell are you?" asks Aron Beck. He lays his paddle on the table and walks over to the police officer. He looks the red-haired giant over from head to toe and finally at the book that he's holding.

"My name is Hörður. I'm a police officer."

"I would never have guessed," says Aron, smirking. "What brings you here? I don't remember having booked an interview today."

"Just paying a courtesy visit," says Hörður. He looks the prisoner directly in the eye, and Aron meets his gaze. Aron is about a head lower than the police officer, broad-shouldered and muscular, yet without being a bodybuilder in any way. He has an air of either self-confidence or madness—or perhaps a little of each. His ears are pierced, yet lack earrings. He has small scars here and there, perhaps from knife fights, including at his left eye and the right corner of his mouth. Something white hangs at the end of a leather strap around the prisoner's neck.

Aron has only two visible tattoos. On the left side of his neck is the anarchy symbol, a circled A, and on his right forearm is an equilateral triangle with a skull inside it. The triangle is pointed toward Aron's elbow, and there are small symbols on either side of it, runes or letters.

"It isn't polite to stare, cop," says Aron. He acts as if he's relaxed, but the tendons in his neck tense, like a snake preparing to strike, and his half-closed eyes flash.

Hörður ignores the comment. He turns his attention to Aron's pendant, which is a bone with a hole through it. As far as Hörður can tell, it's a knucklebone. A rune or sorcerer's stave resembling a swastika has been burned onto it.

Aron grabs the pendant in the fingers of his left hand. "It's from a seal's flipper. An amulet. It gives me strength during difficult times."

Hörður nods, then lifts the book and smiles faintly. "I have a book of yours. I thought you might want it."

Aron blinks. He's unfamiliar with this police officer, and is therefore suspicious. This could be a trap.

"That's all," says Hörður, with a shrug.

Aron glances at the surveillance camera, which is monitoring him over the police officer's shoulder. "Let's go into my cell."

"Are we done here?" asks the fat prisoner, still standing at his end of the ping-pong table.

"Yeah, Bibbi," snaps Aron.

"I win, three-zero," says Bibbi proudly.

"Have it printed on a t-shirt, then it'll last longer," barks Aron. He walks ahead of Hörður into cell number eight. There are ten cells in this block. "When I get out of this cast, I'm going to stuff that retard's yap with ping-pong balls. His ass, too."

Hörður bends his head as he steps into the prisoner's living quarters. The cell is neither big nor lavish. At a guess, it's two meters wide and four meters long, with the door at one end and a tiny window at the other. On one side are a bookshelf, a desk, and another shelf holding an audio system and a video-game machine. On the other wall is a narrow wardrobe and an unmade bed. On the desk is a 28" flat- screen TV, and beneath it a chair. The space between the bed and the desk is barely more than fifty centimeters. The bookshelf holds a few worn paperbacks, mainly thrillers, and quite a few CDs, DVDs, and computer games. On top of it are a few tealights, a life-sized plastic skull, and incense in a special holder.

Aron sits down on the bed and kicks the chair over to the police officer.

"Have a seat. Make yourself at home."

Hörður sits down on the chair.

Aron lights a cigarette, crosses his legs and lets the arm in the cast rest on his knee. He tilts his head and regards the police officer as he blows smoke out one corner of his mouth.

There's something feminine about how he's sitting and comports himself. Something *gay*, in fact.

"What would you do if you got to be a woman for one day?" asks Aron, with a mischievous grin. It's as if he's read the officer's mind.

Hörður feels slightly awkward. "I suppose there's little risk of that happening."

"An uncomfortable question?" Aron asks, smiling widely. "I don't think so. I would lie back and let myself be fucked all day long."

Hörður clears his throat. "I heard that you were going to sue the prison."

"You just change the topic? What'll it be next? The weather?" Aron blows smoke rings. "But, yeah. Our safety isn't guaranteed here at all. It's like being in a sweatshop. It isn't normal to break your arm at work, is it?"

Hörður smiles faintly.

"Isn't that a bit odd, for a declared anarchist to submit a formal complaint and go to court? Aren't you seeking protection from the system you pretend to be fighting against?"

Aron shakes his head. "As long as I have a national ID number and pay taxes, I'm a part of the system, whether I like it or not. Is this your secret mission, to get me not to sue the prison? The book's just a cover, huh?"

"No, not at all." Hörður hands him the book. "I just came to return it. True story."

Aron takes the book and looks it over carefully. "It was stolen from me. Where did you find it?"

"At a storage facility," replies the police officer. "Among the belongings of the deceased Mummi."

Aron stiffens when he hears his friend's name. "Is that so … okay. I see. But, as I said, the book was stolen from me. But I didn't miss it at all. It's a bunch of damn rubbish. Still, thanks for bringing it to me."

"There were other books there," says Hörður. "I didn't check whether they belonged to you or not."

"Probably not." Aron gives a quick snort. "Mummi had lots of books. He was a smart kid. He had a Bible and some sort of dictionary, among other things. Maybe the dictionary was there, too, huh?"

Hörður frowns. "Actually, yes."

Aron shrugs. "As I said, it belonged to Mummi. The Bible, too. I'm not the dictionary type, do you understand? And I don't believe in God."

Hörður nods. He's trying to see the tattoo better, the one with the skull. The symbols next to the triangle are letters—l, j, and e.

Aron blows smoke out of his nostrils. "Take a photo, cop. It'll last longer."

Hörður looks up and smiles. "What does your tattoo mean?"

Aron shrugs. "Everything. Nothing. Know your enemy."

"What enemy is that?" asks Hörður. "Society? The system? The police?"

"Is this an interrogation?" asks Aron coldly. "If so, I must point out that you have neither read me my rights nor given me a chance to call my lawyer."

Hörður raises his hands, palms outward, in capitulation. "Sorry. I'm just a big fan of tattoos. And skulls."

"Is that so ... okay," mutters Aron.

"There was a skull among Mummi's things." Hörður turns halfway to the side and points at the plastic skull on top of the bookshelf. "Not unlike that one, only darker. Is that a model?"

"Yep." Aron taps the ash from his cigarette into an ashtray sitting on top of the audio system, next to two bottles of 8x4 deodorant. "I glued it together and then sprayed it that color. I've got enough time on my hands here, you know. We do puzzles, play games, and put together models. It's like being at summer camp."

"Is it?" asks Hörður.

Aron clamps his lips shut, and reddens around the eyes. He puts out the cigarette and gets up quickly from the bed. "You've returned the book. Was there anything else?"

"No, not really." Hörður gets to his feet and pushes the chair back beneath the desk.

"You must have enough keeping you busy these days," says Aron. "What with the murder and all. I saw the reports on TV. Extensive media coverage, understandably."

"Exactly," says Hörður.

"But they've got someone in custody, right?" says Aron. "So you're probably breathing a little lighter, you cops?"

"Yes, yes."

"Do you know what Iceland's main problem is?" asks Aron, with a sarcastic gleam in his eyes. "I mean apart from its location, the weather, and low population."

"What is it?"

"Murders are solved too quickly, which, of course, has to do with the low population," says Aron. "The result is that we never have any proper serial killers. They're always caught before they manage to place their mark on society."

"Most people would consider that a good thing—not a problem," says Hörður.

"Most people are also as soulless and unoriginal as amoebae," says Aron contemptuously. "Other than the serial killers. They're original and have style; they're go-getters, while others are stuck daydreaming."

Hörður sighs. "You're a bad apple, that's what you are."

Aron lets the officer's words go in one ear and out the other. "I've read countless books about serial killers.

Accounts of their actions as well as studies of their behavior and inner nature.

Having done the same, Hörður's interest perks.

"One of them, I don't remember his name, started out an ordinary person," says Aron, "but then he got in a motorcycle accident and suffered a serious head injury. The day he regained consciousness, he knew that *something* was wrong, he just didn't know what it was. I read about him in a book by some psychologist."

Hörður nods. He knows the story, but he, too, can't remember the man's name, being one of the lesser-known serial killers.

"Soon after he got out of the hospital, he started raping women," says Aron. "At first, he went to town on his wife like a mad dog, but when that wasn't enough, he began raping. His sex drive was uncontrollable, as was his anger. Burning inside of him was a rage that he couldn't stifle. He tried discussing it with psychologists and psychiatrists, but none of them found anything wrong with him, nothing that could be measured or pinned down. He had simply become malevolent, and ended up killing women after raping them."

"And then he ended up on death row in Florida, if I remember correctly," says Hörður.

Aron beams. "Right you are, cop! You're not as stupid as you look."

Hörður doesn't know whether to be offended or proud.

"Or what," says Aron. "This guy was well suited as the subject of study, because he had the experience of being both normal and insane, besides being much more intelligent than your average criminal. In one interview that the author of the book conducted with this man while he was on death row, the conversation in fact turned to the other prisoners, who were nothing but utter monsters in the opinion of our man—animals, not humans. He pointed out to the psychologist that on death row there were no windows, which made it impossible to know whether it was day or night outside, let alone whether the moon was new or full. But despite that, the murderers on death row howled every time the moon was full. They simply felt it."

Aron looks at the police officer with a smirk and a menacing gleam in his wide-open eyes.

"And?" asks Hörður. He really wants to get out of this anarchist's cell, but manages to control himself. He knows very well that the prisoner presents no real threat to him, no *physical* threat, that is, but nonetheless, there's something very unpleasant and threatening about his presence.

Something illogical that's difficult to put his finger on.

Something *evil*.

Aron grins broadly. "The moon will be full on Sunday, copper."

Hörður shrugs. "Which means?"

Aron winks at him conspiratorially.

"Well, goodbye." Hörður bends his head as he steps out of the cell, turns left, and walks back toward the blue door. On the wall to its right is a button.

"Goodbye yourself, copper," says Aron, with a soft laugh. "I've changed my mind, by the way. You are as stupid as you look."

Hörður's temper flares, but he swallows his anger and continues on his way as if not noticing the remark. If he so much as touches one hair on this prisoner's head, he'll be in big trouble. He could even lose his job.

"Say hello to your wife for me," Aron calls after him. "Or maybe you don't have a wife? You aren't wearing a ring, in any case. You don't have anyone to love? Are you lonely? No one understands the red-haired giant?"

Hörður's mouth goes dry and his heart hammers in his chest. The words are meant to hurt him, and that's exactly what they do. He feels like crap. It's as if he's been in the presence of radioactive waste—or sheer evil, pure and simple.

"Fucking loser," calls out Aron.

Hörður approaches the steel door and can't wait to press the button, to get out of Block 3. If only the officer would hurry up. He knows that Aron is standing in front of his cell and watching his every move. He feels the anarchist's piercing eyes boring like glowing iron wires into the back of his neck.

When Hörður returns to the control room, he's told that Vigfús is waiting for him in the car outside the prison, along with the detainee.

"How'd it go with our man?"

"He was in good form."

Hörður says thanks, and leaves the same way that he Vigfús came in. He looks over his shoulder, and feels a chill. Aron Beck is like the prison enfleshed, oppressive and scathing. Being in his presence is like breathing in cement and sand. The blood is poisoned, the muscles are paralyzed and breathing becomes harder.

The man's a fucking creep.

Hörður gulps in the fresh air outside the thick stone walls. He really wants to lie down on the ground, close his eyes and gather his strength for fifteen minutes or so. But that's impossible, of course.

He pushes his way through the turnstile gate and out into freedom. There are a few cars in the parking lot, but only one with its engine running, Unit 213 from the Reykjavík Police Force. Vigfús sits moodily behind the wheel, and in the back seat is a timid young man wearing a baseball cap on his hanging head, with his hands in his lap.

"Took you long enough," mutters Vigfús resentfully, as his partner gets in and sits down in the passenger seat.

"I wasn't that long," says Hörður. He fastens his seat belt, turns halfway around in his seat, and regards the detainee. Gísli Már is wearing new running shoes, tight jeans and a short jacket with cuffs, a so-called bomber jacket. His baseball cap bears the logo of the New York Yankees. The prisoner is pale, appearing almost in shock, which may in fact be the case. He glances either to the side or at his cuffed hands.

"How are you doing back there?"

Gísli Már doesn't appear to hear the question, but then shrugs his shoulders slightly.

"Leave him alone," says Vigfús. He backs the car up and then drives in a semicircle out of the parking lot, taking a left onto the road that connects the towns of Hveragerði, Stokkseyri and Eyrarbakki.

Hörður glances out the driver's side window, at the barricades blocking the narrow road leading to the village from the north, the ditch and the tractor with the pneumatic drill. The road crew is nowhere to be seen, and the tractor is no longer running. It's an all-wheel drive Massey Ferguson, red and gray with a cab.

"What did that friend of yours have to say?" Vigfús asks cynically.

"Very little," says Hörður.

"Well now," mutters Vigfús.

"He said that the dictionary you took isn't his," says Hörður.

Vigfús grasps the wheel so tightly that his knuckles whiten. "Why did you ask him about that?"

"I didn't, actually." Hörður puts on his Ray-Ban sunglasses to shield his eyes from the glaring autumn sun, high in the sky. "He just told me that, unasked. How he came to bring it up is as much of a mystery to me as to you."

Vigfús seems relieved. "That's what you get when you talk to idiots."

They drive in the direction of Þorlákshöfn, with sand dunes and withered grass on one side, and endless gravel flats on the other. Vigfús clearly intends to take Þrenglsavegur Road.

Hörður looks back at the prisoner, who appears sad and helpless, and on the verge of tears from despair.

"Does he have to be cuffed?" asks Hörður in a low voice.

Vigfús nods. "Those are the rules."

"Yes, I know but …" Hörður feels sorry for this kid; he has to admit it. "He's no thug—just an ordinary young man. It's not like he's dangerous."

"Tell that to the deceased," mutters Vigfús.

Hörður turns to the prisoner. "Do you have a lawyer?"

Gísli Már clears his throat. "Yes. An acquaintance of my dad's. He brought me clothes and a toothbrush and so on."

"Good to hear," says Hörður. "I'm sure he'll do his best. No need to worry."

Gísli Már doesn't reply. Hörður thinks of the evening at Ölver and the little that's known about what took place there.

"You said you drank two glasses of Coke at Ölver," says Hörður. "Is that right?"

Gísli Már nods.

"We're not allowed to question the witness," says Vigfús.

"I'm not questioning him," says Hörður. "I'm just repeating what he already said during questioning."

"All the same," mutters Vigfús. "We shouldn't be speaking to the prisoner. Least of all about his case."

"Yeah, yeah." Hörður turns back to the prisoner. "How much time passed between you finishing your first glass and ordering the next?"

"Hörður!" says Vigfús determinedly.

"Relax, man," replies Hörður.

Gísli Már clears his throat again. "Fifteen minutes, or maybe a little longer. I'm not sure."

Hörður nods thoughtfully. His friends drink beer, whereas Gísli Már drinks Coke because he's driving. "So did you go to the bar to order a new glass?"

Gísli Már shakes his head. "My friend Benni did. He went to the bar and ordered three beers and a Coke for me."

"I see." Hörður scratches his head. This Benni goes to the bar and orders four drinks: three beers and *one* Coke. He waits while the bartender fills the order. But he doesn't watch the bartender; instead, he turns his back to the bar and keeps watching the match. The bartender puts the drinks on a tray and takes payment from Benni, who has his mind on the match.

Everyone is focused on the match, including the bartender. Everyone except for two shady characters hanging around at the bar. Would anyone have noticed it if one of them emptied the contents of a little vial or syringe into the *one* glass on the tray?

"You don't remember anything that happened that evening?" asks Hörður.

Gísli Már shakes his head.

"Have you confessed?"

"No," says Gísli Már. "But maybe I should. They say that I did it. I don't know if I have the strength for all this questioning. I've got nothing to say; there's nothing I can add."

"You've got to be strong," says Hörður. "And you absolutely must not admit to anything. How can you admit to something that you don't even remember doing? That would be perjury."

"Will you please stop now?!" exclaims Vigfús angrily. "You can't be …"

He stops when his cell phone starts ringing.

"What the hell is this?" mutters Vigfús. He slows down, steers with one hand and grabs his pocket with the other. "Can't I get five minutes peace and quiet?"

"You're not going to talk on the phone while driving?" asks Hörður, grinning sarcastically.

"None of your business …" Vigfús retrieves his phone and peeks at the screen before answering. "What's that bastard want? Yes, hello!"

Hörður turns back to the prisoner. "I don't find it out of the question that you might have been drugged. That someone slipped liquid X into your second Coke at Ölver. That could explain your amnesia."

"Liquid X?" asks Gísli Már, bewildered.

Hörður nods.

"Today? Not tonight?" says Vigfús into his phone. "But … yes, all right. Yes, talk to you later. Goodbye."

"Was that your nephew?" asks Hörður. "The one who wants to buy your stamps?"

"Hm?" Vigfús sticks his phone back in his pocket and refocuses on his driving. "Yes, exactly. My nephew. That was him."

"But why would anyone slip me liquid X?" asks Gísli Már.

"What's he talking about?" asks Vigfús.

"Nothing," replies Hörður. He turns to the prisoner and signals him to keep quiet.

"I asked you not to speak to the prisoner," says Vigfús, authoritatively. "There are certain rules that apply to the transport of prisoners, and it's our duty to follow them."

"Nor are we allowed to talk on the phone while driving," says Hörður grumpily. "And in fact, we're not supposed to do personal business while working. If it were up to me, I'd ban the use of cell phones at work ..."

He stops when his own phone starts ringing.

"You were saying?" says Vigfús with a smirk.

"Funny," mutters Hörður. He pulls his phone from his jacket breast pocket and looks at the illuminated display. It shows a cell-phone number that he doesn't recognize.

"You're not going to answer it?" asks Vigfús sarcastically.

"No." Hörður cuts off the call and puts the phone back in his pocket. "Probably a wrong number. Besides, I'm at work."

Vigfús clicks his tongue. "Don't get me wrong, but sometimes you take this job a little too seriously. Some people are cops, others just try to act like cops. A cop knows when he should be a cop and when it's safe for him to relax. The ones just acting are *always* cops; they've got sticks up their ass and rules and regulations printed on their foreheads. Do you understand what I mean?"

Hörður nods. "A bit like you, just now, when you tried to prohibit me from speaking to the prisoner?"

"No, you don't understand," Vigfús mutters. "To those who *aren't* cops, we're *always* cops. But within our own ranks we're not cops, just men—do you understand? A cop who can never relax is unbearable. It's not like we're the president's bodyguards or anything! No, we're insignificant servants of the law, and poorly paid, at that. I'm just asking you to lighten up toward me and others in our department. Don't be one of those damn clown-cops."

"No worries. I'm relaxed." Hörður leans back in his seat, crosses his arms and looks out the dusty windshield at the endless road ahead. The autumn sun casts a reddish glow on the homogeneous landscape, which, at this particular moment, is reminiscent of Tatooine, Luke Skywalker's home planet.

Vigfús parks the car in the alley behind the police station, and they lead the handcuffed prisoner in through the back door. Gísli Már is pale and downcast. They step into the elevator and Vigfús pushes the button for the 3rd floor. The elevator is at level -1.

"Does he go straight to the Swimming Pool?" asks Hörður. The CID's interrogation room is a windowless, green-blue room that's never called anything other than the Swimming Pool.

"Yep," says Vigfús. The door shuts and the elevator jerks into motion. "They're probably waiting for us there."

Hörður pushes the button for the 1st floor. He doesn't want to meet Engilbert twice in one day. "If you don't mind, I'd like to check something on the Internet. I'll just see you when you come back down."

"Up to you," mutters Vigfús.

The elevator opens on the first floor. As Gísli Már steps out, Hörður pats him on the shoulder.

In the communal work area, Hörður goes straight over to the desk phone, next to the printer and photocopier. He selects 0 to dial out, and then enters a three-digit number.

"Information, how can I help?" asks a cheerful female voice.

Holding the handset between his ear and shoulder, Hörður takes out his cell phone and opens his call list. At the top is a missed call. "Yes, can you tell me whose number this is?"

He reads out the number.

"It's Ester Guðmundsdóttir, hairdresser, Birkimelur 10."

Bíbí? Hörður feels a tingling in his stomach. Why did she call him? To scold him?

"Would you like me to connect you?" asks the information operator.

"No. Absolutely not." Hörður hangs up. He should never have asked Bíbí out on that date. It's best just to stay single. Relationships are a pain, that's just how it is. Now he can't get his hair cut at Klapparstígur anymore, for example.

It's best by far, and safest, never to do anything—of that, Hörður is convinced. You should just live your life according to a certain routine, and stick to it. Period. Happiness is found in doing everyday things over again and again, in resting contented in the beauty of repetition. Life then develops a comfortable rhythm, becomes music that you learn by heart and can hum along to during the daily grind.

All exceptions to the daily routine interfere with this rhythm and create imbalances in life. Those who enjoy the unexpected and want constantly to try out and experience something new are pretty much lost, as such individuals are generally both rootless and unhappy, constantly searching for something that they never find because they're always on the run, *looking* for what was never lost.

Goodbye, Bíbí, says Hörður to himself. Goodbye, all women. This cop doesn't need anyone.

❧ ❧ ❧

For lunch, Hörður and his partner go to Múlakaffi, as always when they're on day shift and nothing unexpected comes up. Thursdays are good days at Múlakaffi; there's always something special on the menu. Today it's breaded lamb chops, boiled potatoes, red cabbage, peas, and melted butter. Unexpectedly, Hörður has a good appetite, lamb chops being one of his absolute favorites. Not even Vigfús's smacking lips bothers him now.

The two partners have barely sat back down in their car when the radio crackles. *"Dispatch calling Unit 213, come in."*

Vigfús answers. "Unit 213 here, over."

Hörður shakes a cigarette from its pack and lights it, then rolls down the passenger-side window halfway.

"We've got report of a half-dead cat at Melaskóli Elementary. It was likely hit by a car. Can you check on it?"

Hörður scowls and blows smoke out his nostrils. Vigfús clears his throat before answering: "On our way, over and out."

"I guess we'll have to put it out of its misery, the poor thing," mutters Hörður.

"We'll see," says Vigfús.

"What a shitty assignment," says Hörður. If there's anything he truly hates, it's having to put down animals. That, and being sent to homes where everything is awash in alcoholism and violence—to see crying children who live in constant fear and never get to experience the freedom and happiness of youth.

"No two days the same," says Vigfús philosophically as he drives off. "I've said it often before, and will say it often again. No two days the same."

Hörður rolls his eyes. "It's not as if this hasn't happened before. This is at least the fourth half-dead cat that's been reported since I became a cop."

"Same thing," says Vigfús stubbornly.

"Maybe," mutters Hörður, just to keep the peace. Although their work is certainly diverse, it's also more or less predictable. The days may not be exactly the same, but within them are certain waymarks, fixed variables that are as unchangeable as the course of the sun. Morning coffee. Traffic monitoring near schools, speed monitoring in particular places. Lunch at Múlakaffi. And then there are the usual assignments: something suspicious is found, a car is broken into, or a half-dead cat is reported. And writing up reports.

Vigfús drives down Miklabraut Road, toward the western side of town.

Hörður scratches his head. "Don't you find it strange how often we get random assignments just when we sit back down in the car after lunch?"

"What do you mean?" asks Vigfús.

"Just that," says Hörður. "Every third time we sit down in the car outside Múlakaffi, we're called up on the radio. What I'm wondering is whether reports come into dispatch at precisely this time, or whether dispatch waits with various minor assignments until we're done eating?"

"Good question." Vigfús gives this some thought. "I think it's the latter, that they wait to call us."

Hörður nods. That's what he thinks, too. If so, it emphasizes his belief that the ordinary routine matters. That police officers on duty are allowed to eat their lunches in peace and quiet, and thereby find contentment in the routine, matters more than whether a car break-in is investigated as soon as it's reported or twenty minutes later. Such minor crimes are almost never solved, anyway.

At Miklatún Road, Vigfús's cell phone rings. He curses softly, looks at the display and answers the call. "What do you want?"

Hörður shakes his head, disappointed in his partner.

"Now?" asks Vigfús. "It can't wait …? Okay, then … Yes, I'll find it."

"Who was that?" asks Hörður.

"Oh, just my nephew." Vigfús signals a right turn and takes the exit that ends at the intersection of Snorrabraut Road and the old Hringbraut Road.

"Where are you going?" asks Hörður. "We're supposed to be going to the west side!"

"I've got to meet him now," says Vigfús apologetically. "Unfortunately."

"Are you joking?" Hörður throws up his hands. "You're going to sell your nephew *stamps*. It can't wait?"

"No," mutters Vigfús. He turns north onto Snorrabraut. "We're on an assignment!"

"The cat can wait," says Vigfús angrily.

"No. It's *half dead*—not dead," says Hörður angrily. "The animal is suffering as we speak."

"It'll take me just a moment, damn it!" Vigfús growls. His cheeks are flushed and his voice quivers. "What are you going to do? Tell on me? File a complaint with internal affairs?

"Calm down, man," says Hörður. "No need to make a big drama out of this. But you know you're wrong, otherwise you wouldn't be so irritated."

Vigfús snorts.

"And besides, there is no internal affairs," says Hörður grumpily. "Or is there?"

"No," mutters Vigfús. "I don't think so."

We're like an old couple, thinks Hörður, with a shudder. He knows full well that most, if not all, of the members of the police force wrangle occasionally—anything else would be unnatural. Yet he has the feeling that most partners treat each other more equitably than what he's used to. It's probably the age difference between him and Vigfús. His partner is of course no old man, but it's as if he can't wait to retire. He's been tired of the job for a long time, and that weariness makes him bitter and difficult to be around. He's probably a good example of someone "cooling down"—who has lost all interest in his job, and with it, his joy and sense of purpose.

Vigfús turns west onto Hverfisgata Street. To their right is police headquarters in all its glory, but it's as if Vigfús makes a point of ignoring the white and blue building. At least he appears to avoid looking at it, like a sinner pretending not to see a church.

Does he have something on his conscience?

Hörður looks out the side window and lets his mind wander. Should he ask for a transfer, maybe? Request a new partner? No, he could never do that. Vigfús would be so hurt. It would be barely be worth it.

But one day, he'll apply for a position in the CID. Then, hopefully, he'll move between departments, and not just from one squad car to another. Then he'll have an unmarked car at his disposal, and a new partner. Unless he gets to work alone. Not all of the detectives have partners. Some of them work alone.

Vigfús slows down and keeps his eye on the house numbers on the other side of the street, then parks the car halfway up on the sidewalk a short distance from the intersection with Vitastígur. He pulls the parking brake and opens his door. "I'll be quick."

"Okay," says Hörður. He sounds like a teenager, realizes that, and wants to shout with irritation. Somehow, he and his partner's relationship has developed into this. Vigfús is the old, grumpy dad, and Hörður the son who brings him nothing but disappointment, an immature teenager who dreams of leaving home because his old man is so unbearable.

What a cliché. He could just puke.

Vigfús goes to the back of the car and opens the trunk. The sun is low in the sky; in some places it illuminates the street or reflects off the windows, in other places the shadows are both long and deep.

Hörður lights a cigarette and opens his window a crack. He wonders if the poor cat is still alive. He envisions it lying at the curb, both its hind legs broken, whining in pain. Around it are crying children, students from Melaskóli Elementary. One boy tries to poke at the cat with a stick, but a girl stops him. The girl squats down to pet the cat, but it hisses at her. A teacher appears and ushers the kids back onto school grounds, looking at the cat with an expression of pity and wondering why the police haven't come.

Vigfús slams the trunk shut. Holding something with one hand beneath the lapel of his jacket, he glances to both sides and hurries into the dark alley between houses.

What is it that he's hiding? His stamp collection? Hörður blows smoke out his nostrils. Why is he hiding it beneath his jacket? Hörður looks up at the sky and down at the street. It's not going to rain—at least there's that.

Hörður regards the alley. Does Vigfús's nephew live in a back building? Damn, this is shady. One might think that the stamps were stolen. He knocks the ash from his cigarette out through the crack in the window.

He'd never seen these stamps. They'd probably been arranged in a stamp book? Why hadn't Vigfús shown him the collection? Had he had it in the trunk of their squad car for a long time? Hörður doesn't recall having seen it there.

Vigfús put the dictionary in the trunk; he remembers that. The dictionary that he took from the deceased Mummi's belongings. The dictionary that Aron Beck said wasn't his. Why did he point that out, unasked?

Why should he have remembered the dictionary?

Hörður takes a drag of his cigarette. There's something really strange about all of this. Vigfús had acted a bit awkward when Hörður asked him why he was going to take the dictionary. And got angry when Hörður said that he was going to return the hypnosis book to Aron, as if he absolutely did not want him to meet that anarchist. And then Aron mentioned the dictionary, for some reason. And Vigfús tensed up when Hörður told him this.

What's the deal with that goddamn dictionary?

Hörður steps out of the car, flicks away his cigarette and goes to the back of the car. He opens the trunk. It's all as it should be. But there's no dictionary. He doesn't recall Vigfús taking the book home. He would have noticed it. Did he take it with him just now?

Was it the dictionary that he was hiding beneath his jacket?

Hörður closes the trunk and walks into the alley, whose walls are covered in graffiti and which smells of cat pee. The alley ends at a shoddy back garden. Leaning against a red wall is a broken-down bicycle, and lying on yellow grass is a worn car tire. A flagstone sidewalk ends at a basement door of a blue back building. The door is open. Hörður walks quietly down the cracked concrete stairs and stops in the doorway. Inside, it's half dark. Through the doorway come the sound of voices and the smell of cannabis smoke blended with incense.

"Hurry up, I'm in a rush," he hears Vigfús says. The person to whom he's speaking mutters something indistinct.

What the hell is going on?

Hörður doesn't wait, but slips through the crack in the door, steps into the basement apartment, and finds himself standing on one of the Turkish rugs covering the floor. It takes his eyes a few seconds to become accustomed to the darkness, and he himself to take in what he sees. The apartment is painted in dark colors, and the windows are covered with shirts, cloths, and bandanas. On a wide sofa covered with numerous rugs sits a gangly hippie of around thirty, long-haired and barefooted, with a leather strap tied around his head and wearing an Oriental tunic.

Vigfús's back is turned to Hörður. He's standing slightly to one side of the hippie, with his hands on his hips, impatiently watching his every move.

The hippie is leaning over a long coffee table, counting out thousand-króna bills from a thick bundle that he's holding, laying the bills one by one onto the table, slowly and deliberately. The table is cluttered with all sorts of stuff, including a fine-looking hookah, a big brick of hash, and a pocket knife with a blackened blade.

And the blessed dictionary, which is lying open next to the steadily growing stack of bills on the table. A hole has been cut into the book—the pages are nothing but a frame of around a centimeter wide. In the hole is a rolled-up plastic bag, holding something blue—which are in fact tablets.

Ecstasy, guesses Hörður.

"What the fuck is going on here?" he asks, in a soft, but deep voice. He's insecure and nervous, that is, deep inside, but so full of righteous anger that he feels as if no one and nothing can stop him.

Vigfús stiffens, but the hippie looks up calmly and stares inquisitively at Hörður. The hippie is so stoned, his brain so fried, that he doesn't have the sense to be scared, let alone to try to hide what is clearly going on.

"Hörður, what ..." Vigfús's face turns bright red, and he hesitantly steps aside when his partner comes rushing up to the table.

Hörður grabs the book and lifts the bag from the hole in its pages. In the bag are ecstasy tablets, as he suspected; between three to five hundred of them, he estimates, blue and each imprinted with a pentagram.

"What's going on, man?" asks the hippie, looking at Vigfús.

"Hörður." Vigfús grabs his partner's left forearm loosely.

Hörður shakes him off, turns halfway and looks Vigfús straight in the eye. "What the hell are you thinking? Are you selling stolen goods? What's wrong with you?"

"What's with your friend, huh?" asks the hippie.

Hörður looks at the hippie, then shouts and overturns the coffee table so violently that the hookah smashes into the wall and shatters and banknotes rain over the room.

Vigfús takes a few steps backwards and raises his hands in surrender.

"Hey!" The hippie gets up from the sofa. "What are you doing, man?! This is my home. You've got no right to be here. I'll sue you!"

"Are you going to call the cops, you fool?" barks Hörður. "I am a cop, you idiot! Go ahead and sue me. The name is Hörður Grímsson."

The hippie points at him accusatorily. "Yeah, I'm gonna …"

"Shut up, Fribbi," says Vigfús in a shaky voice.

Hörður snorts like a bull, and then rushes out of the apartment and up the stairs with the book in one hand and the bag of tablets in the other. He's already in the alley when Vigfús calls out after him.

"Hörður! Wait!"

Hörður acts as if he doesn't hear his partner. He sits down behind the wheel of their squad car and slams the door behind him. Vigfús comes running up, stops next to the car and looks questioningly at Hörður through the side window. Hörður stares at him furiously and signals him to get in on the passenger side. Vigfús does so.

Hörður sits there silently in the driver's seat with the closed dictionary in his lap.

"Hörður, I …" Vigfús pauses, takes a deep breath and starts over. "You need to get off your high horse, young man. You'd be better off keeping quiet about this. I've been doing this job for far longer than you. What you just witnessed is nothing unique. This is how things are done around here. You'll have to accept it."

Hörður taps the book with his index finger. "Do you know what tablets these are?"

"Do I know?" Vigfús hesitates. "It's ecstasy. It's always in circulation. It doesn't matter if this stash is destroyed or not."

"These are the same tablets that Gísli Már found in his jacket pocket the day after the murder," says Hörður. "Blue, with pentagrams. These tablets are part of the murder investigation. They connect the murder of the MP, Þórólfur, with the anarchist, Aron Beck."

"Oh?" Vigfús is unsure of how to react, or of what to say. "And what are you going to do with them?"

"What?" Hörður asks, shocked. "I'm going to hand them over to the CID, of course."

Vigfús's face flushes. "And what are you going to say?"

Hörður sighs. "I'll forget what I just saw there. But on one condition."

"Which is?"

Hörður looks hard at his partner. "That as long as we're partners, nothing like this ever happens again."

"Agreed," mutters Vigfús.

"It's all the same to me what you do." Hörður drives off the sidewalk. "But there's no way I'm going to let you destroy my reputation."

Vigfús snorts. "When I joined the police, I was like you: a righteous clown. And one day, after this job has sickened your life the same way that mold ruins a house, you'll be just like me."

"Right," says Hörður coldly.

"Awaiting you is nothing but disappointment, adversity, and boredom," says Vigfús. "Believe me, boy."

Hörður takes a U-turn at the next intersection.

"Where are you going?" asks Vigfús.

"To the station, where else?" Hörður steps on the gas and tears eastward down Hverfisgata.

"But the cat?" asks Vigfús sheepishly.

"Ask Schrödinger." Hörður puts on his Ray-Bans.

"Huh, who?" asks Vigfús.

"Forget it." Hörður drives over a hundred kph, with one hand on the wheel, staring hard at the road. The sun is reflected in his black sunglasses, resembling a glaring moon on a pitch-black night.

Hörður steps out of the elevator on the third floor of police headquarters and storms down the long corridor toward the CID, beads of sweat on his forehead and *The Place of Words* by Jón Hilmar Jónsson in one hand. Then he stops abruptly, furrows his brow and scratches his head.

Isn't he in too much of a rush? This is important business. What he's going to present to the department is *big*. Something that's not only crucial to the murder investigation, but also his career as a police officer.

Shouldn't he be better prepared? Have everything nice and clear. And preferably in print. Come well *prepared* to this meeting.

Yes.

Hörður takes a deep breath. He turns on his heel, goes back into the elevator and presses 1. His heart is hammering in his chest, and his back and palms are sweaty. He shuts his eyes, tries to relax. To calm down. No agitation.

Think logically. Work professionally.

Hörður sits down at a free computer in the communal work area, cracks his knuckles and immediately gets down to work with pen and paper. He's going to gather data, trace sources, and record everything that he finds. Gather details and create a coherent picture. He's going to think like a detective, work like a detective, and then go meet with the detectives on the third floor on a level playing field. He's going to deliver some important puzzle pieces for the investigation, and at the same time, present himself as excellent detective material.

He starts by writing down some facts. Gísli Már had the ecstasy tablets on him, blue, and imprinted with a pentagram. The same kind of ecstasy pills were hidden in the belongings of the deceased Mummi. There was also a book owned by Aron Beck, a textbook on hypnosis. The ecstasy tablets connect the murder of the MP Þórólfur with Aron Beck. Gísli Már doesn't remember the murder and has to be considered an unlikely suspect, despite it seemingly having been proven that he killed the MP. He remembers nothing, and his blood contained traces of something that could have been GHB.

Hörður underlines the word *facts*. Next, he writes *theories*, followed by a colon. He bites his lower lip gently, thinks things over, and then writes what he thinks. Did someone slip Gísli Már a drug? Could he have been hypnotized? Is the anarchist Aron Beck behind the murder? If so, who was or were his accomplices? Why a member of parliament? Was that a coincidence? Does it mean something?

Hörður lets this suffice for now. He starts up the computer, opens the browser, and again looks up the interview with Aron Beck. He goes over it, sentence by sentence, noting down every little bit of information he thinks worthwhile.

He comes to the point in the interview when Aron aims his spear at the system, that *three-headed giant that stands for oppression, injustice, and violence.*

Are you talking about the separation of powers? asks the reporter.

Hörður notes this down. The three-headed giant. What, again, was the separation of powers? Wasn't it into three branches: legislative, judicial, and executive? He writes the words side by side on a new sheet of paper. Under legislative branch, he writes Parliament, and at the same time, the hairs rise on the back of his neck. He's on the right track—he can feel it!

What if this isn't an isolated murder, but an organized murder conspiracy against the three different branches of government? Then wouldn't the judiciary branch be next? Which means what? That a judge will be murdered next?

I'm talking about the Enemy with a capital E, says Aron in the interview. *It's disgusting to see how the public in this country both feed this giant and pretend not to see it. It's democracy in the form of a monster. Parliament ensures the continued existence of oppression and inequality in society, the courts dole out injustice like some hellish gospel, and the cops silence and beat anyone who dares to object to this abomination.*

"The separation of powers," mutters Hörður. He shuts his eyes and, in his mind, goes over the conversation that he had with Aron. He envisions him sitting on his cot in his cell. The police officer's attention is drawn to the tattoo, the triangle with the skull inside it. What letters were they again, next to the triangle?

L, j, and e, weren't they? The legislative, judicial, and executive branches! What did Aron say when Hörður asked about them? He avoided the subject, but then said something. *Know your enemy*, wasn't it? Yes. Enemy with a capital E. The three-headed giant!

Hörður snaps his fingers. This can't be a coincidence. But Aron, of course, isn't working alone; that's out of the question. He's locked up. The police officer's attention is directed to the photograph accompanying the interview, the group shot of the black-clad anarchists. If Aron has an accomplice or accomplices, they could very well be hidden in this ugly group.

He has barely looked at the photo when a current of energy flashes through his head and he gets goose bumps on his forearms. Why didn't he notice this earlier? One of the anarchists has a spider-web tattoo on his neck. He's one of the shady characters that Hörður saw at Ölver. And it looks to him as if the other one is there as well, but he isn't one-hundred percent certain.

Hörður reads the photo's caption. *In the photo are, from left to right: Orri, Hákon, Guðmundur Vífill, Aron Beck, Tryggvi Leó, Þorsteinn, and Egill Þór.* The one with the spider-web tattoo is Tryggvi Leó. The one who Hörður thinks was with him at Ölver is Egill Þór.

He writes all of this down and prints out the interview, then goes onto *domstolar.is,* the Icelandic judicial system website, and looks up the verdict in the squatting case. There he finds the full names of all involved. Tryggvi Leó's patronymic is Helgason, and Egill Þór's is Birgisson. His heart starts pounding again; he's flying, he's hot on the trail—he's burning up! The judge who pronounced verdict in the case is named Aðalsteinn Kvaran. He prints out the verdict.

His theory is shaping up. Hörður takes a deep breath, and then writes a summary of what he knows and what he suspects, building a credible theory out of all of it. Following that, he goes and retrieves all of his printouts from the printer, taps the papers together and leaves the communal work area with the dictionary in one hand and the stack of papers in the other.

The door of the CID is shut and locked, as always. Hörður takes a look at the tablet on the wall and sees that Engilbert is in. He knocks on the door, straightens his back, and clears his throat.

It's Engilbert who opens the door. He looks coldly at the police officer, his bloodshot eyes gleaming with something uncomfortably reminiscent of rage.

"Hello." Hörður tries to act both composed and confident, despite being both nervous and frightened. "I have something to show you. It concerns the murder investigation. I consider it rather urgent. Otherwise, I wouldn't be bothering you."

Engilbert says nothing, and instead steps aside and gestures to Hörður to enter the domain of the CID. Engilbert's bearing is stiff, almost formal, reminiscent of a butler in a British TV series.

Hörður bows his head as he enters the department. "I've never been in here before."

He's heard members of the CID speak of its offices as The Cave, without knowing the origin or reason for this designation. The room is both long and wide, the atmosphere is rather heavy, and the curtains are drawn over the windows. The space is divided into twelve cubicles, each of them the office of a detective. On the floor is a gray-speckled carpet, and long fluorescent lights burn on the ceiling.

Around seven or eight detectives are sitting working at their computers, and none of them looks up.

"I'm going to let my boss know that you're here." Engilbert knocks three times on a dark wooden door in the end wall of the room. "I'm sure he'd be very keen on meeting you."

"Your boss?" exclaims Hörður. "Are you talking about …"

"Come in!" sounds a deep voice from the other side of the door. Hörður stops in mid-sentence, with a bewildered expression.

Engilbert opens the door to his supervisor's office and gestures to Hörður to enter first, which he does, but hesitantly. His legs are numb and he feels a bit queasy, being completely unprepared to meet the man whom he has secretly worshiped for almost ten years. The man he dreams of having as his own boss.

The office is big and dark and cold, much more reminiscent of a cave than the work space of a criminal investigator. Along the walls are dark book- and file cabinets, and the only light in the room comes from a green-shaded lamp on top of a huge hardwood desk at the far wall. Sitting in a high-backed leather chair behind the desk is Steppenwolf himself.

"This is Hörður Grímsson, police officer number 9909 in the general section," says Engilbert, lightly pushing Hörður, who walks tentatively to the desk. In front of it are two low leather chairs.

"I was in fact planning on inviting him to come meet me," says Axel M. Axelsson, removing his reading glasses. He's broad-shouldered and stout-necked, and is wearing a black jacket and white shirt, with a black tie and gold watch on his left wrist. He's tanned and fit, and his hair is thinning and receding.

Axel is one of Iceland's most experienced police officers. He was educated in the United States and the UK, and has personal connections with the FBI and Interpol.

He was going to invite me to come see him? thinks Hörður. Why? Is that good or bad? For some reason, he has a bad feeling about all of this.

He walks to the table, sticks the dictionary under his left arm and holds out his right hand. "Hello."

Axel looks at him as if something is wrong with him, before signaling him to have a seat. Hörður pulls his hand back quickly, his legs give out and he plunks down in one of the chairs. Engilbert sits down next to him, leans back comfortably and crosses his legs.

The silence is unbearable.

Hörður clears his throat. "Well, let's see ... the reason I'm here—thanks for seeing me—is that I've discovered a certain connection between ..."

He pauses when Axel holds up his hand, which is the size of the dictionary resting in the police officer's lap.

"A complaint showed up on my desk," says Axel M. Axelsson. Then he stares silently into the eyes of the red-haired giant.

"A complaint?" asks Hörður in surprise.

Axel gestures at Engilbert.

The detective inhales through his nose. "You were assigned to pick up the detainee at Litla-Hraun, you and your partner Vigfús, right?"

"Yes, that's ..."

"Gísli Már Brynjarsson," continues the detective, "who is in custody for the murder of the MP, Þórólfur Hannesson."

"Yes, we ..."

"Did you communicate with the prisoner on your way back?" asks Engilbert coldly.

"Yes, a little," says Hörður, his voice hoarse from stress. He looks down at the floor, avoiding eye contact with the head of the CID. "We exchanged a few words."

"A few words?" snorts Engilbert. "Not only did you put the idea in the suspect's head that someone slipped a drug into his drink at Ölver, but you *insisted* to him that he, the suspect, *must not* confess to the crime. Am I right?"

Hörður swallows. "The former is an extremely credible scenario and the latter is technically or theoretically correct, because ..."

"Yes or no?" barks Engilbert.

Hörður nods his head quickly. "You're right, but ..."

"Aren't you familiar with the procedure to be followed when a prisoner is transferred?" asks Axel in a low voice. "Didn't you attend the Police Academy? You did graduate, didn't you?"

Hörður nods again. "I know the procedure. But this case is really unusual, not to mention ..."

Axel hammers the table with the palms of his hands, so hard that it sounds like gunshots, and the lamp bounces.

Hörður stiffens in his chair, hardly daring to breathe.

"It's not your job to give your opinion on particular cases," growls Axel. "And it's absolutely not your job to ..."—he looks at Engilbert. "Get involved," interjects the detective—"to interfere with suspects, witnesses, or the investigation of cases. Do you understand that, Police Officer Number 9909?"

"Yes," sighs Hörður.

"We're under tremendous pressure to solve this case," says Axel. "From the media, from the public, from Parliament and the National Commissioner of the Icelandic Police. A member of parliament has been murdered in public. It's unprecedented. It's not enough for us to have someone in custody; we need a confession, preferably yesterday."

Hörður nods.

Axel takes a deep breath. "You'll receive a reprimand. What the consequences will be isn't clear for the time being. A temporary suspension can't be excluded."

Hörður feels slightly dizzy, as if he's stuck in a Kafka-esque nightmare. He can't believe that this is happening.

"Do you realize how serious this is?" asks Steppenwolf.

"Perfectly," replies Hörður, in a frail voice.

"That's all then … for now," says Axel M. Axelsson. "You'll continue to perform your duties until the commissioner decides what to do with you. You can go. "

Axel puts his reading glasses back on and directs his attention once more to the report that he has on the table in front of him.

Engilbert gets up from his seat, but Hörður sits stock still. The detective gives him a little shove, but the police officer doesn't move. He stares at his big hands, one of which is holding a dictionary, and the other a stack of papers.

It's now. Or never.

The head of the CID looks over the upper rim of his glasses and regards the police officer. "You're still here?"

Hörður clears his throat. Does he have anything to lose? He's not sure. "Gísli Már was slipped liquid X at Ölver. He was taken from there by two men, whose names are Tryggvi Leó and Egill Þór. They took Gísli Már someplace off the beaten track. There, he was hypnotized and given certain instructions. He was then dropped off in the city center, where he followed the instructions that he was given. That is: to kill a member of parliament. The person behind all this is Aron Beck, who is behind bars at Litla-Hraun Prison.

Whether Gísli Már confesses or not is irrelevant in this context, no matter what anyone might think of my assertions."

"What are you talking about?" asks Engilbert, irritably.

Axel stares rigidly at the police officer. "Do you have any evidence to support this theory?"

Hörður places the dictionary on the desk and opens it, revealing the bag of ecstasy tablets. "Are these the same kind of pills that Gísli Már had on him?"

Engilbert lifts the bag and examines its contents. "Where did you get this?"

"Vigfús and I were given an assignment on Tuesday," says Hörður. "A skull was found at a storage facility on Grandi. The skull is old, and completely irrelevant. The things there belonged to Little Mummi. We found this dictionary there, along with other books. For example, a textbook on hypnosis that was marked as belonging to Aron Beck."

"You discovered a stash of ecstasy on Tuesday," says Engilbert. "Why are you turning it in only now?"

Hörður looks at Axel. "We didn't open the book until today. May I continue?"

Axel nods.

"The ecstasy tablets connect the murder of Þórólfur to the anarchist Aron Beck," says Hörður. "But I think that in the larger context, the tablets are a kind of *red herring*—they're there to throw us off track."

Engilbert snorts. "Us?"

"What do you mean?" asks Axel.

"We're supposed to believe that the suspect was under the influence of drugs," says Hörður. "That he committed the murder in some sort of psychotic state. Because it's the only logical explanation. Why should Gísli Már have killed the MP? He has a clean record, and is lacking a motive.

We're supposed to believe that he was high on drugs. And we're also supposed to believe that the trace materials found in his blood are from ecstasy, when the truth is that he was given GHB."

Engilbert shakes his head. "Anyone can speculate, but what we need is evidence."

"You mentioned a few names earlier," says Axel. "Where did they come from?"

"I was at Ölver that evening," says Hörður.

"You were?" asks Axel, before turning to look at Engilbert. "Did you know that?"

The detective nods.

"I saw those two guys there." Hörður lays the group photo of the anarchists on the table. He points at Tryggvi Leó and Egill Örn. "I'm one-hundred-percent certain about Tryggvi, and fairly certain about the other one."

"Put out an alert for them," says Axel to Engilbert. "We need to question these two."

"Of course," says the detective, with a grumpy expression.

Hörður's confidence grows. "In this interview, Aron Beck speaks of the enemy with a capital E, the three-headed giant, by which, he probably means the separation of powers into three branches: legislative, judicial, and executive. He's obsessed with it."

"You say that he's behind this," says Axel. "But I don't see how that can be."

"That makes the two of us," mutters Engilbert.

"It sounds of course like a conspiracy theory," says Hörður, half apologetically. "But I think that Aron is not only the brains behind the MP's murder, but also that he has a bigger plan in the works—that he's planned other murders. Two more, to be exact."

"Wait!" Axel holds out his hand. "Tell me first what he had to do with the murder of Þórólfur."

"He organized it," says Hörður. "He's studied hypnosis and must have taught his accomplices the techniques. They slip GHB into some innocent individual's drink, and then they take him to some out-of-the-way place, as I said earlier. GHB transforms people into mindless tools. That's how Gísli Már was after drinking Coke spiked with GHB. They hypnotize him, give him instructions and drop him off near the Parliament House."

Axel ponders this.

"I don't know," says Engilbert. "GHB turns people into zombies. A person on GHB has neither the strength nor the concentration to carry out such a deed."

"Let's say you're right, that this is how it was," says Axel. "Why do you think there'll be more murders?"

"I think that there'll be three in all," says Hörður. "I think that Aron is going to attack *the three-headed giant*, hoping to spread chaos and fear in society—anarchy. The MP symbolized the legislative branch. Next is the judicial branch. And finally the executive branch."

"So a judge will be murdered next?" asks Axel, with a bewildered expression. "When, then, may I ask?"

"When, I don't know, but sooner rather than later, I'm afraid," says Hörður. "And yes, I think that a judge will be next."

Axel laughs joylessly. "Let's say you're right; what can we do? Keep watch on the courthouses, yes. But all the judges in the greater Reykjavík area? There are thirty-eight district judges. No, their number was raised to forty-three! And there are eleven on the Supreme Court. We don't have the manpower for that—not even for twenty-four hours."

"I know," says Hörður. "But if I were to bet money on it, I'd put it all on one person." He leafs through his stack of papers, finds the printout of the verdict and the name that he was looking for. "Aðalsteinn Kvaran, district judge."

"Why him?" asks Axel.

"It was Aðalsteinn who sentenced Aron to prison," says Hörður. "That's not to say that he'll definitely be next, but he's definitely a strong candidate. I have no doubt that Aron remembers him."

Axel shifts his attention to Engilbert, who clearly finds this all highly dubious. "What do you say about all this?"

"This is speculation, nothing but speculation," he says. "I don't really think that this theory holds water. It's too far-fetched. And as I said; people on GHB are completely out of it."

"Maybe they gave him a small dose, or a new type of GHB," says Hörður. "All I'm certain of is that Gísli was slipped something."

"Find those guys and question them," Axel tells Engilbert. "The goons that were at Ölver. They need to explain what they were up to. There are still too many things that need clearing up in this case."

"You can say that again," mutters Engilbert.

"Gísli Már is guilty, but we lack a motive, as he pointed out," says Axel. "This with the GHB sounds both believable and unbelievable. I don't know about the hypnosis. But I suppose it's certainly possible that the boy didn't know what he was doing. There's something strange about this murder."

"I agree," interjects Hörður.

"But as far as the judges go, I don't know." Axel sighs heavily. "I'll bring it up with the Police Commissioner, in any case. We'll see what we can do. But one thing must be crystal clear." He looks straight at Hörður. "Not a word of what was discussed here may go beyond the walls of this building. Not one single fucking word! Is that understood?"

Hörður is lying on the cot in his basement apartment, reading. After work he went to the Sundhöllin swimming pool and relaxed in the hot tub for almost two hours, allowing the stress and fatigue to leave his body. He definitely needed it. His day had been more or less a rollercoaster ride. But despite being scolded and having a reprimand hanging over his head, he's not at all unhappy with himself. The meeting with Axel had started badly, but Hörður had still managed to turn defense into offense and present his ideas, and he'd been listened to—well, to a certain degree, anyway.

He reaches for his coffee cup, which is on top of the stack of CDs on the dresser, and takes a sip of the strong, warm espresso. Instead of eating at Vitabar, he'd ordered some food to go from a Thai place on Laugavegur Avenue. What he really wanted was a burger, but since he'd decided not to drink this evening, he felt safer not going into the bar. There are probably also more nutrients in the Thai food than in Vitabar's greasy offerings.

Inside the bathroom, the water pipes buzz, and the pages of his book rustle pleasantly as he turns them. The book he's reading is *Slaughterhouse 5*, by Kurt Vonnegut, which is one of his favorites, along with Conrad's *Heart of Darkness*, *Pan* by Hamsun, and *The Stranger* by Camus. He's read these books more than once and more than twice, and enjoys them more each time, as if he gets deeper into the texts and the books' ideologies with each reading.

In this, *Slaughterhouse 5* is no exception. It's about an American soldier by the name of Billy Pilgrim, who is a prisoner of the Germans when the Allies bomb Dresden at the end of World War II. The city, which was not military important, was transformed into a flaming hell that wiped out both buildings and residents. The prisoners of war survived, though, as they were shut inside a concrete building that had previously been a slaughterhouse. What makes the book both deep and fun to read is the fact that long after the war, Billy is kidnapped by aliens who take him to their home planet. Following this experience, Billy starts jumping from one period of his life to another, like someone switching channels on a television set. For example, he jumps between World War II, his marriage following the war, and the planet Tralfamadore, where he was kept in a zoo. The book is like Billy's life; not a linear narrative with a logical progression, but rather, a random collection of memories, good and bad, which together form a whole that is more bound to objective experiences than anything that might be called a lifetime. The memories are objective because Billy has experienced them all before; he knows in advance how they turn out, which works to distance him from their emotional core—he's free from tension, anticipation, and fear, and has gained distance from his own life—a life that takes place beyond time and space. It's not bound to birth and death, beginning and end, but rather, is by nature an unpredictable repetition.

Billy Pilgrim is a very ordinary man, neither exceptionally intelligent nor a hero of any kind, and that makes the narrative funny, realistic, and interesting—it's easy for the reader to see himself in the main character. The time-travel element gives the book depth and a kind of higher meaning, and in the opinion of Hörður Grímsson, it holds the keys to some of the greatest mysteries of the universe—the answers to questions about life on other planets, life after death, the soul, time, and eternity itself.

Hörður takes a sip of coffee, sighs with pleasure and sinks himself deeper into the text of Master Vonnegut. The words change into images, sounds, and impressions—he's swept away by the author's magic and floats about in a timeless nirvana, but then the phone rings and the magic disappears, as if at the snap of fingers.

"What the hell?" He puts the bookmark back in the book, lays the book aside and sits up on his cot.

Who's calling? No one ever calls him. He doesn't really know why he has a cell phone, in general.

The phone is on the floor, connected to a charger plugged in somewhere beneath the cot.

Hörður looks at the display. It's Bíbí. Again. What does she want? He is about to answer, but feels a knot of anxiety in his stomach and changes his mind. No, he has nothing to say to her.

He lowers the volume of the ring tone, puts the phone on the floor and makes himself comfortable on his cot again. He opens the book, finds the place where he left off and starts reading. But his concentration is gone; the text falters and refuses to come alive. His head is full of whirling, random thoughts, like a cliff teeming with birds, and his body is restless, agitated—he has a pain in his neck, his legs ache, and his scalp itches, and then he suddenly has to pee.

"Damn disturbances, all the time!" He jumps up from the cot, stretches and cracks his neck, and goes into the bathroom. He has just started to pee when someone knocks on the door of his apartment.

❖   ❖   ❖

At a corner table in the bar Kaffibarinn, three girlfriends sit and drink Bacardi Breezers. They're all twenty-four years old, and are named Edda, Jóna and Sólrún. They've been best friends since attending the Commercial College of Iceland together, and meet here every Thursday after work, have two, three drinks, chat, and dance. Edda is studying business at the University of Iceland, whereas both Jóna and Sólrún work in retail—Jóna as an associate at a fashion store in the Smáralind shopping mall and Sólrún as assistant manager at a shoe store in the Kringlan shopping mall.

There's a smattering of people at Kaffibarinn, most of them regular patrons. From nine o'clock onwards, the number of patrons increases, and the place is usually packed during the final one-and-a-half hours before closing time on weekdays.

"But you don't know each other very well, do you?" Edda asks.

"No, not that well," replies Sólrún. She is blonde and slender, and is wearing black, high-heeled boots, pantyhose, a black leather skirt and a red blouse. Her black wool coat is draped over the back of her chair, along with her purse. "But we've met quite often, of course, at Christmas parties and funerals and such. He was at my dad's fiftieth birthday party this summer, but I didn't talk to him."

They're talking about a relative of hers who is being held in custody under suspicion of murder.

"How are you related?" asks Jóna.

"Oh, I hardly remember," says Sólrún. "Or, yes, I think that his mother is my grandfather's sister."

"The pastor?" asks Edda cautiously, as Sólrún's paternal grandfather is a convicted sex offender.

Sólrún nods. "We knew each other a bit when we were kids. Once he fell off his bicycle and got a concussion and cut on his forehead. I'll never forget it. There was blood everywhere."

"Oh, wow," says Jóna. "It's like some people are cursed. You know, sometimes it's just one drama after another."

"Exactly," says Edda.

"Maybe he suffered brain damage?" suggests Jóna.

"I mean, a head trauma like that can have serious consequences. Maybe …"

She stops when Sólrún glares at her.

"My cousin Gísli is just fine," says Sólrún. "I mean, he's nothing like my grandfather. I was stunned when I heard that he'd been arrested. I really don't believe that he did this. It must be some misunderstanding."

Her girlfriends nod, but don't seem quite as convinced. The bar's DJ has started spinning records. Just now, Daft Punk is on. Every table is occupied and there's a smattering of people on the dance floor.

"Should we dance?" asks Edda.

"Yes!" says Jóna.

"All right," says Sólrún, smiling. "It's why we're here, isn't it?"

They get up from the table, hang their jackets and purses on the backs of their chairs, and take their Breezer bottles with them onto the dance floor. They pick a spot between a square column and the DJ's cage, forming a triangle as they start dancing. Their table is in sight, and they give it glance now and then.

Standing on a chest-high shelf on the column are three half-empty glasses of beer.

Edda takes a drink from her bottle and places it on the shelf. Jóna and Sólrún do the same. Once they're free of their drinks, it's easier to dance—they wave their arms, turn around in circles, and laugh loudly. Their everyday troubles are forgotten, as well as boyfriends, parents, and all worldly woes.

They're having a blast, allowing the blaring music to take control and losing themselves completely in the dance. They don't notice it when two black-clad men pull out little syringes containing a clear liquid and empty them into their bottles—especially as it happens in only a matter of seconds.

The floor bounces lightly, the lights flash and the bass pounds. They dance in rhythm with the beat, look into each other's eyes, and laugh happily, enjoying life to the fullest. In between songs, they drain their bottles. The carbonation tickles their throats, the taste conjures smiles, and the alcohol quickly sifts into their blood—as does the GHB.

Someone knocks.

What the hell is going on? Hörður stops peeing; washes his hands quickly and then goes and opens the door to his little apartment so forcefully that the person standing in front of it is terribly startled.

It's Bíbí.

"Oh!" She lays her hand on her chest and takes a small step backward.

Hörður is so surprised that at first, he's completely tongue-tied. He just stares at her as if she were a ghost.

"How did you find me?" he asks.

"You're in the phone book," she replies.

A mistake, thinks Hörður.

"How did you get into the building?" he then asks.

"Oh, sorry." Bíbí smiles apologetically. "Your neighbor let me in. I tried to reach you by phone, and I rang the bell, too, but you didn't answer."

"It's broken," mutters Hörður. The light goes out in the stairwell, and the darkness swallows Bíbí.

"Can I come in, maybe?" she asks. "I won't stop long. I just wanted to have a word with you."

"All right." Hörður lets her into his cramped abode and shuts the door. "Still, I'm pretty busy right now."

Bíbí looks around and doesn't like what she sees. "Do you really live in … this?"

Hörður blushes with anger and shame. He's offended by her words, but is also forced to take account of his own circumstances and how messy his place is. The apartment is tiny and smells of cigarettes, garbage, sweat, and coffee. He has neither tidied up nor cleaned the place since he moved in; there are full trash bags and dirty clothes lying here and there on the floor, and coffee stains on the floor and walls.

"It's my home," he mutters, hurt and annoyed. "It's maybe not the nicest place in town, but it's good enough for me."

"Sorry, I didn't mean to offend you. Not at all," says Bíbí. She looks around for something to sit on, but sees nothing except the cot. "I wasn't criticizing. But this … apartment is right at the limit of being habitable, no matter how you look at it."

"As I said," Hörður says irritably, "it's good enough for *me*. Did you come here just to insult me and my life, or was there something else?"

"You probably think I'm a terrible person, but I'm not." Bíbí wrings her hands nervously. She lifts the moka pot from the burner, turns it around and puts it back down again.

Hörður looks anguishedly at the moka pot, which isn't precisely in its same spot. He tries to restrain himself, but then reaches for it and moves it about one-and-a-half centimeters.

Bíbí takes note of this.

"Why did you come here?" Hörður asks agitatedly. He feels as if a Tyrannosaurus Rex has barged in on him. There's no room in this apartment for anyone else but him. It's as if this small, cute and nicely smelling hairdresser fills up the entire space and is on the verge of bursting its walls and ceiling. She's everywhere, so near him—so near to everything he owns.

"You just left me yesterday," she says. "Twice, in fact. I fully understand that you needed to have a word with that colleague of yours, but we were on a date, and I sat there a long time all by myself. Then you went to talk to him again, and ordered yourself a drink. I waited outside in the cold and watched you through the window. You had obviously forgotten about me, so I just went home."

"Yeah, I know," mutters Hörður. "It wasn't supposed to go like that, but it was just bad timing, workwise."

"It was a nice date while your attention was on us," says Bíbí. "I really enjoyed chatting with you. You're not like everyone else. I would certainly have liked to see you again. That's why it was so disappointing when you just dropped out. You completely forgot about me."

Hörður nods. "This is what it's like being a cop. Sometimes there's no room for anything else. That's just how it is."

"But isn't life more than just work?" she asks. "Don't you've any hobbies? Don't you want to share your life with someone? Create a home, maybe have children?"

Hörður scratches his head, with a stubborn look on his face. "Not necessarily. I feel just fine as things are. I'm not missing anything."

"But why did you ask me out on a date?" Bíbí asks. "You seemed like you had a lot on your heart when you came back to the barber shop to ask me out. It was so sweet, so nice. It was obvious that it mattered to you. That's why I said yes."

"Maybe you just felt sorry for me," he says.

"Why should I feel sorry for you?" she asks.

"I don't know," mutters Hörður. "Aren't women always looking for some loser to save?"

"Not me," says Bíbí.

"Oh, okay," says Hörður, as he opens the door to the darkness of the hallway. "And I'm not looking for anyone or anything. Bye."

Bíbí starts, as if he'd splashed cold water over her. "I think you're a good man, Hörður Grímsson. But I also think that you don't allow yourself to enjoy all that good that you deserve."

She steps out of the apartment and disappears into the darkness.

Hörður closes the door and leans against it, immediately regretting his behavior. But he couldn't help himself. He really felt completely overwhelmed, having her inside his apartment. But her absence is ten times more difficult. The silence has deepened, loneliness gnaws at his heart, and his apartment seems twice as small as before.

He wants so much to scream.

❧ ❧ ❧

The crowd on the dance floor has become tight, warm, and sweaty. The bass rumbles, the floor quivers beneath the dancers' feet, and their eyes are blinded by the lights. The atmosphere is great, as always, but Edda, Jóna and Sólrún have lost their rhythm and wander around like sleepwalkers trying to find their beds again. They grope with their hands and stare into space, their mouths half open and their pupils like black holes.

Someone grabs Sólrún by the hand and speaks loudly into her ear. "Come. You're coming with me. We're getting out of here."

"But …" She doesn't want to go, but it's as if he's in control of her, this man.

"Don't go!" calls out Edda. She holds onto Jóna and fumbles for Sólrún, but can't reach her. A black-clad man leads her away from the dance floor. They disappear into the noise, the intoxication, and the light.

"Wait here," says another black-clad man. He holds their hands tightly and speaks to both of them at once. "You're not going anywhere. Not right away."

"No," says Edda, but with a nod. She doesn't want to be there anymore, but doesn't know how to get away. She holds onto Jóna, they stand there unmoving within the blurred faces and bodies that writhe like a mass of snakes.

The black-clad men are gone. Sólrún is gone; she floated off into the darkness. Edda and Jóna are stuck inside a warm fog that spins in circles and blurs their vision.

Black Car

Bjarkargata has always been one of the most sought-after streets in the city. It's considered a wonderful place to live, the location being so ideal. In fact, this street's short length is inversely mirrored in the high number of privileges of those who inhabit it. The street lies between Hringbraut Road and Skothúsvegur Street, with elegant houses on one hand and the woody grove of the western part of Hljómskálagarður Park on the other. The houses are very similar in appearance, having been built at pretty much the same time, around sixty years ago—two stories, a basement and attic. The roofs are steep, stone steps lead up to the main door and a deep driveway leads to a garage. The windows are large and some of them arched; the houses are close to the street and have small back yards.

It's one a.m. There are few people out and the traffic is as light as it gets. Yet there are always at least a few cars on Hringbraut. Hljómskálagarður Park is dark and silent. Birds sleep in its trees, and cats creep between the trunks. Quite a few cars are parked along Bjarkargata, one of them with its engine running. It's a police car that's been parked, facing south, in front of a certain house in the center of the street. Inside it, two police officers sit drinking coffee from paper cups.

The nearby Pond is calm and smooth as a mirror. Over it hangs the moon, which will be full in three days.

A black car is driven west along Skothúsvegur Street, over the bridge that divides The Pond in two. The car is a BMW, ten years old but in good condition. Inside it sit two black-clad men, one behind the wheel and the other in the passenger seat. Sitting in the back seat is a young woman, blonde and slender, wearing high-heel boots, pantyhose, a black leather skirt, a red blouse and black wool coat. She's holding her wallet in her hands, and staring determinedly out the windshield.

The driver turns south onto Bjarkargata without signaling, and hits the brakes when he sets eyes on the police car. For a few seconds, nothing happens, and then the right-side back door opens and the girl steps out onto the street. She shuts the door behind her, puts her purse over her left shoulder, and steps up onto the sidewalk, as the driver of the BMW backs it out onto Skothúsvegur, before heading toward the city center.

The girl walks down the sidewalk toward the house being watched by the police officers. Her gait is awkward, stumbling on her high heels as if she's plastered. She holds her purse in one hand, and supports herself now and then with the other on the stone walls that separate the houses from the sidewalk.

The police officers smile faintly as they watch her in their rear-view mirror.

The girl stops next to the police car and looks up the darkened house, which is numbered. She opens the gate and enters. The police officer sitting in the passenger seat looks at his partner, who shrugs. The girl walks up the stairs, which are on the north side of the house, then stops in front of the door and rings the bell, which sounds solemnly inside the house. The large door is of carved hardwood, and is set with a vertical window.

When no one answers, the girl rings the bell again. A light switches on in the entrance, and a second or two later, the door opens. In the doorway stands a man of about sixty, tall and grey-haired. Aðalsteinn Kvaran, district judge. He's wearing pajamas beneath a silk robe, with slippers on his bare feet.

"I thought it was the police," says the judge. He peeks out the door and sees the back of the police car. "Who are you?"

"They sent me, the policemen," says the girl. She stares hard at the judge with eyes that are both glossy and empty at once. Her voice is both fragile and unclear, as if she's drunk or has perhaps screamed it hoarse. "Let me in, you've got to let me in."

The judge hesitates, before stepping aside. "I don't understand. Did they send you? Why? Are you a friend of my son? Have you come to meet Bjarki?"

"Shut the door," says the girl. "You're letting the cold in."

"I ..." The judge sighs, but does as the girl asks. "What damn nonsense is this? Bjarki lives in the basement. If you've come to meet him, then ..."

He stops when the girl grabs his left shoulder with her right hand. She stares into his eyes as she sticks her left hand in her purse and pulls out a knife, without the judge noticing.

The strap of her purse slips off her shoulder, the purse falls to the floor, and her left hand draws back. The girl's eyes shoot sparks and her face is deformed with fury.

"Listen to me, young woman. I ..." The judge stops when the girl drives the knife into his abdomen—and then he utters a half-smothered cry. His legs give out, but before he collapses to the floor, the girl manages to stab him twice more.

"Die, you pig!" she spits, trembling with agitation and wobbly on her feet. The knife falls out of her hand and bounces along the tiled floor. The judge is lying curled up in his blood, holding his stomach and moaning in pain.

"Aðalsteinn?" calls a woman's voice from within the house. "Honey?"

The girl walks into the house and turns right. The judge's wife comes running down the carpeted stairs. She doesn't notice the girl, who has disappeared into the darkness of the living room.

The wife's footsteps stop, and she bursts into a piercing scream.

Friday

It's half past seven in the morning. Bjarkargata is a flurry of activity. The street has been closed off on both ends by police cars and yellow tape; only its residents are allowed on it, to go to work and to school. The squad cars' blue flashing lights stand out in the dark. Broadcast vans from the television stations are parked on Skothúsvegur, and journalists and photographers are all over the place, particularly in the grove on the opposite side of the street—whence come occasional flashes of camera bulbs. Around thirty police officers are standing guard outside the house toward which all eyes are directed—it's brightly lit, outside and in, and members of the CID and Forensics Unit hustle in and out its door. The district coroner completed his work three hours ago, and shortly thereafter, the body was removed from the scene.

Hörður and Vigfús stand guard at the intersection with Skothúsvegur, within the yellow tape that's tied to the gate of the house on the corner. It's only three degrees Celsius outside. The two officers are wearing hats on their heads and gloves on their hands, and stamp their feet and dream of hot coffee and pastries. Vigfús is calm as can be, but Hörður is on edge. Not only had he been right when he predicted that a judge would be murdered next, but he'd also guessed the name of the judge whom he considered most likely to be the next victim. When he heard what had happened, he nearly passed out; he had a hot flash, everything went blurry.

"Damn day shifts," mutters Hörður. "We always miss out on everything. I can't wait to get back on night shifts."

"Speak for yourself," Vigfús mutters grumpily. They haven't said anything more about the ecstasy tablets and the events surrounding their discovery—despite these things clearly being boxed but not forgotten.

Hörður looks over his shoulder toward the judge's house. He desperately wants to have a look at the crime scene, *participate* instead of standing guard. But that isn't an option. He punches himself lightly to warm up. Two murders in three days. What a mess. On Tuesday, the two partners were standing at the end of this street, doing radar speed monitoring of the traffic on Hringbraut. The day of the fatal collision, which manifested itself ahead of time in the form of a death-shadow.

Looking back, the shadow was perhaps an omen of more than just one death by traffic accident.

"Excuse me, gentlemen!" says one of the journalists who's been hanging about there since the partners showed up for duty. It's a man of around thirty, one of the directors of the current-affairs program *Spotlight* on National Television.

His name is Haukur, if Hörður remembers correctly. He looks slightly hawkish, as well, with his hair combed back and a crooked nose. A real newshawk.

"We don't do interviews," says Vigfús.

"No, I know," says the television journalist. He's dressed in a black wool coat, and is carrying neither a microphone nor a recorder. The cameraman who's been hanging at his side isn't visible either. "I was just wondering, just like the Icelandic public, what actually went on here tonight?"

"We know nothing more than you," says Vigfús. "A man was taken away in an ambulance after being attacked. We can't say anything more at this time."

"Can't say, or won't say?" the journalist asks.

"You know the answer to that," mutters Vigfús, before stepping off the sidewalk onto the street, where several high-school kids have gathered outside the yellow tape. He tries shooing them away with a few choice words. Two police officers step over to assist him.

"He was dead, wasn't he?" the journalist asks softly. "The judge. Aðalsteinn Kvaran."

Hörður nods.

The journalist steps all the way up to him. "The street's residents say that there was a police car outside the house all last evening, and that it was there when the murder was committed. A car with two officers in it. Is this right?"

Hörður clear his throat. "We're not allowed to comment on the matter at this time—and you know that. A statement will doubtless be made to the media before long."

"Why was the house being watched?" the journalist asks. "Had the judge been threatened?"

Hörður glances at Vigfús, who is still dealing with the teenagers—undoubtedly late for their classes at Reykjavík High School or the Reykjavík Women's High School. "Not directly, but indirectly."

"Indirectly? What do you mean?" the journalist asks. He's not at all aggressive; it's more like he's chatting about the weather.

Hörður shrugs.

"Could this be connected to the murder of the MP?" asks the journalist, in the same tone of voice used by people when they say: I wonder if it'll rain today? Beyond Skothúsvegur are The Pond, City Hall, and the Iðnó Culture House, with the back of the Parliament House slightly visible between the buildings. The two murders were committed within a thousand-meter radius.

Hörður bites his lower lip. Thoughts dash and flutter in circles in his head, like startled birds in a cage. He knows too much, but can't say anything. It's as if his mind is a kettle on the verge of bursting from the pressure of hot steam, desperately needing release before the kettle explodes.

"If you ask me, yes," he concludes.

The television journalist nods contemplatively. "First an MP, then a judge. Sounds like some sort of conspiracy against public servants, or something? First the legislature, then the judiciary. Did they receive any threats?"

Hörður shakes his head.

"Has anyone put two and two together?" asks the journalist.

"Maybe," mutters Hörður.

"Was it you?" asks the journalist.

"I'm not allowed to go into any details about this case," says Hörður.

"No, of course not." The journalist sniffs nonchalantly. "Were the police keeping watch on the homes of all the judges? Or just Aðalsteinn's?"

Hörður goes on the defensive. "You ask too many questions."

"The home is being watched," the journalist says thoughtfully. "Yet still, the judge is murdered. In sight of the police. That doesn't look too good."

"No, not at all," says Hörður. "But as I said, no threats were made, or anything like that. *If the* house was under surveillance, which is something I can't discuss, it was only as a sort of safety measure."

"But then someone just strolls in and murders the judge?" asks the journalist. "A young girl, I understand."

"I don't know what happened," mutters Hörður, frustratedly. "But if people had paid more attention to what *someone* had to say, this would probably never have happened."

"So someone warned the police," says the journalist. "But that warning wasn't taken seriously. Is that what I'm to understand?"

"No, not really," says Hörður. "The house was under surveillance, that's true. But apparently, the officers responsible weren't paying close attention."

"So you're saying this was a screw-up ?" the reporter asks empathetically.

"I've said too much," mutters Hörður.

"First, a talented athlete and exemplary student murders an MP, and now a young girl has killed a judge," says the journalist. "This just doesn't make any sense. Rumor has it that Gísli Már had ecstasy in his possession. Could this be connected to dangerous drugs?"

"I can't say any more about this," says Hörður.

"Forgive my curiosity," says the journalist. "I'm just thinking out loud. A young man goes with his friends to watch a football match, and then suddenly, he has killed a man. He wasn't even drinking. There's something missing here, if you see what I mean?"

Hörður nods. "I was there, actually, at Ölver. Not as a police officer, but as a citizen. I don't think it unlikely that someone slipped Gísli something."

"Oh?"

"There were some suspicious people there," says Hörður, with a mysterious look on his face. "I can't say any more."

"No, of course not," the journalist says, sympathetically. "But I expect you've told your superiors about this? Passed on this information."

"Of course," says Hörður.

"What was your name again?" the journalist asks.

"It doesn't matter what my name is," says the red-haired giant.

"Hörður Grímsson!" someone calls out.

He turns around. Engilbert comes walking up, quickly, his unbuttoned trench coat swinging to and fro. The detective pulls disposable gloves off his hands and gestures to Hörður to follow him.

"But I ..."

"Come with me," says Engilbert as he slips beneath the yellow tape. "Orders from above."

Hörður hurries off. With a resolute expression, the journalist follows the officer with his eyes. Hörður follows the detective to the intersection with Tjarnargata, where Engilbert gets into an unmarked Ford Explorer, white with colored side windows.

Hörður hesitates, before getting into the car and sitting down in the passenger seat. "Where are we going?"

"To the station, where else?" Engilbert starts the engine, takes a mint from a small box and pops it in his mouth, and drives off. "Axel is waiting for us."

The detective is clearly under a great deal of strain. He's pale, and his eyes are bloodshot and have dark rings beneath them. His hair is greasy and there's dandruff on the shoulders of his trench coat. The mint that he crunches can't hide the smell of alcohol on his breath.

"What can you tell me about what happened last night?" asks Hörður.

"This is uncomfortably similar to the murder of the MP." Engilbert drives down Skothúsvegur toward the bridge, through the roadblock at Bjarkargata. "The girl's name is Sólrún Davíðsdóttir. No criminal record, works at a store in Kringlan. She had blue ecstasy tablets on her. The knife is exactly the same. The victim was stabbed in the abdomen three times, with great force. When the judge's wife came to him, he was still alive. She went out and called to the police officers. By the time the ambulance arrived, the judge was dead."

Engilbert turns left onto Fríkirkjuvegur Road.

"But the girl?" asks Hörður.

"At first it was as if the earth had swallowed her," the detective says. "But she was found in the judge's living room. She was lying there face down, as if she were praying or something. When one of the police officers shook her, she opened her eyes, but had no idea where she was or what had happened."

"Where is she now?" asks Hörður.

"She was taken straight to the hospital last night for a blood test and medical exam," says Engilbert. "While there, she had some sort of fit. They had to sedate her. From what I understand, she's in shock, but I hope to be able to question her today. Not that I expect that questioning her will yield anything, unfortunately."

Hörður, looking pensive, nods. "Is anything known about her activities earlier in the evening?"

"Yes." Engilbert turns up Hverfisgata. "We were able to locate two of her girlfriends who were with her at Kaffibarinn. Jafet is taking their statements now. It seems likely that they were all slipped drugs. They hardly remember anything."

Hörður scratches his head. "This is all very similar to Tuesday's events, that's true. Do you know whether the girl held the knife in her left or right hand?"

"Left," says the detective.

Hörður opens his eyes wider, questioningly.

"But she's also left-handed," adds Engilbert. "I asked her to write her name down. This about the right or left hand is irrelevant."

"I see," says Hörður. He's listening. He's learning. He's determined not to make any mistakes. "I was just thinking about the murder of the MP. Gísli stabbed him with his left hand, despite being right-handed."

"There's often something that doesn't seem to fit," says Engilbert. "But it usually turns out that it doesn't matter."

"Aron is left-handed," says Hörður. "Or at least I think he is. His left arm is in a cast, due to a work accident. He was playing ping pong yesterday, but was obviously playing with his bad hand, the right one."

"Aron is behind bars at Litla-Hraun," says Engilbert irritably.

"Yes, indeed he is," says Hörður.

"We mustn't get stuck on irrelevancies," says the detective. "It's a common error, even though we try to avoid it."

"Yes, of course," says Hörður.

"Facts. Evidence. The overall picture," says the detective. "Who, how, and why."

"I see," says Hörður. "But there's something really strange going on. I've never been so dissatisfied with being right. It would be so much more convenient if the murder of the MP had just been some sort of random bullshit."

"I know," says Engilbert. "It appears as if this has all been organized, with everything pointing at these anarchists. That's why Axel wants to bring you on board the investigation."

On board the investigation. Hörður struggles not to smile out to his ears. This is the big opportunity that he's been dreaming of.

He clears his throat. "What about the police officers keeping a watch on the judge's house? Did they see anything?"

"The girl was dropped off by a black car, a BMW," says the detective. "She was let out two or three houses away from the judge's home. The car backed out onto Skothúsvegur and disappeared. They didn't get a look at the driver or catch the car's license plate number."

"What about the men who were at Ölver, Tryggvi Leó and Egill Þór?" asks Hörður.

"Yes, indeed." Engilbert is waiting at a red light at the intersection with Snorrabraut. Ahead of them is the police station. "When they didn't answer their phones yesterday, we put out an informal alert for them. They still haven't been found. A formal, public alert will be issued for them, and the search expanded."

"They must have been in that BMW, then," says Hörður. "Have you spoken to the staff of Kaffibarinn?"

"We got in touch with one of the bartenders and one of the bouncers, and showed them photos of Tryggvi, Egill, and Sólrún," says Engilbert. "The bartender remembers three girlfriends and two men dressed in black, but he isn't certain whether one of them had a tattoo on his neck or not. But he didn't see them together, the men and the girlfriends. The bouncer vaguely recalls Sólrún leaving the place with one or two men, but isn't certain. It was very busy, and dark both inside the place and out."

"I see," says Hörður. He absorbs every word the detective says, like a sponge. They walk together into the building and take the elevator up to the third floor.

"This will end when we find Tryggvi and Egill, of that I'm convinced," says the detective. "But this is a complicated case, which is why we've got to take every last detail into account. It's one thing one to arrest people, and another to get them convicted. Our case has to be completely airtight."

"Of course," says Hörður contemplatively.

Engilbert looks at his watch, a gold watch with a leather strap from the shop Gilbert's Watches, on Laugavegur Avenue.

"Axel is waiting for us in the Operations Room."

Hörður nods as if he knows what the detective is talking about. *The Operations Room.* Wow. He feels like a kid going to Disneyland for the first time. He envisions a large wall with a map of the greater Reykjavík area. Photographs and notes have been thumbtacked to the map, and locations connected with red threads. To the sides of the map are more photos and sticky notes, with prominent question marks here and there.

The activities of the CID are controlled from a conference room at its back, ordinarily called the Operations Room or just The Room. Inside the room is a long table with six chairs on each side and one at the end nearest the door. Above the table is a projector. On the far wall is a white markerboard.

When Engilbert and Hörður walk in, Axel M. Axelsson has his back turned to them and is writing something in the top corner of the markerboard. He turns around and puts the lid back on a green felt-tipped pen. His jacket is draped over the back of a chair at the end of the table. The head of the CID has loosened his tie and rolled up his shirt sleeves.

"Well, boys," says Axel. Above his right shoulder can be seen the words that he has written on the markerboard. It's a phrase in Latin:

Semper Ubique Prima.

"Anything new?" asks Engilbert. He takes off his trench coat and lays it over the back of one of the chairs.

"Yes and no," says Axel. "Traces of GHB were found in the young woman's blood. The ecstasy tablets found in her purse are of the same make as the ones that Gísli Már had on him. But they don't contain GHB. I would guess that these tablets were all from the same bag, the one found inside the book from the storage unit."

Hörður nods in agreement. He takes off his hat and places it on the table, then takes off his jacket and hangs it on the back of a chair.

"She also had a needle mark on her right forearm," says Axel. "It was new, and the skin around it was red. Who injected her, or with what, we don't know. But we can't rule out that both Sólrún and Gísli Már were injected with GHB or a similar anesthetic."

Hörður opens his eyes wide, inquisitively. "So the drug wasn't slipped into their drinks?"

Axel shrugs. "Yes, or maybe both methods were used. These needle marks are a mystery."

Hörður nods in agreement.

"Gísli Már hadn't received any injections in the days preceding the murder of the MP," says Engilbert. "Nor does he have diabetes. Since Sólrún also has a needle mark, it must be related to the murders."

"No doubt," says Axel.

"Is anything known about the knives, where they came from?" asks Engilbert.

"The Forensics Unit thinks that they're commercial butcher knives," says Axel. "Used in meat packing, to trim cuts. It's almost impossible to know where they came from, but we're asking around."

Hörður frowns. Meat packing? That rings a few bells in his mind.

"When can I question the girl?" asks Engilbert.

"Later today, I would think," says Axel. "She's in intensive care at the City Hospital. She was given some medication last night. We'll speak to her once she wakes up."

"But her girlfriends?" asks Engilbert.

"They went to Kaffibarinn to dance, as they do every Thursday," says Axel. "Drank Bacardi Breezers from the bottle. They were only on their first bottles, according to them. They left them on a shelf while they danced. What happened next isn't quite clear. Apparently, one of the bouncers sent them home in a taxi. According to him, the girls were smashed. They insist that they weren't. One of them threw up when she came home, and the other passed out. The latter one's boyfriend called an ambulance. Blood samples from both of them are being analyzed as we speak. They hardly remember anything, although one of them says that a man took Sólrún, and she hadn't been able to stop him. That it was like a bad dream."

"A bad dream—so true," says Engilbert.

"I would like to believe that this was the case of an atrocious act committed in a psychotic state caused by the ingestion of bad drugs," says Axel. "But this theory is pretty shaky. On the one hand, it appears as if innocent individuals were slipped something that they would otherwise never mess with. Unless they injected themselves with something, which is of course a possibility. However, we know that someone drove the girl to Bjarkargata and left her there. This leads me to believe that the same sort of thing happened when the MP was murdered. But both strongly suggest that these horrific acts were organized by an unknown perpetrator or perpetrators."

"Which means that the alleged perpetrators are also victims," says Engilbert in a tone of surrender. "What a nightmare."

"Dream or no dream." Axel tosses the felt-tipped pen to Hörður, who catches it nimbly. "We need to wake up, boys—that much is certain."

Hörður looks questioningly at the pen, and then at Engilbert, who shrugs, and finally at Axel, who steps aside and points at the blank markerboard. "It's all yours, big man. We're at square one. This case is *tabula rasa*, and it's your turn."

Hörður hesitates, but then goes to the markerboard. His mouth is dry and his heart starts beating faster. What should he write? He's so stressed that he has trouble thinking clearly, and the only thing that he remembers at the moment is what Engilbert said in the car: Don't get stuck in irrelevancies.

He takes the lid off the pen, clears his throat and draws three vertical columns on the board, then writes the headings of the columns at the top of each one.

Who—How—Why

Hörður underlines each heading, then starts writing in the columns. He talks things out while writing—which helps him concentrate—and occasionally looks at Axel, who watches his every movement. "As I said yesterday, I believe that Aron Beck is the one behind all this, the one organizing these crimes behind the scenes and telling his accomplices what to do. His accomplices are Tryggvi Leó and Egill Þór. They're the real perpetrators, the hands that do what the head tells them to do. Gísli Már and Sólrún are victims; I agree with that. But as things stand now, they'll be charged with murder, or manslaughter, at best. To prevent any further murders, we need to find both Tryggvi and Egill. But in order for the ringleader to be punished instead of innocent civilians and insignificant minions, we need to demonstrate his connection to Tryggvi and Egill, and show in black and white how he went about making ordinary people commit murder."

In the column *Who*, he has written the names of the three men, with Aron at the top. He moves to the next column—*How*.

"One question," says Axel. "Why this emphasis on Aron? They were all in that anarchy group. Couldn't either Tryggvi or Egill be the ringleader? Maybe they're responsible for what's going on, not Aron?"

"Yes, theoretically," says Hörður. "But in the interview in *DV*, only Aron is questioned. There, he appears not only as the spokesman for the anarchists, but also the brains behind them. He tries to present his group as educated members of the resistance, organized activists who adhere to a particular world view and have strong views on world affairs. As he would have it, they could even be called philosophers. But in actuality, they have various things in common with cults and extremist groups, and are basically militant nihilists. All of this is derived from the things that Aron himself has stated. I just don't see anyone else in the group as being of his caliber, without, however, being able to substantiate this assertion."

Engilbert clears his throat. "I spent two hours last night reading through Tryggvi and Egill's criminal records, and I have to agree with the police officer. They aren't the sharpest tacks in the box, and I consider it almost out of the question that they could organize anything more complicated than the house burglaries or gas-station robberies for which they've already been convicted. We're talking about typical petty criminals."

"But there are others in that anarchy group, right?" asks Axel. "What about all the rest? Couldn't any of them be behind these things?"

Hörður blushes. "As I said, I saw Tryggvi and Egill at Ölver. I didn't make any assumptions about any of the others in the group being involved, apart from Aron, of course."

"But I did." Engilbert pulls out a sticky note. "The three that we haven't mentioned are named Orri, Hákon and Þorsteinn. Orri works as a dishwasher at Hotel Borg. He worked until just past one a.m. both last night and Tuesday night. Hákon and Þorsteinn both work on a fishing boat operating from Grindavík. I got hold of the father of one of them, and he told me that they'd gone to sea on Monday and wouldn't return until next Monday. I called the fishing company and they confirmed it—the boat's at sea."

Hörður breathes a sigh of relief.

"Well, that's clear, then," says Axel, before gesturing to Hörður. "Go on."

Hörður turns back to the board. "What we know, or believe we know, is that the drinks of the victims, the alleged perpetrators, were spiked with GHB at pubs and clubs. We'll call these alleged perpetrators *subjects*, to avoid confusion. The anarchists are the perpetrators. When a particular subject is turned into a mindless tool under the influence of the GHB, that subject is taken away from the scene and brought to an out-of-the-way location, where he or she is hypnotized."

"Why should this be done in an out-of-the-way place?" asks Engilbert. "Why not in an apartment, or just in the back of a car?"

"Yes, a car might work, that's true," says Hörður. "But I find it unlikely that the subject would be dragged in and out of an apartment. It would increase the likelihood of witnesses, of people finding their activity suspicious and calling the police. Too risky."

"I agree," says Axel.

"But a car is certainly an option." Hörður writes *car* in the column, under *out-of-the-way place*. "I ran through Aron's hypnosis handbook. It provides instructions from A to Z, written in plain language for the public. The environment matters, for the subject to feel comfortable and so on. Hypnosis requires peace and quiet, among other things. The subject sits on a chair or lies on a sofa. He looks at a certain object or a light, and focuses on it while the hypnotist speaks. That's why I said an out-of-the-way place. In the back of a delivery van is certainly possible. In the back seat of a black BMW, I find unlikely, but it's not out of the question."

"If those goons are too stupid to be able to organize anything," says Axel, "how are they supposed to be able to hypnotize someone?"

"Exactly what I was thinking," says Engilbert.

"The anonymous author of the book claims that anyone can learn hypnosis," says Hörður. "But they need to follow the instructions, of course—that is, *study* them. And they need to practice. Both require at least a minimum amount of intelligence, diligence, and patience. So it's unlikely, though not impossible, that they mastered the techniques. I'm leaning toward the former. But how did they do so, if that turns out to be right? That's the big question."

"Do you have the answer?" asks Axel.

"Maybe. But first, one question," says Hörður. "What are the odds of Aron having a cell phone in his prison cell?"

"Little or none," says Engilbert.

"It's highly unlikely," says Axel. "His cell is searched regularly, and I think it would be easier said than done to hide both a cell phone and a charger in it."

"Fine—so Aron doesn't hypnotize the subject over the phone," says Hörður. "But Tryggvi and Egill could play *a recording* of his voice. Not only do I find that more believable, but it would be much better suited to our investigation of the case."

"Why do you say that?" asks Engilbert.

"In order to connect Aron directly to these crimes, we need hard evidence," says Hörður. "For example, a script with instructions for hypnosis, preferably in his own handwriting, or, even better, a *recording* in his own voice, in which he hypnotizes some undetermined subject."

Axel grunts. "We've already searched both of their apartments, but found nothing of the sort."

"They could have something like this on them," says Hörður. "But it's most likely that evidence could be found in their car, or at this imaginary out-of-the-way place. A script like the one you mention, or a recording, GHB, ecstasy tablets, or hopefully more knives."

"We just have to find them," says Engilbert.

"But why?" asks Axel, pointing to the third and last column. "Why this murder? What's the motive?"

"To spread chaos, disruption, and fear in society," says Hörður. "As I said yesterday, the anarchists have an enemy with a capital E, the three-headed giant that I believe to be the separation of powers into three branches—the foundations of democracy."

Axel sighs. "Very well. Our priority is to find these goons. Personally, I believe that they're responsible for all of this. It's this hypnosis thing that I'm not convinced about. It's too much hocus-pocus bullshit for my taste. Still, we can't rule out the possibility of these being random acts of violence, committed under the influence of drugs. That theory that Aron is the ringleader is good, though rather far-fetched. But I'll call him in for questioning today. To start with, he'll have the status of a witness. I don't have enough evidence to go beyond that, not right now. Shall we say two o'clock?"

"Two o'clock what?" Hörður asks.

Engilbert nods. "That's fine by me."

"It's decided, then. "I'll call the prison warden and send someone to go pick up the bastard. The three of us will interrogate him at two o'clock. At the same time, his cell will be turned inside-out. Who knows—maybe something will be found that connects him to the murders."

"The three of us?" asks Hörður.

Axel nods. "It's an exception, rather than a rule, for the head of the department to be present. But this is a very special case. Not only is it a double homicide, but the victims are far from being down-and-out junkies. Not that

that matters—but it *does.* The pressure we're under is enormous, and the department's reputation is on the line. As it's I who run the department, I'm responsible for the process from start to finish. If we screw this up, I'll lose my job. It's as simple as that."

"I see," says Hörður. "But you said the *three* of us. In other words, you want me to question him, too?"

"It's your theory. He's your man." Axel looks at his gold watch. "You'll be there to back us up. But I want you to be well prepared. *Very* well prepared. We have a few hours until then. That should be enough. Among other things, I want you to go back to that storage unit and fine-comb it, high and low."

"It could be too late," says Hörður. "The custodian could have emptied it already."

"Then what are we waiting for?" Axel asks brusquely.

"Nothing, of course." Hörður puts on his jacket and hat. "Who's going to drive me there? My squad car is with Vigfús on Skothúsvegur."

"Loan him your car," says Axel to Engilbert, who gives the others an angry, resentful look.

"Don't scratch it," says the detective, tossing the keys to the red-haired giant.

Hörður walks quickly to the alley behind the police station and heads over to the white Explorer. He opens it with the remote-control key and sits down behind the steering wheel. He starts the eight-cylinder gasoline engine, then moves the leather upholstered seat backward half a meter and tilting it slightly back. Next, he adjusts the rear-view mirrors, cranks the heater all the way up, turns on the radio and sets it to The X.

He backs the SUV out of its space and drives out of the alley and down to the intersection with Sæbraut, where he waits at a red turn signal light. The powerful engine purrs beneath the hood, and the heater blows warm air onto the windshield. Hörður smiles slightly, with a proud look on his face, and squints in the glare of the strong autumn sun. All he's missing are his Ray-Ban sunglasses, which are in the glove compartment of his squad car. But it doesn't matter, *nothing* can dampen the exquisite feeling of sitting *alone* in an unmarked SUV belonging to the *CID*, on his way to *survey a scene* as part of a *murder investigation*. Nothing!

The lights turn green. Hörður shifts the automatic transmission to Drive and steps on the gas. The engine growls loudly, the SUV tears off with such force that Hörður just manages to steer it through the turn. Such power! He turns onto Sæbraut Road, straightens the car and hits the gas. The engine lets loose with a war cry and the SUV reaches a hundred kph in just a few seconds. On the radio, one song ends and another begins. It's the hit "Chop Suey!," by System Of A Down. Hörður cranks up the volume, rolls down his side window and sticks his elbow out.

He slows down as he drives out to Grandi. The car has become steaming hot, but the engine doesn't show it—its over-300-horsepower engine has what seems endless energy. He parks the SUV in the parking lot of the Geymslur Storage Facility, shuts off the engine and steps out into the cool sea breeze.

He finds the custodian sitting in his office on the building's ground floor. "Remember me?"

Guðjón looks up from his paperwork. "What happened with the skull?"

"Nothing really. It turned out to be old," says Hörður. "Are Mummi's belongings still here?"

Guðjón shakes his head. "I emptied the unit last Wednesday."

"What happened to all his stuff?" Hörður asks. "Did you manage to get hold of any of his family members?"

"They didn't want anything to do with it," says Guðjón. He gestures behind him with his thumb. "So I took it to the recycling center over there."

Hörður curses under his breath. "What containers did it go into?"

"I put the clothes in the Red Cross container," says Guðjón. "The rest went into the Good Shepherd container. The dresser and the books and all that. Why do you ask?"

"It doesn't matter," says Hörður. He hurries out to the car and drives over to the recycling center, which is a 2-minute drive away. It's closed. A sign on the gate says that the center will reopen at 12:30.

Hörður notices movement behind the gate. He honks the car's horn and steps out of the SUV. A man in pale green work clothes approaches the gate from the other side. "We're closed."

"I need to get in," says Hörður. "Police business."

"What sort of police business?" the man asks.

"On Wednesday, a man came here with someone's household effects," says Hörður. "He says that he put it in the Good Shepherd container. Is the container still here?"

The man shakes his head. "It was taken yesterday morning."

"To the second-hand market?" Hörður asks.

"Yes," says the man. "But the market doesn't open until twelve."

"We'll see about that," mutters Hörður, as he gets back in the SUV. He's full of energy and enthusiasm, and isn't about to let an everyday thing like opening hours stop him.

Hörður parks the SUV in a shady alley behind the Good Shepherd building, between open and closed shipping containers on one side and a stone wall on the other. He steps out of the car, tosses his burning cigarette onto the asphalt and crushes it with his foot as he walks toward the windowless back door. He knocks heavily on the green-painted iron door a few times. While waiting for someone to answer, he peeks into a nearby garbage container, which is half-full of useless furniture, including an old teak dresser with narrow legs and burn marks.

He climbs into the container, pushes back a desk and opens the drawers of the deceased Mummi's dresser. They're empty, as he expected. At the same moment, the back door of the Good Shepherd opens and a young girl wearing a green apron peeks out at the lot. Seeing nothing at first, her eyes open wide when she spies the red-haired giant in the garbage container, lifting a teak dresser to shoulder height.

"Hello, dear," he says. "Do you know where the stuff that was in this dresser went?"

"No-oo," says the girl. "What kind of stuff was it?"

Hörður lets the dresser fall back into the container, then jumps down from it and dusts off his clothes. "Candles, incense, essential oils and that sort of thing. Also some voodoo dolls. But mainly books. Some of them were fantasies and the like, but there were also books in English about spiritual things, hypnosis and that sort of stuff. That's what I'm most interested in finding."

The girl invites him into the building. "You're welcome to have a look inside. Does it have to do with a police investigation?"

"Yes." Hörður looks around. He's in a very large room, a kind of a hall where everything that comes here is sorted. First, the things are divided into two categories: unusable and reusable. What can be reused is then separated into numerous different categories, such as furniture, photograph frames, books, clothing, toys, tableware, electronic equipment and so on. The unusable stuff ends up in trash bins and containers like the one in which Hörður was rummaging.

Besides the girl, there are two other employees, another girl and a young man, all wearing green aprons.

"Do you know when this dresser came in?" asks the girl.

Hörður nods. "On Wednesday. It came in the container from the Sorpa recycling center at Grandagarður."

"Then it must have been emptied the same day or the morning after," says the girl. "Whatever it contained that was usable will be in the store now. You're welcome to look around there. Everything else would have gone into the trash, like the dresser."

"I'll have a look around, then." Hörður goes to the store area, which is very large, half-lit, and empty of customers. He's been there before and remembers the layout fairly well, and heads in the direction of the bookshelves, located at the store's center. Their long rows hold books by the thousands, rather than the hundreds. The section containing books on spirituality isn't very large, however. There, Hörður finds numerous self-help and New Age books, but sees none of the books that were in Mummi's dresser.

Among the corny, positivity-loaded New Age books, he finds a tattered copy of *Sorcery in Iceland*, by Matthías Viðar Sæmundsson. Hörður grabs it and leafs through it. The book is, on the one hand, a historical study, in which the history of sorcery in Iceland is traced in detail, and on the other hand, an exposition of one particular, notorious Icelandic sorcerer's handbook, written on vellum in the seventeenth century and considered so dangerous by the secular and Church authorities that it was banned and men burned for the mere fact of possessing a copy.

On one of the book's spreads, Hörður finds images of two sorcerers' staves, one of which he recognizes. It's the same symbol that was painted in black on the front of the house on Vatnsstígur, which had been taken over by the anarchists. According to the book, the stave's name is Ginfaxi; it's said to be "similar to Gapaldur," and with it, an attempt is made to call forth "tremendous power" with the aid of the rune, Þurs (Giant).

"I guess that didn't go very well," mutters Hörður to himself.

He flips back a few pages and reads the opening of one of the first chapters of the book:

Why are people fascinated by pure evil, when it conflicts with their needs and honest wishes; from what depths springs this ambiguous and dangerous inclination, this red-haired soul-demon that breaks out through every orifice of the body and turns a man into a gorgon with a poisonous arrow on each finger, suddenly desiring what appalls him the most?

"Good question, Matthías, my man," mutters Hörður, before continuing:

This must be an innate inclination, because the worship of evil appears to have existed in every age in human society. The explanation must be apparent, even if it is difficult to distinguish at first glance.

Aha. Hörður closes the book and puts it back in its place. He looks up and sees an employee. It's the other girl.

"Sorry," he says. "The books that came in on Wednesday or Thursday morning—could they have sold out already?"

"Yes, it's possible," says the girl. "Especially if they're sought-after. A lot of collectors come here on a daily basis. What books were they?"

"*The Satanic Bible*, for example," says Hörður. "*Necronomicon*, which is a handbook for devil worshipers, *The Anarchist Cookbook*, and then a few about hypnosis and such."

"If they aren't here, then they've been sold," says the girl. "I don't remember *The Satanic Bible*, but a tattered old Bible came in the other day. It's still in the box of junk books, out back."

"Okay, thanks," says Hörður. He walks back to the door leading to the sorting area. Next to the door are framed paintings, empty frames, and mirrors. One of the mirrors is in an ornate frame. Hörður recognizes it as the mirror that was in the storage unit.

Hörður goes to the back of the building, and finds the box of junk books. In it is the Bible from the Mummi's dresser. Like the dictionary, it's hollow inside. He rummages through the box, but finds no other books from the storage unit.

He thinks about the mirror that he saw inside. In the storage unit, there was also a box of framed photographs.

"Hey," he calls out. "What do you do with framed photographs?"

The young man looks up, slowly turns halfway around and points at a wooden box on the floor. Despite his young age, the man has the appearance of a sloth.

"Is this place some sort of reserve, or what?" mutters Hörður irritably. He walks over to the wooden box, lifts it onto a table, and starts going through the pile of photos. He soon finds what he's looking for: the photo of Little Mummi taken in a slaughterhouse. His eyes immediately go to the knives. Affixed to the slaughterhouse wall is a horizontal board, and nailed to the board are sections of a rubber hose, which are used as a sheath for the meat-trimming knives.

To Hörður's eyes, these appear to be the same type of knives with which the murders were committed.

"Bingo," mutters Hörður, smiling. He looks around and spies another wooden box on the floor. Inside it are broken picture frames. He pokes through the box's contents and finally finds a frame with dark glass—the black mirror that was among the deceased Mummi's belongings.

Hörður's face appears like a specter in the darkness.

He tilts the frame, blows dust from the glass and examines it back and front. Just as he remembers, it looks to him as if the glass has been painted black on the inside. There's nothing noteworthy about the frame, but he takes it with him anyway, along with the photo.

Hörður sits at a vacant desk in the communal work area, rolls his shoulders and takes a deep breath. To one side of him is an irregular stack of papers—printouts of verdicts, newspaper interviews and articles, and handwritten notes and short summaries that no one can read but him. Sitting on top of the stack are the three things he brought with him from the Good Shepherd: the Bible, the photograph, and the framed darkness.

The photo is on top, as he believes that its contents are directly tied to the murders. He just needs to find a connection between Aron and the meat-packing facility. If the anarchist worked there as a teenager, as well, he would undoubtedly have handled such knives, and if luck is on Hörður's side, he would have stolen them from there, too.

He starts by opening the phone book to the yellow pages and looks for meat-packing companies. There can hardly be that many in the greater Reykjavík area. He should have time to call them all and check if they have employee registers that go back as far as ten years. There turn out to be sixteen such companies, six of which are elsewhere in the country. That leaves just ten, most of which are in Reykjavík, with two or three in Hafnarfjörður and Kópavogur.

Hörður picks up the phone and is about to enter the first number when he sets eyes on the name of the company second on the alphabetical list:

Einar A. Beck's Meat-Packing Company

His eyes widen. This easy? Can it be? He enters the number and waits. The phone rings for a long time, before an older man answers.

"Meat-packing, Einar here."

"Hello. My name is Hörður Grímsson and I'm a police officer. Is it possible that you're related to Aron Beck?"

No response.

Hörður pushes the receiver to his ear. "Einar, are you there?"

"Is he … dead?" Einar asks. He no longer sounds like an older man, but more as if he's at death's door.

"No, not at all," says Hörður. "I'm just investigating a case that might involve him. How are you related?"

"He's my grandson—I can't deny it," says Einar. *"This boy has caused me so much unhappiness and pain. I thought that he was dead, that someone might have killed him. And felt relieved to hear it—that's the worst."*

"Yes, indeed." Hörður clears his throat. "Listen, tell me. Did he ever work for you? At your meat-packing facility?"

"Yes, he did—I can't deny it," says Einar. *"They were here one or two summers, he and his friend Mummi. Mummi was a good kid. But he was in bad company. Aron never lifted a finger. Except when he was vandalizing or otherwise damaging something."*

"Did he like the knives?" asks Hörður.

"You called to ask me that?" says Einar, tiredly.

"Did any knives go missing?" Hörður asks. "The meat-cutting knives?"

"There was always something going missing," says the old man. *"Money. Meat. Equipment."*

"And knives?"

"Everything that wasn't nailed down," says Einar. *"I can't help you any further. It was a long time ago. And I can't do anything to help my namesake."*

"You've helped me plenty. Bye now," says Hörður, and he hangs up. His conversation with the old man hadn't exactly been cheerful, but the police officer is beaming. He got what he needed. It couldn't have gone any better.

Hörður turns on the computer, cracks his knuckles, and glances at his watch. He has plenty of time to write a short summary before joining Axel and Englibert at the cafeteria for lunch.

Where should he start?

How about by making a list of what was in the storage unit? He looks at the stack of papers, and tries to pull a few sheets from it—a copy of his report on the discovery of the skull—without removing the Bible and the picture frame. But he doesn't succeed—the Bible slips onto the keyboard and the picture frame with the black glass falls to the floor. The glass breaks and two knife-shaped shards go bouncing along the linoleum floor.

"Fuck!" Hörður blushes with anger and shame. Did the damn thing really have to break? What a klutz he can be! He picks up the shards and tosses them into a trash bin, and then examines the picture frame, which is otherwise undamaged.

But what is this?

Beneath the glass is a photograph. Where the shards had been, he glimpses thin legs and white sneakers.

Hörður turns the frame over and removes the back cover. Then he takes out the photograph and turns it over. It's an old color photo, showing an eleven-year-old boy standing near an Icelandic lake. It's Little Mummi. Hörður recognizes his eyes. In the background is a wooded area, and in the distance, a few boys can be seen launching a kayak onto the lake; all of them are out of focus. Mummi is wearing shorts and a t-shirt, with the letters YMCA embroidered onto the chest. He looks directly at the camera, but doesn't smile.

Summer camp in Vatnaskógur?

Hörður parks Engilbert's SUV in one of the parking spaces outside a row of townhouses on the east side of the city. According to the National Registry, this is where the pastor lives, in number 16. If Ingimar is still a pastor, that is to say. Maybe he's been defrocked, as it's called. Convicted rapist and all that.

Hörður's parking space is at the end of the row, which is part of a lush, quiet suburb. Half a century or so ago, there were no houses here; at most a stable here and there, and a few small farms. Nor was it so terribly long ago that there was a windmill on the otherwise empty Skólavörðuholt, and a foul-smelling brook running down Lækjargata Street. At that time, Reykjavík was just a small village—and pretty much still is.

Hörður leaves his hat and jacket in the car. He walks up a few stone steps, and then up a paved path in front of the row of townhouses. The pastor's house is at the end, standing in the shadow of a tall maple. On the weatherbeaten front door is a dark mark, where there had once been a small plaque bearing the inhabitants' names.

Why has the plaque been removed? Hörður rings the doorbell, which chimes loudly inside the house. He waits, then takes a few steps back and looks at the front of the two-story house. The windows are dark, and no one comes to the door.

It's chilly in the shadow of the tree.

Behind each townhouse is a fenced garden. The sun is shining on that side, and there the police officer walks, on the silent rubber soles of his shoes. Each house has a back door leading out onto a sunny deck, with steps down to the garden. On the upper floor are small balconies, adjacent to a room that the officer guesses to be the largest bedroom. Each garden is lovelier than the next: newly mown, lushly green, and sporting well-groomed roses and summer blossoms.

All except one.

The pastor's garden is overgrown and utterly neglected. The bushes are untrimmed, there are no summer blossoms, and the lawn is thickly grown with buttercups and dande-lions. On the faded deck, laundry hangs on a rack; all male clothing. The sun gleams on dusty windows whose curtains are drawn tightly over them.

Hörður looks around, and then climbs over the low fence into the garden. He wades through the tall grass and weeds and hops up onto the deck. The back door is locked; he tries to peek through the windows but can't see inside.

What is he doing? What is he looking for? He isn't sure, yet is convinced that the pastor is one of the key puzzle pie-ces in the picture that he's trying to fit together. What hap-pened in Vatnaskógur is perhaps a kind of starting point; at least it isn't unlikely that the alleged abuse inflicted on Little Mummi marked the start of his sad end.

Next to the back door is an open window, narrow and tall. Glancing over his shoulder, Hörður sticks his left arm in through the window and stretches his fingers toward the latch that unlocks the back door. He gets close, but not close enough.

Hanging on a wire hanger on the laundry rack is a light blue shirt. Hörður tosses the shirt onto the rack, grabs the hanger, and sticks it and his arm back through the window. He paws around with the wire, manages to hook it around the latch and yank it upward.

Voilà!

The back door is no longer locked. But so what? Is he really going to enter someone's house without authorization?

Hörður pushes aside both legitimate doubts and com-mon sense, opens the door and slips inside. There, it's done! No turning back now.

He's in a dusky room that is mainly empty. Apart from an armchair, a newspaper rack, and a television, there's nothing else in the spacious living room. Not even a painting or floor lamp. The carpeted floor is marked with depressions left by the legs of a sofa-set and cabinets, and shadows on the light-colored walls indicate where pictures once hung.

The living room has obviously been emptied. Someone has moved out. The pastor is probably divorced. His wife has most likely left him. But she didn't leave yesterday or the day before. It was probably many months ago, even a few years. This house has neither been dusted nor vacuumed in a long time.

Hörður slinks across the room and up two steps, to find himself standing on a platform that may have been a dining area, and adjacent to it, the hall. On the other side are the entrance and the door he stood before just a few minutes ago, with a small, messy kitchen on the other side. Between the entrance and the kitchen is a steep staircase leading to the upper floor. Beneath the stairs is a small door, which Hörður opens, revealing a dark staircase leading down into the basement. The smell of sewage, mold and detergent wafts up from the dark basement.

Should he start upstairs or down?

Hörður shuts the door and ascends the stairs to the upper floor—something pulls him there: either instinct or intuition. He comes to a short hallway with closed doors at both ends; two at one end and one at the other. The first door on the left-hand side leads to a small room that was a child's bedroom at one point, but now looks like an empty storage room. On the right is a bathroom, which reeks of urine. Next on the left is a bedroom, with a double bed that's clearly been slept on on only one side. The place is stuffy and hot and smells like a retirement home. Opposite the bedroom is the pastor's office, the room that the police officer was looking for.

He walks into the office and looks around. In it are a desk with a desktop computer, a bookcase, a file cabinet, a single sofa bed and a large wooden chest. On the walls are crosses, icons, and various framed photographs.

Hörður regards the sofa bed. Was it here that he raped the young man? He turns on the computer, which is old and takes a long time to start. He wonders what's on the hard drive. Financial records, or child pornography? As the computer is booting up, Hörður opens the desk drawers but finds nothing of note, just pens, paper clips, and a white candle. He tries opening the wooden trunk, but it's locked. He wonders what's in it. Photos of naked men or boys? Sex toys? Should he force it open? Or ask Axel to get him a search warrant?

Hörður is looking around for something to use to spring open the lid of the chest, when he sets eyes on one of the photographs hanging on the walls of the office. Or … it's more than one. On one wall is a whole series of photographs that are almost all the same, taken at the same place, but at different times.

He steps closer and takes a better look at the photos.

In all of them, groups of boys are either sitting or standing in front of summer houses or cabins. Most of the boys are wearing shorts and t-shirts, all of which are embroidered with the logo of the YMCA.

The summer camp at Vatnaskógur.

Hörður scrutinizes the photos, examines the dates and narrows down his search. After a few moments, he finds the right photo, and then the boy he was looking for. There he is, Guðmundur Vífill Marínósson, around ten or eleven years old. Mummi is sitting in the front row, noticeably small and looking completely miserable. The boy standing behind him has his hand on Mummi's shoulder. It's a slim boy with black hair, high cheekbones and piercing eyes.

Aron Beck.

With the boys in the picture is a young man wearing a Scouting uniform. Some sort of leader. In the back row stands an adult male, partially shadowed by the awning of the building behind them. The man is blond, tanned, and bearded. He's wearing a gray suit and black shirt with a clerical collar.

Reverend Ingimar Jósefsson.

Hörður runs his eyes over the group of boys—over their innocent faces, some of which look as if they've seen a lot for their age; others appear sad, and some distressed. What memories did they bring back home with them from that summer vacation?

Hörður thinks he's found Tryggvi Leó, and perhaps Egill Þór, too. But he's not certain. Maybe they were all there, the anarchists. Maybe just a portion of them. But did the pastor rape them all? Or just some of them?

Would that change anything?

Hörður takes the photo down from the wall and wipes the dust off it. He lays the frame face-down on the desk, removes the back and takes out the photograph. The computer emits a familiar beep. He looks at the screen. The computer is asking for a password.

Typical!

Hörður shuts off the computer. At the same moment, the front door opens with a click. The hairs rise on the back of the police officer's neck, and it's as if the blood clots in his veins.

Reverend Ingimar has come home.

Hörður hears footsteps, the jangling of keys and a stifled cough. What should he do? What *can* he do?

Run?

Hide?

His heart pounds in his chest and he breaks out in a sweat. He broke into someone's house, and is about to be caught in the act. What the hell was he thinking?

From below comes the sound of running water, and then the clatter of crockery. The pastor is doing something in the kitchen. Having a glass of water or making coffee.

Hörður bites his lower lip.

Should he wait between hope and fear?

Or turn defense into offense?

He looks at his watch. Time is slipping away. He's got to do something. He's working, he's a *police officer*! Break-in or not, authorization or not—he's not going to let an old sexual offender frighten him!

With that thought in mind, he plucks up his courage, takes the photo and leaves the office with it, then marches down the creaking wooden stairs like a circus elephant heading into the ring.

In the kitchen someone slams down a glass, and the feet of a chair scratch along the floor. The pastor has become aware of this visitor—the uninvited guest who addresses him authoritatively before he appears in the hall.

"Ingimar Jósefsson!"

The pastor doesn't respond. He rushes out of the kitchen, but stops abruptly when he sets eyes on the red-haired giant towering over him.

"Who are you?" barks the old man. "And what are you doing here?"

Hörður stares at the man, but doesn't answer.

Ingimar is rather tall himself. His hair is white and he has a white beard that's poorly groomed and yellowish around his mouth. His face is pale and swollen, his nose is veiny, and his eyes are bloodshot. At one time, he must have been fit, but that time has passed.

"Haven't I had enough?" the pastor yells. "When will the police stop persecuting me and my family? When will this end?"

"What are you talking about?" asks Hörður. Then he remembers that Gísli Már is the pastor's nephew.

"This is my home!" Ingimar splutters with rage—or is it fright? The pastor notices the photograph. "What's that you've got there?"

"I'm with the police," says Hörður.

"You don't say!" says the pastor, his voice trembling with rage or fear. "But you have no right to be here!"

"The back door was open," says Hörður.

Ingimar looks over his shoulder. "That's a lie! I ..."

Hörður raises his left hand to silence him. "You may frighten little boys, but I'm not one of them."

The pastor is about to say something, but stops. He stares at the police officer with eyes overflowing with malice and disgust.

Hörður shows him the photograph. "I came here to gather information for a case that I'm investigating. I'm taking this photo with me as evidence."

"On whose authority?" asks Ingimar. "If you don't have a warrant, I'll press charges against you for burglary and theft!"

"You want me to get an official warrant?" asks Hörður in return. "That's not a problem, on my part.

For example, I would like to have a look inside your trunk. The one up in your office. And the hard drive on your computer."

The pastor opens his mouth, but shuts it again. He has bad breath, there are dark shadows in his glaucoma-damaged eyes, and there's yellowish spittle at the corners of his mouth. The man is a monster. An old, filthy monster.

Hörður is disgusted. He wonders where this monster took the boys at Vatnaskógur? To his room? Or to the chapel?

"What did you do to those boys?" asks Hörður coldly. "Did you touch them? Or did you make them touch you? How far did you go?"

"The case was dismissed," says Ingimar hoarsely.

Hörður snorts, goes to the entrance, and opens the front door. "You'll get your photo back."

"When?" asks the pastor confrontationally.

Hörður turns around in the doorway when an unexpected thought pops into his head. "I found a photograph in Guðmundur Vífill's personal belongings. A photo of him, taken in Vatnaskógur when he was a child. Do you know who took the photo? Was it his mom or dad?"

The pastor looks at the police officer as if he were the devil himself, but doesn't answer him.

"Did you take it, maybe?" Hörður asks.

"Go to hell," mutters Ingimar.

"You too," says Hörður, before slamming the door behind him. He shudders, and hurries back to the car. He has a bad taste in his mouth and tries spitting to get rid of it. The first thing he does after getting back in the SUV is light a cigarette.

It's at moments such as these that he wishes there were a God. That there were a Heaven—and a Hell. That there were both purpose and justice in the world, and that there were a place reserved in Hell for people like Reverend Ingimar Jósefsson.

Hörður walks back and forth in the corridor in front of the Swimming Pool, the CID's interrogation room, with his stack of papers in one hand and the hollowed-out dictionary in the other, beads of sweat on his pale forehead and a queasy stomach. He's waiting for Axel and Engilbert, whom he hasn't seen since their lunch of lamb curry at a corner table of the cafeteria. There, he'd told them about the work that he'd done that morning and handed them a printed summary, which they barely looked at. He didn't, however, tell them about his visit to Ingimar's house, and hoped like hell that the pastor hadn't already filed charges against him for breaking and entering. He only told them that he'd found the photo from Vatnaskógur at the Good Shepherd, which was a kind of half-truth. Axel and Engilbert were mainly interested in the possible origin of the knives, and were going to send a police officer to pick up some knives from Einar's meat-packing facility in order to make comparisons. They were least interested in the Vatnaskógur angle, and the fact that Gísli Már was the grandson of the man whom Mummi accused of sexual misconduct. Too weak, too far-fetched, in their opinion.

They were about to interrogate Aron regarding his relationship with the two wanted perpetrators and the two murders, and therefore their entire focus should be on those ties, and then, number one two and three on the *physical* connections, as Axel put it.

Then Hörður was sent back down to prepare himself better—to fill in any holes and make their case no less than airtight, to quote Axel once more. Hörður wasn't given so much as one little compliment, not even an indirect one, let alone any encouragement, a smile or a pat on the back. The only kudo was getting to sit with them at the corner table, which is Axel's table.

The curry hasn't sat well with Hörður, who's more for boiled haddock and potatoes, and instead of focusing on the work that he was asked to do, he has already spent an hour and a half running to the toilet every seven minutes, where he squirms and sweats as his digestive system and intestines empty with a vengeance.

Hörður looks at his watch. It's three minutes past two, and as far as he knows, Aron Beck is waiting for them in the windowless interrogation room, along with two police officers. Despite his arm being broken and weighing hardly more than eighty kilograms, the anarchist is on the Police Commissioner's list of the country's ten most dangerous criminals. He's both devious and unpredictable, and is serving a sentence for crimes against the government authorities.

Hörður takes a deep breath and tries to calm his nerves and his upset stomach. He feels like an actor a few minutes before a premiere. He's never interrogated anyone before, just written dry reports for traffic offenses and public drunkenness. Now it's the big stage—a murder investigation and a serious criminal, smug, a smooth talker, and capable of anything.

Has the interrogation already begun? Hörður is about to knock on the door when he hears footsteps. Axel M. Axelsson and Engilbert Gústafsson approach quickly, as focused and concentrated as professional football players, despite the two men being different in appearance and demeanor. Axel is dressed elegantly, as if on his way to mass, and is wearing a nice cologne. Engilbert is unkempt and scruffy, like the main character from a thriller by Raymond Chandler, with bloodshot eyes and a match between his dry lips.

"Well then," says Engilbert.

Axel hands Hörður a yellow folder. "For your papers. So they don't end up all over the floor."

"Thanks," says Hörður, hoarse from stress. He places the dictionary between his thighs, opens the folder, slips the untidy stack of papers into it and snaps the elastic bands around it.

"We have the results from the blood sample that was taken from Sólrún, as well as the samples from her girl-friends, Edda Bæringsdóttir and Jóna Andrésdóttir," says Axel. "Of course, the results of the analysis of the two girlfriends' blood aren't really reliable, as the samples were taken approximately twelve hours after they met at Kaffibarinn. But the results match up, which is a good sign. They all had a small amount of alcohol in their blood and just a *trace* of GHB—next to nothing, really."

"Yet still a trace," says Hörður.

"Yes, which is far better than nothing," says Axel. The good thing is that this corroborates their testimony. They appear not to have been drunk at all."

"Shall we?" Engilbert points to the closed door.

"Betti and I will direct the interrogation," says Axel. "I'll be sitting opposite the witness, and you'll be to my right. I'll let you speak now and then. Just keep calm and take all the time you need. Time is on our side. We'll speak slowly, pause for effect, and say nothing, if necessary—draw things out. Instead of pressing the witness, we'll bore him, and encourage him to speak by indirectly letting him put in a word or two. Few people can endure silence for very long. Are you in?"

Hörður nods. He drinks in every word. He's being given his own personal masterclass in police science and doesn't want to miss anything.

"Then let's get to it." Axel opens the door and lets Engilbert and Hörður precede him into the room.

The scene is a greenish blue; the color reminds him of the water in swimming pools, which makes the room appear bigger than it really is—it almost seems as if it would be possible to swim into the walls and disappear into the deep. In the middle of the room is a simple table, square, on metal legs. Aron Beck is sitting at one side of the table, flanked by two uniformed police officers, and he smirks as he watches the three men walk in. He's wearing black sweatpants and a black, glossy sports shirt that's so tight-fitting it seems glued to him. He has shaved off his hair and eyebrows; his head is as hairless and smooth as a baby's bottom and his flared nostrils give him a snake-like appearance, while his staring eyes appear to have expanded in size. Around his neck hangs the knucklebone with the rune on it. His left forearm is still in a cast, which has something scribbled on it.

On the table are a digital recording device, a notepad and pencils.

"A three-person delegation, no less," says the anarchist. "Led by none other than Steppenwolf, freshly shaven and looking sharp. I'm honored—I really must admit. I can't complain."

Aron smiles widely and pretends to be relaxed, but his muscles twitch slightly here and there, and there's a touch of both suspicion and angry fear in his eyes

"Thank you for coming," says Axel as he sits down in the folding chair in the middle. Engilbert and Hörður sit down next to him. "You're here as a witness, as I'm sure you know. This interrogation is formal, but you're not in custody for this crime. Not for the moment."

"I apologize for this, but my friend Bibbi wrote it," says Aron, showing them his cast. The sentence that's been scribbled on it in black marker is:

COPS ARE PIGS

"Very mature," mutters Engilbert.

"Were you drinking yesterday, Betti?" Aron asks cheerfully. The detective lets his words go in one ear and out the other.

Hörður lays the dictionary and the folder on the table in front of him. Aron glances at the book, and his jaw muscle twitches.

"You're also allowed to have a lawyer present," says Axel. "If you'd like."

"I'm good," says Aron. "I haven't done anything wrong, and I've got nothing to hide."

"Very well," says Axel.

Aron runs his eyes over the three men. "But wouldn't it have been better to have at least one woman here? For the gender quota, you know. This won't look good on paper."

"We'll ask the questions here." Axel turns on the recorder and states the date and year, the name of the witness and the names of the interrogators.

"Witness?" Aron looks menacingly at the head of the CID. "Witness to what, if I might ask?"

"We'll ask the questions here." Axel clears his throat. "Do you know either Tryggvi Leó Helgason or Egill Þór Birgisson?"

Aron blinks. "I'm familiar with them, yes. As you know."

"They're wanted on suspicion of involvement in two murders," says Axel. "I'm sure you're aware of this. That they're wanted. The murders can hardly have escaped your notice."

Aron shrugs and blinks.

"You don't have any opinion on this?" asks Engilbert. "Your friends are wanted for murder. You don't care? Do you think they're guilty? Or innocent?"

Aron says nothing. He just looks at the detective as if he were a boring television program.

Hörður fidgets in his seat. He feels that this interrogation is starting off badly, that Axel's original plan has already been turned over on its head. Maybe old Steppenwolf has lost his mojo.

"They'll be caught," says Axel. "And they'll be found guilty of two counts of murder, and of conspiracy to commit a third. Evidence will be found on them that not only links them to these deeds, but also to you, the ringleader and brains behind these horrific acts."

"Whatever." Aron pretends to yawn. "You're a treat. What evidence is that, might I ask?"

"The knives with which the murders were committed are from your grandfather's meat-packing company," says Axel. "Where you and Guðmundur Vífill worked as teenagers."

Aron snorts. "All the meat-packing companies use the same knives. You've got to be kidding! You think you'll find *my* fingerprints on those knives? I'm in jail, in case you hadn't noticed."

"This won't look good in court," says Axel calmly. "When building a case, all such connections matter a great deal.

They add to the credibility of the charges, and at the time weaken the defense's case."

Aron sighs. "I have no idea what Tryggvi and Egill have been doing or not doing in the past weeks or months. But you can't pin crimes on me that are committed while I'm locked up. Such charges will never look good in the courtroom, old man."

"The knives aren't all," says Axel.

"Whatever," says Aron.

"Hörður, would you like to take over now?" asks Axel, but the question is of course not that, but an order.

Aron looks at Hörður. "You look familiar. Have we met?"

The police officer clears his throat. He feels warm, and the uneasiness in his stomach makes its presence known again. "As Axel pointed out, it's not just the knives that connect you to the alleged perpetrators and the two killings. On Tuesday, I went out on a call. An old skull was found among some personal belongings stored at Grandi. There, among other things, I found this dictionary here, which has been hollowed out inside. In the empty space was a bag of blue ecstasy tablets—the same type of ecstasy tablets that were found in the possession of those who committed the two murders."

"Oh, right," says Aron. "You've got the two murderers in custody. So why are you looking for Tryggvi and Egill?"

"We'll get to that later," says Engilbert. "Go on, Hörður."

"Yes, so ..." Hörður wipes the sweat from his forehead. "The same type of ecstasy tablets were found and ..."

Aron interrupts him. "You said that Mummi owned the stuff in the storage unit. What does the X have to do with me?"

"Things belonging to you were found among his possessions," says Hörður. "Books with your name in them. At least one book. A handbook on hypnosis. You're familiar with it, right?"

Aron looks straight at the police officer. "No. I've never had such a book."

Hörður can't help but smile. "You can't deny it. I returned the book to you yesterday."

"No, you didn't," says Aron. "But now I remember you. You were doing something there at Litla-Hraun."

"You returned the book to him?" asks Axel in surprise.

"Yes, I …" Hörður clears his throat again. "Though naturally, I didn't know then that it was evidence."

Aron throws up his hands. "I don't know what book you're talking about."

"Your cell is being searched right now," says Engilbert. "The prison officers have undoubtedly found the book."

Aron grins. "No, because there is no book."

"There are witnesses," Hörður says hoarsely. "My partner Vigfús saw the book. As did the prison officer who let me into your cellblock."

"What officer was that?" asks Aron.

Hörður blushes. "I can't remember. He didn't introduce himself. It was a young man. I would recognize him again."

Aron shakes his head. "I'm sorry to say it, dear fellows, but none of what you're saying holds water."

Axel grunts softly.

"The ecstasy tablets are a fact," says Hörður. "They connect you to …"

"Hold on, hold on!" Aron raises his hand and silences the police officer. "You said you found the X on Tuesday, but you didn't say anything about it when we chatted yesterday. Why not?"

"The dictionary was found on Tuesday," says Hörður. "But the tablets weren't found until yesterday. After we went to Litla-Hraun."

"That sounds pretty strange," says Aron.

Engilbert clears his throat, as if to agree with the witness. Axel curses under his breath.

"Tell me something else," says Aron. "Was the search through Mummi's stuff formal? Were this dictionary, and with it the X, taken from the scene as evidence, and recorded as such?"

Hörður's face reddens. "No, because we didn't know then that ..."

"What kind of fucking circus is this?" ask Aron irritatedly. "Are you just fucking with me? Or are you just completely fucking incompetent?"

"You'd better watch what you say," says Axel angrily.

"The thing is this," says Hörður, his voice shaky from stress. "Your friends spike innocent people's drinks with GHB and then hypnotize them and order them to commit murder. These people are hypnotized according to your instructions, or by using a recording that you made. You've killed an MP and a judge, and next is probably a police officer, because you're attacking the great Enemy with a capital E that you talked about in your interview with *DV*—the three-headed giant that's the symbol of the separation of powers into three branches, whose initials are tattooed on your arm: l, j, and e—the legislative, judicial, and executive branches."

Aron laughs loudly. "What a fantasy! First of all, I'm behind bars, and haven't had any communication with anyone outside of prison. Second, I don't know how to hypnotize people and never have. Third, that interview you're referring to is complete bullshit from A to Z. And fourth, this isn't an 'e' in my tattoo, but an 'a', as everyone can see—in other words, 'l j a,' which, if you want to know, stands for League of Junior Anarchists—an unofficial nickname I gave to our gang, you know—and not what you said, copper."

"Bullshit." Hörður leans forward and looks at the tattoo. It still looks to him like an 'e', but the middle line connects close enough to the bottom for it to be read as a kind of 'a'. "This is an 'e,' for 'executive'—but aren't leagues or federations contrary to the spirit of anarchy?"

"Some cop tried to sell Mindless Fribbi a bag of blue X tablets yesterday," says Aron, out of the blue. "Was that you? Or your partner? Is that the reason why you didn't say anything about the X? You were going to sell it?"

Hörður's face pales. "How do you know this? Locked up, as you are. Do you have a phone in your cell, maybe?"

Aron looks away. "No. But news like that gets around, from one person to another. It's just something I heard, you know … through the grapevine, as they say."

"What's he talking about?" asks Axel.

"He's just spewing venom." Hörður feels slightly fearful, but also angry, and he allows his anger to break through and smother his fear. "Pay no attention to what this viper says. This slippery bastard thinks that …"

"Hörður," says Axel, in a paternal tone.

"I'm sorry, I …" The police officer takes a deep breath. "He's just fucking with us. He wants to make me angry and …"

Aron smirks devilishly.

"Take a little break," says Axel, softly. "Engilbert and I will continue."

"Of course." Hörður stands up clumsily. He accidentally knocks over his foldable chair, stands it back up and hurries to the door. It isn't until he's in the corridor and has shut the door behind him that he realizes he's left his folder on the table.

But it doesn't matter. Nothing matters anymore. He blew it. The opportunity slipped through his fingers.

Hörður goes up to the cafeteria on the third floor. It's empty, apart from the employees who are finishing washing the dishes. He wants nothing more than to swallow an entire glass of sleeping pills, but the opposite will have to do—old, pitch-black, workplace coffee. Holding a cup of the stuff, he strolls over the freshly mopped floor and plunks down in a seat by the window.

Aron Beck showed up much better prepared than him. He'd knocked all the weapons out of the police officer's hands, undermined his credibility, overwhelmed him and thrown him entirely off balance.

Hörður hides his face in his hands. Why hadn't he foreseen this? How could he be so stupid?

He feels numb; his mouth is dry and his heart is racing, as if he's had an accident or experienced some other kind of shock. Which is indeed the case. He won't get an opportunity like this again. That's just how it is. His dream of joining the CID has turned into a nightmare.

A promotion? His career? He can forget these things.

Hörður takes a sip of the bad-tasting coffee. He looks out the window and tries to distract himself. The view isn't very exciting—Hlemmtorg Square, asphalt, buses, and

Rauðarárstígur Road. The only beautiful house in sight is the old gas station, which is like a radiant drop in an ocean of spiritless, concrete blocks. The Hemmur bus station is one of the country's ugliest buildings. Reykjavik is in fact a rather ugly city, poorly organized, and cold. Not just cold as in gray and spiritless, but literally so windy and cold that its residents prefer not to leave their houses, and when they're forced to, it's in cars that they drive straight out of their garages.

Concrete, cold and dust.

Necropolis—the city of the dead.

Hörður is drinking coffee that's like tar: liquid darkness. He's full of darkness. Soon the winter darkness will lie heaviest over the city—when it will be dark more or less all day, every day.

Depression, darkness and frost.

Just splendid.

He slurps his tar coffee and stares indifferently out the window. Damn, he wants a cigarette. A blue car is parked in front of the police station, not far from the old gas station. It looks to be a twenty-year-old Volvo. An old man steps out the car, gray-haired and with a full beard, dressed in light-colored coat. He opens the rear door and takes a red sports bag from the back seat. The old man shuts the door and locks the car, then looks up at the building before going to the main entrance.

Hörður's eyes open wide. Damn it! It's Reverend Ingimar, of all people. What does he want?

Is he going to press charges against Hörður for breaking into his house?

Hörður gets up from the table, so stressed that he sees everything in a haze and can barely keep his balance. He leaves the cafeteria and takes the elevator down to the first floor, where it opens onto a landing. He hears Ingimar before he opens the door to the lobby. The old man is arguing with the police officer behind the glass.

"… and I demand a proper explanation!" says Ingimar angrily.

Hörður closes the door behind him and walks hesitantly toward reception.

"Excuse me, is there anything I can do to help?"

Ingimar turns around. "You!"

The old man is furious, and for a moment he seems about to attack Hörður, who is prepared for anything.

The police officer behind the glass throws up his hands. "I don't understand what this is all about."

"I just want an explanation!" yells Ingimar, who is highly agitated. His eyes are about to pop out of his head and he trembles with agitation. "Why does my family have to suffer? First, my nephew is arrested, and now my granddaughter. Suspected of murder? What's this madness supposed to mean?"

"Wait." Hörður can hardly believe his ears. "Is Sólrún your granddaughter?"

"She's my son Davíð's daughter, yes," says Ingimar impatiently. "I've brought her some clothes. Ideally, I'd prefer to take her home with me, but you won't let her go. What's wrong with you people?"

"I've got to go." Hörður opens the door to the staircase with his card, leaves the lobby and shuts the door behind him. The pastor shouts something after him but he can't hear what it is.

He enters the communal work area, goes and gets the photograph from Vatnaskógur, and takes the elevator to the third floor. He runs down the corridor and knocks pro forma on the door of the Swimming Pool before opening it and going in of his own accord.

The interrogation room is stuffy and warm. Aron looks up with an arrogant expression and gives Hörður the evil eye.

"What's the meaning of this?" Axel asks brusquely. "You can't just rush in like this in the middle of an interrogation!"

"Sorry," says Hörður as he sits back down on his foldable chair. He lays the photograph face-down on the table in front of him. "But there's a reason for my rudeness. A very good reason."

"And that is?" asks Axel.

"I have new information. Important information," says Hörður, staring hard at Aron, who looks away and rocks in his seat, as if having a sudden hot flash—he's like a snake, coiling up when threatened.

"I'm not sure this is a good idea." Axel frowns and crosses his stout arms.

"Trust me," says Hörður. He pulls the elastic bands off the folder, takes out his papers, and finds the printout of the newspaper interview. He clears his throat before reading a short excerpt from the interview: "*The rich are made richer, ownership is nothing but violence in the form of laws, public assets are raffled off to the chosen few and criminal complaints filed in response to the rape of children and teenagers are dismissed because the offenses are past the statute of limitations! In return, I ask: When does the shame pass the statute of limitations, when do the damage and the pain become null and void?* Are you familiar with these words?"

Aron snorts.

"It's a direct quotation from the witness in an interview published in *DV*," says Hörður. "In the interview, Aron outlines what he believes to be wrong with the society in which we live. The anarchist's criticism is threefold, and he blames the separation of powers for everything he finds wrong, especially the legislative and judicial branches. The first two targets of his criticism are of a general nature, but the third, which is about the statute of limitations on sexual offenses against children, is more passionate than the others, and seems personal. And in fact, the reporter asks the interviewee if he's referring to a particular case. Aron answers, and here's another direct quotation: *Yes and no; this happens on a daily basis. And it doesn't matter whether it's women or men who file complaints. Children don't file complaints, they're scared, and feel threatened and intimidated by their abusers. But when they come of age, have matured and gained courage, then, perhaps, they may step forth, but only to be humiliated again. Whereas the abusers go free and continue to work, teach, and proclaim the word of God. May they all burn in Hell, if Hell in fact exists.*

"And?" asks Aron, irritably.

"*And proclaim the word of God,*" Hörður repeats.

"I think it would be best for you to inform the witness as to where you're taking this," says Engilbert.

"Thirteen months ago, three young men pressed charges against Reverend Ingimar Jósefsson for sexual offenses that took place when they were teenagers at summer camp in Vatnaskógur," says Hörður. "These men's names are Guðmundur Vífill, better known as Little Mummi, Tryggvi Leó and Orri Atlason."

Aron blinks.

Hörður taps his finger on the photo accompanying the interview. "They were all part of the group of squatters on Vatnsstígur. All of them are friends of Aron Beck, and belonged to his anarchist gang."

"And?" asks Aron again, irritation is gradually turning to fury. Engilbert seems agitated, but Axel gestures to him to steady himself. Steppenwolf's curiosity has clearly been aroused.

Hörður turns over the photograph from Vatnaskógur. "They were of course together at Vatnaskógur, as well—but also there was our witness, Aron Beck, along with Egill Þór, the other man wanted in relation to the murder of the MP and the judge."

Aron laughs coldly. "Where are you going with this, copper?"

"I ask the witness to answer questions, but otherwise keep quiet," says Axel. "Go on, Hörður."

"Thanks," says Hörður. "Reverend Ingimar was convicted for sexual offenses against a young man and is therefore hardly innocent of the charges that were dismissed. I find it fairly likely that other boys besides the three who pressed charges were raped at Vatnaskógur. Perhaps Aron was also raped, as well as Egill Þór."

Aron Beck's face reddens and his eyes flash with anger. "I refuse to sit here and listen to this bullshit!"

"Calm down," says Axel, in a paternal tone.

"But this is only speculation," says Hörður. "What, on the other hand, is a fact, is that the two murders committed this morning and on Tuesday night weren't directed first and foremost against the separation of powers, but against Ingimar Jósefsson."

"What's that?" blurts out Engilbert.

"Go on," says Axel.

"The victims aren't the main issue, but rather, the unwilling subjects who wielded the knives," says Hörður. "Gísli Már is Reverend Ingimar's nephew, and Solrún is his granddaughter."

The match drops from Engilbert's lips. Axel does a slightly better job of concealing his astonishment.

Hörður nods. "They weren't chosen randomly, but because of these blood relations. Their drinks were spiked with GHB, and they were abducted and hypnotized. They were forced to commit murder to make Ingimar Jósefsson suffer."

Aron laughs coldly. "Why would anyone kill someone just to take revenge on someone else? Why not just kill this Ingimar?"

"Good question," says Hörður. Once again, he turns to the interview in *DV.* "And here is the answer, in your own words. *The system is like a mean-spirited kid who pulls the wings off of flies just to see them suffer. Things are boxed but not forgotten. When the Revolution takes place and the oppressed come to power, the oppressors will not be squashed like bugs, but instead, they'll be given a taste of their own medicine.* End quote."

Aron throws up his hands. "This interview isn't proof of anything! I'm in jail. I haven't come close to any of the things you're accusing me of. If you don't stop this harassment, I'll sue you for … for harassment."

"Easy there, friend," says Axel in a deep voice.

"One question." Aron takes a deep breath. "If the choice of the so-called subjects wasn't random, how on earth did the wanted men find precisely the people they were looking for only a few days apart? It sounds pretty far-fetched."

"Hörður?" says Axel.

"It sounds far-fetched, certainly, but it's anything but that, when you look at it closer," says Hörður. "Gísli Már is an active member of the Arsenal Fan Club, which is why it was known beforehand that he would be at Ölver that evening, as always when Arsenal has a big match. And I understand that Sólrún and her girlfriends customarily met at Kaffibarinn on Thursdays to dance. Right?"

Engilbert nods. "That's correct."

"In other words …" Hörður taps his stack of papers into shape and sticks them back in the folder. "Our case couldn't be clearer. The murders were organized by Aron Beck and carried out as I've described. The motive was first and foremost to torment Ingimar Jósefsson, the torturer of those same boys, but also to deliver a blow to the government and cause havoc and dissolution in society."

"What bullshit!" spits Aron. "Do I really have to sit here and listen to such crap? I've had it up to here with you—and then some! Will you please drive me back to Litla-Hraun now? I feel filthy, and really need to take a shower."

"You'll have to wait a bit for that, young man," says Axel. He smiles apologetically at the witness, then directs his attention to the police officers standing to cither side of him. "Take this man downstairs and lock him up. You know the protocol."

Aron sits up. "Wait! What the hell are you saying, man?"

"You no longer have the status of witness," says Axel. "You will be formally charged with the murders of Þórólfur Hannesson and Aðalsteinn Kvaran, in addition to being under suspicion of the planning of more murders. You'll be taken to a judge later today. I'll be asking for a remand of a week to start with. That's all for now. This interrogation is over."

"Stand up," says one of the police officers. Aron obeys reluctantly, and the officers cuff his hands behind his back.

"You," says the anarchist. He stares hard at Hörður, his eyes black with hatred and fury.

"Remove this man," says Axel. The officers obey; one of them opens the door to the corridor and the other pushes Aron ahead of him through the doorway.

"You haven't heard the last of me!" shouts the anarchist, before the door is shut.

Engilbert, Axel and Hörður remain sitting there, staring silently at nothing. It isn't until Aron Beck is gone from the room that they realize how overwhelming his presence is, whether he speaks or says nothing. On the one hand, he's aggressive in both word and demeanor, tense as a taut spring and staring at everything and everyone like a predator on the prowl for a kill, and on the other hand, he's like a kind of human black hole that sucks in all energy, all light, and all life without having to lift a finger.

"Tiresome fellow," says Engilbert, to break the silence.

Nodding in agreement, Axel reaches for the recorder and switches it off.

Hörður looks at his watch. It's five minutes to three. His shift ends at three. But he's more than willing to do overtime today. He just saved his own neck, and with style, at that, and he'll eat his own hat if Axel doesn't throw him a bone in the form of a compliment or kudo of some sort.

"That went pretty well," he says, just to say something.

"I wouldn't really say that," says Engilbert tiredly. "In actuality, we've got next to nothing on the bastard."

"This could have been much worse," says Axel. "But could have been better, too. We definitely have a long way to go in terms of burden of proof, that's for sure."

"Maybe he's just innocent," says Engilbert. "It's not entirely impossible that Tryggvi and Egill are acting alone. And this hypnosis theory is both far-fetched and weak. We don't even have that damn book, let alone other evidence. In fact, our case against Aron is based on speculation, and nothing else."

Axel sighs. "Yes. That's correct."

Hörður sinks deflatedly in his chair, like a balloon whose air is let out. And there he thought that they were pleased, that the interrogation had gone as planned and Aron was in deep shit. He clearly has a lot to learn.

"How did you find this out about Sólrún?" asks Axel. "That she's the granddaughter of Reverend Ingimar?"

"Ingimar was down in the lobby earlier," says Hörður. "He was bringing clothes for Sólrún, and complaining about the way the police are treating his family."

"I hope he doesn't take this to the media," says Axel pensively. "It's best that I contact him later, try to calm him down."

"What was that about the ecstasy tablets?" asks Engilbert. "Aron said that a police officer tried to sell Mindless Fribbi blue ecstasy tablets. He's most likely talking about Friðbjörn on Hverfisgata."

Hörður groans, as if he's been punched in the stomach.

"Is there any truth to this?" asks Axel cautiously.

"Sadly, yes," replies Hörður, hoarsely. "But I was able to prevent the transaction. I don't know what Vigfús was thinking, but I promised him that I would keep it to myself.

He didn't realize that the tablets were connected to the murders."

"That man is a fucking idiot," says Engilbert.

"There are always a few rotten apples in every barrel," mutters Axel.

"Unfortunately."

"What happens next?" asks Hörður softly.

Engilbert clears his throat. "I'm going to question two of the bartenders who were working at Kaffibarinn last night, as well as one of the bouncers. I'm thinking we should set up a photo lineup and see whether they pick Tryggvi and Egill out of photos of ten or twelve similar-looking men. I'll also try to get something out of Sólrún—and then I have to write up a few reports. But I guess I'll start by visiting the morgue and getting the results of the autopsy."

"Is that German woman here in Iceland?" asks Axel.

Engilbert nods. "She arrived on the noon plane on Wednesday, to do an autopsy on Þórólfur. She has two other autopsies to do, a suicide and a hospital death. She was supposed to be going home today, but delayed her flight, of course."

"Right," mumbles Axel.

"That German woman?" asks Hörður.

"Our forensic pathologist," explains Axel. "No Icelander has been trained in the subject for decades. So we have to send for experts from abroad."

"I see," mutters Hörður.

Axel looks at his gold watch. "Yes, well. I need to go meet with the prosecution before Aron is brought before the judge. But I'll start by calling the pastor. And then *Spotlight* wants to interview me tonight, live. I can't say I'm excited about that, but in light of the circumstances, I find it difficult to say no. Fortunately, I should be able to ease the concerns of both the media and the public a bit. Not to mention if Tryggvi and Egill are found before the broadcast."

"They'll be found," says Engilbert.

"But what about this with Vigfús and the ecstasy tablets?" asks Hörður.

Axel curses. "We'll be watching him in the future. He's off the hook for now, at least officially. If we start an investigation and it leaks to the media, it will only weaken our case even more, besides damage the police force's credibility."

"I see," says Hörður. He feels relieved. "I highly doubt he'll ever do something like that again."

"I certainly hope not," says Axel.

"Listen," says Hörður hesitantly. "If you want, I can go with you to your meeting. With the prosecution. If I can be of any help."

"Yeah. No. That's unnecessary," says Axel. "Your shift is over for today. But thanks anyway. You did great. The meeting is just a formality. I'll give the prosecutor on duty details of the case, and then we'll see how things go."

You did great. Hörður finds it hard not to jump up and celebrate like some idiot at a football match. Where Steppenwolf is concerned, this compliment must surely score a seven or eight on a scale of one to ten. He wants more than anything to have the compliment printed on a t-shirt.

The kudo boosts his courage. "Please don't misunderstand me, but the reason that I'd like to go to this meeting with you is that I'm worried that the prosecution will focus too much on the physical evidence, or on the lack of it, rather, while ignoring the larger context, which might be called the social one and is based on the world view that Aron expounds in his interview in *DV*."

"The social one?" exclaims Engilbert.

"What are you talking about?" asks Axel.

"On the one hand, these murders are a form of retaliation against the sexual offenses that the perpetrators experienced as adolescents," says Hörður. "When the charges were dismissed thirteen months ago, this ball began to roll; the thirst for revenge manifested itself and the plan gradually began taking shape in the head of the ringleader, the victim Aron Beck. On the other hand, the murders are a political performance rooted in the ideology of Aron Beck the anarchist. The motivation for it is personal, but the plan is political, *social*, and its consequences harm the society that the anarchists resent so much. In their eyes, the government is a tool of society that's founded on democracy. They're devotees of anarchy, and want to bring it about. This political angle is important, in my opinion. Aron is the brains behind all this, the ideologue and prime mover. I would highly emphasize these factors in our arguments, because a case that's based on a dry murder charge rather than ideology is too narrow, and therewith too weak, as you've pointed out. We don't have any hard evidence to rely on, which is why we need to base the charge on these social factors—on a political conspiracy."

"You watch too much TV," says Engilbert.

"I understand what you are getting at," says Axel pontifically. "But I can tell you in advance that the prosecution has neither any interest in the social aspects of such a serious accusation, nor the time to bring such a case before a judge who can't wait to get home for the weekend."

"Fine then," says Hörður. "But isn't it complicated to charge a person with murder when that person played no direct part in it? You know, theoretically."

"Not at all," says Engilbert. "Not theoretically. Unless you can't fulfill the burden of proof."

"Organizing something and assigning others to carry it out is as serious as carrying it out yourself," says Axel, as if instructing a student. "Aron will be charged with the murders, as the main perpetrator. And secondarily, he'll be charged as an accomplice. Tryggvi and Egill will be charged as accomplices, and secondarily as the main perpetrators. The three men's joint involvement would probably be classified legally as a conspiracy, which always carries stiffer penalties."

"I see," says Hörður. "But what if nothing is found in Tryggvi and Egill's possession that would implicate Aron in the case? He appears to have destroyed the book on hypnosis. Maybe nothing was found in his cell."

"If no substantial evidence is found, we're on slippery ice," says Axel. "Then we'll be forced to rely on Tryggvi's confession, or Egill's, or that of the both of them. We'll try to make them suspicious of each other, so that at least one of them is tempted to turn on the other in the hope of a plea bargain. But if they either refuse to talk or take the blame, I'm afraid that Aron will slip through our fingers. He's as slippery as an eel and our nets are in very bad need of mending, unfortunately."

"I'm sure something will be found," mutters Hörður. He hates himself for having given Aron back his book on hypnosis. What was he thinking?

"There's still one thing I need to do," says Engilbert. "Call Litla-Hraun and find out if anything was found in Aron's cell."

"Yes, let's stop mucking about." Axel stands up, followed by Engilbert and Hörður.

"In regard to the pastor," says Hörður hesitantly. "I actually got the group photo from him, the one from Vatnaskógur. But it's possible that I acquired it by, how shall I say it, unconventional methods."

Axel sighs. "Unauthorized, you mean?"

"Something like that," mutters Hörður.

Axel shrugs. "I'll handle it. Don't worry."

"Thanks," mutters Hörður.

Engilbert opens the door to the corridor.

"Listen," says Hörður, as they exit the room. "Is there any chance you can let me know how it goes? I've become involved in the case, and … am pretty excited about it, to tell you the truth."

Axel nods, and pats Engilbert on his shoulder. "Would you give Hörður a call this afternoon, when we know a little more?

"Yeah, I guess," replies Engilbert grumpily. "But I can't promise anything."

"Thanks," says Hörður, lifting his folder in his right hand in a goodbye gesture. In his left hand, he holds the dictionary.

Axel and Engilbert proceed west down the long corridor, in the direction of the research department. Full of envy and admiration, Hörður watches them, then goes to the elevator and takes it down to the first floor. They'll be working late in Hörður's Promised Land, even until the middle of night, whereas he's about to sign out like any old office worker.

When Hörður goes to open his locker in the changing room, he realizes that he's still holding the yellow folder, with all his papers in it. He looks at the folder and wonders what he should do with it. Let Axel have it? Put it in the closet?

Take it home?

The greatest thing about Iceland is its water. Its weather is awful. The winter darkness is hellish. And despite the summers being quite nice, they're far too short, and sometimes it rains all the time. Iceland's national character is bourgeois, its culture can be fit into a sandbox and the small population ensures that even those who inhabit the capital city live in a little village where everyone knows everything about everyone else. But the cold water flows clean and clear straight from the taps, and the hot water literally gushes up from the earth!

What a privilege—what a luxury.

Hörður relaxes in his favorite corner in the hottest tub at the Sundhöll swimming pool. He rests his arms on the edge of the tub, stretches out his legs and tilts his head back. When he gets himself situated like that, there isn't much room left in the otherwise spacious hot tub. He swam a bit before getting into the tub, which is something that he doesn't do very often. He was going to let two hundred meters of breaststroke suffice, but then added four hundred meters of freestyle. After that, he swam a leisurely two hundred meters of backstroke, and ended with another two-hundred meters of breaststroke. A kilometer in all. Not bad.

The sun is setting, the sky over the eastern part of town is a beautiful red, with a dark undertone. The weather is still and cold, steam rising from the hot tubs. The gurgling of the water is pleasant, and its heat is cozy.

Now, Hörður is on weekend break. A long, hard work week is behind him, and his accumulated fatigue passes slowly but easily from his body. However, he would definitely have liked to work longer. He thinks about Axel and

Engilbert, who are still working, and will undoubtedly not stop until all the puzzle pieces in the double homicide investigation have been put together.

He wonders how the meeting with the prosecution went, and whether Tryggvi and Egill had been found and arrested. Will Aron be remanded into custody? What will come out of the interrogation of Sólrún? Is Axel preparing for his TV interview?

Hörður lets his eyelids droop and goes over the day's events in his mind, from leaving the murder scene with Engilbert until he finished his shift. He did well, didn't he? Yeah, pretty well. Could he have done better? No question. The visit to the pastor wasn't exactly by the book, and Aron was able to throw him off balance. But he managed to save his own neck. This thing with the ecstasy tablets was uncomfortable, to put it mildly. Aron's interrogation, however, ended with an indictment. That was something, or what? Actually, Axel and Engilbert weren't as pleased as he was. What he'd interpreted as a great victory, they maintained was a quasi-defensive victory.

That remains to be seen.

And then, Engilbert is going to call and give him a report on the development and status of the case. A phone call after work from a member of the CID! Now that's something. Hopefully Betti will remember. Surely he'll remember, right?

Hörður cracks a smile. Yes, all in all, it was a good day. He decides to be content with himself, for a change. He glances furtively to both sides and then gives himself a quick pat on the shoulder, hoping no one else will notice.

He relaxes in the hot water, exhales and lets himself sink down until his ears are below the surface. Silence takes over, as heavy as the water that envelopes him. He himself is weightless. Half-submerged, he rocks slowly back and forth, like an astronaut outside Earth's atmosphere. His heart beats calmly, his mind empties, he experiences a kind of timelessness and while it lasts, he's perfectly happy.

Feeling slightly dazed when he comes home from the swimming pool, Hörður decides to lie down a bit. He sets his phone's ring tone to vibrate, lies down on his cot and lays his phone on his chest, sticks the headphones in his ears and presses play. He falls fast asleep to "Sabbath Bloody Sabbath" by Black Sabbath cranked to the max in his ears, disappearing completely into the heavy, melodic music and dreaming that he's at a dark, sweaty concert with the old masters.

Time and space dissolve into a hazy bliss. Hörður leans up against the amplifier stack of Tony Iommi, the legendary guitarist and godfather of heavy metal, and lets the seductive noise flow straight into his heart, at the same time as he watches the fingers of the left-handed magician dance over the neck of his instrument, stretch the strings and bend them. The music flows over him, through him, along every nerve, every muscle and every vein, and the electricity jolts his heart …

Bzzzz! Bzzzz! Bzzzz!

The dream gradually dissipates, his rational mind floats back up to the surface of consciousness, and then everything clicks in place and Hörður wakes with a start. Engilbert! He rips off the headphones, sits up and just manages to grab his phone before it falls to the floor.

He pushes the green button and puts the small phone to his ear. "Hello!"

"Did I wake you?" asks the detective, who sounds as if he himself was on the verge of falling asleep.

Hörður looks at his watch. It's twenty minutes past six. "No, not at all. What's up?"

"This and that," says Engilbert lazily, as if he can't be bothered to talk. *"They didn't find anything in Aron's cell. Not so much as a speck of dust, let alone a hypnosis handbook or a phone."*

"Damn it," says Hörður.

"Yes, damn it. Aron was brought before the judge around half past four. He was remanded into custody for twenty-four hours."

"Twenty-four hours, that's all?"

"That's the amount of time that the judge gave us to arrest Tryggvi and Egill and demonstrate that they take their orders from Aron, either in the form of a confession or by presenting substantial evidence. The fact that both perpetrators are in custody doesn't help us at all, see."

"They haven't been found yet, Tryggvi and Egill?"

"They turned themselves in about an hour ago. As soon as they heard that they were wanted, according to them. They said that they were at someone's house in Hveragerði, where they'd both been playing poker since around dinnertime yesterday."

"Does that hold up?"

"Their friends corroborate their statement, but we've already done a photo lineup. One of the three bartenders who were on duty at Kaffibarinn picked out Tryggvi Leó from the photos, but said that he wasn't completely sure, and wasn't at all sure whether the person he was referring to had a tattoo on his neck, but was fairly confident that he'd had a tattoo on the back of one hand, which doesn't add up.. One

of the bouncers picked out Egill Þór, but wasn't sure either. In other words, not at all decisive, but enough to cast doubt on their alibis. Tryggvi and Egill, on the other hand, admit to having been at Ölver last Tuesday. They completely deny everything else, including being in contact with Aron."

"Was anything found on them, in the car or ..." asks Hörður.

"Nothing. The black BMW hasn't been found. It was probably stolen. They drove an old Mazda belonging to Egill Þór."

"Damn. But were they brought before a judge?"

"Yep," says Engilbert. *"They're to be held in custody for four days. In order for that to be extended, we need a confession, or something that connects them directly to the murders: witnesses or physical evidence. We're stuck in a rut."*

Hörður thinks things over. "What we need is to find the place where the hypnosis was done."

"If that place exists," says the detective. *"Tomorrow we'll hold a real lineup. Hopefully, the bartenders and bouncers will point out both of them, Tryggvi and Egill. We desperately need that."*

"Will that hold up in court?" asks Hörður. "I mean, you've already done a photo lineup. I mean, the witnesses will have already seen photographs of the suspects, before the real lineup takes place. That must pose a problem."

Engilbert says nothing.

"Are you there?" asks Hörður.

"I hate this case," says the detective in a drowsy voice, as if he were drunk. *"Two murderers in custody who don't remember anything, have clean criminal records and have no beef with the murder victims. Gísli Már is probably having*

a nervous breakdown. He swings between silence and being ready to confess to anything. Sólrún is still in intensive care at a psychiatric unit, so heavily medicated that she's barely present. Catatonic schizophrenia, said the doctor. She's on the verge of losing her mind, and it's entirely uncertain whether she'll ever recover. It's certain that the two of them committed the murders, but they're useless as witnesses and no judge in his right mind would accept a confession from them. At worst, they'll end up in the forensic psychiatric hospital at Sogn."

"Yeah, this is a bloody mess," says Hörður. "But we mustn't give up."

Engilbert laughs hopelessly. *"Nor should we hang ourselves on something that's not only far-fetched, but also unbelievable and almost impossible to prove. Of course we're not giving up immediately, but neither can we make fools of ourselves. Our case needs to be credible. It has to be backed up with the testimonies of witnesses and physical evidence. Otherwise, this will become one big media circus, with the CID playing the clowns. That must not happen."*

"What are you saying?"

"I'm just thinking out loud," says the detective. *"Of the two evils, it's better that the two people who actually committed murder serve time in prison for a few years for manslaughter, than for the CID to lose all its credibility by cooking up a huge charge that stands on shaky legs, based on ideology and alleged hypnosis and that smells very strongly of paranoia and conspiracy theories. We could all lose our jobs."*

"We mustn't give up," repeats Hörður. "There's too much at stake. Aron Beck mustn't be set free."

"Gísli and Sólrún's attorneys will plead temporary insanity due to drug use," says Engilbert. *"It being the only*

theory in this case that still holds water. All that we have are the ecstasy tablets and two unlikely murderers who may have injected themselves with some crap. It could be worse. They'll never receive heavy sentences. The damage has been done already, anyway. They murdered two people. They're already suffering."

"There could be more murders," Hörður reminds him. "The nightmare isn't necessarily over."

"It's over," says Engilbert. *"Even if we can't prove anything against Tryggvi and Egill, they're still out of the game. They're hardly so stupid to try to keep this going, if they're even guilty in the first place. And Aron's already behind bars. Actually, it would be smartest for them just to give up now. If we fail to prove anything against them, it won't look good for the department, and they'll automatically be seen as the victims of harassment and prejudice. I predict that this is over, that it will end like this."*

"Yeah, maybe," mutters Hörður.

"Win some, lose some," says the detective.

"What did the forensic pathologist have to say?" asks Hörður.

"Not much, really," Engilbert mutters. *"I was present at the autopsy on the judge. It was ..."*

The detective pauses, and a cold shiver shoots up Hörður's spine and the hairs on the back of his neck stand up, as if the cold that he imagines to be characteristic of morgues has streamed to him over the phone.

"She didn't find anything new, so to speak," says Engilbert, finally. *"But she did think that the perpetrator was one and the same person. She doesn't watch the news, as she doesn't understand Icelandic."*

"Were the injuries so similar?" asks Hörður.

"As I understood it, yes. Actually, the attacks were slightly different. The judge was stabbed hard, with more force. But the knives are of course of the same make, and the stab wounds apparently highly similar. They were ..."

The detective pauses again, and Hörður hears the rustling of papers.

"Here it is. The stab wounds go slightly from left to right, which indicates that the perpetrator is left-handed. But it all depends on the circumstances, she points out. It isn't strange that the injuries are similar, taking everything into consideration. Same kind of weapon and ..."

"The same hand," concludes Hörður.

"Exactly. But none of this is of use to us."

"Will I see at you at Vitabar later?" asks Hörður. "I'm going to head over there and have something to eat."

Engilbert inhales through his nose. *"No, I don't think so. I'm too tired. And there's too much to do. Which isn't a good mix."*

"Okay, I understand," says Hörður. "But thanks for calling. I ..."

A clicking sound is heard from his phone. The detective has hung up.

It's rush hour at Vitabar; the babble of voices and clinking of glasses bounce between the walls, the ceiling fan stirs the cigarette- and fryer smoke, and the air is as warm and muggy as in the engine room of a steamship.

Hörður is sitting in his usual seat, sipping on a dark Beck's in a half-liter mug and groaning with pleasure. On a plate before him are the scanty remains of a steak with pepper sauce, thick-cut fries, and coleslaw. He decided to treat himself, in honor of his day—after all, he'd been of assistance to the CID, had an unmarked SUV at his disposal, and taken part in the interrogation of a suspected murderer as the right-hand man of Axel M. Axelsson, better known as Steppenwolf. How about that! Without wanting to be too optimistic, he feels as if it's more likely than not that they'll end up working together. At least he'll be a part of this investigation, that much is certain. What comes next will probably depend on his overall performance, and perhaps on the outcome of this case. If all goes well, it should help fast-track his career within the police force.

But he's on the map, damn it! Not only does Axel know who he's, but he *gave* him a folder and instructed Engilbert to *call* him, thank you very much. If this isn't having *one foot inside the door*, as they say in America, then what is?

He lifts his beer glass, toasts himself in his mind and gulps it down. Now this is life!

Also on the table are the day's newspapers, *Fréttablaðið*, *Morgunblaðið*, and *DV*. The murder cases are on the cover of *DV*, which went to print later than the morning papers, which, however, devote a lot of attention to the murder of Þórólfur. On the contrary, the media's websites are crowded with the most recent news and rumors, and the comment sections are full of conspiracy theories. In the main, the police have refused to comment, although just this afternoon, they did issue a press release announcing that a total of five individuals were in custody in connection with the case, including both perpetrators. The theory of psychosis due to the ingestion of toxic ecstasy tablets is the most popular one, and both *DV* and *visir.is* speculate on the murder of both an MP and a judge, stating that this indicates that this was no coincidence, not least due to the fact that the judge was murdered in his own home.

The headlines are of various types, mainly in the form of uncomfortable questions:

DANGEROUS DRUG IN CIRCULATION? (*Morgunblaðið*)

THREE ANARCHISTS IN CUSTODY (*visir.is*)

WERE THE MURDERS ORGANIZED? (*visir.is*)

IS NO ONE SAFE? (*DV*)

WHO WILL THE NEXT MURDERER BE? (*dv.is*)

A substantial fear has gripped society—fear that the media certainly stokes with irresponsible speculation, although the silence of the police works like oil added to the fire—that's as clear as day.

Hörður's phone beeps, much to his astonishment. Was someone sending him a text message? He who almost never receives the same.

Is it from Engilbert? He looks at the message. It's from Bíbí. He gets a knot in his stomach.

The only man in the world—was he happy?

What does she mean by this? Does she expect him to answer?

Hörður puts away his phone and looks at his watch. It's seven thirty. *Spotlight* begins in a few minutes. He gets up and elbows his way to the bar, and finally manages to get the bartender's attention.

"A double Highland Park on the rocks, please. And a cigar, the best you have. Put it on my account. And could you turn up the TV?"

Hörður takes a sip of his drink, lights the cigar and leans against the bar. The TV is up in the corner, near the ceiling just to the side of him. *Spotlight* is starting—a blonde woman introduces the show's subject matter, and behind her, two men can be seen sitting at a small, round table.

It's Axel M. Axelsson and the young television journalist who spoke to Hörður at the intersection of Bjarkargata and Skothúsvegur.

What's his name again?

"… Spotlight went and met one of her girlfriends, who wishes to remain anonymous."

A girlfriend? Hörður missed what the host said, but he puts two and two together. One of Sólrún's girlfriends. They've managed to locate her, these professional snoops. He wonders what she has to say.

On the screen, a young woman is sitting on a chair in an apartment somewhere in town, perhaps just at her home. She's back-lit, a black silhouette against a large window. Her voice has also been slightly altered—making her sound like a robot.

"… then I just passed out. But I don't remember it at all. I don't remember anything after we started dancing. My boyfriend called the ambulance. They brought me to the emergency room and pumped my stomach."

"Was a blood sample taken?" asks the host. *"Was your blood sent for analysis?"*

"No, not then. Not that night," replies the girlfriend. *"That was done this morning. Someone called from the police, and I was sent to have a blood sample taken."*

"Twelve hours after your drink was spiked?"

"Yes."

"Did your boyfriend go with you to the emergency room?"

"Yes."

"Did he tell the doctors that there'd been three of you at the bar? Did he ask that the police be notified? Did he want them to contact your girlfriends?"

"Yes."

"Was that done?"

"No, not that I know of."

Hörður scowls. What a fucking mess! If this turns out to be true, that is.

"Did you drink a lot at Kaffibarinn?" asks the host.

"No, not at all. Just one drink, as far as I remember. Then everything just went

black."

"You were chatting, and then started dancing, right?"

"Yes."

"What were you chatting about?"

"For example, about Gísli Már, who supposedly murdered the MP. He's Sólrún's second cousin."

"What the fuck," mutters Hörður. He wonders if *Spotlight* has realized the bigger picture. That one of the people in custody pressed charges against Ingimar, Sólrún's grandfather and Gísli's uncle, for sexual offenses? Hardly. Journalists don't have access to databases like Löke. They can look up court cases and verdicts, but can't access complaints that are under investigation or have been dismissed.

"Really?" asks the host.

"Yes. She doesn't know him very well. Still, she said that she believes he's innocent. Said he was a good kid."

The program switches back to the studio—and the live broadcast. The young television journalist welcomes Axel. His name is Haukur, that's right. His name is on the screen. Haukur Sólmundsson.

Hörður sips his whiskey.

"There we saw a clip from an interview with a girlfriend of Sólrún Davíðsdóttir, who is in police custody in connection

with the murder of Aðalsteinn Kvaran," says Haukur. *"It appears that these girlfriends' drinks were spiked with some sort of drug the evening the murder was committed. One of them ended up unconscious in the emergency room of the National and University Hospital. Why weren't the other two checked? Why weren't blood samples taken from them that night?"*

"First of all, we don't know for sure whether they were slipped drugs or not," says Axel. *"There were traces of a toxin in their blood, but we don't know where that toxin came from, whether it was ingested unintentionally or not. Regarding the blood sampling, it isn't customary for emergency room staff to send blood samples for analysis."*

"Shouldn't some warning bells have rung, though?" asks Haukur.

"Maybe," says Axel. *"You'll have to ask someone from the hospital about that."*

"Good answer," mutters Hörður, sucking on his cigar.

"As was stated in the interview, they're related, Gísli Már Brynjarsson and Sólrún Davíðsdóttir," says Haukur. *"Do you think that's a coincidence?"*

"They're related to some small degree, as was stated," says Axel. *"But they barely knew each other, as was also stated. It could be a coincidence, yes. But as I said, we don't know how the toxin came to be in their system. The same type of ecstasy tablets were found on both of them, Gísli Már and Sólrún. The big question is: where have these tablets come from?"*

"They might have gotten them from the same source, you mean?"

"I can't discuss the various aspects of the case, as you know," says Axel. *"But we're making a good progress. We've*

got people in custody and one of the things we're investigating is the origin of these ecstasy tablets."

"There are three people in detention, apart from Gísli Már and Sólrún," says Haukur, *"and according to* Spotlight's *sources, they're all declared anarchists and part of a group of squatters that took over an abandoned house on Vatnsstígur a year and a half ago. Is that right?"*

"As I said, I can't comment on individual aspects of the case," says Axel dryly.

He's doing well, thinks Hörður, blowing cigar smoke out his nostrils.

"The fact that the two victims are an MP and a judge must raise certain questions," says Haukur. *"In other words, it looks as if this is no coincidence. No explanation has been given as to how Gísli Már left Ölver and went to the city center, but according to* Spotlight's *sources, Sólrún was driven to Bjarkargata late last night. What do you have to say about this?"*

"As I said ... "

"Sorry to interrupt you," says Haukur. *"But did the police have any knowledge that a judge would be murdered?"*

Axel starts. *"No, not at all. Why ... "*

"Was the home of Aðalsteinn Kvaran being watched by the police?"

Hörður's face pales, as does Axel's.

"As I said ... "

"Do you deny that Aðalsteinn's home was being watched?" asks Haukur firmly.

"I can neither confirm nor deny it."

"Was only his home being watched, or other judges' homes, as well?"

"What the fuck," mutters Hörður.

"I can't answer this, unfortunately."

"I have it on authority that Aðalsteinn's home was being watched, that two police officers were sitting in a squad car in front of the house when the murder was committed," says Haukur. *"This fact can mean only one thing. That you had a well-founded suspicion that someone would attempt to murder Aðalsteinn. But it all came to nothing. First, what we have here is an absolute failure on the part of the police, as Aðalsteinn was murdered under the police's watchful eyes. Second, questions arise concerning the nature of these murders and the responsibility of the police force, which appears to have suppressed knowledge that had to do with public safety."*

"What sources are you referring to?" Axel asks angrily.

The knot in Hörður's stomach tightens.

"Þórólfur Hannesson was working on a controversial alcohol bill and Aðalsteinn had a reputation for the lenient treatment of rapists, for example, twice delivering a dissenting opinion in which he demanded that the accused be acquitted. In light of these facts, I ask: are we talking about political murders, organized by anarchists? If so, who's next? And will that person be warned? Will it be a minister? The President? Do you have all of those involved in custody? Or are the criminals still running loose? And how are the ecstasy tablets connected to all of this?"

Axel grunts. *"I neither can nor wish to answer particular questions concerning an ongoing investigation. But we're making good progress; everyone involved is in custody and neither the public nor anyone else is in danger at present. On the other hand, there may be some toxic ecstasy tablets in circulation, blue and imprinted with a pentagram. If anyone becomes aware of them, please contact the police."*

"Was the National Commissioner informed of this?"

"Was he informed of what?"

"I have sources that say that Aðalsteinn's home was being watched. Why was it watched? Did the police suspect that the judge would be murdered? Why were those suspicions kept secret from the National Police Commissioner? Who knew this? These are questions that you must answer."

Axel slams his palms onto the table. *"What sources are you referring to?"*

Haukur lifts a sheet of paper and gives it a glance. *"I spoke to a police officer on the scene this morning. Hörður Grímsson. He confirmed this, and hinted that it had been he who brought these suspicions to the attention of his superiors."*

Hörður is as if paralyzed. He stands at the bar with his cigar in one hand and glass in the other and gapes like a fish on dry land. His eyes stare into space, and everything goes blurry. The noise inside Vitabar transforms into an annoying buzz, and he feels suddenly feverish, as he breaks into a cold sweat.

No.

This wasn't happening. He can't believe this. What has he done? What was he thinking?

He's history.

He'd allowed himself to fly high, so terribly high. Like Icarus, he adorned himself with waxed feathers—borrowed feathers—and flew too near the sun. The fall is so long, so terribly long.

And the landing correspondingly hard.

That fucking Haukur. Why did he talk to him? Why did he say so much?

Why did he have to put himself out there like that?

Hörður blinks, pushes himself away from the bar and tries to find both his focus and balance. He stumbles about like a drunkard, bumping into other customers, spilling his drink and burning holes in jackets and coats with his cigar.

"Sorry. Pardon me. Sorry."

Hörður staggers around on shaky legs, his heart beating rapidly and feeling slightly dizzy as he heads for his table. He's trying to make it to shelter, to a safe home port, like a damaged sailboat on a stormy sea. But the table is no longer his; four high-school kids are sitting there eating hamburgers.

What's going on? It's as if he no longer exists. He's invisible, purposeless, and useless, has become a ghost that no one can see. But then through the smoky haze, he sees a hand. A hand that's waving, beckoning him to come. Someone is throwing him a lifeline. Someone sitting in a corner, smirking over a half-empty beer glass. A black-clad bird with a bent back, a crooked smile on his lips and a malicious gleam in his eyes. On the table in front of him are a notebook and pen.

The flightless, squawking skua—the young writer, Ófeigur.

"Hello, friend!" Hörður says as he plunks down in the seat opposite the poet. He takes a sip of the whiskey, puffs his cigar and smiles generously, despite feeling so bad that he wishes he would die. But maybe he smiles precisely because of that. He has only two options. Surrender himself to the pain, face his own actions—his own stupidity—and writhe in shame, self-hatred and despair until he loses his mind or kills himself. Or, escape from it all, talk about something else, act as if it didn't happen, give in to denial—darken his mind, numb his feelings and drink himself into forgetting.

Crash into oblivion.

"Hi," says Ófeigur, grinning.

"Cheers!" says Hörður, raising his glass. "Bottoms up!"

They clink their glasses, and then gulp down the liquor until nothing is left in them. Ófeigur licks his lips, while Hörður scowls and gasps. The whiskey tears into him, burning its way into his stomach and his heart skips a beat.

Each sip is a step in the direction of the black hole that he desires.

"Are we celebrating something?" Ófeigur shakes a cigarette out of a nearly empty pack and lights it.

"Celebrating?" exclaims Hörður. He puffs his cigar, looks at the ice cubes in his empty glass, then slams the table with his palm and turns around halfway. "Waiter! Waiter! We need whiskey! Whiskey and beer!"

Ófeigur laughs. "You're all right."

"You not so bad yourself." Hörður takes a good look at the writer, this bloodless young man whom he first met about a year ago when he bought a book from him, a short novel that the author had printed at his own expense and sold in bars and cafés.

Hörður bought the book because he felt sort of sorry for that timorous wretch who went from table to table and received one "no" after another. He, too, was lonely, and his book purchases were a form of human interaction, or a preface to them. Maybe he saw himself in that bitter and seemingly misfortunate writer. But then he read the book, and was fairly impressed.

The book is titled *Deeds of Darkness*, and is about a man in prison who tells the story of his life, from his very first memories of himself until the day that murders a child in cold blood. The book is narrated in the first person, cold and concise, but with a tragic undertone that makes the main character human in an extremely sorrowful way. Hörður began to like the emotionally cold, almost mechanical villain, who never had a chance in human society—like the book's black-clad author. The book didn't sell well and received rather bad reviews; its fate was the same as the protagonist of the story.

"Are you working on anything?" he asks the writer. Hörður isn't talkative by nature; he finds it both more comfortable and more *natural* to remain quiet, rather than babble on about everything and nothing. But he's worried that Ófeigur will ask him about work, and therefore decides to fill the silence instead of dreading that the writer will do just that.

"Yeah, sort of," replies Ófeigur reluctantly. "I'm jotting down this and that, anyway. I have an idea brewing. I don't know what will become of it. Maybe nothing. Maybe a long novel."

"Tell me more about it." Hörður's throat is dry. He clicks his tongue and looks over his shoulder. Where are their drinks? Isn't the bartender on his way? Didn't he hear him?

"I actually got the idea when I read an interview with the MP who was killed," says Ófeigur. "That Þórólfur."

"You don't say," says Hörður, drumming his fingers impatiently on the edge of the table. At the same moment, the bar owner himself appears with a tray of drinks—two double whiskeys on ice and two mugs of dark Beck's.

"Here you are." The bar owner is fat and bald, and is wearing a green apron. He exhales like a whale and wipes the sweat off his red face.

"Bless you!" says Hörður, patting him on the back. "Put this on my account. And bring another round after twenty minutes, my dear friend. No, make it fifteen minutes!"

"Sure thing," says the bar owner, before waddling off.

Hörður takes a sip of whiskey, groans and chases the sweet aftertaste with a drink of cold, foaming beer.

"I'm completely in favor of selling alcohol in the supermarkets. I don't find it a problem, but solely for personal reasons," says Ófeigur. "Increased access to alcohol will accelerate society's decline and my own death. Drinking is the suicide of cowards, which suits me well. It's all that freedom bullshit that gets on my nerves."

"I see," says Hörður.

"As it's just a pretext. The bill is about retailers' right to make more money," says Ófeigur. "But the Independents are always talking about freedom; it's their mantra, the noble heart of free-market capitalism. Not being able to buy or sell anything they want, they call constraint. People should have the freedom to choose and reject, the freedom to own everything and the freedom to sell it profitably. Freedom, Freedom, Freedom."

"Exactly," mutters Hörður.

"But freedom doesn't actually exist, except as a concept," says Ófeigur. "Society works by limiting the freedom of individuals; there's an agreement that no one can do whatever he pleases, a contract about constraint. If we were free, we could do anything—drive at any speed we liked, show up to work drunk, *not* show up to work and kill someone, if we felt like it. All laws and all regulations have one purpose: to limit freedom. And even in a state of complete chaos, freedom would still be limited by time, space, and the laws of nature. The weaker, for example, would always be less free than the stronger. I can't become a child again; I can neither make myself smaller nor larger, nor live forever. I can't stop breathing without dying; I have to drink and eat, and in order to be able to eat and drink, I have to do something. This is what I want to write: a big book about the freedom that doesn't exist."

"Nothing less!," says Hörður. "And won't you do just that?"

"Yes, but …" Ófeigur sips his beer. "I'm just so fucking unfree. I need time to write, but in order to be able to afford rent, food, and cigarettes, I have to work. After slaving away at the print shop for eight or ten hours, however, I have no energy left for creating; I'm dead inside. But if I quit my job, I would lose my apartment and have no place for doing my writing. I'm like Sisyphus rolling the same rock up the same slope, but never making it all the way to the top."

Hörður blows life into his cigar. "You mustn't give up. You're a good writer, a smart guy. You're the *real deal*. The adversity will only make you stronger."

"Maybe," mutters Ófeigur. "But deep down, I just want to give up. Why let it bother me? What does one more book matter? People don't care about books. Why should I roll this goddamn rock up this goddamn slope? Why not just sit on my ass and look up into the sky?"

Hörður cracks a smile. "Camus used Sisyphus as a metaphor for the futility of human life. Only death frees us from bondage. But think about this. If Sisyphus had only rolled the rock up the slope once, we would never have heard about him. But because he didn't give up, he gained fame, immortality. And maybe he found purpose in the futility? Life may be meaningless, but if you accept that, maybe it's not all that bad."

Ófeigur grins. "You'll give us pessimists a bad reputation, talking like that, Pollyanna Grímsdóttir."

Hörður laughs. "Yeah, maybe. I was just trying to cheer you up. I want you to keep rolling your rock—and to write that book."

"Thanks," says Ófeigur. "But maybe it's just a waste of time. Such a philosophical book isn't likely to be popular. I should maybe just write crime novels; apparently they sell quite well."

"A person should do what he's best at," says Hörður. "In my unwavering opinion, in any case."

Ófeigur smiles faintly. "I'm not just wrestling with a big rock and a slope, Mr. Policeman. There are also all sorts of obstacles in the road, phenomena such as those so called *good people*, the literary elite and the Butterfly School."

"The Butterfly School?" exclaims Hörður, with a laugh.

Ófeigur scowls. "Yes, the sensitive poets, the lyrical short-story writers, and the sentimental modernists who whimper like rural pastors and write *magnificent* books that nobody bothers to read but everyone pretends to understand."

Hörður laughs heartily. "You've grown bitter and senile—long before your time!"

"Oh?" says Ófeigur, before taking a drink of beer. His expression is sullen.

Hörður snaps his fingers. "Do you know what you were doing? You were standing up straw men!"

Ófeigur shakes his head. "These aren't imaginary enemies. They're real powers, and they're very careful to make sure that people like me don't get ahead. They protect their own interests."

"Fine, fine." Hörður takes a sip of whiskey, swallows it and shuts his eyes. The alcohol sifts into his bloodstream, softening every sensation and filling his head with a pleasant buzz. Oblivion draws closer.

Who are his straw men, if any? What imagined enemies does he set up when the going gets rough? What excuses does he pull out of his sleeves when he makes a mistake or life treats him badly?

"Otherwise, I'm mostly listening to music these days," says Ófeigur. "Old Chicago blues. Muddy Waters, Buddy Guy, Little Walter, Robert Johnson, and all those other awesome black musicians. Incredible stuff."

"Very good." Hörður swigs his beer. What powers are working against him, slowing him down or pointing him in the wrong direction?

The first thing that comes to mind is that fucking depression—the black dog that follows him like a shadow and sucks all the energy out of him, all his will to live, gnaws on his heels and wants him dead.

"But Robert Johnson isn't a Chicago blues man. He's from the Mississippi estuaries. A delta man." Hörður puffs his cigar until the writer disappears behind the odorous smoke.

And then, of course, there's the self-doubt, the self-hatred—the demon that sits on his shoulders and either makes good-natured fun of him or tears him down. The demon that makes sure he doesn't ask for a promotion and doesn't date any women. The demon that says that Hörður doesn't deserve anything good, and that Hörður believes. The demon that wants to have Hörður all to itself, which is what the black dog wants as well. They can't stand competition. They don't want Hörður to be proud or happy, because then there's a chance that he'll forget about them, that they'll fall off their pedestals and turn into nothing.

But which are they? Straw men, or real opponents? thinks Hörður, before finishing his beer in one long gulp.

"Are you all right?" asks Ófeigur.

"Yeah," mutters Hörður. And he mustn't forget that fucker Bacchus—the gentleman with the black heart, the playboy who pats him on the back and asks if he wants *one* drink, whether he doesn't deserve to have *one* beer, to reward himself a bit and relax, meet other people, and so on? But then he can't stop, his thirst is like an itch that grows stronger each time he scratches.

With a shudder, Hörður tosses back his whiskey—swallowing it like some awful-tasting medicine. The worst thing is that he always forgets how horribly hungover he got the last time he drank, how badly he felt the next day—the headache, the vomiting, and the cold sweats, the feverish daze and nausea.

Not to mention the awful feelings—the regret—oh, man.

Never again, he swears it! But then, two or three days pass, everything is forgotten, and before he knows it, he has poured himself a beer and has a gleam in his eyes.

Just one glass!

"Waiter!" he calls. "We're drying up over here!"

It's night.

Hörður staggers across the street, so drunk that he can hardly keep his balance or see anything clearly. Everything is hidden in a haze; it's pitch black outside, although now and then the drifting clouds reveal the bright moon.

He finds the house, feels his way along the wall and teeters to the right door. He supports himself on the wall and pats the pockets of his green army jacket. My keys, where are my house keys—doesn't he have his fucking house keys? Cigarettes, matches, crumpled banknotes and change, but no keys.

"Godda …"

Hörður hesitates, grabs the doorknob and jiggles it, but it's locked, of course. He knocks on the door, nearly shattering the glass in its window. He stares at the doorbell, at the white slips of paper next to the black buttons.

What's that guy's name again? The boring one. Yes, that one. He squints; everything is out of focus but he pushes the button, holds it in.

Answer your door, you idiot!

"Hello?" asks a quiet voice. It's Leifur, Hörður's neighbor. Hörður leans toward the door, bends down and speaks straight into the intercom. "Itt is me! Hröur!"

"Will you please go away," says Leifur, in a shaky voice. *"You can't fool me. Go away, or I'll go and get Hörður. He's a police officer."*

"No, issme!" calls Hörður, but Leifur has hung up his intercom phone.

"Fluckn idjit," mutters Hörður. He backs down the stairs, nearly topples, regains his balance but missteps and lands flat on his stomach.

"Ow-ie!" Hörður crawls along the ground, and catches a glimpse of something in the gutter. Are those … huh?

He bends down, gropes for the object and grabs his keys. So he had them all along?

Hörður goes back to the front door, makes several attempts to put the key in the keyhole, and finally succeeds.

He shuts the door behind him, and then tumbles down the stairs and ends up on his back in the basement.

"Come on." He rolls over onto his stomach, crawls over the lacquered concrete floor and manages to stand by supporting himself up against the walls. Luckily, he didn't lock his apartment door when he went out.

Everything is spinning before his eyes.

Hörður collapses onto his cot and is asleep before he hits it.

SATURDAY

*B*ONG! BONG! BONG!

Hörður wakes to the clanging of an imaginary bell, which sounds like the infernal start of "Hell's Bells" by AC/DC. And then, of course, the song gets stuck in his brain, infecting it like a virus and taking over his system.

I'm a rolling thunder, a pouring rain. I'm comin' on like a hurricane. My lightning's flashing across the sky. You're only young but you're gonna die.

He whines in misery, but is neither able to fall asleep again nor get the noise out of his fragile head. The steaming hot darkness of his basement apartment threatens to suffocate him, the autumn sun shining on the curtains in his tiny window and the light burning like acid—he's a writhing Count Dracula, tormented by the light.

Oh, miserable me!

I won't take no prisoners, won't spare no lives. Nobody's putting up a fight. I got my bell, I'm gonna take you to hell. I'm gonna get you, Satan get you.

"Aw, shut up," mutters Hörður, anguished, his breath reeking.

Hell's bells. Yeah, hell's bells. You got me ringing, hell's bells. My temperature's high, hell's bells.

He's hot, his mouth is dry, his head is splitting and his stomach is gradually filling with a nauseous pressure, churning and expanding, wanting up, wanting out …

No! Hörður leaps of his cot, rushes into the bathroom, throws himself onto his knees and, screaming and gasping, vomits into the toilet.

Never again. Never ever again …

Hörður sits hunched on his cot, smoking the first cigarette of the day. He's cold, he's miserable, and is quivering like a reed in the wind. His hair is greasy and his skin is clammy, his eyes are bloodshot and his lips cracked.

He's waiting for the first coffee cup of the day. His moka pot is heating up on the electric burner.

If only he won't get sick from the smell of the coffee. His headache isn't getting any better; he can feel his rhythmic pulse in his head—a soft ax splitting a block of wood per second. His belly aches and his nose is clogged with mucous and vomit.

He has two aspirins, but doesn't want to take them until he's a hundred-percent sure that he won't puke them up.

Doesn't he have any Coke? Or beer? He has quit drinking, but desperately needs a bit of the hair of the dog. He isn't reset to zero; he's still in the minus. He needs something to bring himself back to normal, to *straighten himself out.*

Hörður opens the fridge, which is as empty as an open grave. Damn.

The water boils in the moka pot; it makes gurgling sounds and the coffee-scented steam drifts up through its nozzle.

Nausea gushes up in his stomach. Fuck. He simply can't handle vomiting any more. His stomach is more than empty—it's inside out. Last time, nothing came out but brown bile.

Isn't there just a drop of whiskey here somewhere?

He puts down his cigarette, gets down on his hands and knees and peeks under the cot. There it is—a bottle of White Horse whiskey. There's almost nothing left in it but a tablespoon, maybe, but he pours it tremblingly into his coffee cup. The coffee is ready, and he takes the gurgling pitcher from the burner and fills his cup.

The smell of the freshly brewed coffee is wonderful—his mouth waters, and he takes a little sip of it.

Ah!

After finishing his cup, Hörður swallows the painkillers and pours himself another. There are a few drops left in the whiskey bottle, and he lets them fall into the coffee. There, that's better.

Now he just needs to wait for the tablets to work, and he'll be right as rain.

Feeling relieved, Hörður sighs. He'll get through the day. He takes a drag of his cigarette and blows the smoke out his nostrils.

Then he spies the yellow folder, and simultaneously breaks into a cold sweat.

Hörður suddenly remembers why he got so drunk. The interview with Axel on *Spotlight*. He's gotten the head of the CID into a terrible mess. Steppenwolf was raked over the coals on live TV.

Fuck.

He's already nervous about showing up for work on Monday. But maybe he doesn't have to go? He might have lost his job.

What will he do then?

Hörður has taken a long cold shower, smoked eight cigarettes, and drunk three batches of espresso. He has opened his curtains and the little window, and let in some air. He sits on his cot and goes over and over the stack of papers in the yellow folder, while listening to *Exile on Main Street* by the Rolling Stones.

Has he overlooked something?

He desperately tries to find a new angle, an exit route, a straw to cling to—something important that sheds a new light on the case and could possibly get him out of this mess.

He can't end his short career in the police like this, with reproach, humiliation, and shame. He has to make up for his mistake, show what he's made of and save what can be saved. But no matter how often he goes through the date, he finds nothing new—he flips through his papers, reads, examines, and stares but nothing happens.

"Bloody fucking hell," mutters Hörður hopelessly as he lets the papers fall to the floor. Hiding his face in his hands, he lies down on the cot and closes his eyes. Inside of him is a void, a lightless black hole that echoes with hopelessness and misery. He tries to empty his mind, but the events of the last days rush through his consciousness like a videotape on fast forward, from when they went to check on the storage unit to the interrogation of Aron Beck.

If only …

If only they hadn't been given that assignment on Tuesday. If only other officers had gone to check on that fucking storage unit. Then he wouldn't feel as badly as he does now—then he wouldn't be unemployed. Then he would show up for the evening shift on Monday and complain like an ungrateful fool over the monotony of his job, instead of just enjoying driving around the streets of the city and responding to some minor calls, without being overwhelmed by the burden of responsibility and worries of a police detective.

Why …

Why did he have to go and stick his nose into the CID's business?

Why couldn't he just do his job and leave it at that? Every man's dream contains a shadow of his fall … and all that.

What a mess.

To make matters worse, he can picture the smirk on Aron Beck's face, as he stands there cockily in Block 3 of Litla-Hraun Prison and watches the police officer leave. What did he say again? *I've changed my mind, by the way. You are as stupid as you look.* Yes, something like that.

But before that? He said something about the moon, didn't he? Yes, it was the story of the prisoners on Florida's death row. About how they howled at the full moon, but without *knowing* that it was full. Then he smiled smarmily and added something—something that seemed not to matter at the time, but perhaps did, in retrospect. It wasn't *what* he said, but more like *how* he smiled. In that arrogant smile there was a kind of subtext—something that hinted that he might have been saying something other than what he did, something *more*.

What did he say? Wasn't it something about the moon? He called Hörður *copper*. Something about the moon, *copper*.

The moon will be full on Sunday, copper. Yes, that's how it was. The moon will be full on Sunday. Why did he say that? Yes, the moon *will* be full on Sunday, but what about it?

That's just something that everyone who wants to know, knows. Still, he said it in such a way that it was as if he were talking about something other than this obvious fact.

Full moon. Sunday. Second Sunday in October. Does that mean anything? He isn't sure.

October 13th.

October 13th?

This date rings some bells. Opening his eyes, Hörður sits up and gathers his papers. Isn't that date in here somewhere? He leafs through the stack, running his eyes quickly over the text in search of numbers. When he finds what he's looking for, the hairs on the back of his neck rise.

Little Mummi's ID number—131077. His birthday was in October. He would have been twenty-five years old tomorrow, had he lived.

A full moon on Mummi's birthday.

What does that mean?

If the murders are about revenge, if they're directed against Reverend Ingimar, as Hörður is convinced that they are, then they're not only revenge for what he did to those boys, but first and last blood revenge for Little Mummi, who committed suicide after the complaint was dismissed.

His death is symbolic. As is the revenge. Three organized murders committed within the space of a week. The first is on Tuesday night, the second after midnight on Thursday, and the third and final one will be committed after midnight on Saturday and before midnight on Sunday—on the birthday of the martyr.

Does this make sense? Yes.

Why hadn't he realized this long ago? Enraged, Hörður clenches his fists tightly.

This is how Aron set things up. But now his plan has been ruined—to put it mildly. All those involved are in custody, more innocent citizens won't have their drinks laced with GHB, and no more murders will be committed in the name of Guðmundur Vífill Marinósson.

Hörður lies back down on his cot. Still, he has to tell someone about this, doesn't he? If these speculations have any truth to them, they'll be useful for the case. If he's lucky, this information will matter a great deal, and maybe increase the likelihood of him keeping his job.

But whom can he call? Engilbert? Axel? He feels dizzy just thinking about it. They would probably prefer him to drop dead.

Hörður shuts his eyes and wishes that this was all just a nightmare—that he'll wake up soon, and then everything will be as it was before his life and career went to hell.

The wilderness is long and wide, endless in all directions. The sun is high in the sky, glaring white and relentless—the heat is debilitating. There's no wind; the silence is heavy as a rock. At the horizon, the Fata Morgana quivers.

Hörður is on horseback, riding slowly across the ochre-colored eternity. He's wearing a long leather coat and a cowboy hat on his head. The water has dried up, and he's dying of thirst. His horse limps along, step by step, toward nothing.

But then shadows appear within the quivering mirage. Are they houses? Or is he hallucinating? He squints, stares through the heat. Yes, they're houses—there's a little village ahead. He urges on his horse, which speeds up and gallops over the sunbaked earth. They pass tall cactuses and reddish cliffs.

Hörður rides into the town. The main road is empty, a gentle wind swirls up dust and rolls tumbleweeds along the road. On both sides are houses with high facades and verandas, a post office, hotel, and the sheriff's office. The horse's hoofbeats are amplified, *clomp, clomp*—in the distance, a crow caws.

Hörður dismounts his horse in front of a saloon. Outside of it are a hitching post and a trough of water. The horse snorts and gulps down the water. Hörður's spurs jingle as he walks up three steps to the veranda. Through the door come the sounds of a piano playing and the murmur of voices. Above Hörður's head is a hand-painted sign, weathered and faded:

Saloon

Hörður pushes the saloon's door and walks into the dark room, where patrons sit at round tables here and there. The piano music stops, shady faces look up from their drinks and card games and eye him. He stops, looks over the place, and then walks straight over to the bar. The jangly piano music starts again and the patrons return to their drinks and cards.

"Whiskey, please," says Hörður, in a hoarse voice. He leans against the bar and rests one foot on a low metal bar in front of it.

"Of course," says the bartender, a gangly, middle-aged man dressed in a white shirt and vest. He lifts an unmarked bottle, pulls a cork from it and pours rye whiskey into a heavy glass.

Hörður empties the glass in one gulp. "Another, please."

"Of course," says the bartender, who is no ordinary bartender, but rather, Detective Inspector Engilbert Gústafsson.

"Betti?" says Hörður in surprise.

"That's me," says the bartender.

"Well I'll be," says Hörður, as he removes his dusty hat. "So, tell me, have they been apprehended, the two outlaws, Tryggvi and Egill?"

"Yes, they're in the sheriff's custody," says Betti. "They gave themselves up about an hour ago. As soon as they heard that they were wanted, according to them. They were at a house in Nowhereville, where they said they'd been playing poker since around dinnertime yesterday."

"Does that hold up?"

Betti wipes the bar with a cloth. "Their friends corroborate their statement, but we've already done a photo lineup. One of the three bartenders who were on duty at the Saloon picked out Tryggvi Leó from the photos, but said that he wasn't completely sure, and wasn't at all sure whether he'd had a tattoo on his neck but was fairly sure he had a tattoo on the back of one hand, which doesn't add up. One of the bouncers picked out Egill Þór, but wasn't sure either. In other words, not at all decisive, but enough to cast doubt on their alibis. Tryggvi and Egill, on the other hand, admit to having been at Ölver last Tuesday. They completely deny everything else, including being in contact with Aron."

"Was anything found on them, in their carriage, or ..." asks Hörður.

"Nothing. The black carriage hasn't been found. It was probably stolen. They were riding an old mare of Egill Þór's."

Hanging behind the bar is a framed picture of a steamship, sailing a choppy sea. Thick smoke rises from its smokestacks.

Hörður downs his drink. "Damn it. But they were brought before a judge?"

"Yep," says Betti. "They're to be held in custody for four days. In order for that to be extended, we need a confession, or something that connects them directly to the murders: witnesses or physical evidence. We're stuck in a rut."

"I've got to find something that ties them to the murders," says Hörður. "These men shall hang!"

"There's not just them," says Betti. "There are others."

"What do you mean?" asks Hörður.

"The tattoo," says Betti. "Think about the tattoo. Not about the man."

"The tattoo?"

Betti gives a little smile. "What it is. Where it is."

Hörður wakes with a start. His heart is pounding and he's drenched with sweat. He lifts himself and looks around him in surprise. He's at home—where else?

Had he fallen asleep? Was he dreaming?

He sits up and swings his legs out of the cot. It was Engilbert. He said something about a tattoo. What it was? Where it was?

Which tattoo?

Hörður opens the yellow folder, and goes once more through his papers, without finding what he's looking for. In fact, he doesn't really know what it is he's looking for. He's tries to recall his dream, but what he remembers best is his thirst—and the whiskey that he drank. He mouth goes dry at the thought.

He would really like just one shot of whiskey. Or a small beer—ice cold and frothy.

But he has quit drinking, right?

Yes.

Concentrate! They were talking, he and Engilbert. It was a repeated conversation, discussing something they'd discussed before, in reality. Was it the phone call? What did Engilbert say on the phone? He said that Tryggvi and Egill had turned themselves in, and then something about the bartender being unable to identify them. There was a photo lineup, the bartender picked out Tryggvi but said he'd had a tattoo on his hand, but not on his neck.

Something like that.

What it is. Where it is.

Tryggvi's tattoo is of a spider web. That's what it is. It's on his neck. That's where it is.

But the bartender said that the man he saw had had a tattoo on his hand. But he didn't say anything about *what* the tattoo was, did he? He can't remember.

Hörður sighs and covers his face with his hands. He doesn't understand his dream, and doesn't know what he's looking for. Suddenly, however, her realizes everything, as if fingers were snapped.

Of course!

He leafs quickly through his stack of papers, finds the *DV* interview and examines the image of the anarchists. One of them has a prominent tattoo on the back of his right hand. It's a pentagram. He goes over the names in the caption. *The photo shows, from left to right: Orri, Hákon, Guðmundur Vífill, Aron Beck, Tryggvi Leó, Þorsteinn, and Egill Þór.* The one with the star tattoo is second from left—Hákon.

Hörður puts the interview aside and finds the verdict in the squatting case, which gives Hákon's full name. His patronymic is Úlfarsson, as Engilbert said. Other members of the group who haven't been found are Þorsteinn Gunnarsson and Orri Atlason. The latter is a dishwasher at

Hotel Borg, if Hörður remembers correctly, and according to what Betti said, the other two are at sea.

Or are they?

"This isn't fucking finished yet," mutters Hörður as he looks up Engilbert's number on his phone.

He finds it and pushes the green button.

"At the moment, this phone is either switched off, outside the service area, or ... "

Hörður hangs up.

Damn it!

He calls police headquarters.

A man's voice responds. *"Reykjavík Police."*

"Yes, hello. Officer Hörður Grímsson here. To whom am I speaking?

"My name is Daniel."

"We've never met, I think," says Hörður. "I really need to reach Axel M. Axelsson, the head of the CID. Can you put me through?"

"I'm not allowed to put anyone directly in touch with Axel," says Daníel.

"This is very important and concerns the murder investigations currently underway," says Hörður. "I have new information."

"I can't put you directly in touch with Axel," says Daniel.

"But can you give me his number?" asks Hörður.

"No, sorry."

"Damn it!" says Hörður. "What about Jafet? Can you give me the number for Jafet Sigurðsson?"

"Yes, hold on a second," says Daníel. He leafs through a phone book and reads the detective's number. Hörður writes it in pen on his left forearm.

He calls Jafet. It rings and rings, then connects to his voicemail. *"This is Jafet Sigurdsson. Leave a message after the beep, and I'll call you back."*

Beep.

"Yes, hello. This is Officer Hörður Grímsson. Engilbert's phone is switched off and I don't have Axel's number. The thing is, I have information pertinent to the investigation of the two murders. I would appreciate it if you could pass this information on to Axel. Tell him that Tryggvi and Egill weren't at Kaffibarinn on Thursday evening. Apparently, everyone from the anarchist group is involved in these murders. It appears that Hákon Úlfarsson and Þorsteinn Gunnarsson are at sea; that claim has to be verified. I firmly believe that Hákon was at Kaffibarinn, and with him either Þorsteinn or Orri Atlason. An alert needs to be put out for these men. If they aren't found, the third murder will be committed after midnight tonight, or tomorrow. Got it? Bye."

Hörður ends the call. Then he remembers something else and calls Jafet again.

Beep.

"Yes, this is Hörður again. I know that the third murder will be committed tonight or tomorrow because all of these murders are revenge for little Mummi, Guðmundur Vífill, whose birthday is in fact tomorrow. Aron told me that the moon will be full on Sunday, which is true. But he meant something else, and thought that I wouldn't figure it out. I'll explain it all better to Axel if he calls me. Tell him to call me, okay?"

Fuck! He forgot something else.

Beep.

"One more thing. This is Hörður again. The revenge is directed against Ingimar Jósefsson, as Axel knows. For this reason, certain measures have to be taken. It would be best if Axel or someone met with Reverend Ingimar or someone from his family and got him to make a list of his closest relatives, mainly the younger people—Aron seems to choose young people as his subjects, them being perhaps easiest to approach. Then you need to contact these people and warn them, ask them to stay at home until these men have been arrested. This is important! Goodbye."

No! There's *one more* thing. Damn it.

Beep.

"It's me, Hörður. You probably think I'm crazy, but there's just one other thing that I have to mention. Potential victims. According to my theory, the executive branch of government is next. Aron is locked up for assaulting police officers. Which is why I believe that a police officer will be his next target, or a supervisor or department head within the police. But the president of Iceland also belongs to the executive branch, as well as the prime minister and every other minister. Also the district administrators, and the board of the Central Bank. It wouldn't be a bad idea to increase security around these officials, and ask police officers to be alert. That's it for now."

Hörður puts his phone down. He's shaking, and his throat is terribly dry. Did he do the right thing? Yes. He can only hope that Jafet will listen to his messages and pass them on.

But would Axel call him? Or is he still angry because …

Hörður starts when the phone rings. He's quick to answer, without even looking at the screen. "Yes, Axel?"

"No, fool," says Þórhildur Sverrisdóttir on the other end.

"Oh, hi," says Hörður. "Sorry. I was expecting another call."

"No problem," says Þóra. *"I just wanted to remind you about the wedding. The ceremony starts at six."*

Hörður groans. "Oh, fuck. I forgot all about it."

"I thought so," says Þóra.

"Do I've to go?" he asks miserably. "My suit jacket was ruined the other day, and I've got nothing to wear to it."

"First, I'll kill you if you let me down," Þóra says sternly. *"Second, I'll pick you up at five sharp. Third, stop moaning, get off your ass and go buy a new jacket."*

"Yes, but …" He looks at his watch. It's five minutes to four. "It's Saturday. The shops are only open until four."

"Then what are you waiting for?"

It's four o'clock on the button when Hörður rushes in through the door of the leather-goods shop Kós on Laugavegur Avenue.

"Are you still open?" he asks, panting. In the middle of the room stands a middle-aged saleswoman, who was on her way to lock the door.

"Yes and no," she says.

"I need a jacket," says Hörður, speaking fast. "It's an emergency. I promise to be quick."

The saleswoman sighs. "Well. What style are you thinking of? What color? What kind of leather? Buttoned or zipped?"

Hörður runs his eyes over the selection and breathes in the aroma of the leather. Dozens of leather jackets—short, long, narrow, wide—hang on long racks. The colors range from creamy white to black, but most of them are brown, reminiscent of caramel, brandy, or chocolate.

The shop also sells overcoats, vests and hats, as well as belts and other accessories.

"Maybe brown, or black," says Hörður, just to say something. He looks through the jackets, pushing them to and fro on the racks. There's too much of a selection, really—giving him serious choice overload. "Definitely not short. Buttoned, I think. Other than that, I'm not sure. Isn't leather just leather?"

"We have bull leather, cow leather, and calfskin," says the saleswoman. "Thick leather, thin leather. Delicate leather, strong leather. Soft leather, stiff leather. The quality varies, and is reflected in the price."

"I see," mutters Hörður in surrender.

"You're not a small man," says the saleswoman. She draws a tape measure down from one of his shoulders, and grabs the police officer's hand. "Let me take your measurements. There aren't many jackets you can choose from. Most of them are tailored to fit the average person. Still, I do have a few that should fit a giant."

She fetches three jackets and asks him to try them on. Hörður takes off his army jacket and tries out the leather ones, one by one. The first is too narrow at the waist, the second isn't long enough, and the sleeves of the third are too short.

"I'm afraid I don't have any more jackets in your size," says the saleswoman.

"Shit," mutters Hörður. He has always had difficulty finding clothes that fit. Every now and then over the years, he's occasionally come across some dream garment, but it never fit him. Always the same old story.

Dream garment?

What was he wearing in his Wild West dream? Wasn't it …?

⚜ ⚜ ⚜

Hörður hesitates on the sidewalk in front of a row of houses on Bergþórugata Street, chain smokes, and glances over and over at his watch. It's four minutes past five. Þóra is late, of course. So typical! Who was she to insist that he be on time?

He's freshly shaven, smells of musk, and has put a little gel in his hair. He's wearing newly polished motorcycle boots, black pants, a white shirt, and a purple cravat. And of course his new leather coat, which is very long and black, heavy and glossy and smells of the tanning process and leather oil.

Hörður smokes his cigarette down to the filter, lets it fall to the flagstones and stubs it out with his foot. He hardly ever buys new clothes, and when he does, it's generally something that he already has—new black pants, a new white shirt, and so on. He's had his green army jacket for ten years, and his motorcycle boots for seven.

He'll never forget how insecure and frightened he was the first few days he wore his army jacket. He felt like it was so *new*, so strong-smelling and eye-catching. He felt like everyone was looking at him, and came close to throwing the jacket out. He would probably have done so if he hadn't already thrown out his *old* jacket, which had worn out years ago.

But if he felt insecure in his army jacket, he's close to feeling tormented in his brand-new leather coat. The garment is not just *big* and noticeable, but also uncommon and therefore even *original*, which is worst of all. The last thing that Hörður Grímsson wants to do is stand out, to attract *attention,* or—he nearly faints at the thought alone—to be considered *out there.*

What was he thinking?

Cursing silently, Hörður lights another cigarette. But he still likes the coat. It's really nice. It's cool and smart—a classy garment. It also suits him well. Or what? Yes. Or, at least he feels good wearing it. The coat is just such a huge statement, which is the worst. It says: *Here I am, deal with it or go to hell.*

Which is totally tough. Just a little difficult at first. He'll get used to it. Get used to wearing such a garment. Get used to being noticeable, being a guy who dares to wear a leather coat and doesn't give a shit what others think.

Yes, exactly. He blows smoke out his nostrils. It *has* to be all the same to him. That's the point. Fuck other people and what they think. This is his coat, his style, his statement.

"Deal with it, punk!" he mutters angrily.

"What?" says someone behind him.

Hörður stiffens and turns around slowly.

"Were you talking to me?" asks Leifur, his neighbor. Out of breath and wearing a track suit, he's obviously just been out for a run.

"No, no. Just thinking out loud," mutters Hörður, putting on his Ray-Ban sunglasses. What's this idiot doing here? If he says something about the coat, he'll kill him with his bare hands.

"Did you notice that junkie who was here last night?" asks Leifur.

"What junkie?" asks Hörður.

"He rang my bell," says Leifur. "It was around one or one-thirty. I was fast asleep. It was a crazy junkie. Probably a criminal. He was trying to get into the building. For what purpose, I hardly dare think about."

"Oh?"

"Yes," says Leifur. "A sly bugger. He said his name was Hörður, but I wasn't fooled. I told him to get lost or he'd be sorry. I said I would go get Hörður—the *real* Hörður—if he didn't leave right away."

Hörður breaks into a cold sweat. "And?"

"Fortunately, he left," says Leifur, who's still upset by the incident. "But the door is all scratched, as you can see. He was probably trying to open it with a wire or skeleton key."

"This is a dubious neighborhood," mutters Hörður. Then he raises his hand and waves when he glimpses a white Yaris that appears like a messenger from heaven. Finally, she's here!

"You're right," says Leifur. "Which is why I've been wondering whether the owner's association should set up a surveillance camera and …"

Þóra stops the car, looks at her friend and bursts out laughing. "Sorry, I've got to run," says Hörður, as he walks out into the street. "I'm late for a wedding."

"Cool coat," says Leifur.

"Thanks!" Hörður tosses away his cigarette, stuffs himself into the small car and shuts the door behind him. "Why can't you ever come on time, you? And what's so funny?"

Þóra drives off. "Nothing. But then when did you become a Goth?"

"A Goth?" Hörður annoyedly exclaims.

"They're the only ones who wear such coats," says Þóra teasingly. "Well, besides SS officers and child molesters."

Hörður's face reddens with anger. "Listen, just let me out here. I don't feel like going with you to this stupid wedding, since you feel I look so ridiculous."

"Easy now," says Þóra, patting him on the thigh. "I'm just teasing you. Don't be so sensitive. Your coat is tough. I just didn't expect you to buy that kind of garment, that's all."

"What kind of garment?" he asks suspiciously.

"So, you know … noticeable," she says.

Hörður grumbles. Exactly what he thought. He isn't cool. He isn't a cowboy. He's the Garðskagaviti lighthouse.

"You're tough, I mean it," says Þóra, who, however, is still having a hard time keeping a straight face. "You'll be the coolest guy at the wedding. No question."

"Do you think so?" he asks doubtfully.

"No, I don't think so," says Þóra, as she drives down an exit ramp, then under a bridge, and east onto Miklabraut. "I *know* so."

"If you say so," mutters Hörður, a bit more content, but not at all convinced.

"There's beer in a plastic bag on the floor in back," says Þóra. "Have one and relax."

"Beer?" Hörður asks, turning around. Hasn't he quit drinking? Or is he just taking a break?

He sees the bag, and in it, catches a glimpse of the dark green necks of Heineken bottles—his favorite beer.

"Thanks, but I'm not going to drink now," he says.

"Why not?" asks Þóra.

"Just, no reason," he mumbles.

"Did you hear about the protests?" she asks.

"What protests?"

"Outside the police station," she says. "Up to three hundred people. It was organized through social media. Eggs have been thrown at the building, and a few windows broken with rocks. The protest was supposed to be peaceful, but some black sheep have probably joined in with the group."

Hörður's stomach knots with anxiety. "What are they protesting?"

"I guess Axel was given a grilling on *Spotlight* yesterday," says Þóra. "I didn't actually see it, but from what I understand, the police had some knowledge that a judge would be murdered. Even that Aðalsteinn was personally at risk. They say that his house was being watched, but the officers on duty weren't as alert as they should have been. Did you see *Spotlight?* Do you know anything about this?"

"No," says Hörður. He knows that he should spill the beans and tell his friend everything that's been going on, but he just doesn't feel up to it. The shame is weighing him down. He feels as if he can hardly breathe.

If only he could forget about all this.

"Anyway, that's the reason," she says. "The protesters are demanding that Axel resign, and that the police be required to inform the public and warn people if dangerous criminals are roaming free, and/or if they have any knowledge of impending atrocities."

"Fucking hell," mutters Hörður.

"There was an interview with the police commissioner at noon," says Þóra. "He said that the police had been keeping watch on Hljómskálagarður Park the past few nights because of tips about mysterious activities going on there—as you know, more than one woman has been raped in that park. That's why a police car was parked on Bjarkargata when the judge was murdered. He also said that there was no further danger—all of the involved individuals are in custody."

"I wish they were," says Hörður. He picks up the phone and writes a text message to Jafet:

Did you get my messages?

He pushes send.

"All the same, the protests weren't canceled," says Þóra. "People are both angry and scared, perhaps understandably.

Two murders in just a few days, and it seems that both murderers are the man or woman next door. There are no ties between them and the deceased. Toxic ecstasy tablets in circulation. They'd better figure these things out, because otherwise, I'm afraid that society will go haywire, and there'll be hell to pay."

"Maybe I'll have one." Hörður turns around in his seat, fishes a bottle from the bag, opens it with the end of his lighter, and takes a drink of the foaming beer.

"There you go."

Hörður's phone beeps. It's Jafet, returning his message, and the answer is short but sweet:

Yes, have forwarded them.

"The case is in its final stages, I think." Hörður sticks his phone in his pocket. "This case is certainly complicated and unpleasant, but the public needs to remain calm. Anarchy isn't the answer—that much is certain."

"That's true," says Þóra. "But the police administrators still need to speak more clearly, and immediately inform both the media and the public about the state of affairs."

"Yes, yes," mutters Hörður.

"I just hope that this isn't right about the judge," she says. "That the police had knowledge that he would be attacked."

"Can we talk about something other than work?" asks Hörður, before pounding his beer.

"Did I buy the right kind?" asks Þóra, grinning.

"Yes," says Hörður, forcing a smile. He takes a closer look at his friend. She's wearing a denim jacket over a short summer dress, leather ankle boots and a pink scarf around her neck, pink lipstick, and gold hoops in her ears. She has a large number of hairpins in her hair, and she's not wearing glasses, as she normally does.

"What are you staring at?" she asks.

"Nothing," he says. "Are you wearing contacts?"

"Yeah," she says. "I just find it so difficult to put them in. I'm always dropping them, or I don't hit the right spot. That's why I'm so late."

"You look good. Really good."

Þóra blushes. "Thanks. That's great praise. From a Goth, I mean."

Hörður laughs. "Shut up."

By the time they get to Heiðmörk, Hörður has opened his third beer. Þóra drives slowly along the pothole-marked gravel road that ends at the old farm Elliðabær. On one side is Elliðavatn Lake, and fields and the woods on the other. At the farm, all the parking spaces are taken, and quite a few cars have been parked along the road.

"Is it a big wedding?" asks Hörður anxiously.

"No, no," says Þóra, as she parks the car alongside the road. "Maybe a hundred people."

Hörður opens the door. "The food had better be good, and the speeches short. We won't be here late into the night, will we?"

"Stop your nagging!" exclaims Þóra. She locks the car, and they walk together over the main hayfield. They follow several guests who seem to know where they're going. "How was your week?"

"Just, different," mutters Hörður. He looks suspiciously at the guests walking ahead of them. If he isn't mistaken, most of the couples are of the same sex. The women have short hair and are a bit boyish-looking, and the men are wearing colorful clothing, some with bleached hair and earrings.

"Thanks for coming with me," says Þóra, putting her arm around him—or making an honest attempt to do so. He's broad, and his new leather coat is slippery.

He mumbles something indistinct.

As they approach the clearing, the group of people gradually tightens, and voices and laughter are carried on the breeze. The sun is setting, birdsong is heard in the woods, and the air smells sweetly of birch and soil.

Hörður is watching a male couple, both of whom are laughing and comporting themselves like seven-year-old girls.

"What sort of wedding is this?" he asks as they enter the clearing.

"What do you mean, 'what sort'?" asks Þóra.

"Gather round, gather round!" calls a woman, waving like a preschool teacher to the group. "Form a semicircle. Gather round so that everyone can see!"

Everyone gathers round and the group spreads out on both sides, and before Hörður knows it, he and Þóra find themselves toward the front of the semi-circle. Standing at the end of the clearing are two women, dressed and adorned in their finest. One of them is around forty, Hörður guesses. She's coarse and fat and rather ugly, he thinks. The other woman is much younger, around Þóra's age. She's quite pretty, but her head is shaved bald, she has a ring through one of her nostrils, and piercings in one eyebrow and her lower lip. Standing next to the two women is a third, the one who ordered everyone to come closer. She's the pastor, smiling widely and bidding everyone a heartfelt welcome on this beautiful day to rejoice with this loving couple who are to be joined together and blah blah blah.

"Lesbians?" Hörður whispers loudly.

"Hush!" Þóra hisses.

"Which one's the groom?" Hörður whispers mischievously.

Þóra kicks him.

"Is your ex here?" whispers Hörður.

"Yes."

"Where?"

"She's about to be married," whispers Þóra, hoarsely.

"She is?" He regards the couple once more. "Which one is it, the bulky one or the one with all that jewelry crap?"

"The one with all the crap," Þóra hisses. "Now shut up! The ceremony is starting."

"Easy, easy." As he finishes the rest of his beer, Hörður runs his eyes over the guests' faces. The lesbians are finding it difficult to keep it together, and the gays are starting to tear up.

Hörður rolls his eyes. Then he looks to the left, feeling as if someone is looking at him. But when he sees who it is he stiffens and gets goose bumps. It's Bíbí. She's standing next to a tall man, and she looks straight into Hörður's eyes and gives him a little smile.

Hörður is so surprised that he gapes. He doesn't smile back at her or greet her in any other way. She looks away, turning her attention back to the wedding, leaving Hörður so confused that he neither sees nor hears what's going on in the clearing.

What's she doing here? And whom is she with?

Furtively, Hörður glances once more at Bíbí. She's wearing tightly laced army boots, a black leather jacket over a red dress, with bright red lipstick and nail polish to match. Hörður feels himself growing warmer—shit, she's tough!

What had he been thinking?

Hörður curses himself in silence. He secretly watches Bíbí. She wipes a tear from one corner of her eye, and then whispers something to the tall man, who is bearded, with black, shoulder-length hair, and is dressed in a black suit with a wool coat draped over one arm. He kisses Bíbí lightly on the head, and puts his free arm around her.

Inside, Hörður cools down fast. He wishes that the earth would open up and that he would plunge into its deepest darkness.

The ceremony is over and the group walks across the field in the direction of two large party tents standing behind Elliðabær, on a flat bank of the lake. The sun is gone, but the sky is still red. It's dark in the woods, but the tents are lit up and strings of multicolored lights hang between fence-posts and trees in the surrounding field.

"I can't be here," Hörður whispers to Þóra. "I've got to go."

"What is this bullshit?" she says. "We just arrived. You're not going anywhere."

He looks around but doesn't see Bíbí. "There's a woman here. I went on a date with her this week. It didn't end well. Then she unexpectedly came to visit me the next day, and I kind of threw her out. I don't know what I was thinking."

Þóra sighs. "You're such an oaf!"

"And now she's here," he says. "With some guy. I can't handle this."

"Oh please, relax," says Þóra. "My ex is one of the brides. How do you think I feel?"

"I don't know," he mutters. "Why did you come if you find it uncomfortable? And why the hell did she invite you?"

"Oh, she's the sort of person who wants everyone to be friends," says Þóra. "And I had to come so that she wouldn't think I was still hurting or angry at her or anything like that."

"Are you still hurting?"

Þóra shrugs.

"I understand," he whispers.

They've entered the party tent, inside of which are three long tables, with a name card at each seat.

"You don't even get to choose where you sit?" says Hörður. He takes off his coat and hangs it on a hook on a freestanding coat rack.

Þóra reads the cards. "One might think you'd never gone to a wedding."

"It's my first one, actually," he says.

"Really?"

Hörður nods.

"Here we are," says Þóra, and they take their seats, which are toward the center of the table nearest the woods.

Hörður finds it both strange and amusing to see his name on a card at the wedding of people he doesn't know at all. He looks around, but Bíbí is nowhere to be seen. Maybe she's gone. Much to his surprise, her absence makes him more disappointed than relieved. He likes her, he has to admit to himself.

The fool that he is.

He reaches for an open wine bottle and pours himself a glass.

"Would you like some?"

"Yes, please," says Þóra.

Hörður takes a sip of the wine. In the tent next to theirs, the long tables bend beneath the weight of all the banquet food. Hörður can smell the aroma of roasted game meats, and his mouth begins watering. Maybe this won't be so bad after all.

Þóra chats with the person next to her, a chubby man with a gray beard. Hörður drinks his wine and looks around, at the guests who are already seated and the others still looking for their seats. To his left are two empty seats. He looks at the name card closest to him.

Ester Guðmundsdóttir

He gets a knot in his stomach. Ester? Isn't that …

"Hi, Hörður," says Bíbí as she sits down beside him.

"Hi," he manages to moan.

"Do you know the brides?" asks Bíbí.

"No," says Hörður. "I'm here with my friend Þóra. She's the ex of one of the lesbians. The thin one."

Bíbí smiles slightly. "I see. I'm also here with a friend, Einar."

"I see," says Hörður. He glances at Einar, who is pouring himself some wine. He has hung his jacket on the back of his chair, and is wearing a black vest over a white shirt, and a lime-green tie.

"Would you like some?" he asks Bíbí in a soft bass voice.

"Yes, please, thank you!" she replies cheerfully.

Looking away, Hörður drains his glass in one gulp. He feels awful.

"I heard you mentioned on *Spotlight* yesterday," Bíbí says. She could just as well have punched him in the stomach.

Hörður groans, as if she'd done just that.

"You're a famous man," she adds.

"Don't say that," he says. "Didn't you catch the context? I got the head of the CID in big trouble. He was practically executed on live TV, and it was *my* fault."

"I'm sorry to hear that," says Bíbí.

"That's what you get for thinking you're someone," says Hörður, both hurt and bitter.

"What do you mean?" she asks.

"Oh, just …" he says. "I thought I had some business with the CID. But it turned out to be a misunderstanding."

"You were just trying to help, weren't you?" she asks.

"Yes, but then I ruined everything," Hörður mutters. "It doesn't pay to be ambitious, to cling to foolish dreams. You just have to accept things as they are. No one knows what they have until they've lost it."

"Did you lose your job?" Bíbí asks.

"I don't know," he mutters. "I tried to make up for my mistake, but I have no idea whether it helped or not. I was on the right track with this case. Until that fucking TV journalist led me into a trap. Vanity was my downfall. Vanity and stupidity. I who lived under the delusion that I didn't have any silly defects such as vanity, ambition, and complacency."

Bíbí pats him softly on his left forearm. "You're not stupid, Hörður Grímsson. And ambition isn't a defect. You just made a mistake. It's human."

"Yes, maybe," says Hörður. He looks at his forearm, at the place where she touched him. He can still feel her fingers, warm and soft.

"We're all human," Bíbí adds, smiling.

Hörður refills his glass. "Yes, that's right. But what does it mean to be human? Aren't we all just talking monkeys in clothes?"

Bíbí laughs. "Maybe."

"Shall we make a toast?" he asks.

"Yes, why not?" she replies, lifting her glass. "To what should we be toasting?"

Hörður smiles wistfully. "To lost opportunities."

"Okay," says Bíbí. They look each other in the eye, clink their glasses lightly, and take sips of their wine. Bíbí blinks and looks away, but Hörður gets butterflies in his stomach.

Someone taps a glass with a knife. The guests fall silent and all eyes are directed at the host, a young man wearing a light-red suit.

"The answer is both yes and no," whispers Hörður, a moment before the host bids everyone welcome. Þóra pokes him with her elbow.

"To what?" whispers Bíbí, confusedly.

"The only man in the world is neither happy nor unhappy," whispers Hörður. "He has no idea how he feels."

There are only a few people at the Næsti bar on Ingólfsstræti, the evening being quite young. In an hour or so, all the seats and tables will be occupied, and around midnight, the place will be as tightly packed with people as a shoal of herring. At the moment, two bartenders are on duty, and a third will come on at ten. They're wearing black clothing, in pressed trousers, a shirt and vest. One of them is blond and tall, the other is dark-haired and short. The blond bartender's left eyebrow is pierced, and the dark-haired one has a tattoo on the back of his right hand—a pentagram.

Three men occupy a corner table, and two girlfriends are sipping white wine by the window. At the bar, a young man with a cup of coffee in front of him is chatting with the blond bartender, a former classmate of his from Sund High School. The dark-haired bartender is putting away glasses that are still hot and damp, just out of the dishwasher.

The blond bartender's name is Benedikt Arnarsson, and his old classmate is called Elías. The dark-haired bartender's name is Hákon Úlfarsson. Hákon had worked at the bar all summer, before getting work on a fishing boat. He still takes a few shifts though, whenever he's on land.

"When did you last see them?" asks Elías.

"It was probably at my uncle Davíð's fiftieth birthday party," says Benedikt. "Davíð is Sólrún's dad. We're cousins, but I haven't really spent any time with her since we were kids."

He tops up Elías's coffee from a glass pot holding a freshly brewed batch. "His birthday was this summer, at the end of July. I'm pretty sure that Gísli Már was there, too. But I didn't speak with him. I know Sólrún better."

"Where was this birthday party?" Elías asks.

"Where?" asks Benedikt. "Someplace in Kópavogur. Why do you ask?"

"What sort of refreshments were served?" asks Elías. "Cold or warm? From a catering service, or homemade?"

"Just appetizers and the like. Soup, too, I think," says Benedikt. "Why are you asking me about this birthday party?"

Hákon is still putting away the clean glasses. He's not in any hurry, and acts as if he's not listening to the two friends' conversation.

"Because there's something peculiar about it all," says Elías. "Do you know if either of them owns a cat, Gísli or Sólrún?"

"No, I don't know," says Benedikt. "Why do you ask?"

"Has either of them has gone abroad in recent months or weeks?" asks Elías. "To France, for example?"

"Is this an interrogation, or what?" Benedikt asks. "Why are you asking all these strange questions?"

Elías leans forward and lowers his voice. "Toxoplasma gondii."

"Toxo—what?" asks Benedikt. He looks at Hákon, who appears to be immersed in what he's doing.

"It's a worm, a parasite," says Elias. "It's carried by rats, and is transmitted from them to humans via cats. It's belie-ved that around thirty to fifty percent of all people in the world are infected with toxoplasma gondii, but the ratio is highest in France: eighty-four percent."

"And?" Benedikt asks.

"The parasite takes over the host's brain functions," says Elías. "Rats that are infected by the parasite act reckless; they even threaten predators, including domestic cats. The parasite controls them; it *wants* the cat to catch it and eat it, because then it will inhabit a larger host and be a step closer to man, its ultimate target. When a cat becomes infected, it starts peeing indoors, according to the parasite's *command*. The owner of the cat makes contact with its urine, and voilà—the parasite is transmitted to the man!"

Benedikt laughs out loud. "I've never heard anything like it! Have you heard of this, Hákon?"

"Of what?" asks Hákon indifferently.

"Parasites that control rats and cats," says Benedikt. "Toxoplasma something. It spreads to people through cat piss ... and then what?"

"It starts controlling the person," says Elías. "The host starts suffering all sorts of maladies, such as typhoid fever and schizophrenia. The parasite takes control of the brain and can make the host do anything, but its purpose is always the same: spreading to more people, and finally taking over the world."

Benedikt shakes his head. "Sorry, but I find this really hard to believe. What do you think, Hákon?"

"Sounds pretty far-fetched," says Hákon.

"Schizophrenia, Benni. Think about it," says Elías. "Your uncle and aunt commit murder. They've never done anything wrong, but one day they murder innocent people, in cold blood. Which is more unbelievable: your relatives turning into murderers in a single night, or *known* parasites taking control of their central nervous systems?"

Benedikt sighs. "I don't know. Are you saying that there was something wrong with the food at Davíð's fiftieth birthday party?"

"Maybe," says Elías. He looks at his coffee cup, and then pushes it aside. "You should probably have yourself checked out. Just in case."

"Weren't they on ecstasy?" asks Hákon.

"Yes, as far as I understand," says Benedikt. "Which really surprises me. Gísli, for example, is an athlete through-and-through. He's hardly ever touched alcohol. I don't know about Sólrún."

"The parasite made them take the X," says Elías. "Maybe it wanted them to go dancing. That way, they would meet a lot of strangers who could be easily infected. Now they're in custody. The parasite may have spread to the police and health professionals. Maybe the entire system will be infected soon—all public servants. Then it won't be long before all of society goes bonkers."

"That would be crazy," says Hákon, grinning. "Would everyone be wandering around in some sort of psychotic state, then? Like in a zombie movie?"

"Something like that," mutters Elías.

"You've always been a fan of such conspiracy theories," says Benedikt, smiling at Elías. "I remember when you were obsessed with aliens. After you read the article about the oblong skulls found in South America."

"The Paracas skulls in Peru aren't human," insists Elías. "It's been scientifically proven."

"All right, then," says Benedikt. "But I'm not buying this about the parasite. I'm inclined to think this is all just a coincidence. A peculiar coincidence, an extremely unpleasant coincidence, but a coincidence nonetheless."

Hákon nods. "That's what I think, too."

"It's all too strange to be a coincidence," says Elías, stepping off his barstool. "I've got to get going. My girlfriend's waiting at home. Thanks for the coffee, Benni."

"You're welcome." Benedikt removes his untouched coffee cup. "Stop by again later."

"Will do," says Elías, before going out into the evening darkness.

Benedikt's phone starts vibrating in his vest pocket. He looks at the screen but doesn't recognize the number, which is for a landline phone. He sticks the vibrating phone back into his pocket.

Hákon wipes off the bar top. "Should I make two staff coffees?"

"Yes, please." Benedikt pushes a curtain aside and takes his coffee cup with him into the back room, where he pours its contents into a steel sink before placing it in a tray for dirty glasses. The phone is still vibrating. Benedikt takes it out again and answers it.

"Hello?"

Out at the bar, Hákon pours coffee into two cups. He then pours a shot of Grand Marnier into each cup—making so-called staff coffees. He glances at the curtain separating the bar from the back room, then fishes a small syringe containing a clear liquid from his vest pocket and empties the contents into one of the cups. Then he puts the empty syringe back into his pocket and stirs the coffee gently with a teaspoon.

When Benedikt reappears, he hands him the cup containing the GHB.

"One staff coffee, as you ordered."

"No thanks," mutters Benedikt. He's holding his jacket, and has a distant look on his face.

"Is anything wrong?" asks Hákon.

"The cops just called," says Benedikt. "They want me to go straight home and call them back once I'm there. Something to do with the murders. Still, they wouldn't give me any clear answers."

"But you're working!" says Hákon.

Benedikt shrugs and puts on his jacket. "I've got to go. Sorry."

Hákon shakes his head. "Fucking bullshit. Are you sure you can't stay a half an hour longer?"

Benedikt looks over the room. "It's pretty dead right now."

"At least have one staff coffee with me," says Hákon. "I've already mixed in the liqueur."

"I have to go," says Benedikt, before walking in front of the bar, through the room, and out into the evening.

"Damn it," mutters Hákon. He pours both of the coffees down the sink, takes out his phone and calls a number on speed dial.

"It's me," he says when someone answers. "The cops are on our trail. They warned Benedikt."

"Get out of there," says a man's voice at the other end. *"Make yourself disappear. We'll talk later."*

Hákon hangs up and looks around. One of the three men sitting at the corner table is now standing at the bar. "Yes?"

"A round of lagers, please," says the man.

"Just a moment," says Hákon. He pushes the curtain aside and disappears into the back room.

The man waits at the bar. The bartender doesn't return, but after a few minutes, two police officers come walking in and go and stand next to the man. He nods at them.

"Isn't anyone working?" asks one of the police officers.

"He went to the back," says the customer.

"Wait here," says one police officer to the other, before stepping behind the bar and into the back room. There's no one there. The officer sets eyes on a back door that's open halfway. He peeks out through it.

The door opens onto a dark, empty alley that smells of garbage and urine.

Hákon Úlfarsson has vanished into the night.

At Elliðavatn Lake, it's pitch-dark except for the illuminated party tents and the strings of multicolored lights running to fenceposts and trees. The long tables have been removed, all except the high table occupied by the wedding party and another serving as a bar. The chairs have been lined up along the tent walls, and at the end of one of the tents, a band is playing pop songs, old and new.

Hörður is sitting to one side, drinking beer from a can, listening to the music with one ear and watching the wedding guests dance. He's wearing his coat, it being a bit chilly even though the tents are heated with powerful gas heaters. Þóra, who is dancing with her two girlfriends, gestures to Hörður to join in. He shakes his head and smiles apologetically. He would sooner go riding a bike in a spandex outfit than dance in front of other people.

He has lost sight of Bíbí, which is perhaps for the best. He's tired of thinking only about her and getting butterflies in the stomach every time he sees her. She has probably just gone home.

I wonder if she left with that Einar? Wonder if they're …

Hörður tries not to think about it. The thought of her doing something with another man makes him jealous.

Damn. He messed it up with Bíbí, just like he messes up everything else. It's his destiny—everything that he touches changes into its opposite. Murder investigations become farces, and romantic dates become Greek tragedies.

Here's to that! Hörður lifts his beer can to his lips and takes a sip of the lukewarm beer. He's in mid-sip when Bíbí suddenly appears, as if by magic.

"Don't we owe each other one dance?"

The beer goes down the wrong pipe, and Hörður coughs with his mouth closed, twitches, and inadvertently blows the beer out of the nostrils.

"Do I take that as a yes?" says Bíbí, with a mischievous smile on her lips.

Hörður hesitates, and then nods and stands up. He wipes the beer off his face with the back of his left hand, tosses the beer can aside and takes Bíbí's outstretched hand, which is warm and incredibly soft.

"Good," she says, leading him to the dance floor. At the same moment, the drummer counts the band into a new song. It's "Careless Whisper" by Wham, which the singer says is one of the bride's favorite songs.

"I have to warn you, though," says Hörður as he places the palm of his right hand on Bíbí's lower back. "I'm a really terrible dancer."

"We'll see," says Bíbí. She grabs his left hand, entwines her fingers with his and leans her head against his chest. Then they dance a slow dance—so slowly that they merely rock gently in place, barely moving at all.

"I'm never gonna dance again. Guilty feet have got no rhythm."

Hörður's heart beats so fast that he fears it will knock Bíbí out. She must hear it knocking on his rib cage. He breathes in the scent of her hair, gently laying his cheek on the top of her head. He looks at his giant paw closed around her delicate fingers, and feels the heat from her tiny hand resting like a little bird in the embrace of a lion.

He can hardly believe that he's dancing. Him, who never dances! She caught him by surprise, he wasn't prepared for such a thing, but then said yes before he could think up a hundred reasons for saying no. But he's glad he accepted the invitation. Dancing with Bíbí is both fun and nice. More than nice—it's wonderful. He hopes that the song never ends; he wants to dance like this forever. Their feet move slowly to and fro, controlling themselves; he just goes along with them. The two of them slowly rotate, two bodies that adapt to each other—two souls that melt together in a slow dance and gradually become one.

Þóra is slow dancing with a young woman. She smiles beautifully at Hörður, and he smiles back at her. Then he lets his eyelids droop, drinks in Bíbí's warmth, breathes in her fragrance, merges with the music and disappears into the moment.

"I'm never gonna dance again ..."

He's happy, joyful. He's floating on a cloud; he's dancing among the stars in the sky. They're alone in the universe—the universe is alone in them.

Hörður is perfectly happy for a moment at a time, heartbeat upon heartbeat. He experiences pure joy—the joy of immortality.

"We could have been so good together. We could have lived this dance forever."

Legs move, hearts beat in rhythm. Then the melancholy song ends; then the dance ends. They separate, look into each other's eyes and applaud the band.

Hörður feels shy, but he wants more. Another dance, anything. But before either of them can say a word, the next song begins. It's "Love Me Do," by the Beatles. Hörður stiffens up. He's not sure he's confident enough for a song like that. The only dance move he knows is a stiff, side-together-side step.

"Would you mind?" Bíbí's friend Einar asks. He doesn't wait for an answer, but grabs his friend and spins her around, before they both start dancing their hearts out.

Hörður smiles apologetically at Bíbí, who shrugs and gives him a what-can-you-do look.

Hörður leaves the dance floor and goes straight to the bar. He fishes a beer can from a tub of ice and strolls out under the open sky. *We could have been so good together. We could have danced this dance forever.*

We could have. But the opportunity slipped through his fingers.

He walks to the edge of the woods, sits down on a fallen tree trunk and looks out over the dark lake, toward the city glowing in the distance. Overhead is the vault of the night sky, with its thousands of stars and a bright moon that draws out the outlines of the forest, gleams on the water and will be full in one day. He turns his back on the reception, but the sounds of it still reach his ears. The water ripples when a fish tries for a fly, and a soft rustling sound wafts from the woods.

Hörður sips his beer and thinks about Bíbí. He likes her, he admits to himself, but he knows best of all that he doesn't deserve such a woman, and that a woman like her would never put up with a man like him. She's warm and kind, and he's distant and cold. She'll end up with a man like that Einar, with whom she came—a handsome, tasteful man who doesn't get drunk all the time and knows how to behave around people. He himself will undoubtedly end up alone, maybe in a hut in the woods—perhaps with a dog and a shotgun, like Lieutenant Glahn in *Pan* by Hamsun.

He isn't what a woman like Bíbí is looking for. She wants an ordinary man who enjoys ordinary things. A man with whom she can establish a home and have children. A man who has a lot of friends, plays golf or bridge and barbecues on weekends. A man who stands by her and supports her. A man who isn't silent and heavy. A man who isn't a psychic troll who doesn't like modernity and feels like everything was better in the old days. A man who should have lived two hundred years ago—two thousand, even.

No, Hörður Grímsson is no dream prince. He's a loner. The strong, silent type who is attractive to women, but whom they soon give up on. Like Humphrey Bogart in a good old Hollywood movie. Women pursued him, but he always ended up alone, anyway, haggard and bitter, with three days of stubble and a shot glass of whiskey.

Women! What are they besides drama and bother? Beautiful, certainly, but apart from that they're flighty and unpredictable. If it weren't for the sex drive, no man in his right mind would go near them.

"Better an empty bed than sharing it with the wrong person," mutters Hörður. If his fate is to spend the rest of his life alone, he isn't going to fight it. He spends a lot of time alone, but is never lonely. The two are very different. He isn't bored in his own company, far from it. He has his books and music, his own thoughts. He appreciates silence, and the peace that comes with living alone. No hassle. It's only immature souls who can't enjoy being alone. Not only can he do so, but he does so—and needs to do so.

Solitude isn't poison. It's an elixir—the wine of the soul.

Exactly! Hörður raises his beer can, toasts himself in his mind, and takes a sip of the lukewarm beer.

"Is there room for another butt on this tree trunk?"

Hörður starts; again the beer goes down the wrong pipe, but this time doesn't shoot out his nose. He manages to swallow, looking in surprise at Bíbí as she sits down next to him.

"Am I bothering you?" she asks.

He shakes his head. "I just needed to step away for a bit. Get some fresh air. Breathe in the silence."

She nods. "Me too. Receptions are nice, but it's easy to have enough. The commotion can be overwhelming sometimes—the voices, the eyes, the music. Sometimes I just disappear."

Hörður open his eyes wider, questioningly. Does she really mean this? Or is she just saying what he wants to hear?

They sit there silently for some time. Their silence is far from being tense or uncomfortable.

Finally, it's Hörður that breaks it. "They're beautiful, these autumn evenings."

Bíbí nods.

He clears his throat. "You asked me a question on Tuesday, when you were cutting my hair. I didn't answer it."

"How did you decide to become a police officer?"

Hörður nods. "Some say it's a calling, others that it's simply a matter of education, but I suppose you need both. You've got to have some interest in it to start with, but why people take interest in a job like this is of course simply a mystery—nothing less. It isn't for the pay, that's for certain. And it's not the work hours or the assignments, and even less the respect that the job gets these days. We do all the dirty work and get little or no thanks for it. No, it's easier said than done to explain why any man in his right mind would become a police officer, which may be where you can find your answer. We may not be in our right minds, and if we ever were, we're not any more after doing this thankless job for some time. But when you get right down to it, I think the fact is that you can always take the man out of the police officer, but you can never take the police officer out of the man. Education or no education, this is a birth defect, damn it. I've always been a cop, and always will be a cop."

"Good answer," says Bíbí.

He inhales through his nose. "I also want to apologize to you."

"Oh?" she says.

"Our date didn't go exactly as I imagined," says Hörður. "I got lost in work—I admit it. You gave up on me, and I understand that well. But I'm sorry about the way I treated you."

"No problem," mutters Bíbí. "You had a lot going on at work. Murders aren't committed every day. Your mind was elsewhere. It happens to the best of us."

"And the rest of us, too," adds Hörður.

Bíbí smiles. "I know you're not perfect. But I don't believe that you're a bad man."

"It depends on how you look at it," he says. "And look, I owe you another apology. I wasn't what you'd call welcoming when you showed up at my place the other evening."

Bíbí nods. "You found it uncomfortable, right? For me to show up like that, so unexpectedly?"

"Yes," says Hörður.

"I noticed," she says softly. "You don't feel comfortable having visitors. People entering your personal space. It makes you feel suffocated. You feel even worse if a visitor touches the things in your home or moves them. Then it's as if your world is starting to collapse. You want things in their places, as you've decided are best. That's when you feel safe. That's when you feel good."

Hörður gapes in astonishment. "How do you know this? I couldn't have explained it better myself! Are you … are you psychic?"

Bíbí laughs. "No, not at all. But … you mustn't misunderstand me. I have a cousin who's autistic. I'm *not* saying that you're autistic, not at all, but you're probably on the spectrum, like so many. Which isn't bad or anything like that—it just explains some things."

He frowns. "Are you saying that I have Asperger's?"

"It doesn't matter what it's called," she says, patting his broad back. "All I'm saying is that if you find it uncomfortable having unexpected visitors show up at your home, it's neither unhealthy nor wrong. You're *allowed* to feel uncomfortable."

"Yeah, okay," says Hörður. "Still, I was rather rude to you. And I'm sorry. You didn't deserve it. But this week has been so difficult, too. If that's any excuse."

Bíbí nods. "Difficult week, yes. But you've seen it worse. Haven't you also had a difficult life? Lost all of your closest relatives in one day, and before you were twenty. That had to have its effects."

Hörður nods.

"Did you get any help?" she asks. "Like trauma counseling? Have you gone to see a psychologist or psychiatrist?"

He shakes his head.

"How do you carry all this inside you?" she asks gently. "The loss? The grief? The regret?"

Hörður grunts. "Don't forget the guilt. They're dead, but I'm still alive. I should be happy, but instead, I feel guilty. I'm the boy who survived. And I feel miserable."

Bíbí strokes the back of his hand. "I wish I could say that I understand you. But I don't. No one can understand such feelings. No one except for those who've experienced the same."

Hörður shivers, as the night has grown cooler. "It's as if death has a special fondness for me. Or that it singles me out. At least, it lets me live while it snatches away everyone else. Everyone who matters to me. Even my little siblings."

"Oh, my dear friend," Bíbí says, moving closer to him. "But your memories of them live, don't they? They all live in your heart."

Hörður laughs coldly. "Sorry, but such phrases don't help much. The heart is just a muscle and the soul doesn't exist, any more than God, and my family is dead and buried. Even though I certainly remember them, it's not like they're alive. The only one still living is me. I think, I remember—I suffer."

"I didn't mean any harm," Bíbí mumbles.

"I know, I know." Hörður sighs. "Forgive me. I can be a bit cold. It's just so difficult to talk about this. I'm still so angry. Angry at life, at fate, and at God. Still, I don't believe in God, per se. If he existed, such things would never happen. He would protect the innocent, wouldn't he? Would God, the creator of the world, create something like cancer? As if it isn't enough to die! We know that one day our lives will end—so why do we have to be eternally worried about diseases and accidents—avalanches! No, no beneficent God would create such a world. There's no creator and no eternal life. The only thing that's eternal is the emptiness—the darkness and cold that fill the universe."

"I understand very well that you feel that way, that you think this way," says Bíbí empathetically. "But it must also be difficult to feel like that, to be suffering, without faith or solace of any kind."

"You get used to it," mutters Hörður. "But it's not like I'm suffering all day, every day—I'm not nailed to a cross or anything like that. Usually I'm just working, reading a book or listen to music. When I forget myself in my daily routine, it's easy to exist. Then, I'm preoccupied with something insignificant and feel like my life has purpose, without actually thinking about it, you know. When you're busy with something, you're *not* thinking. At those times, you just *are*. But as soon as I start thinking about things outside of the commonplace, about the big picture, that's when the emptiness and futility come—why wake up in the morning or go to work? Why not just drink myself to death?"

"Why die, if you can live?" asks Bíbí in return. "At least life can surprise you. But death is final. Choosing death over life is such a huge surrender. Do you understand what I mean?"

Hörður nods, and then cracks a smile. "You're really something else, I must say. Such dark talk usually gets people to run away or call the Emergency Line. You probably have thick skin, even if you don't look like you do."

Bíbí laughs softly. "Never judge a book by its cover."

"Right," he says." I can be more pessimistic than the devil, I do admit it. Still, I don't always mean everything I say. Sometimes unadulterated pessimism is more refreshing than a strong cup of coffee."

"Maybe," she says.

"And they do live in memory—you're right," he admits. "Mom, Dad, my brother and sister. But not in such a way that I feel as if they're alive when I think about them. It's more complicated than that. I might be doing something, reading or repairing my motorcycle or out driving, and then a song comes on the radio, or I smell a certain smell—something that evokes a vibrant memory, and then it's as if I go back in time for a few seconds, or just for a single moment.

"Voulez-Vous" by Abba, and suddenly I'm in our old house in Súðavík. Mom is vacuuming. She's wearing a flowery dress and slippers, with her hair in a bun and singing her heart out. I catch a whiff of Ajax and freshly baked doughnuts.

"I spray WD40 on a rusty screw, and Dad appears in an overall and his hair tied in a ponytail, mumbling something grumpily, irritatedly. I want him to see me, for him to say something, but he disappears as soon as he appeared.

"The sounds of video games conjure up my brother, silent but warm. Once I saw some Star Wars toys and felt his presence right away. I felt like I never knew my brother well enough, and therefore miss him most; it's so weird.

"Someone sharpens a pencil, and my sister's laughter echoes in my head. The smell of pencil shavings can conjure her up, as well as oranges and pink hairpins. She was very much like me and our mom; my brother was more like Dad. My sister was very smart. I also think she was psychic, like me and my mom. But we never got to talk about it, any more than so much else.

"For me, life is kind of like that. A series of moments, experiences and memories, some good but others not so good. Some moments live, others don't. Some we remember, others we don't. What happens between these moments is dead time, what we call days and years—the emptiness that fills our lives. When we experience moments, old or new, we feel like we're alive, and nothing else matters. Then the emptiness takes over, the life struggle, the work and the futility.

"I'm trying to put this into context, create some sort of image or an impression or whatever it's called, but it's easier said than done. If I were a poet, I could undoubtedly put it all into one splendid phrase, but I'm neither Hamsun nor Gunnar Gunnarsson. Do you have Gyrðir Elíasson's phone number?

"Does life have a purpose? I don't know. Sometimes I feel as if everything we do is futile by nature. Showing up for work and being ambitious and all that. The more pressure that I put on myself, the more ambition that I show, the greater the chaos that I create around me. Purpose, ambition, a goal—it's all the same rainbow, and a rainbow retreats if you try to catch it. Isn't it just as good to sit on your ass, relax, and look at the rainbow from a distance?

"Maybe life is like a tranquil river running from the beginning of time to the end of the universe and we're trouts who spend our entire lives in the depths, down in the darkness. But from time to time we awaken, we swim up and push our consciousnesses through the surface and experience something unforgettable—light, colors, and feelings merge in a kind of rainbow that perhaps shares a part of eternity with us."

He pauses, and in the silence are the night, the forest, the water, and the moon—and the two of them on a log under a roof of galaxies.

"Are you psychic?" asks Bíbí, after a few moments.

Hörður hesitates before nodding. "But it isn't like I see dead people or can talk to them. I see shadows appear before death snatches away one more soul. A kind of black ghost that's a premonition or something like that. I don't know what it's called, but I call these visions death-shadows. When it happens, I feel terribly cold, and for a moment it's as if I'm watching the world through the eyes of death. We become one, death and I. I'm in death and death is in me."

"Ugh," says Bíbí. "It sounds awful."

Hörður agrees. "I've never told anyone about this. Not one single living soul. Until now, that is."

She leans toward him. "Thank you for sharing this with me."

He puts his arms around her. "Thank you for listening, for being there. It felt good to say these things. They've been weighing on me my whole life, like a nightmare."

"Sometimes it's good to keep quiet," says Bíbí. "But sometimes it's better to speak up."

"Yes," he says. "I told you these things so that you would understand me better. There's a reason for me being the way I am. I don't know if I could bear losing more loved ones. That's why it's easiest for me to love no one."

"But don't you want to get married one day?" she asks.

Hörður shakes his head. "Don't take it personally, but a person who isn't married can never get a divorce. A person who isn't born can never die. He just lives in a dream."

"But can't that dream be shared?" Bíbí whispers in his ear.

Hörður feels a tingling in his stomach. "Yes, perhaps."

Black Magic

Hörður is traveling through a forest. It's night, and the woods are covered in darkness, though now and then the moon can be seen peeking through the crowns of the trees. The earth is covered with leaves, evergreen needles, and twigs; the indistinct tree trunks stretch high into the sky. He goes deeper into the forest, which conceals something that both repels him and pulls him forward.

Something that he fears, but that he has to see.

It's cold in the woods, which smell of rotting wood and leaves; the fallen trees are covered with moss and there are mushrooms everywhere, yellow, white, red. Ahead of him is a clearing; he bends his back and creeps forward, and then peeks out between trees. In the clearing, a fire is burning. Someone has dug narrow channels into the ground—channels that form a pentagram. In the channels, oil burns.

That someone is crouched down inside the pentagram. It's a naked male of an undetermined age, long-limbed and so skinny that he's nothing but skin and bones. His hair is black and so long that it covers his face. His bony body is as white as milk, covered with magic runes that are either burned or cut into his flesh. Around the man is all sorts of bric-a-brac, utensils, and tools—skulls and bones, bowls and knives, shells and pebbles. On a pole hangs the carcass of a black cat, and beneath it lies a dead raven.

Hörður lies there hidden, and watches the man brew something sinister. In a bowl, he mixes ground bones, blood from the cat, bile from the raven, and thick fat that he scoops out of a clay jar. Then he skins the cat and strings its hide tight on a frame, skin side facing him. He smears the mixture from the bowl onto the skin; the concoction is black, and finally, the skin is transformed into a black mirror. The man faces the mirror toward the moon, and it takes on a silvery hue.

The man stands up, yet he's still all bent and crooked. He mutters some spells, intertwines his fingers and holds them up to the moon, casting their silhouette onto the mirror. At first, the silhouette bears no resemblance to anything, but then it starts to take shape. The man murmurs and mumbles, moves his fingers, and conjures up a little demon in the mirror.

The demon has hooves and a tail, a goatee and curved horns.

It straightens up, smiles widely, and jumps out of the mirror.

Hörður is startled. He hides behind some trees, but continues to watch what is happening in the clearing. The conjurer continues to cast a silhouette on the mirror, while the demon that he created has acquired a life of its own—it stands outside the mirror and moves like the silhouette that the conjurer controls.

The demon leaps into action, shooting through the night and landing on the living-room floor of a darkened home. Smirking, it slinks into a bedroom, where Bíbí is sleeping beneath a white duvet.

No! Hörður leaps out of his hiding place and screams loudly. But Bíbí doesn't hear him.

The demon looks at Hörður, a gleam of hatred in its beastly eyes, and then it smirks once more and pulls out a curved dagger. It bends over the bed, intending to cut Bíbí's throat. The dagger is raised; its menacing tip glistens.

Hörður starts running, then stops and looks over his shoulder. In the clearing, the conjurer stands there bent-backed, casting the silhouette on the mirror.

Deeper in the night, the demon hovers bent-backed over Bíbí.

Hörður hesitates. Should he run toward the conjurer or the demon—toward the puppet or the puppet master? Which one is the real enemy? Which one is more dangerous? Which one is closer?

What should he do?

What?

Sunday

When Hörður opens his eyes, he's not certain at first of where he is. His heart is pounding, he's sweaty and his hands tremble.

Had he been dreaming something?

The room he's in is larger than the basement apartment that he's renting, and the sun shines differently through the windows. He's lying on a living-room sofa with a blanket over him. He blinks while his brain processes this limited information. On the walls are photographs and paintings; the apartment is large and bright and tidy.

Was it here that the demon landed?

Hörður shudders. Suddenly he remembers the dream. What a nightmare! He sits up, pulls off the blanket and rubs his neck. On the coffee table are an empty bottle of white wine and two glasses. Right, he remembers it now. He's at Bíbí's place. They shared a taxi-ride home from the wedding. She'd had half a bottle of white wine in the fridge, left over from one of her friends' visits. They finished the bottle, and then went to sleep—she into her bedroom, and he on the sofa.

Nothing had happened. And yet. They kissed. But neither of them wanted to go any further. She's undoubtedly an upright girl. He's simply too insecure, too shy. And anyway, there was no rush. They would be meeting again.

Or, what? Yes—wouldn't they?

Hörður scratches his head and looks at his watch. It's nearly ten o'clock. Sunday morning. He's thirsty, and a bit groggy. He wants a cigarette and a cold Coke.

He slinks into the bathroom, pees and splashes cold water on his face. The bedroom door is closed. He goes into the kitchen and opens the fridge. There's no Coke but he drinks a little orange juice straight from the bottle.

He looks out the living-room window. The apartment is on the third floor of an apartment building on Birkimelur Street, on the west side of town. Beyond a large roundabout are Hotel Saga and the University Cinema, and a little farther north are the Shell gas station and National and University Library. Blinded by the sun, he turns away.

Hanging on one wall are countless family photos. Bíbí clearly has a large family. He himself has none.

Hörður looks around. The apartment is so different from his own that it's not even funny. Why would Bíbí want a man like him? Wouldn't she rather be with an ordinary man? Some fit, well-educated business administrator or CEO who also has a large family and dreams of a house in the suburbs, a dog, and a few children? Hörður himself can't imagine helping to propagate mankind.

Bíbí is a lovely girl. He likes her. But is there any future in this? Is there any future in *him*?

They talked together. They had some drinks. They had fun. Still, they didn't sleep together. Isn't that an indication of something? Wouldn't they have slept together if they'd been sure?

He doesn't know.

Hörður sighs. Is he overthinking this? No doubt. But that's not to say that he's wrong.

He's desperate for a cigarette. He finds his leather coat in the entrance and pats its pockets. In one of them he finds a crumpled pack holding two cigarettes. Should he go out on the balcony?

No, it's probably best just to get going. Take a leisurely stroll home.

Bíbí might be embarrassed if he's still in the apartment when she wakes up. She may have morals or something.

Hörður puts on his motorcycle boots and coat and slinks out onto the landing, shutting the door gently behind him. He walks down the carpeted staircase and out into the cool morning air.

He puts on his sunglasses, lights a cigarette and blows smoke through his nostrils. What a luxury! Nothing compares to the first cigarette of the day. Still, he should quit. It's fucking poison. Goddamn fucking wonderful poison.

Hörður walks north along Birkimelur. There are few cars out on the streets, the city is quiet and there's practically no pollution. At the corner of Birkimelur and Hringbraut is the bakery at which Hörður and Vigfús sometimes stop. From its door waft the aromas of bread and cakes. Hörður's stomach is upset. He's hungry, but still too hungover to have an appetite.

He crosses Hringbraut and walks over to Ljósvallagata, then along the western wall of the Hólavellir Cemetery. The cemetery's trees shield him from the strong rays of the autumn sun. He can't get the dream out of his head, the nightmare about the conjurer and the demon that he sent to kill Bíbí. Why does he dream such horrendous crap? The dream was very realistic, as was the fear that he felt—his fear of the demon and evil. Of course it had only been a dream, but the smirk on the demon's face is as if burned into his mind.

Why can't he ever dream anything beautiful?

Hörður doesn't know the answer to that question. He feels quite numb inside, but it's refreshing to walk in the cool air; his blood flows faster and the grogginess in his head gradually disappears.

The streets are empty; not a single soul around. Just like in the book about the only man in the world.

Hörður turns the corner of the cemetery and continues north along Garðastræti Street. At the intersection with Hávallagata Street, he looks left, and sets eyes on a sparse grove of trees at the corner of Hólavallagata. Between the leafless trees, he catches a glimpse of the back of the Catholic Cathedral standing on Landakot Hill. He stops there, before walking westward along Hávallagata and into the garden on the hill. There, the yellow, red, and brown leaves of the trees lining the path rustle.

He's facing the church, dark gray and splendid—it's the Baroque, chiseled in stone, with a rectangular tower and stained-glass windows. The Cathedral of Christ the King is the northernmost cathedral in the world, and the only *real church* in the country, in the opinion of the police officer. His mother was a Catholic, as was as everyone else on his mother's side. Although Hörður considers himself an atheist, he still finds it difficult to turn his back completely on Catholicism. Maybe out of respect for his mother's memory.

Maybe because he really wants to believe in a higher power and eternal life—in the opposite of death and all the evil that he experiences both in dreams and his waking life. The thought of a universe without hope or purpose is somehow so depressing.

The Catholic Church acknowledges the existence of evil spirits and the devil himself. Hörður does, too—he has seen the devil smirking. And the Catholic Church believes in both magic and miracles. At its core is the eucharist, the holy sacrament, when bread and wine are transformed into the body and blood of Christ. The ceremony isn't symbolic, it's literal. The transubstantiation is a magical act, in which bread and wine are changed into Christ.

Hörður opens the heavy church door, removes his sunglasses, and walks through the vestibule and into the elegant nave. The church is silent and peaceful and smells like an old library. He dips his fingers into water that's been blessed, goes down on one knee, bows to the crucified king hanging over the altar, and crosses himself at the same time.

He puts some coins into a donation box, takes four candles and lights them before the statue of Mary at the back of the church. Then he kneels before the statue, presses his palms together and recites the Lord's Prayer and the Hail Mary for his parents and siblings.

Hail Mary, full of grace …

Hörður feels warm, and then as if he's floating, and finally, it's as if his body dissolves or melts. His eyes fill with warm tears and before he knows it, they well up and stream down his cheeks. He gets a lump in his throat and sobs.

What's going on? He *never* cries! He just misses his family so much. He misses them so terribly much.

Hörður opens his teary eyes and looks up at the Mother of God, and at the same time, the church bells begin to ring. He starts, stands up, and wipes away the tears with the back of his hand.

At the altar stands a tall priest in full vestments. The church door opens and in walks a family from the Philippines. Following them come a few Polish people. All are dressed in their Sunday best.

Hörður looks at his watch, which shows twenty minutes past ten. Sunday mass is starting in ten minutes, and the congregation files in. He hurries out under the open sky and walks onto the lawn east of the church.

He sits down on the grass and lights his last cigarette. Ten minutes ago, he was on his way home to his cramped and airless basement apartment, but now he can't think of going there. He doesn't want to spend the day by himself. He longs for something other than depression and silence.

Hörður finds the right bell and presses the button. An uncomfortably long amount of time passes before she answers.

"Hello?"

He bends down and speaks directly into the intercom. "Hi, it's me—Hörður!"

"Oh!"

"Is this a bad time?" he asks hesitantly.

No answer.

He hears a click as she hangs up the intercom phone, and then a loud buzz as the door is unlocked.

Hörður hurries to open the door to the foyer, and then goes up to the third floor, carrying a bag stuffed with pastries from Björn's Bakery. Just as he steps onto the landing, Bíbí opens the door to her apartment. She's barefoot, is dressed in a thick bathrobe, and has a towel wrapped around her head.

He's flabbergasted. "Were you in the shower? I guess I should have called ahead. I can come back later."

She smiles and gestures to him to come in. "Don't be silly. I just thought you'd gone home."

"Well, no ..." He steps over the threshold and hands her the bag. "I just popped out to the bakery. Bought a few things. To have with coffee, you know."

"Oh, that's so sweet!" Bíbí looks into the bag, then stands on her toes and kisses him on the cheek before marching into the kitchen.

She radiates warmth following her shower, and smells of coconut oil.

"I didn't know what you like best, so I just bought some of this and some of that," says Hörður, taking off his boots and coat.

"I'm going to make some coffee," Bíbí calls out from the kitchen.

"Sounds great," says Hörður. He follows her into the kitchen and sits down at the table, which is by the window. On the windowsill stands a radio, which Hörður switches on. It's set to The Wave, upon which the eleven o'clock news are being read.

"Did you sleep all right on the sofa?" Bíbí asks. As the coffee drips into the pot, she arranges the pastries on a tray. The bag contains three types of buns, two croissants, two *pains au chocolat* and half a length of Danish pastry with icing.

"Just fine," says Hörður.

"Good," she says, smiling at him. Feeling slightly embarrassed, he smiles faintly. He has a huge crush on her, but doesn't quite know what to say or what to do.

If there were such a thing as a manual on gender relations, he really wouldn't mind having a look at it.

Hörður listens to the news with one ear.

It appears that no murder had been committed during the night. He's relieved. But there haven't been any reports of any new arrests, and Axel M. Axelsson is still under great pressure from the media and Parliament.

Were Hákon, Þorsteinn and Orri still on the loose?

"Do you think he should resign?" Bíbí asks. "The head of the CID?"

Hörður feels slightly dizzy. If Axel loses his job, it will be his fault. "Yes and no. He's very good at his job. But I understand the criticism, up to a certain point."

"Is it true what was said on *Spotlight?*" Bíbí asks. "That it was you who predicted that a judge would be murdered?"

Hörður gets a knot in his stomach. "Yes, it's true. But I shouldn't have told that damn TV journalist about it. And if those fools who were watching the house had done their job, the judge would still be alive, and Axel and I wouldn't be at risk of losing our jobs."

"You could lose your job?"

Hörður nods.

"Oh, I hope it all works out." Bíbí adds cheese, butter, and jam to the tray, and places it on the table. "Lucky me, receiving such a wonderful delivery!"

"My pleasure," says Hörður.

She fetches cups and saucers, then pours them freshly made coffee.

"Thanks," says Hörður. He slices a bun, butters it, and puts cheese and jam in between the two halves.

Bíbí has a *pain au chocolat.* "Shouldn't we just enjoy the day and put aside all of our worries until tomorrow?"

Hörður smiles at her. "You're a ray of sunshine, you know that?"

She blushes. "You're cute."

"I am?" he asks in surprise.

"Maybe you'd also like to take a shower?" she asks nonchalantly. "I can loan you a towel."

"Well … no, no. It's okay," he says. "I'll just shower at home. I don't have any clean clothes to change into, anyway."

"Oh, right," says Bíbí. "But I was wondering if we might maybe lie down a little bit after breakfast. Together, you know. In my bed."

Hörður blushes brightly, but his face isn't the part of his body that fills with blood. "Oh, I see. Maybe I'll just go ahead and take a shower."

"Good," says Bíbí, smiling mischievously.

What a day! Hörður is so happy that he wants both to laugh and cry. Laugh because of the joy that's flowing through every nerve in his body, tickling his heart and brain. Cry because of his grief over lost time—all those days and nights that he spent by himself, spinning around in hopelessness, darkness, and cold, like a human Pluto on the outskirts of the solar system.

He cuddles up to Bíbí on the living-room sofa, wearing only his underwear, but wrapped in a warm down duvet. She's wearing pajamas, with her legs pulled up beneath her and half-covered by the same type of duvet. The lights are low; on the coffee table in front of them are a bowl of mixed candies and a bottle of Coke, and there's a DVD in the player—the French movie, *Amélie.*

Hörður feels so good that it doesn't even irritate him to have no cigarettes. He hasn't smoked since sitting on the lawn outside of the Catholic cathedral. Maybe he should just quit? He feels as if he can do anything, as long as he has Bíbí by his side. After spending the entire day more or less in bed and ordering pizza for dinner, they're already at the hang-out-on-the-couch-and-watch-DVDs stage of their relationship, or so it seems. It's as if they've fast-forwarded through several weeks, even straight past the honeymoon stage. But it really isn't like that. After all the passion, sweat, heat and pillow talk, it's a nice change just to sit quietly, relax and watch a movie.

Still, Hörður would have preferred to watch something else—there's no denying that. He can't really connect with the super-cute Amélie, and Paris, that metropolis of culture, is an extremely high number of light years away from the down-to-earth fishing village where he grew up. But of the few DVDs that Bíbí owns, this was one of the better ones—sort of. Most of her DVDs are different seasons of the *Friends* series, along with a few tearjerkers. As long as he gets to snuggle up with a woman like her, however, he doesn't really care what they watch. He would even make the effort to watch a couple episodes of *Friends*, even if he wanted just to spank those spoiled slouches who find everything awesome and spend half their time hanging around in cafés.

He prefers visiting old Hollywood, going on black-and-white journeys with James Cagney, Bogart or Edward G. Robinson. All *real actors* who played in *real movies*. No special effects, no glamor, no bullshit.

Clint Eastwood was also good in the old days, say, up to around 1980. After that date, hardly any good movies have been made. That's just how it is, no matter what anyone says. *Titanic? Lord of the Rings?* Rubbish!

Does Bíbí like black-and-white gangster movies? She knows who Humphrey Bogart is, in any case—she mentioned him at Vitabar. Maybe he should buy a few DVDs to see if he could get her interested. He could start with something easy, *Casablanca* or *Citizen Kane*, before moving to the hard-boiled thrillers. Whiskey, cigars, and old-fashioned machine guns—Tommy guns.

The prohibition years in the United States, such a great era! But the only thing that can match the golden age of jazz and Al Capone is, of course, the Wild West. Hörður literally worships movies like *High Noon*, with Gary Cooper, and the spaghetti-westerns of the Italian Sergio Leone, which sport merciless deserts, the immortal music of Ennio Morricone and the only and only Man with No Name, who wanders about on horseback with a gun at his side, silent as the grave, gritty and self-sufficient.

A Fistful of Dollars. For a Few Dollars More. The Good, The Bad and The Ugly. No love bullshit or romance! Hörður smiles to himself, and then breathes in the fragrance of Bíbí's hair. How can anyone smell so good?!

He could just eat her up.

Bíbí's ears perk, and she reaches for the remote and pauses the movie. "Is your phone ringing?"

"Is it? Oh, yeah, it is." He pulls off the duvet, abandons the warmth of the sofa and walks in his underwear to the entrance, where his phone is ringing in the inside pocket of his leather coat.

Hörður looks at the lit-up screen. He doesn't recognize the number, which belongs to a cell phone, but he answers it anyway. It could be Axel.

"Yes?"

"Hörður?" asks a male voice on the other end. It isn't Axel. It's a young man speaking in a tense voice, as if he's nervous.

"Who's asking?"

"My name is Orri. I've got to talk to you. Are you at home?"

"Orri who?" asks Hörður. "This isn't …"

"*Orri Atlason. We've got to meet. It's important!*"

"Aren't you wanted by the police?" asks Hörður authoritatively.

"*Yes, but I don't dare turn myself in. I'm worried that they won't believe me. But most of all, I'm worried that they'll let me go. If I turn myself in, Hákon and Þorsteinn will know where I am. They're looking for me. I'm in danger!*"

"Aren't you a friend of theirs?" asks Hörður. He peeks into the living room. Bíbí is looking at something on her phone.

"*No, not at all,*" says Orri. "*We fell out after the squatting incident. I'd had more than enough. They're extremely dangerous people. Aron is completely insane. He's behind all of this. He not only organizes the murders, but he commits them, as well.*"

"What are you talking about?" asks Hörður. "He's behind bars at Litla-Hraun."

"*You've got to believe me,*" says Orri, with despair in his voice. "*But my phone is running out of battery. Can we meet?*"

"Why are you calling me?" asks Hörður.

"*I watched* Spotlight *yesterday—and the journalist said that you predicted that a judge would be killed next. If that's true, it means that you know what Aron is doing. It means that if anyone believes what I have to say, it would be you.*"

"Okay," says Hörður. His curiosity has been awakened, but he doesn't know what to do. This could be a trap. Shouldn't he himself be laying a trap for Orri? Agree to meet him, but send the police instead?

"Plus, I know that you're honest."

"Oh?" asks Hörður in surprise.

"Fribbi told me what happened. How you prevented your partner's drug sale. I'm not bullshitting you, Hörður. Maybe you think I'm trying to trap you. But I'm not. I'm asking you to trust me. I'm putting all my trust in you. My life is in danger."

Hörður sighs. "Fuck it. Where are you?"

"Outside your home. Hiding right nearby. Are you at home?"

"How do you know where I live?" asks Hörður angrily. "Who gave you my number?"

"Easy, man. It's all in the phone book."

Hörður curses silently. "I'm not at home, but I'll be there in ten minutes, okay?"

"Thanks. I'll be here. But if you sick the cops on me, I'll disappear. They won't catch me, and you won't get to hear the truth."

"I'm the cops, you fool," snaps Hörður.

"You know what I mean," says Orri, before hanging up the phone.

Hörður puts his phone back in his pocket and heads back to the living room. "Something's come up. Work related. I need to pop home. Someone's waiting for me there. I need to talk to him. Still, it shouldn't take long."

"No problem," says Bíbí. "I'll use the time to call Mom. She called earlier."

"Okay," he says.

"But you don't have a car," says Bíbí.

Hörður shrugs, and then gathers his clothes and pulls on his socks. "I'll just walk. Or take a taxi."

"Don't be silly," says Bíbí. "You can take my car."

It's dark outside the apartment building. Hörður walks out to the parking lot and presses the remote-control key on the keychain that Bíbí gave him. There's a loud beep, and the lights on a red Nissan Micra parked at the outskirt of the parking lot blink.

What is it with women and compact cars? thinks Hörður as he stuffs himself into the car, which is even smaller than Þóra's Yaris. He pushes the seat back as far as it will go, but still struggles to get his legs and feet in position and shut the door. He himself is fond of large American cars.

Hörður starts the engine, backs out of the parking spot and drives off. He feels like a sperm whale in a sardine can. The car has little power, but will still get him where he's going. Hörður drives east on Hringbraut, north on Njarðargata, and pulls up in front of his building on Bergþórugata before he knows it. The street is dark, despite the lit streetlights along it. He parks in an empty space a short distance from the door to the stairwell of his building, and practically has to crawl out of the car.

As Hörður re-tucks his shirt into his trousers, he looks around in the twilight, but doesn't see Orri anywhere. As far as he recalls, Orri is short, slim, and shaved-headed. Not unlike Aron, but not quite as insane-looking.

Just below the Technical College is a dark alley. Next to it is a lit streetlight, in whose gleam walks a young man in jeans and a blue coat. It's Orri Atlason. Hörður recognizes him from the photo in *DV*. He's certainly short and slim, but has let his hair grow out; it's black and hangs down in front of his eyes.

Hörður gestures to him to come over.

Orri jogs across the street, glancing furtively to both sides. "Can we go in?"

"We'll see," says Hörður. "What have you got to say?"

"They're looking for me! "I can't …" Orri pauses when car lights appear further west down the street, one block from Vitabar.

"What?" Hörður looks in the direction of the car, and shields his eyes from the glaring lights with his hand. The driver stops, the engine purrs as it idles and the exhaust pipe pumps carbon dioxide into the atmosphere.

"It's them," says Orri. "Damn it, man! Let's go inside, huh?"

"Are you sure?" Hörður looks at the car. The glare from its headlights prevents him from seeing inside it.

"Yes, I'm sure!" says Orri, frustratedly. "Now there's no way I'm getting away. I'm history."

"We'll see about that," says Hörður. He opens the front door. They step in and onto the landing, and Hörður shuts the door behind them. He switches on the light and leads Orri down to the basement.

He opens his apartment door, switches on the light, and lets Orri in ahead of him. "You'll have to excuse the mess. Have a seat on the cot."

"Thanks." Orri sits down on the unmade bed, while Hörður stands over him like a rock giant. "Got any cigarettes, by any chance?"

Hörður shakes his head. "You said that Aron was the murderer, right?"

Orri nods.

"Explain it to me further," says Hörður.

"You'll probably think I'm insane or lying, but if you won't believe me, then no one will," says Orri. He rocks back and forth and scratches at his left hand with his right. It's as if he's in withdrawal. "It's about hypnosis, for the most part, anyway. Aron has studied hypnosis, among other things."

Hörður nods. "I know. Go on."

Orri looks at him. "Have you heard of astral projection?"

Hörður shrugs. "Yes and no. Do you mean when you leave your body and look at it from above, like you're floating?"

Orri nods quickly. "That's the simple version, yes. Aron has combined the two, hypnosis and astral projection. He's been developing this for a long time, and was able to master it. He's doing things that have never been done before. Not that I know of. And Mummi was his main guinea pig."

Hörður frowns. "What's he been doing?"

Orri clears his throat. "It's based on deep meditation. He sets up a kind of altar, consisting of a mirror, two candles, and a skull. At first, he used an ordinary mirror but then he started using a black one. He paints glass on one side with black lacquer, then turns it around and has a black mirror. You can hardly see anything in it except your own eyes. He ordered the skulls off the Internet, from some guy in Amsterdam. They're from Nepal."

"I see," says Hörður. "Go on."

"He meditates in front of the altar," says Orri. "He stares into his own eyes in the mirror, recites some mantras and enters a kind of trance. But somewhere else there's another altar, exactly the same, with someone else is sitting in front of it. He usually practiced on Mummi, but has used all of us for it. Me just once. Afterward, I decided to quit, leave the group."

"Wait," says Hörður. "Where's the other altar? In the same room? In the same house?"

Orri shakes his head. "It can be anywhere. Aron has a handsfree headset, and speaks by phone to the person he's hypnotizing."

"But he doesn't have a phone at Litla-Hraun, does he?" asks Hörður.

"Yes, he has a phone," says Orri determinedly. "Otherwise, he couldn't do this. They take the person to be hypnotized into a dark room with an altar."

"Where is this room?" asks Hörður excitedly.

"I don't know where it is," says Orri. "When Aron was practicing, he was usually at home, and the one he was hypnotizing was at Mummi's house—and anyway, it was usually Mummi himself."

"I see," says Hörður. "Go on."

"They position the person to be hypnotized in front of the altar," says Orri. "Aron sets up an altar in his cell, and then calls at a predetermined time."

"From his cell?" Hörður tries to recall everything he saw in Aron's cell at Litla-Hraun, but there was nothing in it resembling an altar. Or was there? There was at least one skull in there, though it was made of plastic.

"The person to be hypnotized is usually on GHB," says Orri. "Then all their defenses are down and it's easier for Aron to get inside that person's head. He speaks directly into their ears through little headphones."

"So he hypnotizes the subject and sends him or her out to carry out his orders?" asks Hörður.

Orri shakes his head slowly, before looking straight into the police officer's eyes. "It's a bit creepier than that, I can tell you. He hypnotizes both the subject and himself. Then he leaves his body and goes *into* the subject's body, by means of astral projection. The subject's spirit falls asleep, and Aron takes over its body. He controls the other body; it's *he* who goes and kills people. It's Aron."

Hörður blinks and whistles softly. "Fucking hell. That bastard. So that's how it's done. That's why the subjects all kill with their left hand. Aron is left-handed—that *was it* the whole time!"

"You believe me?" asks Orri in surprise.

Hörður sits down next to him on the cot. "This is the only possible explanation. Still, no one will believe it. Not to begin with."

"I know," says Orri.

"Why are they looking for you *now*?" asks Hörður. "You've known this the whole time."

"Because I'm wanted by the cops," says Orri. "They know that you know that I know something, understand? They don't want you to find me. They're worried I'll tell you everything."

Hörður nods.

"I'm so dead," Orri mutters.

Hörður thinks things over. "But if the subjects are on GHB, then why isn't Aron on GHB, too, when he takes over their bodies? Wouldn't he also be like a mindless tool?"

"It was like that at first," says Orri. "But he found a solution to it, though I don't know what it is. It took him months to develop this technique, almost two years. It's all written up in a book of his. A book that he created. It's his own sorcery manual. Its cover is made of black leather. He calls it Blackhide."

"Have you read it?" asks Hörður.

"No," says Orri. "No one's allowed to look at it. Aron is very careful about that book."

Hörður shakes his head, with a skeptical expression. "Still, it's hard to buy all this. Astral projection? Fucking hell. Is that even possible?"

"Yes," says Orri.

"Sounds like some fucking nonsense from a horror movie," Hörður mutters bitterly. He's prepared to believe it, although reluctantly, with reservations. But he knows it will be easier said than done to sell Engilbert or Axel this sort of mumbo jumbo.

"This isn't nonsense," says Orri. "Unfortunately."

"He isn't just a killer," says Hörður. "He's a goddamn serial killer."

"Aron is a demon," Orri says in a low voice, as if fearful of someone listening in. "What he's doing is black magic of the worst sort. When he did this to me, I was depressed for many days afterward. I had no energy, no interest in anything—I was completely *empty*. It was as if the breath of life had been sucked out of me. He often did this to Mummi. He used him, preyed on him and then tossed him aside. Mummi never recovered. It's one of the reasons why he killed himself. Not just because of that thing with the pastor. Or ..."

Orri falls silent, looks away.

"Or what?" asks Hörður.

"Nothing," mutters Orri. He keeps scratching himself and staring at the overflowing ashtray on the floor. "Are you sure you don't have any cigarettes?"

"Why do you allow Aron to treat you like this?" asks Hörður. "Why did you take part in this crap?"

"It ..." Orri sighs. "It's complicated ... a long story. You don't know what he's like. He ..."

Orri stops again, shrugs.

"He has some kind of hold on you, doesn't he?" asks Hörður gently.

"Maybe," whispers Orri, with a furtive expression.

"You've got to tell me everything," says Hörður. "You've got to confide everything in me. Otherwise, I can't help you. You've got to trust me."

Orri nods, but doesn't say anything. He rocks back and forth, continues to scratch himself, and avoids looking the police officer in the eyes.

"Is it the abuse?" asks Hörður softly. "You were all together in Vatnaskógur. Maybe all of you were victims of the pastor? Not just you and Mummi, but Aron and the others, too?"

Orri clears his throat. "Abuse is abominable, but you just swallow it, you know?"

"Is that so?" asks Hörður doubtfully.

Orri scowls, as if he's bitten into a bad apple. "This thing happens to you, but life just goes on. You don't go whining about it your entire life. What for? I want to kill that fucking pastor, but I don't want to be locked up for murder, see?"

"But it hurt you," says Hörður.

Orri nods. "You either break or bend. Something broke inside Mummi. Aron bent. I'm tougher than Mummi. But Aron isn't just tough, he's a sick mother fucker. The rest of us tried to forget about it. He became obsessed with it."

"How?" asks Hörður.

"He stole the pastor's camera," says Orri.

"Camera?" exclaims Hörður in surprise.

"Ingimar took pictures of us," says Orri. "Not in the chapel, though. Not when he, you know. But afterward, just in the area. By the lake and all that. He probably has an entire album of photos of little boys at summer camp."

Hörður nods. He keeps it in that trunk of his. The locked wooden trunk in his office at his house.

"Only …" says Orri. "Aron stole the camera from the pastor's room. It was the last day, the last year we were there together. He kept the camera for years. Then he developed the photos and gave us all one of them when we turned twenty, an enlarged photo of ourselves. He had us perform a kind of ritual. We bought frames, and we painted the glass and created miniature black mirrors."

Hörður nods.

Orri continues. "Behind the black glass was the photo that he gave each of us, of a little boy who had just been raped. It was supposed to be symbolic. The ritual took place in darkness, in the past and the subconsciousness, but we were its offspring—anarchists who had survived, defeated the darkness and merged with it."

"I found Mummi's mirror, and the photo," says Hörður.

Orri rocks in his seat, as if he itches all over. "Aron is twisted, sexually. I don't know if he's gay, but …"

"Go on," says Hörður.

"All gangs have their own rules, their own customs," says Orri reluctantly. "If someone breaks the rules, he's punished by the others. Maybe forced to eat a lit cigarette or drink and entire bottle of vodka, and then beaten up. Things like that. But in our gang it isn't like that. Aron uses a different form of violence. We all do. But he's the one who invented it, was the first to use it. The punishments are …"

"Sexual?" finishes Hörður.

Orri grimaces, as if he feels nauseous.

"Okay," mutters Hörður. "But beatings and rape have been common in the underworld for a long time. Sadly, this is nothing new. Still, people have been able to turn a new leaf and start a new life."

Orri nods distractedly.

"This isn't the hold that Aron has on you, is it?" asks Hörður. "You wanted me to think that, but I don't. It's something else, isn't it? Something more, something bigger."

Orri swallows.

"You've got to trust me," says Hörður.

"What I tell you mustn't go any further," Orri whispers. "You've got to promise me."

"All right," says Hörður, reluctantly. "I promise. The seal of the confessional is in effect here."

"Good," says Orri, hoarsely. "Do you remember Ársæll? Sæli from Stórholt?"

Hörður nods. "He disappeared a few years ago. From what I understand, he's a bigwig coke-dealer in South America."

Orri shakes his head. "Together, they smuggled ecstasy into the country, he and Aron. Blue ecstasy tablets imprinted with a pentagram. Then half the shipment disappeared. Aron accused Sæli of stealing it. I don't know what happened, but …"

"But what?"

"All I know is that the tablets that disappeared all reappeared the other day. At Fribbi's place on Hverfisgata."

"We found them among Mummi's possessions," says Hörður pensively.

Orri sighs. "As I say, I don't know who it was that took the tablets. But it probably wasn't Sæli."

"What happened to him?" asks Hörður.

Orri clears his throat. "He's in a hole in the lava not far from Hafnarfjörður. By some old fish-drying racks. We were all there when …"

"The whole gang? The house-squatting group?"

Orri nods. "His corpse is missing one finger. His left thumb. Aron made something out of the knucklebone."

"The pendant," mutters the police officer. From a seal's fin, Aron had said. Who goes around with a human bone around their neck?

Hörður shudders at the thought.

"I really need a cigarette!" Orri squeezes his fists in frustration. "I'm dying for some nicotine!"

Hörður ignores him. "So this is what holds you all together. You have an ugly secret. You're all accessories to murder. If one of you leaves the group, the others will become suspicious."

Orri laughs coldly. "Suspicious—yeah, right. People have been killed for less. And now I'm wanted!"

Hörður nods. "What do you think they'll do to you if they catch you?"

Orri scowls. "One of only two things. Either kill me, or make me the next subject. Who would believe a witness who has just killed someone?"

"You've got to turn yourself in," says Hörður. "We'll talk this over with the head of the CID, and explain to him the hypnosis thing. You're the key witness that we desperately need."

"You won't tell him this stuff about Sæli, will you?"

Hörður curses under his breath. "No, not yet. It can wait."

"Wait?" exclaims Orri. "You promised!"

"I won't mention you, okay?" says the police officer. "But I can't act as if I know nothing about a corpse in a hole in a lava field. You've got to understand that."

"Fine," mutters Orri.

Hörður takes out his phone. "I'm going to see if I can get in touch with someone from the CID."

"Do you think they'll believe me?" asks Orri skeptically.

"They'll have to," says Hörður. He calls Engilbert, but the detective's phone is turned off.

"I need to know in advance whether they believe that I'm innocent or not," says Orri. "If they don't believe me and arrest me, I'll be in deep shit. They'll hold me for twenty-four hours and then throw me out, because they won't have anything on me. Then Hákon and Þorsteinn can just lie in wait for me at their ease."

Hörður nods. He calls the CID, but no one answers. The phone rings out.

Hörður sighs. He calls Jafet's number, and gets his voicemail. "Yes, hello. Hörður here. Officer Hörður Grímsson. I've got Orri Atlason here with me. He has very important information and is prepared to testify against Aron. Please call me, or ask Axel to call."

Hörður hangs up and looks at his watch. It's half past nine. Bíbí is waiting for him. He really needs either Jafet or Axel to call him back right away.

"Are we just going to wait here?" asks Orri.

"Yes. Or. I don't know." Hörður scratches his head, wondering whether anyone's at work in the CID.

"That was probably them, earlier." Orri rubs his palms together. "In the car that stopped. I saw them earlier today. They were in a white Escort. Yesterday it was a blue Mazda. They drive stolen cars, and change them regularly."

Hörður looks at his watch and exhales like a whale. "What do you say about coming with me to the station? There may be someone working at the CID, despite no one answering the phone."

Orri shakes his head. "Out of the question! If I don't have witness protection, I'm dead."

"Then do you want to wait here while I go to the station?"

"Not a chance," says Orri. "They're here outside. They know where I am."

"Okay," says Hörður. "But do you think you can wait at the home of a friend of mine? It's on the west side. I'll drive you there and then pop down to the station."

Orri shrugs. "Maybe. Yes, that'll work. If they don't follow us there. I have to be sure."

Hörður lifts his phone again. "Let's try that. First, though, I need to call my friend and ask her if I can leave you at home with her."

Hörður opens the front door a crack and peeks out to both sides. He left the lights off in the stairwell, and Orri stands in the darkness behind him. He notices nothing suspicious; only parked cars and brightly lit houses.

"Come on," he says. They hurry to the small car and get inside. Hörður starts the engine, and then drives down to the intersection with Barónstígur and turns right. It's twenty minutes to ten on a Sunday evening; there are few people out and about, and they would probably notice it if someone were following them.

Hörður glances now and then in the rear-view mirror, but Orri fidgets in his seat like a hyperactive kid, looking frightenedly in all directions.

"Try to stay still," says Hörður frustratedly. He shifts to third gear and steps down hard on the gas pedal. The car is so powerless that it does his head in. They drive at sixty kph down Hringbraut to the west side of town.

"Are you sure you don't have any cigarettes?" asks Orri.

Hörður looks in the rear-view mirror. There are several cars driving in the same direction as them, and at least one of them is white. But he can't tell if it's a Ford Escort. It could just as well be a Toyota or Mazda. Or a Honda Accord.

"I'm sure," he mutters. "Stop asking."

"Could we stop at a shop?" asks Orri.

"Not an option," says Hörður. "The sooner that I get rid of you, the better. How about showing a little appreciation instead of hassling me like some damn kid?"

"Sorry, man," Orri mumbles.

Hörður sighs wearily. He drives through the roundabout by the National Museum and then left at Björn's Bakery.

"Are we there yet?" asks Orri.

"Yes," mutters Hörður. He looks in the rear-view mirror. The white car is following them like a shadow, but is still too far behind them for him to see what kind of car it is. All he sees is the glare of the car's headlights.

They drive past the Shell gas station. Bíbí's apartment building is on the right, on the opposite side of the street. Hörður drives through one quarter of the roundabout next to Hotel Saga and turns right down Espimelur.

He slows down and watches the traffic in his rear-view mirror. The white car continues through the roundabout and disappears. It could have been an Escort, but he's not sure.

"Was anyone following us?" Orri asks nervously.

"No." Hörður drives into the parking lot in front of the apartment building and parks the small car. "I suspected someone was, but that turned out not to be the case."

"Good," says Orri.

They step out of the car and walk over to the building's easternmost staircase, nearest Birkimelur. Hörður rings the bell and Bíbí lets them into the staircase. Hörður pushes a switch on the wall to light the entire staircase, from the entrance to the top floor. Each landing has a large window overlooking the parking lot.

At the same time, a white Ford Escort drives slowly into the parking lot of the Shell gas station on Birkimelur. In the car are two men dressed in black. They stare at the apartment building on the other side of the street, at the lit staircase and the two men walking up the stairs. One of them is a head higher than the other and is wearing a long, black coat.

Bíbí opens her door with a smile and lets them into the apartment. She has gotten dressed, and is wearing light linen trousers and a salmon-pink blouse.

"Sorry about this," says Hörður apologetically. "I wouldn't bother you with this if I had had any other choice."

"It's all right," says Bíbí.

"This is Orri," says Hörður. "Orri, this is Ester, called Bíbí."

They shake hands.

"Stay here," Hörður says to Orri. "Behave like a man and do what Bíbí tells you to do."

"What do you think I am?" says Orri, insulted.

"We'll leave that unanswered for now," says Hörður. "Go in and sit down somewhere and wait for me, okay?"

"Okay," Orri mutters. He takes of his shoes and strolls into the living room.

"You'll be quick, won't you?" asks Bíbí.

"Absolutely," says Hörður. "I'm just going down to the police station to check if anyone's on duty in the CID," he says. "Hopefully, I'll find someone who can take Orri and keep him safe the next few days and nights."

"Is he in danger?" asks Bíbí.

"Yes—that can't be denied," says Hörður reluctantly. "But no one knows that he's here. For safety's sake, don't let anyone in. Except for me, of course."

"Okay," says Bíbí. She has difficulty concealing her worry.

"Again, I'm sorry," says Hörður. "I'll be quick. I promise. And then it'll be as if it never happened."

Bíbí smiles reassuringly. "Don't worry about me. Just hurry."

Hörður nods and kisses her on the cheek. "See you later."

"See you," says Bíbí. He returns to the staircase, and she shuts the door behind him.

"Do you have any cigarettes?" asks Orri, when she appears in the living room. He sits on the couch and rocks back and forth. He's still wearing his coat, but has unzipped it.

"No, I don't smoke," says Bíbí. "But I can make some coffee. Would you like coffee?"

"Huh? Yes, of course," says Orri.

Bíbí goes into the kitchen. She rinses out the coffeemaker's pot, fills it halfway with cold water and pours it into the machine. Then she takes out a coffee filter from one of the kitchen cabinets, places it in the funnel and scoops ground coffee into the filter before switching the machine on.

She hopes that Hörður will be quick. Naturally, she doesn't mind doing him a favor, but it's a bit odd, to put it mildly, having a complete stranger hanging around in her home. A person she knows nothing about—except that he's in some sort of danger.

Lost in these thoughts, Bíbí starts and utters a half-stifled cry when Orri suddenly appears in the kitchen.

"I didn't mean to startle you," says Orri.

"It's okay," says Bíbí. She grabs a cloth and wipes the kitchen counter with it, despite the counter not needing it.

"I'm going to pop out and buy cigarettes," says Orri. "My nicotine craving is doing my head in."

"Don't you want to wait for Hörður?" asks Bíbí.

"I'll be quick," says Orri. "I'll just go to the gas station."

"Well, suit yourself," says Bíbí. She follows him to the door, where he puts on his shoes.

"I'll just ring the bell," says Orri as he opens the door and steps out onto the landing. "Do you need anything?"

"No, but thanks for asking," says Bíbí.

"See you," says Orri, and then he's gone.

After checking to see if the door is securely shut, Bíbí goes to the living room, walks over to the window and pulls open the curtains. She sees Orri jog across the street and go into the brightly lit gas station. Just as he said; he's going there to buy cigarettes.

She draws the curtains back over the window.

Hörður uses his access card to enter the police station on Hverfisgata Street. The building is mainly vacant at the moment, but there's always someone in the control room, besides the fact that those on evening- and night shift often have business at the station. He takes the elevator up to the third floor and goes to the CID and knocks on its door, with no result. He looks at his watch. It's two minutes past ten.

He curses under his breath, takes out his phone, and again tries calling both Engilbert and Jafet. Engilbert's phone is still turned off and Jafet doesn't answer; after a few rings, his voicemail clicks in with its message and usual beep.

Hörður clears his throat. "It's me again. Hörður Grímsson. Can you please call me? Or ask Axel to call. It's important."

He hangs up, sticks his phone back in his pocket and heads back to the elevator.

Orri enters the empty gas station and goes straight to the counter. The station smells of floor wax and grilled hot dogs. There's no one at the counter.

"Hello?" he calls out.

After a few moments, a lanky, pimply young man appears. "Yes?"

"I'd like a pack of red Winstons," says Orri. "And matches."

The lanky young man grabs both, runs them over the price scanner and places them on the counter between them. "Anything else?"

Orri tosses two crumpled thousand-króna bills onto the counter.

"No."

As the lanky attendant counts out his change, Orri peels the cellophane off the pack, opens it and sticks one of the cigarettes in his mouth.

"There you are," says the attendant.

"Thanks." Orri puts the change in his pocket and marches out.

"No smoking on the premises," the attendant calls out after him.

"Idiot," mutters Orri. Outside, there's a gentle northern breeze. Orri shelters himself from it on the south side of the station, lights a match and holds the flame up to the cigarette. He's hardly taken his first drag when someone grabs him roughly by the shoulder. He turns around and is punched in the stomach.

The cigarette drops from Orri's mouth and he collapses to the asphalt.

Standing over him are two black-clad men.

"Don't try anything," says Hákon.

"Or you'll be sorry," says Þorsteinn, called Steini.

They pull their former friend to his feet and drag him between them to a white Ford Escort parked in the shade on the north side of the station. Then they throw him into the back seat. Hákon sits down behind the wheel, while Steini gets in the back with Orri, who is still doubled up and having difficulty breathing after the punch to his diaphragm.

Hákon starts the car, backs out of their parking place and turns onto Birkimelur toward Hringbraut, where he turns east.

Steini grabs Orri by the hair and straightens him up in his scat. Then he holds a plastic bottle half-full of diluted Coke up to his mouth.

"Drink this."

"No," groans Orri.

Steini pulls out a knife with a tapered, stainless-steel blade and lays its razor-sharp edge against his throat. "Drink this or I'll cut a hole in your throat and pour it into it."

Orri takes the bottle and sips reluctantly at its contents. He knows very well what's in the Coke, but can't taste any GHB.

"Finish it all," orders Steini.

Orri does as he says. His heart is beating fast, he feels sick and his stomach tightens.

Hörður leaves the police station and gets into Bíbí's car. He's about to start the engine when his phone rings. He hopes it's either Jafet or Axel, and feels slightly disappointed when he sees Bíbí's number on the screen.

"Hi," he says. "Is everything all right? I'm about to head back."

"Yes, or ... " says Bíbí. *"Your friend went over to the gas station a short time ago, but hasn't come back."*

"He left the apartment?" asks Hörður, agitatedly. "How long has it been?"

"Ten minutes or so."

Hörður curses under his breath. What should he do? What can he do?

"Are you there?" asks Bíbí.

"Yes, I'm here," mutters Hörður. Did Orri run off? Or did Hákon and Þorsteinn get him?

"I saw him go into the gas station," says Bíbí. *"He should have been back by now, right?"*

"Yes," says Hörður. They've probably caught him. Fuck!

"I just wanted to let you know."

"Thanks," says Hörður. "I don't really know what to do about this. I'm going to make some calls, and I'll let you know, okay?"

"Okay, bye."

"Bye."

Hörður hangs up and calls Jafet again. The call goes to voicemail, and after the beep, Hörður leaves a message.

"This is Hörður Grímsson again. Will you please call me! Hákon and Þorsteinn have probably abducted Orri. It's not unlikely that the third murder will be committed in the next few hours—even in the next hour! Orri will either be murdered, or hypnotized and made to murder the next victim, who could be a police officer, a minister, or just anybody. I'll … I'll let headquarters know."

He hangs up and calls the Reykjavík police.

"Reykjavík Police, how can we help?"

"Yes, my name is Officer Hörður Grímsson. I need to get an urgent message to all officers on duty. I'd like to ask them to be on the lookout for a white family car, probably a Ford Escort. There are three men in the car who are all wanted in connection with the murders of the past week. I also want to ask all officers to be on the alert. It's possible that the third murder will be committed before midnight, and that this time, a police officer or minister will be attacked."

"Are you serious?"

"Perfectly," says Hörður. "I would also like you to get in touch with anyone at the CID. Preferably Axel himself."

"I'll look into the matter. What was your name again?"

"Hörður Grímsson."

"Right. Goodbye."

Hörður looks at his phone. Did he believe me? Or didn't he believe me? He sticks his phone back in his pocket and starts the car. But instead of driving off, he sits there staring distractedly out the windshield. What should he do? What the hell can he do?

The moon, on the verge of being full, hovers over the city.

Aron Beck is sitting at his desk, playing a computer game, when one of the prison officers peeks into his cell. The prisoner acts as if he doesn't see him.

"It's ten o'clock," says the officer. "Do you need to use the toilet before I lock up?"

"No, I'm good," says Aron.

"Good night, then." The officer shuts the door, closes the latch, and locks it with a padlock. The iron clanks cheerlessly.

The officer's footsteps recede. Shortly thereafter, the Blue Door closes with a thunk.

Aron waits a few minutes, and then turns off both the computer game and the television. He gets up, goes to the door and puts his ear to it. All that he hears is the low murmur of the television set in the next cell. Aron takes a roll of tape from a drawer, drops to his knees in front of the wardrobe, pulls a long length of tape from the roll and bites it off. He wraps the tape into a ball, sticky side out. Then he pushes the sticky ball onto a white plastic piece on the right side of the base of the wardrobe. The white piece forms the top of a plug covering a narrow hole in the base, and when he gently pulls on the tape ball, the plug comes with it. The head of a screw is visible in the hole normally covered by the plug. Aron does the same on the other side. Then he pulls a small Phillips screwdriver from the sock on his left foot, and loosens the screws holding the base board in place.

Bibbi, in the second cell from Aron's, keeps the screwdriver for him during the day. It's too risky for Aron to conceal it in his own cell. They would have found it when they searched his cell last Friday.

Aron presses the tape onto the white base board and pulls it carefully from its place. He grabs one end of it and removes it from the oblong gap.

Inside the gap, he keeps this and that, including money, drugs, and the book that the red-haired cop returned to him.

In this secret storage space of his is also a homemade book bound in black leather, embossed with runes and sorcerer's staves—Blackhide. But what he's after this time is a cell phone with a handsfree headset.

Aron stands up, sits back down in his chair, and turns on the phone, which is set to silent mode. Five-and-a-half minutes later, he receives a message:

We've got Orri. On our way to the house

He answers:

I'll be ready

Aron lights incense scented with musk. After clearing everything off the desk, he positions the plastic skull at its center and places a bottle of 8x4 deodorant on either side of it. He places a tea light on top of each bottle and lights them. Next, he turns off his cell light and sits down in the chair, sticks the headset in one ear and waits.

He takes a deep breath and holds it in, then exhales slowly, relaxing as he does so. His face is mirrored indistinctly in the flat-screen TV, which works like a black mirror.

Hörður was on his way back to the west side of town when he changed his mind at the intersection of Njarðargata and Hringbraut and turned east instead of west. He drives up Ártúnsbrekka Hill and under Höfðabakki bridge.

He has one hand on the steering wheel, and calls Bíbí with the other.

"Yes?"

"It's me," he says. "Has Orri returned?"

"No. Are you your way here?"

"Well, about that." He clears his throat. "I'm actually on my way east."

"East? Where east?"

"To Litla-Hraun," says Hörður. He doesn't know whether he's doing the right thing or not. Nor does he know if the police have paid any attention to him or if the CID has been notified.

He also has no idea where Orri is. All he knows for sure is where Aron Beck is just now.

"The prison?"

Hörður sighs. "Yes."

"Why are you going there?"

What's he supposed to say? That he's going to try to stop a man from doing astral projection, settling in the body of Orri Atlason, and committing murder?

"It's a work thing," says Hörður, just to say something. He looks at the car's gas gauge, which shows half a tank. "I can't really explain it now. But I'll fill the car's tank before I return it. I promise."

"No problem," says Bíbí, but he can hear that she's not happy with these developments.

Hörður signals a right turn as he takes the exit to Suðurlandsvegur Road. "I'm really sorry. This isn't what I wanted to be doing tonight, believe me."

"I believe you."

"I'll call you later, okay?" he says.

"Yes, do that. And be careful."

"I promise." Hörður hangs up and tosses the phone onto the passenger seat. He steps on the gas, pushing the car's tiny engine.

A white Ford Escort drives along Stekkjarbakki Road in the Lower Breiðholt area. To one side are the Stekkir and Bakkar neighborhoods, and to the other, the lower part of the Elliði River Valley, wooded and shrouded in darkness. Ahead is Upper Breiðholt, but that is not the car's destination. Without signaling, the driver turns left, off the asphalt road and onto an unmarked gravel path that leads down into the valley and ends at an old house clad in corrugated iron, standing by the south bank of one of the southern branches of the Elliði river.

The house is dark. Next to it is an old shed, and parked between the house and the shed is a blue Mazda. Hákon parks the Escort in front of the shed and shuts off the engine, then steps out of the car and opens the driver-side back door. The valley is pitch black and silent, yet the purl of car traffic can be heard from the roads Reykjanesbraut and Höfðabakki.

Hákon opens the car's trunk and takes out a black sports bag.

"Get out," says Þorsteinn to Orri, who obeys. The three men walk over the gravel driveway and into the house, which is humid and cold and smells of mold, having neither heat nor electricity.

The house's wooden floor creaks loudly.

Hákon switches on electric lantern. He leads the others, carrying the sports bag in one hand and the lantern in the other. They walk through the house and into one of the rooms toward the back of it. Þorsteinn, last in line, keeps watch on Orri, who is as silent and obedient as a dog. His eyes are dull and empty, his mouth hangs half open, and his movements are mechanical. The GHB has begun to take effect, turning him into a mindless tool in their hands.

Hákon hangs the lantern on a nail on the back of the door. Its light casts a ghostly glow over the room, which is empty apart from an old dresser in the middle, and a wooden chair in front of it. On the dresser are two black candles, tall and thick. Right between the candles is an old skull, brownish and missing both its jaw and a few upper teeth. Behind the candle and the skull is a black mirror. Hákon first lights incense scented with musk, and then the candles.

"Sit down," says Þorsteinn.

Orri obeys, sitting down on the wooden chair.

"Place your hands on your knees and relax."

Orri does as he's told.

Þorsteinn takes out a cell phone fitted with headphones and sticks the headphones in Orri's ears. Next, he types a number into the phone and calls. After two rings, someone answers at the other end.

Þorsteinn slips the cell phone into Orri's coat pocket, steps carefully aside and positions himself next to Hákon. Hákon lowers the lantern's light to a tiny gleam.

They watch Orri and wait.

Orri sits straight-backed, his palms resting on his thighs. He stares at his own eyes in the black mirror. His pupils are dilated.

A voice sounds in his ears, deep and monotone.

"*You see three things,*" says the deep voice. It tickles his ears and bores into his head. "*Two candles and a skull. The skull is a gate; soon we will journey into it, through it. You see two things. The candles have merged into one. Inside of you, the gate opens; now it would be good to relax and sink deeper. You see one thing. It's the flame flickering before you. The skull is gone. You're the skull—it is empty because your consciousness has sunk. You relax and allow*

*your consciousness to sleep. You're empty, you feel good.
Enter Eckankar!"*

When Hörður reaches the outskirts of Eyrarbakki, it's
twenty minutes to eleven. He slows to sixty kilometers per
hour. He sees the prison ahead, its grounds lit like a runway.
He turns right onto the road leading to the north side of
the village. A little further ahead, the road is still broken up,
and in the darkness he sees the outline of the big tractor
with the pneumatic drill in tow.

Hörður turns left into the prison's parking lot, parks
the small car and shuts off the engine. The big lot is empty,
apart from three other cars that probably belong to the
prison officers working the night shift. He leaves the keys
in the ignition, steps out into the cool night air and walks
along the double security fence and down the separately
fenced pathway leading to the turnstile gate. He walks at a
medium pace, not knowing quite what to say. Technically
speaking, he has no business being at Litla-Hraun, besides
not even being on duty.

But he has nothing to lose.

Hörður stops at the intercom, clears his throat and
pushes the button. Several long moments pass before someone answers.

"Control room."

The red-haired giant in the leather coat bends down
to the intercom. "Yes, good evening. My name is Hörður
Grímsson, a police officer from Reykjavík. I came here last
Thursday to pick up a detainee."

"And?"

"The thing is, I've been assisting the CID with the investigation of the two murders. We suspect that Aron Beck is

behind them. And not only that, we have a well-founded suspicion that he's in telephone connection with accomplices outside these walls."

"His cell was searched on Friday, but nothing was found."

Hörður clears his throat once more. "Yes, I know. But I have a witness who claims otherwise. Could I be allowed to visit Aron now?"

"His cellblock has already been locked. The prison is locked down for the night."

"This is very important. I suspect that he's organizing something as we speak."

"Are you in the CID? What did you say your name was?"

"Hörður Grímsson. No, I'm not in the CID, in fact, but …"

"Who sent you? Do you have authorization?"

Hörður curses under his breath. "I don't have authorization. I tried to reach Axel, but it's easier said than done."

"I'm going to have to ask you to leave."

"Can't you take a look into his cell? I'll wait here in the meantime."

"First, I don't take orders from you. Second, the prison is locked down for the night, as I told you. Third, Aron will sue us for harassment if we disturb his nighttime peace and quiet, so shortly after we searched his cell."

"Stop being so stubborn!" shouts Hörður into the intercom. "This is a serious matter. The lives of police officers are in danger. Ministers are in danger, and even the President himself!"

"What do you mean?"

"It's a long, complicated story. I don't have time," says Hörður brusquely. Do you have Axel's phone number?"

"Wait, you say you're working on the investigation of the murders, but you don't have the phone number of the head of the department? Did I understand you correctly?"

"Yes," admits Hörður reluctantly.

"I should call the police on you."

"I am the police!" shouts Hörður.

"So you say. I've got you on camera, and if that's the uniform of the Reykjavík police, I'll eat my hat."

"I'm not on duty," mutters Hörður.

"But I am. And I'm asking you to leave the premises immediately."

"I understand," says Hörður resentfully. "But you're making a mistake, just so you know. What's your name, may I ask?"

"Sorry, but you may not!" The intercom speaker crackles when the prison officer hangs up.

"Asshole!" snaps Hörður. He looks at the brightly lit buildings through the sturdily built turnstile gate, and then hurries back down the pathway to the parking lot.

He looks at his watch. It's a quarter to eleven.

Hörður is furious. He walks in circles in the parking lot, takes a deep breath and tries to calm down.

What can he do? Nothing. Not a thing. He'll drive back to Reykjavík with his tail between his legs—that's what he'll do.

"Fuck!" shouts Hörður. He takes out his phone and looks at the screen. Neither Jafet nor Axel have been in contact.

Idiots!

Hörður walks toward the compact car. Shouldn't he call Bíbí and tell her that he'll be back in half an hour or so? Yes, that's a better idea. He finds her number, pushes the green button and puts the phone to his ear.

Hopefully she's not angry at him. He couldn't handle anything like that. Not now.

Orri blinks and pulls the headset out of his ear. He licks his lips, lifts his left hand and waves it to and fro. The candle flames flicker and smoke; the black smoke merges with the darkness of the room.

Hákon turns up the light of the electric lantern. Aron? Are you here?"

Orri exhales and nods slowly.

"Do you want the injection?" asks Þorsteinn. He crouches, opens the sports bag, rummages in it and finally finds a syringe and medicine vial in a brown paper bag. On the vial is an old label, reading:

Epinephrine.

He puts a needle on the syringe, sticks the needle through the vial's rubber sealer, and draws the liquid into the syringe.

Hákon pulls up Orri's right coat sleeve and taps two fingers firmly on the underside of his forearm.

"Here." Þorsteinn hands him the syringe.

Hákon grips Orri's forearm with his left hand and holds the syringe in his right. "You'll feel a little sting. One, two, and …"

He pushes the needle into the muscle and empties the syringe.

"There we are." Hákon straightens up, pats Orri on the shoulder and hands Þorsteinn the empty syringe. "Now we just wait, while the adrenaline burns up the GHB."

Orri grimaces and twitches in his chair, the blood vessels in his neck bulge and his nostrils flare. He takes a deep breath and exhales abruptly, blowing out both candles. The blue smoke rises and swirls, and a burning smell tickles their noses.

"Are you all right?" asks Hákon.

Aron, in Orri's body, gets to his feet, rolls his shoulders and opens and closes his fists. "Never been better."

He turns his head and looks at Hákon and Þorsteinn. The eyes that previously belonged to Orri flash, and his voice is slightly unclear and lisping. "What are you two staring at?"

"Nothing," says Þorsteinn, looking away.

"This is just as fucking weird every time," mutters Hákon.

"How do you think it is for me, huh?" asks Aron, cynically. He shifts his weight on his feet to keep balance, blinks his eyes irregulary and contorts his mouth in between words.

"At least you're not wearing high heels this time," says Þorsteinn.

Aron takes a few steps backward and looks down at himself and along his arms. "What is this I'm wearing? Does the boy have no taste whatsoever?"

"Do you want to change clothes?" Hákon asks.

Aron shakes his head. "No time for any bullshit. Where's that fucking cop? The red-haired giant. He knows too much, just like Orri."

"We don't know where he is," says Þorsteinn.

"What?" snaps Aron. He's so worked up that he nearly loses his balance.

"But we know where his girlfriend is," Hákon hurriedly adds.

"Good, good," mutters Aron. "Then what are we waiting for? We'll kill two birds with one stone. Murder the cop, and pack that bastard Orri off to Litla-Hraun, with a murder conviction under his belt. And I'll be there waiting to welcome him, the dear fellow."

"We'll take the Mazda," says Þorsteinn. "They may be on the lookout for the Escort."

Aron nods.

"What do you need?" Hákon asks.

"Rope and duct tape." Aron contorts his mouth, and Orri's face twists into a grin. "And a knife, of course."

Bíbí is preparing her lunch for tomorrow, as she usually does on nights before work. Tomorrow she's going to have skyr and coffee for breakfast, rye bread with sardines and a hard-boiled egg for lunch, and an apple with her afternoon coffee. She puts four eggs in a pot, pours water over the eggs and puts it on the stovetop to boil, then spreads two slices of rye bread with butter and wraps them in plastic wrap.

Sometimes the other girls at work make fun of her. In general, they find it too much of a bother to take packed lunches with them to work, and usually just pop over to the nearest bakery or shop—but mainly, they find what she brings for lunch both old-fashioned and unappetizing.

For example, she hasn't dared to show up again with cold liverwurst, after the girls fled the break room shouting "UGH!" when they saw it. Bíbí shakes her head at the memory, both upset and sad. It's no joke being a country girl in the capital city, that's for sure. But she's determined not to give up. She doesn't want to live on pastries, soda and sweets, as some do, and even less on diuretic tea, rice cakes and salad. No, healthy home cooking it is!

She takes a tin of sardines in tomato sauce from her pantry and puts it in her lunch box, and places the buttered rye-bread slices on top of the tin. There's room in the box for one boiled egg, even two; the apple and skyr go into her purse.

The eggs are just about to come to the boil. Bíbí looks at the wall clock. Quarter to eleven. She's going to boil the eggs for four minutes, at which point the yolks will be properly firm, but not dry.

She clicks her tongue. What business did Hörður have at Litla-Hraun? Why hasn't he called? He needs to return her car to her before she goes to bed. Surely he'll do that, won't he?

Bíbí starts in alarm when her phone starts ringing. Is it Hörður? Where did she put her phone?

She rushes into the living room, spots her phone on the coffee table and hurries to answer it. She recognizes the number right away, and her heart starts beating faster. She has a huge crush on this peculiar cop—having always had a weakness for the strong, silent type. "Hi! Where are you?"

"I'm still out east. But am about to head back to town. I just wanted to let you know. I'll be there in half an hour. Will you still be up?"

"Yes, of course!" says Bíbí cheerfully. While talking on the phone, she paces the living room and plays with her hair. Her thoughts whirl and she speaks quite fast. Calm down! "I mean, I should be, yes. I often don't go to bed until around twelve or half past twelve. Do you think you'd want to stay, or ...?"

"Stay?"

"Yes, that would be fine, if you wanted to, but I completely understand if ..." Bíbí pauses when the intercom buzzes loudly. Who could be ringing it so late?

"What were you saying? What was that noise?"

"The intercom," says Bíbí. She hurries to the entrance. "I suppose it's that friend of yours, Orri. Wait a second!"

Bíbí puts the cell phone to her chest and answers the intercom.

"Don't answer! Don't let anyone in!" yells Hörður, but she doesn't hear him.

"Hello?" she says over the intercom.

"This is Orri," says a metallic voice.

"Okay," says Bíbí, pushing the button that opens the front door and placing the handset back in its place. She is about to open the door to her apartment, but stops when she hears a hissing sound coming from the kitchen.

"The eggs!" shouts Bíbí, rushing into the kitchen, where the water is boiling furiously in the pot, splashing out and hissing on the hot burner.

"Hold on, I've got a little drama here!" says Bíbí into her cell phone, before laying it on the kitchen table. She dashes over to the stove, turns down the temperature and wipes up the water that spilled over.

"Bíbí!" shouts Hörður over the phone. *"Can you hear me? Talk to me!"*

Bíbí picks up her phone and is about to put it to her ear when she hears a knock on the door.

"Hold on, I'm going to go let him in," Bíbí says into the phone, before hurrying to the door.

"Don't let him in!" Hörður shouts, but she doesn't hear him. *"It's not Orri! Don't open the door!"*

Bíbí opens the door to the landing, which is dark, as the staircase light hasn't been switched on. In front of the door stands a shadow, which is quick to step over the threshold and into the light. A shadow in jeans and a blue coat, holding a black sports bag in its left hand.

"What kept you so long?" asks Bíbí, as she shuts the door. She looks at Orri, who looks back at her with cold, staring eyes.

He puts the sports bag down.

"Is everything all right?" Bíbí asks hesitantly. She doesn't like the way that he's looking at her; the way that he's looking *into* her. She feels somewhat frightened, and the thought occurs to her that this *isn't* Orri.

Something has changed. Could he be on something? Did he go out to buy drugs? She tries to swallow, and her knees go weak. She's still holding her cell phone, but seems to have forgotten about it.

"It's not Orri!" yells Hörður, but his voice can hardly be heard.

"Hörður!" groans Bíbí. She starts to raise the phone to her ear, but Orri grabs her arm. She freezes on the spot.

"Bíbí!" shouts Hörður.

The man who looks like Orri Atlason takes the phone out of her hand and answers the police officer. "Hi! Remember me?"

The lunatic who is at Bíbí's house is also locked in a cell just a hundred meters away. Inside the fortress-like building enclosed within a double security fence topped with barbed wire, with high-voltage current streaming through the inner section.

Hörður paces the parking lot like a lion in a cage, his heart in his throat and his phone pressed against his right ear. "Don't you touch her! Don't you dare!"

"Listen to me," says Aron—says Aron's *voice*. *"I've got my guys watching this apartment building. If you call the cops, they'll let me know and I'll cut your girlfriend's throat. If you don't come alone, they'll let me know and I'll cut your*

girlfriend's throat. If a dog barks, if a car honks its horn, if one shitty seagull lands on a streetlight nearby, they'll let me know and I'll cut your girlfriend's throat. Understood?"

Hörður stops and clenches his left hand into a fist, so hard that the skin whitens. "If you so much as breathe on her, you bastard, I'll …"

"Understood?" barks Aron into the phone. His voice is garbled, distorted, as if he's drunk or has just been at the dentist's.

Hörður feels a cold shiver run down his spine. Bíbí is in mortal danger; that much is certain. "Yes, understood."

"Good. We'll be waiting for you. You're to come alone. Ring the doorbell when you come. No tricks. Otherwise, you know."

Hörður looks at Bíbí's car, and then at the prison. What should he do? Drive to town? Try to talk some sense into the prison officers? He isn't even sure they'll answer him.

"Are you listening, copper?"

Hörður clenches his jaw. "Yes, I'm listening."

"You've got fifteen minutes."

"No," says Hörður. "It's not enough time. I'm … not just one street over."

"Where are you?"

"I'm not in Reykjavík." Hörður runs his eyes over the security fence, the brightly lit buildings and the guard tower looming over the prison. "I'm far away, but closer than you think."

"Ten minutes," says Aron, in an icy voice. *"If you're not here in ten minutes, I'll cut her throat. I promise you."*

"Let's say fifteen," says Hörður. "You said fifteen earlier!"

"Five minutes. And then she bleeds out."

"Aron, don't ..." shouts Hörður, but it's too late. The anarchist has hung up. Hörður stares at the phone. His heart is pounding, his mouth is dry, and his hand is shaking. Bíbí is in danger of her life. Aron has her. He can't even imagine how scared she is.

Hörður sticks his phone in his pocket and looks at his watch. It's five minutes to eleven. He's walks in the direction of the car, stops, and tries to think clearly. No, it's a little less than sixty kilometers to Reykjavík. He walks quickly back toward the turnstile gate and the intercom. Hörður stops and looks at his watch. Four minutes. He's too agitated to talk to the officer. Too scared. He would yell at them, and instead of listening to him, they would sick the police on him.

If they answer him at all.

He tears his hair, turns in a semi-circle, and screams loudly. His desperate, furious cry echoes in the stillness and dies out. High in the cloudless sky hangs the full moon, cold and bright.

He clenches his fists and jaw. Bíbí must not die! If only he could tear down the fence, knock a hole in the prison, and ...

Hörður blinks. Knock a hole? He's hurries over the parking lot, toward its exit, and starts to run.

He's gotten an idea, but has no time to lose.

Aron stands there staring and smirking at Bíbí, and then pushes her ahead of him into the kitchen, where the eggs are boiling on the stove. She forgot to turn on the kitchen hood, causing steam to accumulate on the kitchen windows. The air in the kitchen is muggy.

If the eggs boil for too long, all the water will evaporate from the pot and it will overheat. She's about to turn off the burner, but decides not to. She's so scared that she can hardly breathe, but the thought occurs to her that anything she can do to delay things and interfere with the attacker's plans could make a huge difference.

Aron points at the kitchen table and chairs. "Take one chair and bring it into the hall."

The chairs are wooden, with high backs. Bíbí picks one of them up and carries it into the hall. Her fear makes her feel weak, so much so that she can hardly hold the chair above the floor. She tries hard not to break down and start crying.

"Sit down on it," says Aron. He takes off his coat and tosses it aside. Underneath, he's wearing a gray sports shirt. His palms and forehead are sweaty.

Bíbí does as he says.

Aron opens the sports bag and removes a hank of rope from it. He ties Bíbí's hands together behind the back of the chair, and ties her legs to those of the chair. He tries to do this hurriedly, and to tighten the knots well, but it's as if his hands aren't working properly.

"This will have to do," he says irritably, wiping beads of sweat from his red forehead.

He takes a roll of gray duct tape from the bag, as well as a knife with a blue plastic hilt and a long, tapered, stainless-steel blade. He cuts the rope and tosses the part that he's not going to use to the floor. He's still holding around two meters.

Bíbí whimpers with fear.

"If you scream or try to call for help, I'll tape your mouth shut," says Aron, waving the knife in her face. "And then I'll cut your throat. Do you understand?"

Bíbí nods. She has begun to hyperventilate, and is on the verge of passing out from fear.

On the stove, the eggs rattle in the little that remains of the water in the pot. Two of the eggs have cracked, and strings of congealed egg yolk and white whirl around in the bubbling water.

"I *will* cut your neck, you know?" says Aron smarmily.

Bíbí tries to swallow, but her throat is clamped tight.

"Hörður thinks he can save you," says Aron. "He's scared, like you, maybe even on the verge of losing his mind. He's hurrying as fast as he can, but it will all be for nothing."

Bíbí tries to calm her breathing, without success. Her heart is hammering in her chest, as if she were running hard. Her pulse pounds in her head, which is practically bursting with pressure. She fears that a blood vessel will burst any second now.

"I'm going to hogtie him," says Aron. "Then I'll make him watch when I cut your throat. Do you know why?"

Bíbí is trembling with fear, but says nothing.

"Do you know why?" barks Aron.

Bíbí shakes her head.

"Because Hörður intends to kill my child," says Aron. "That's why I'm going to kill his love. That's the way justice works in my world."

"Your child?" Bíbí asks in a shaky voice.

Aron nods. "The revolution is my child. What I'm doing is art. The revolution is a performance, a living artwork. It's my creation, terrifying and immortal. The deaths of you and Hörður will not mark the end of the beginning, but the beginning of every end. I'm just getting started."

Bíbí avoids his piercing eyes.

Aron looks at his phone's display. Two and a half minutes left. "What's delaying your lover? I just hope he's not doing anything stupid."

"You gave him too little time," Bíbí whimpers. "There's no way he can make it back in just a few minutes."

"Back?" exclaims Aron cynically. "Back from where?"

"From, from …" Bíbí sobs, before coughing and shutting her eyes, to protect them from the acrid smoke wafting from the kitchen.

"From what?" Aron shouts.

"There's a fire!" Bíbí groans. She has barely said the word "fire" when the smoke detector in the kitchen begins to beep. The noise is deafening.

"What the fuck!" Aron rushes into the kitchen. He pulls a chair over, climbs up on it, reaches for the smoke detector, tears it down, and smashes it onto the floor. Its plastic cover breaks into countless pieces, the battery comes loose from its holder and the sharp beeping is silenced.

Aron jumps down from the chair, takes the burned pot off the stove and turns off the searing-hot burner. Then he opens the window and waves his arms to clear the smoke.

In the meantime, Bíbí tries desperately to free herself from her restraints.

Hörður runs to the big Massey Ferguson tractor parked next to the torn-up road. He grabs the cab's door handle, but the door is locked. He takes a large rock from the side of the road and uses it to break the door's window, then reaches in and unlocks the door. He opens the cab and climbs up into the tractor, breathless and sweaty. He's so stressed that he's shaking, but despair overpowers his fear.

He *will* save her!

Hörður checks to see whether the key is in the ignition, which it turns out not to be. Damn it! On the floor to the right of the seat is a toolbox. Among other things, it contains a hammer, chisel, and a few screwdrivers.

Hörður selects a medium-sized, ordinary screwdriver, pushes it into the ignition switch and jiggles it to and fro until something gives—he manages to turn the screwdriver clockwise, the dashboard powers on and the glowplugs in the powerful diesel engine heat up.

Yes! He steps down on the heavy clutch and starts the engine, which sputters at first, before jumping into action—a loud rumbling cuts through the evening quiet, the tractor trembles from one end to the other, and black smoke pours out its exhaust pipe.

Hörður puts the transfer case in the next-lowest gear, then shifts the main gear box to second and releases the clutch. The huge tractor bursts into motion, Hörður jerks to and fro in the springy seat, and he grabs the steering wheel and floors the throttle. Ahead, there's nothing but darkness; he looks for and finds the switches for the lights and turns them all on. The headlights light up, as well as the powerful spotlights on the roof. The light is so strong that he has to squint.

He flies down the road, steering the growling tractor straight toward the prison's double security fence. What exactly will happen when all these tons of steel and all that horsepower hits the fence, he doesn't know. But he hopes it will be something tremendous.

Hörður grips the steering wheel tightly, sets the hand throttle to the max, and watches the fence's dense chain-link mesh approach uncomfortably quickly, then shuts his eyes and grinds his teeth. The diesel engine is on overdrive and the tractor steams ahead in low gear, like a small railroad train without rails.

Then it slams into the fence.

The impact is massive; Hörður is thrown onto the wheel and hits his head against the windshield. He is knocked out and collapses to the floor, but the tractor pushes stubbornly on, it crashing into the outer fence and tearing it down. The outer fence hits the inner, blue sparks shoot in every direction, the tractor's electrical system is overloaded and there's a loud explosion when the high-voltage electricity meets the ground connection, knocking out all power in the area—Eyrarbakki darkens, as well as the prison.

"Where were we?" asks Aron, as he walks out of the kitchen. He wipes something off his hands onto his jeans.

Bíbí stops fighting against her restraints. She has managed to loosen the ropes a little, but is far from freeing herself from them.

Aron looks askance at her and raises the knife with his left hand, letting the light gleam on the slender blade. With his chest puffed out and darkness in his eyes, he walks slowly up to Bíbí.

Bíbí stiffens in her chair. Her first instinct is to lean back, try to retreat. But her reason is stronger than her instinct, and instead of retreating, she pushes herself forward, the ropes stretch tight, and a gap is formed between her and the back of the chair.

Aron leans toward her and puts the knife to her throat. "Where is Hörður? Answer me or I'll …"

Bíbí swallows, feeling the cold, razor-sharp knife blade against the skin of her neck. "He … he went east."

Aron blinks. "East? Where east?"

Bíbí breathes through her nose. He stares into her eyes, and the only thing she sees is evil—in those black holes, there's no humanity to be found.

"Answer me!" barks Aron. He presses the blade harder to her neck, cutting her skin slightly. The tiny slit turns pink, and then red.

"He went to Litla-Hraun," Bíbí whispers.

"What?" hisses Aron. His mouth trembles and he blinks his eyes repeatedly as he digests this information.

I'm not in Reykjavík. I'm far away, but closer than you think. *Closer than you think.*

Bíbí watches as his face contorts with fury. His face whitens, his lips peel back like savage dog's and his eyes transform into glowing lumps of coal.

Aron picks up Bíbí's phone and calls Hörður back. The phone rings and rings, but the police officer doesn't answer.

"I'll kill him!" shouts Aron, smashing the phone against the nearest wall. The phone breaks into pieces that scatter over the floor.

Bíbí stiffens with fear.

"But first, I'll kill you, bitch!" barks Aron. Every single muscle in his body tenses and the knife moves a little upward and to the right. But a fracture of a second before he jerks his hand to the left and cuts her neck, Bíbí kicks against the floor and slings her upper body backwards.

The knife swishes through the air—but misses its mark. The chair topples and slams into the floor. At the blow,

Bíbí's lungs are drained of air; her arms are squashed beneath her, and her head knocks hard against the parquet floor.

Hörður comes to when his phone begins to ring. He coughs, gasps for breath, and tries to scramble to his feet. He lies outstretched inside the tractor's cab and hardly knows what's up or down.

His phone, where is his phone? He gropes at his coat, searches its pockets, and finally finds the phone, which stops ringing just as he answers.

"Hello, Bíbí?"

No answer, just a dial tone.

Hörður calls back immediately, but the caller's phone has been turned off.

"Don't you touch her, you fucker!" He pulls himself to his feet, notices a claw hammer among the debris at his feet, picks it up and uses it to smash open one of the side windows. He crawls out of the cab onto the inner security fence, which is lying nearly flat on the prison grounds. The tractor is on top of the fence, leaning backwards, on the verge of rolling over.

Suddenly, a loud siren starts wailing. Everything is dark, but then lights go on in the prison. Backup power has been activated.

Hörður climbs up along the broken fence, steps onto a sloping iron rod with barbed wire on top, and jumps from it onto the grass-grown prison lot. He lands roughly, stumbles, and nearly twists his ankle. He scrambles back to his feet and runs off, hammer in hand.

The shortest route to the prison entrance is along the fence to the south and around the end of the remand wing, but Hörður decides to go the longer way, along the length of the building to the east, around the north end and then back along the building's length to the west.

The prison officers must realize what has happened, and they will no doubt take the shortest route to the hole in the fence, but Hörður has an extremely limited interest in running into them. This is an emergency, and as such, the officers will have armed themselves with guns.

Hörður runs as fast as his feet can carry him. The siren's wail is deafening, but through it he can hear shouts and cries. He runs around the end of the prison. High above him is the guard tower. Its windows lean outward, making it possible for the officers in it to see him.

He runs along the front wall of the prison. To his right is the gymnasium, and beyond that, the parking lot on the other side of the fence. Ahead is the visitors' entrance; the door is open and in front of it stands an officer holding a stubby shotgun. He has his eyes on the gate in the fence and doesn't notice Hörður until he's about fifty meters from the open door.

"Stop!" shouts the guard, pumping the shotgun and aiming it at the man in the leather coat rushing toward him.

Hörður doesn't slow down. He raises the hammer and throws it as hard as he can in the direction of the guard. The hammer twirls in the air and hits the left side of the officer's chest, just as he pulls the shotgun's trigger. The impact causes the guard to turn to the left, and the shot misses—Hörður hears the pellets whiz past him into the night.

The officer groans. He tries to pump the gun again but Hörður runs him down, grabs the gun from him and enters the building through the visitors' entrance, with the weapon loaded and his finger on the trigger.

Hörður storms into the control room and points the gun at the officer on duty, a middle-aged man with a bald head and a potbelly. "Hands up! No abrupt moves!"

"Easy there," says the officer, raising his hands.

"The keys to Block Three, now!" orders Hörður.

The officer hesitates, then reaches for the hooks upon which the key rings hang. He's about to lift the ring hanging on the middle hook, but stops, and then reaches for the key ring nearest him. He's about to take this ring from its hook when Hörður drives the barrel of the gun into the back of his neck.

"Give me the right key ring or I'll blow your head off!

The officer hurriedly hands him the key ring that was hanging from the middle hook.

"Keep quiet, and don't do anything stupid. I'm not going to hurt anyone," says Hörður.

The officer nods, but Hörður starts running down the long corridor with the gun in one hand and the key ring in the other. When he reaches the Blue Door, he puts down the gun and sticks one of the two longer keys on the ring into the lock. Wrong key! He tries the other long key, and the door opens.

The hatch cover is raised.

"Stop!" yells someone behind him. Footsteps echo along the corridor and someone pumps a shotgun.

Hörður hurries into Block 3, but realizes that he left the shotgun behind. Too late! He shuts the Blue Door and locks it. Then he peeks through the hatch on the door. Two officers come running toward the Blue Door, one of them armed with a shotgun, and the other wielding a black baton.

Hörður's face pales. He has no time to lose!

Block 3 is empty, and lit with dim emergency lighting. The inmates shout, kick and pound the doors of their cells.

They sound as if they're going mad, either from agitation or fear.

Hörður runs to Aron's cell, number eight. There's a steel latch on the door and a padlock in the latch.

Hanging on the key ring are ten short keys.

Fuck!

Hörður picks one key at random and sticks it in the lock. Doesn't fit! He tries the next key. It doesn't fit, either …

The officers have come to the Blue Door. They know very well which key opens it, and will do so in the next few seconds.

Aron nearly loses his balance when the knife cleaves the air, but he hops forward a bit as the chair slams into the floor and manages to keep on his feet. He looks at the knife and then down at Bíbí, as if he can't believe what just happened.

"Don't," Bíbí whimpers. "Don't kill me."

"Shut up, bitch," spits Aron. He stares at Bíbí and walks halfway around the chair, before falling to his knees and clamping her head in between them. He raises the knife high and readies it for the blow, like an Aztec priest preparing himself to cut the heart out of a victim—the razor-sharp blade flashes.

Aron's eyes burn with hatred, with a bottomless hunger that only blood and death can soothe. His nostrils flare, and his tautened lips reveal both his teeth and gums. Every single muscle of his is tensed, and every never stretched.

The moment is like ice that cracks just before it breaks.

Bíbí opens her eyes wide, and the only thing that she experiences and sees is horror and death. She struggles, but simply can't free herself. She clenches her fists, digs her fingernails into her palms, and screams with all her might.

The lights blink in Block 3. The prisoners kick at their doors, curse and raise a ruckus as the officers stick their key into the lock the Blue Door.

Hörður tries to think fast, and to move his fingers even faster. Ten short keys, a block of ten cells. If the keys are in the same order as the cells, then the key to Cell 8 should be the eighth one from the long key that opened the Blue Door.

He starts at the other end, and counts back two keys. This one! He tries to stick the key into the lock, but his hands shake and the lock slips.

The Blue Door opens forcefully, and the two officers push into the corridor. The officer with the baton comes first, followed close behind by the one with the shotgun.

"Stop! Don't open the cell!"

Hörður manages to open the padlock, and then removes the lock from the latch and tosses it aside.

The officers' swift footsteps echo off the walls.

"Stop!"

Hörður pulls back the latch and opens the cell door. He sees Aron, who is sitting in his chair in front of the desk, staring as if in a trance at the black, flat-screen TV—the flames of two candles flicker in the darkness.

Just as Hörður is about to enter the cell, one of the officers throws himself at him, nearly knocking him over, and puts him in a chokehold. The officer kicks the back of Hörður's right knee, and he then feels a heavy blow on his back, either from the baton or the stock of the gun.

"Fuck!" screams Hörður loudly. His body is on fire, his muscles turn to stone, and he sees red. In a frenzy, he shakes the officers off him, slips out of his coat and leaps into the cell. He raises his left leg and delivers a powerful kick to Aron's head with the heel of his motorcycle boot, and the prisoner whips sideways and slumps like a rag doll from his chair.

"I'll kill you!" yells Hörður, foaming with rage and bending over the unconscious anarchist. But before he manages to clamp his paws around him, the red-haired giant is hit so hard in the back of the neck with the baton that he loses consciousness.

Bíbí is lying on her back, tied to the chair and with her head clamped between the madman's legs. She stares at the knife hanging over her, sharp and glossy, at the knife locked tightly in the grip of evil.

She doesn't know if she's still screaming or not. All that she hears is a loud ringing that fills her head, fills the moment, fills the universe—a ringing that cuts through her consciousness, as the knife will cut through her skin, bones, and flesh.

The knife falls …

Bíbí shuts her eyes, the darkness is tinged with red and her heart beats with a heavy rhythm, phrenetic and desperate. The moment lingers; it's an entire eternity of a loud ringing noise, red-tinged darkness, and terror that tears through every thought.

The knife …

Something touches her breast, something slender, something sharp—ice-cold steel that will split her like an apple. Her breathing stops, her heart skips a beat, and every single muscle tenses and freezes—everything stops except for the tone ringing in her head.

The moment passes. Her lungs empty and fill up again, her heart restarts and her muscles relax.

What happened?

Bíbí opens her eyes, and at the same time, Orri falls sideways. Empty-handed and empty-eyed, he collapses to the floor with a heavy groan. His hands tremble, he blinks repeatedly and breathes rapidly through his open mouth.

Bíbí lifts her head as high as she can. The knife is lying between her breasts, its tip pointed toward her face. On her blouse is a tiny slit, beneath it a bleeding wound.

"Oh, God," she cries.

Someone knocks on the door of the apartment.

"Help!" cries Bíbí.

"Bíbí, are you there?" calls out someone through the closed door. It's her neighbor who is asking, the woman from the apartment next to hers. "Something hit the wall, and then I heard you scream. Is everything okay?"

Orri sits up on the floor and looks in surprise around him, then turns over onto his hands and knees and vomits on the floor.

"Call the police!" Bíbí shouts.

"Right away!" her neighbor shouts back.

Orri wipes vomitous drool from his face, sits up and looks at Bíbí. Wearing a sorrowful expression, he appears utterly exhausted. "I don't know what happened, but let me untie you."

Bíbí looks at him. She's still terrified of him, despite the insanity seeming to have left him entirely. She wishes that he would leave, that he would let her be. But most of all, she wants to be free of her restraints.

THE FISH IN THE DEEP

He's empty, he's falling. Inside the skull is an entire universe of nothing. A dark universe, cold and empty, like he himself. Images rush through the universe, through the skull, through his mind. They're old pictures, memories, refractions of his life. He's no longer a person with awareness and perception, he's a half-sphere made of glass, full of water and white particles of fake snow that swirl around before they settle. Every snowflake is a memory, a refraction, is an old moment that he experiences over and over again. These aren't memories, he senses that now. These are real moments, blinks of an eye, events from the past that come alive in him, or he in them. Time is a broken picture, it's scattered all over, a million glass shards that rush through the void and flash like flares, lightning, nuclear explosions in the soul. Unless it's the soul that's broken, that's sprinkled like a rain of shards throughout the universe inside the skull.

In the distance is a flickering light. A light that moves closer and farther away. He is in the depths, but the light floats around on the surface, like bait that he longs to swallow.

The light *is* the surface!

The light is a door—it's a way out. He's got to come closer to the light. He's got to grab the light, pull it toward him, quaff it.

He's got to get to it. He's got to shove the darkness aside. He shall!

MONDAY

Hörður Grímsson is in a hospital room in the intensive care unit of the City Hospital in Fossvogur. He's still wearing the clothes that he was in at the wedding, not having gone home since picking up Orri on Bergþórugata just over twelve hours ago. His shirt is crumpled and is missing two buttons; his trousers are torn and dirty. His leather coat, however, looks almost entirely untouched, apart from some scratches made by the barbed wire on the security fence.

He's standing looking at an unconscious man lying beneath a blanket in a hospital bed, with handcuffs on his hands and ankles. It's Aron Beck. He's hooked up to a respirator, heart and brain monitors, and an IV. His head is wrapped in bandages, and he has a brace around his neck. When Hörður kicked him in the head, he cracked his skull and broke two vertebrae in his neck.

The anarchist's heart beats slowly, but his EEG is flat.

Hörður himself has thick bandages on the back of his head and a roller bandage wrapped around the middle of it. He spent the night at the hospital in Selfoss, where he was stitched up and allowed to recover from the baton blow. A bone in the back of his neck was fractured, he suffered a mild concussion, and was nauseous through the night.

At first, the police in Selfoss had stood guard over Hörður as if he were a dangerous criminal, and he was handcuffed to the bed, for as far as they knew, he was just some crazy person who had broken into the prison. It wasn't until Axel M. Axelsson called the district commissioner for South Iceland that Hörður's handcuffs were removed and all charges against him were dropped.

When a doctor appears at his side, Hörður looks away from Aron.

"Do you think he'll wake up again?"

"I doubt it," says the doctor. "Though it's not impossible. But the longer that a patient's brain shows no activity, the faster his chances of doing so decrease."

"I see," mutters Hörður. He isn't certain whether Aron's decreased brain activity is due to the hypnotic state he was in—as part of his astral projection—or to the blow that he delivered to his head.

Hörður glances at the doctor. He's wearing a name tag on his lapel. His name is Lárus. Doctor Lárus.

"There's one thing I'm wondering about," says Hörður. "The patient, Aron Beck, not only hypnotized himself, but also another man, Orri Atlason, and projected himself astrally and took over Orri's body. When I knocked Aron out, Orri was yanked out of his hypnotic state and woke up again in his own body, but Aron's brain shows no activity. So my question is this: where is Aron's soul?"

Doctor Lárus clears his throat politely. "In the first place, the question isn't a medical one. Science hasn't yet proven the existence of something called the soul. The only difference between we two and the patient lying there is *consciousness*. Consciousness is closely connected to the brain—without a brain, there's no awareness, no *person*. When a patient is in a coma, it's often difficult to determine whether that person can display real life signs or not. By that, I mean whether he's capable of dreaming, thinking, or even hearing. But when the brain shows no activity, as in this case, the chances of there being some kind of awareness are extremely low."

Hörður nods. "But what do you think about this that I described to you? Do you think it's possible for the soul to travel from one body to another?"

Lárus hesitates. "In truth, no. By this I mean that such a thing has never been proven scientifically, as far I know, and therefore, you can't argue for it with any certainty. Science says no. But that's not to say that it isn't possible."

"No?" asks Hörður optimistically.

The doctor shakes his head. "There are so many things that we don't understand, so many things we can't prove. The human brain is a mystery; mostly unexplored territory—*terra incognita*. For example, we know next to nothing about mental illnesses. We just see certain deviations from average behavior and give these deviations names to identify them. Then experiments are carried out with various treatments and drugs, and now and then it happens that, for example, a particular type of neurotransmitter works as a kind of antidote to one of these deviations, in which case we say that we've found a cure for a mental illness, without, however, having any understanding of the disease itself or any idea as to why this particular neurotransmitter seems to suppress it."

"So modern medical science is actually just an old herbalist with an education and wearing a white robe?" asks Hörður. "A witch with a college degree?"

Lárus laughs softly. "Yes, you might say that."

"What will happen to him?" asks Hörður, after a brief silence.

The doctor shrugs. "If nothing changes in the next days or weeks, he'll be disconnected."

"Allowed to die?"

"A person without brain function is already dead, medically speaking," says Lárus.

"Yes, well," says Hörður. He's been staring long enough at the unconscious anarchist. The ECG beeps softly with every heartbeat, but the EEG line is as flat as Álftafjörður in calm weather. "Where can I find Orri?"

"He's up on the next floor, room seven," says the doctor. "The last I knew, he was giving your boss a statement."

Axel isn't Hörður's boss, but he can't be bothered to correct the doctor. "Do you think he'll recover?"

Doctor Lárus nods. "He should, yes. He experienced some dizziness due to low blood pressure and all his neurotransmitter production nearly ceased, but he was in much better shape and on the road to recovery when I looked in on him earlier. I guess we'll be discharging him later today, or tomorrow morning."

"Good to hear," says Hörður. "I'm going to pay him a visit before I go home. I'm starting to want a warm bath."

"That's fine," says the doctor. "Just don't get your head wet. You don't want the wound to become infected."

Hörður limps down a long corridor on the fifth floor of the eastern wing of the hospital, and knocks on the door of Orri's room before he enters. Hörður's right leg is sore from the kick the prison officer gave it. He probably suffered a torn ligament, and bled a bit into his knee.

Orri is alone in the room. He's lying in a bed by the window and smiles faintly at the police officer. The noon sun shines in through the large windows, intensely white and blinding.

"How are you?" asks Hörður.

"I'm tired," says Orri. He's pale and weak, as if needing a blood transfusion.

"Axel just left. I told him everything I know. Except the thing about Sæli. I hope it's enough."

Hörður nods. "I hope so too."

"What about Bíbí?" asks Orri. "How's she doing?"

"She's really something else. She'll be fine." Hörður goes to the window and looks down at the parking lot on the south side of the hospital. He sees the roof of Bíbí's small red car, which is parked at the edge of the lot. Smoke drifts up from the exhaust pipe.

She spent the night at the home of a girlfriend, who then drove her to Litla-Hraun the next morning, where her car was still parked. From Litla-Hraun, she drove to Selfoss to pick up Hörður. They've just returned to the city.

"I feel so bad about attacking her," mutters Orri, looking terribly ashamed. "She was just trying to help, and ..." His voice breaks, the corners of his mouth twitch, and a tear wells in his eye.

Hörður turns away from the window. "It wasn't you who attacked her. You know that very well. It was Aron."

Orri breathes a heavy sigh. "I know, I know. But it was still my fault. I shouldn't have gone to the gas station."

Hörður nods. He couldn't agree more—but he doesn't say so.

"Is she going to press charges against me?" Orri whispers.

Hörður shakes his head.

"Thank God," says Orri.

"Don't worry about this," says Hörður. "You need to focus on recovering, regaining your strength. After the hospital discharges you, you can get all the help that's available. Counseling, medication, anything."

Orri inhales through his nose. "Yes, I know. Thanks. It'll take time. I've gone through this before. The damn emptiness, the loathing. It's like having your soul raped."

"Yes, well …" Hörður makes ready to leave. "Bíbí's waiting for me. Take care of yourself. I'll see you soon."

"Yes, see you soon." Orri puts on a smile. "Thanks for dropping by. I appreciate it."

Hörður goes down to the lounge toward the back of the hospital's ground floor, opens the door of an arched alcove and walks down a few stone steps that lead to the parking lot. He waves at Bíbí, sitting at the wheel of her car a short distance from him. She waves back and smiles at him. He feels a flush of happiness and gets butterflies in his stomach. The sun warms his cheeks; beyond the parked car are yellow fields and leafless trees that stretch up toward the sky, which is clear and blue.

"Hörður!"

He stops, shades his eyes and looks to the right. Axel M. Axelsson shuts the driver-side door of a Mercedes Benz SUV and walks over to the police officer. He's wearing a black wool coat over his tailor-made suit, English leather shoes, and an Italian fedora hat.

"I thought I'd missed you," says Steppenwolf. "But then I had a hunch that you might go out the back door."

"Hello," says Hörður. They haven't seen each other since the interrogation in the Operations Room on Friday. A lot has happened since then. Although Hörður is grateful to the head of the CID for having gotten him out of custody last night, he's still frustrated with him for not having called back after all the messages that Hörður left on Jafet's voicemail.

They stand opposite each other in the middle of the parking lot. Towering over them is the hospital's south wall, like an unscalable cliff.

Hörður takes out a pack of cigarettes, shakes one out and lights it. The first thing he did after getting out of the hospital was buy himself a pack of Camels. He decided that now wasn't the right time to quit.

"I owe you an apology," Axel says in a gentle voice. "Jafet forwarded all your messages to me. I took note of them, but didn't call you because I was so angry at you. The *Spotlight* interview nearly cost me my job."

Hörður reddens. He knows he screwed up. But if Axel had paid full attention to what he said on Thursday, things would never have gone as they did. He would have gotten the judge to a secure location, and enhanced the security around his home.

"But I should have paid better attention to what you said," says Axel, as if he'd read the officer's thoughts. "And those idiots who were keeping watch on the judge's house should have been more alert, too."

Bíbí is still waiting in the car. Hörður gives her an apologetic smile. She's the embodiment of patience.

He blows smoke out his nostrils. Does he deserve a woman like her?

No, not at all.

"So Hákon and Þorsteinn weren't at sea?" asks Hörður.

Axel shakes his head. "The boat was at sea, but what the fishing company didn't know was that two of its crewmembers had gotten others to take their place. Betti should have verified this."

Hörður nods and takes another drag of his cigarette. Personally, he would have called the boat's captain, and not the fishing company.

"I volunteered to resign, just so you know," says Axel. "The pressure was enormous, and I felt that it would be right to step aside, if that would soothe people's anger and calm things down. We couldn't get any work done. The media wouldn't let us alone, and the public was both frightened and angry. Which was no surprise, really. Two murders in a few days, unlikely murderers in custody, misleading information going around and rumors of toxic ecstasy tablets in circulation. And then there was the *Spotlight* thing. It looked like we had information that was being kept secret from the public."

"But ...?"

"The Police Commissioner wouldn't hear of it, and forbade me to resign," says Axel. "He refused to bend to the fourth estate. Police work over politics, he said."

"I see," says Hörður. He isn't sure, however, whether he agrees. Those who screw up should stand down, in his opinion.

"We put out an alert for Hákon and Þorsteinn as soon as we got your information," says Axel. "We met with Reverend Ingimar as well, got him to give us a list of his closest relatives and then let them know, asked them to stay at home. These actions probably saved at least one human life, even two. We owe you a great deal of thanks for your contribution to this investigation, Hörður. It was invaluable."

"Thank you," says Hörður. "But what's next? What about Gísli Már and Sólrún?"

"I'm meeting with the prosecutor this afternoon, but first I'm going to hold a press conference," says Axel.

"That's why I questioned Orri just now. I wanted to be able to answer all conceivable and inconceivable questions from the media. Regarding Gísli and Sólrún, I'll do everything I can to make sure they're not charged with murder. They're going to be released from custody today, as there's no reason to detain them any longer. They'll receive all the assistance that we can possibly provide, being victims in this case, not perpetrators."

"What about Aron?" asks Hörður. "Is it possible to file charges against someone who's in a coma?"

"It's possible, yes," says Axel. "But it's impossible to put him on trial."

"If he dies, then what?"

Axel sighs. "This case is unprecedented, of course. The good news is that both Hákon and Egill have confessed. I'm hoping that Þorsteinn and Tryggvi will do so as well. They were all terrified of Aron, who seems to have had a very strong grasp on them. He was the glue that held this group together. That glue isn't there anymore."

"How will the case be presented?" Hörður knocks the ash off his cigarette.

"With Aron as the kingpin. He'll probably be charged with two counts of murder, as well as kidnapping and attempted murder," says Axel. "Those who carried out the murders will probably be charged with kidnapping, two counts of accessory to murder, and one count of attempted murder. If they cooperate, that will be taken into account in court. What bothers me is the ideology behind the murders, and the methods used. You brought these things up on Friday, as I recall. You talked about politics and social factors. And then there's that astral projection stuff. I don't know about that. As soon as we say the word *black magic*, the judge will roll his eyes."

"I said that the trigger for all of this was personal, but the plan was political, *social,* with consequences that harmed the society that the anarchists hate," says Hörður.

"Exactly," says Axel.

"As far as astral projection and black magic go," says Hörður, "I think that you should put emphasis on the testimony of all those involved, and ignore whether what they describe and talk about is based on scientific evidence or not. I expect that you have Hákon and Egill's testimony as to what they did, saw, and experienced. Bíbí will testify. You also have the testimony of Orri, who is one of the victims, besides being a former member of the anarchist gang, which lends his testimony increased weight. If all of this testimony supports the available facts, isn't that more important than whether astral projection is theoretically possible or not?"

"Possibly," Axel mutters.

"It's probably impossible to prove the possibility of astral projection," says Hörður. "But isn't it also impossible to prove its *impossibility?*"

"I see what you mean," says Axel.

"Also, call the doctor as a witness," says Hörður. "The one in intensive care, looking after Aron. His name is Lárus. I asked him about astral projection, and the answer that he gave me could hold a lot of weight in the courtroom."

"You're a top-notch cop, Hörður," says Axel. "I'll give you that."

Hörður ignores the compliment. A few days ago, it would have gone to his head. Right now, it just gets on his nerves. "It's not like you're lacking physical evidence, either. The knife that Bíbí was threatened with is the same make as the ones used for the murders. If Aron's accomplices lay all their cards on the table, you'll have that much more evidence, won't you? And Aron had a phone in his cell. Did they find anything else there?"

Axel nods. "Among other things, the book that you returned to him. And a handwritten book bound in leather, which at first glance seems to be a journal of various experiments, as well as runes and sorcerer's staves and the like. I need to get an expert to look at it. It's hard to read the handwriting."

"Blackhide," mutters Hörður.

"What?" asks Axel.

"I'd like to have a look at it," says Hörður. "Hopefully, it contains a detailed description of what Aron was doing. This book may prove to be crucial evidence in the case. Not to mention if Aron wrote it by hand."

"The book is handwritten; that much is certain," says Axel. "Most likely with a feather pen and real ink. As if that weren't enough. As far as I could tell, some of the staves were illustrated in blood, as if a bloody fingertip had been drawn over the pages."

"Even better," says Hörður excitedly. "His own handwriting, his own blood—if we're lucky. Even if Aron dies, we have the book, which could act as his stand-in at court, his spirit and his genetic material bound in animal hide."

"Fucking hell," says Axel.

"There's more." Hörður sucks on the cigarette with such abandon that the cherry glows bright and crackles.

"More?

Hörður nods. "Do you remember Sæli from Stórholt?"

"The one who disappeared?"

"He's in a hole in the lava near Hafnarfjörður," says Hörður.

Axel's eyes widen. "How ..."

Hörður lifts his hand and stops the head of the CID in mid-question. "Anonymous tip."

"Very well," says Axel. "But do you know who …"

Hörður nods. "Aron has a bone pendant on a necklace that he wears. A human bone. The knuckle of the thumb of a left hand."

Axel grimaces. "Are you telling me …"

Hörður nods his head repeatedly.

"Can you come with me to my meeting with the pro-secutor?" asks Axel. "You're the one who knows the most about Aron and this case. It would be good to bring these things up there, especially this about the social factor—the political conspiracy. I think it would be most promising to build our case on that."

Hörður looks in Bíbí's direction. Most of all, he wants to forget about all of this and spend the day in her arms. "I don't know. I've hardly slept, and am pretty exhausted. What about Engilbert?"

"He's on sick leave," says Axel dryly.

"Oh?"

Axel clears his throat. "He's been hanging around with Johnnie Walker too much lately."

"I see."

"In other words, there's an opening in the department," says Axel.

Hörður opens his eyes wider, interestedly.

"A temporary one," adds Steppenwolf.

"When is this meeting?" asks Hörður. "I can't promise anything, but …"

Hörður pauses as a shiver runs down his spine. He shud-ders, and then glances over his shoulder and stiffens.

"Can't promise, but what?" asks Axel.

But Hörður doesn't hear him. He hears a buzzing in his ears, and stares at a lonely shadow standing on the asphalt in front of the stairs leading to the alcove of the lounge. It's a death-shadow.

Orri is queasy. He's lying beneath his duvet, trying to relax, trying to fall asleep, but feels nauseous, as hot winds blow around inside his head. He tosses and turns, groans, and lifts the duvet in order to cool himself down, but it's all for naught.

He feels as if he needs to vomit.

"Damn it," Orri mutters as he gets out of bed. He's barefoot, dressed in a white shirt and white pants, both of them the property of the hospital's laundry room. He hurries into the bathroom, throws himself down on his knees and throws up in the toilet. His spew is brown and lumpy; he retches and vomits again, and then wipes the drool off his mouth and sits against the wall.

He's still dizzy, but the nausea is gone. He feels a little better. *Stand up, look in the mirror.*

"What?" Orri looks toward the door, but no one is there.

Who said that?

Stand up, look in the mirror. The voice is deep and gravelly. It isn't outside his head, but within it—deep down in his consciousness.

Was he thinking this?

Orri gets up. He goes to the sink, turns on the cold water and rinses his face. The water is refreshing; his dizziness is subsiding.

Look up.

He turns off the water and looks in the mirror. What he sees in it is a pale face with a half-open mouth and staring, vacant eyes. He looks really bad, to put it mildly. There are red flecks on his forehead, and his hair is both greasy and unkempt.

Look into your eyes, the voice whispers in his ear. *The mirror is a gate, and soon we will journey into it, through the glass.*

Orri is petrified. He hears a ringing in his ear, stares as if hypnotized into his own eyes and listens to the voice that comes from within.

Inside of you, the gate opens; now it would be good to relax and sink deeper. You stand, but relax, even so, and allow your consciousness to fall asleep. You're empty, you feel good.

No, thinks Orri. I mustn't listen; I mustn't obey. These are not my thoughts. This isn't me. It's *him.*

Enter Eckankar!

"No!" yells Orri. He shakes his head, tears his hair, and turns around in circles. "No, no, no! Go away, leave me alone!"

Listen to me.

"Shut up!" Orri rushes out of the bathroom and back into his hospital room. He looks around. What should he do? What can he do?

Call for help? Ask for a sedative?

But what then?

The sun shines through the window, bright and clean, like the sheet on his bed.

Go back to the bathroom. Look in the mirror.

"No!" Orri looks into the light, and then runs ahead. Leave me alone! Go away, get out! Go to hell!"

What are you doing? Stop!

Hörður blinks, and at the same time, the death-shadow disappears. Where it had stood, there is nothing—just emptiness.

"What are you looking at?" Axel asks bewilderedly.

Who is going to die? thinks Hörður. Axel, he himself, or ...

"Bíbí!" Hörður tosses away his cigarette and runs off toward the small car. As Bíbí watches him approach, and seeing the look of sheer terror in his eyes, she becomes frightened.

Hörður slows down and looks all around, and then opens the car's driver-side door. "Is everything all right?"

"Yes," says Bíbí, as she turns down the radio. "What's wrong? Why are you so ..."

She stops when a loud bang comes from above.

Hörður starts in alarm and looks up along the south wall of the hospital.

The wall is bathed in sunshine, reflecting off the windows.

A window on the fifth floor is broken; it gapes like a black mouth lined with sharp teeth. Shards of glass rain down, glittering in the sunshine.

And amid the broken glass, a man dressed in white falls, waving his arms in the empty air as he does. Slowly overturning, he lands on the asphalt with a heavy thud, on his back, precisely where the shadow had appeared.

"No!" shouts Hörður. He rushes off toward the white-clad man, who bounces and lands again. The shards of glass crash clatteringly onto the parking lot and roofs of cars, and then an uncomfortable silence falls over the area.

Hörður drops to his knees, puts his arms around Orri, lifts him carefully. His body is so broken that it's as limp as a rag doll. His clothing is torn and he's bleeding profusely.

His head is cracked open and one cheek is just a red mess. But there's life in his eyes, and his gaping mouth quivers.

"Dear friend," says Hörður, with a lump in his throat.

"What were you thinking?"

"Gone …" Orri whispers with difficulty. "He's gone. I'm free."

"What did he say?" asks Axel, who came running after Hörður. He stands a few paces away, with his cell phone in his hand.

Bíbí steps out of the car and comes closer, hesitantly. She stops a few meters away and covers her mouth with her hands.

Orri shuts his eyes. His throat rattles, and he gives up the ghost in the arms of the police officer.

Hörður hangs his head and rocks gently to and fro, as if putting a small child to sleep.

THE END

About the Author

The Dark Prince of Nordic Noir: Stefán Máni was raised in the rural fishing village Ólafsvík, on the Snaefellsnes peninsula in western Iceland. At the age of twenty-six, he put all his belongings in an old car and moved to the capital city of Reykjavík to publish his first book. For the first ten years as a writer, he was working full or half time as a construction worker, a dishwasher, in a printing press and in a home for the insane. His first major success, at home and abroad, was the haunting thriller *The Ship*. Since then, he has been writing the hugely popular Grímsson detective series, along with occasional thrillers and other work. In 2012 the movie *Black's Game* premiered, based on his bestselling thriller by the same title. The movie is the second most popular and second highest grossing film in Icelandic history.

About the Publisher

This book is published on behalf of the author by the Ethan Ellenberg Literary Agency.

https://ethanellenberg.com

Email: agent@ethanellenberg.com

Facebook: https://www.facebook.com/EthanEllenbergLiteraryAgency/